Book One of The Talamh Nuadh Chronicles

The Servant
of the
Light

STEPHAN COOPER

The reader is strongly advised to consult the annexes at the end of this book for chronological and terminology references.

'Why do the nations so furiously rage together?
Why do the people imagine a vain thing?'
Handel, The Messiah, Part II scene 6.

PART ONE

Innocence

1

"Monsieur le Président?"

"…"

The voice echoed softly, "Monsieur le Président?"

"… Yes?"

"We are almost in Strasbourg, Monsieur le Président."

"Thank you, Barnabé… I apologise. I must have dozed off. You should have woken me up earlier."

"You have a significant day ahead, Monsieur le Président. I did not want to interrupt your well-deserved nap. You require all your strength. Especially…", Barnabé paused. Some things were better left alone, especially today.

The speed train slowed down while the first suburbs of the Alsatian capital passed through the carriage's windows. The voice of the train manager broke through interphone, informing passengers of the impending arrival within the next five minutes and thanking them all for their custom. French President Pierre-Antoine Lascombes looked at his holophone mechanically. The 3D screen displayed a text message: *'Are you ok? Thinking of you.'* He quickly answered. *'All fine. Cannot chat right now. Just arrived. Will call later.'*

His thoughts began wandering. More than a significant day, this was a crucial day. A day not experienced by Europe in decades. A new chapter in its long history, with irreversible consequences for its Member States and their inhabitants. The years of uncertainty were over. Give me just enough time to carry on long enough to witness some achievements, he argued inside. Indeed, the clock was ticking.

The train's abrupt stop brought him out of his mind wandering. The bodyguards assumed their positions, and the presidential entourage began to move and pack while keeping a wary watch on the statesman. One could note the tension around.

"What are the arrangements, Barnabé?"

"Standard security measures, including the train station in complete lockdown, armoured cars with police escort waiting for us at the exit and the closure of all critical roads up to the Parliament."

"Is not this a touch too extreme?"

"Monsieur le Président, we already discussed this. You are not the sole Head of State to arrive by train, and I should not have to prompt the death threats you recently received. On our journey here, the train has already stopped three times—"

"I know, I know."

"—and there will likely be additional disruptions along the way. Even three years on, tensions and resentments persist."

Good Barnabé, always paying attention to details and standing firm in his convictions. "Yes, indeed..." The opposition leader

Charles Le Guen's infamous accusations continued to resonate in the president's mind. '... *an unacceptable betrayal of France's territorial integrity! A knife in the back of those who heroically sacrificed their lives in the First World War to defend our nation's sovereignty!* ... They were foul words. *I am no traitor!* he thought. *This is the best possible outcome. What is at stake here goes far beyond some personal nationalist fantasies.*

The head of security approached him. "Monsieur le Président, another five minutes before we can move on." This day, everything seemed to function within five minutes...

The French delegation and its escort slowly progressed along the Boulevard de Dresde. Too slowly to the president's taste. Pierre-Antoine took a distracted look at the motley crowd gathered on both sides of the road to glimpse at the long procession of state delegations. The sight of people cheering and dancing on this warm sunny day of March, waving flags and messages of support, was comforting. Yet, you could spot among them scattered opposition groups displaying hateful signs against the heads of state and government.

In hindsight, the European referendum campaign had represented a long and exhausting process for all Member States. Extremists on both sides of the political divide have heightened antagonisms, and countless incidents —some fatal— took place in the eight months leading to the vote. The international developments did not help either. Ultimately, the people had decided: the motion was approved by 53.98 per cent two years ago. Even if the result felt short of the polls' predictions, it was still enough to pass, as only a simple majority was required. The referendum was held across the entire Union, not within each nation-state, to present a united front to the outside world and prevent repeating some historical precedents. Words like manipulation, dirty trick and vote rigging burst into the mouths of nationalistic and far-left leaders. Anti-Union protests, sometimes violent, took place throughout the continent. But, in the end, it was a no-brainer, despite the whole process coming close to collapsing at one point.

Even after the initial success, the subsequent round of negotiations proved challenging and laborious. Some EU members failed to take the developing international volatility, a consequence of the destabilisation of the US and the Middle East, and emerging domestic issues seriously. Instead, they persisted in trivial quarrels over pointless symbols and regional identities. Then the decision to make Strasbourg the federal capital was opposed by several states. In the minds of a few nations, there were still deep suspicions about the French Republic's ultimate motives. Given the topography of Europe, some thought Vienna was a more suitable choice. However, it was a resounding no for the Balkans and Central European countries. Brussels was also not a possibility, especially after the traumatic division of Belgium in the middle of the 2040s, which divided the former capital and the defunct state in half. As a result, most European institutions temporarily relocated to Alsace's capital while awaiting consensus on a potential replacement location. A compromise was finally reached by pledging that the future French representative to the Commission would not hold any key position. On the 31st of October 2055, the delegates made public a common position on the future political structure of a united Europe. Strasbourg will become a federal district under the exclusive jurisdiction of the European Parliament, and the symbolic date of the 25th of March 2057 will mark the end of the transition period. *On the date of the Treaty of Rome's 100th anniversary...*

The official vehicle suddenly rocked with a thump. A face warped by hatred appeared behind a window, his scarlet hands frantically banging on the armoured glass. Then, a dark, viscous, red fluid rained on the front and right windscreens.

"Remain seated, Monsieur le Président! We are safe inside," said Barnabé. His earpiece was frantically buzzing. "Security is already responding to the threat." As usual, he reacted calmly and sensitively.

The demented apparition started to yell heinously. "Show yourself, you bastard! I will rip the skin off your vile traitor's body! Your blood and the one of France's enemies will be poured to protect its real patriots. Come out, you scum; face your executioner!"

Several pairs of hands eventually apprehended the assailant within seconds, gagging and handcuffing him before he vanished from sight.

"I am receiving reports that this man broke through the security perimeter," Barnabé went on. "According to our Homeland special units, he received assistance from accomplices employed by one of the private security firms hired for the event. Thankfully, he only carried a bucket containing a red substance mimicking blood. The situation is under control."

"Great!" said President Lascombes, frustrated, "I am going to make the headlines again and be blamed for having deliberately spoiled the day..."

"Do not trouble yourself much, Monsieur le Président, the German Presidency of the Union has already taken the necessary arrangements to delay the ceremony accordingly."

The French President rolled his eyes. "Even better…"

The official convoy finally reached the security of the final metres heading to the entrance of the European Parliament. The imposing structure stood proudly erect, shining brightly in the sunshine of that gorgeous day like a bold crown of glass and concrete. Right at its feet stood German Chancellor Monika Richter, in a dark navy suit and bright yellow shoes, impatiently waiting for her close friend and political ally with a broad smile on her face. The Marseillaise began playing as soon as an usher opened the president's car door.

There we are! The dawn of a new era…

2

Deacon Shenouda Wahba finished washing the altar and the tabernacle following the conclusion of the Sunday service. He was by himself. Despite being a holy day, hardly any parishioners had gathered at the church because of rumours of potential threats against the Christian neighbourhood. Fortunately, nothing unusual occurred. *One cannot condemn people for being scared,* he thought. *We shared enough tears in the past.* At the end of the liturgy, he instructed his colleagues to head straight back to their families and not worry about the cleaning. Being an orphan raised and living on church grounds meant he didn't have any loved ones to look after, unlike them. At twenty-two, he was the youngest ranked deacon in the brotherhood. His dedication, humility, and empathy were well-known and respected in the local Coptic community and fostered his rapid ascent. Most of the church's senior members praised the genuineness of his calling and auguring his future rise to the highest positions in the priesthood. *Time to leave.* On his way out, he briefly glanced at the painted ceiling where the image of the saints and Christ Pantocrator looked at him benevolently.

Once in his cell, he hastily changed out of his religious robe for more suitable clothing, then headed to the main gate of Dayr Mawas' Church of the Virgin Mary. The sun was still high in the sky, meaning he had plenty of time ahead of him. Shenouda wanted to catch an earlier ferry to arrive well in advance of today's evening scheduled tour to get an opportunity to wander around the new excavation site. Besides his spiritual duties, Father Zacharia —the mentor who brought him up and educated him— constantly encouraged him to engage in extra-religious activities from the youngest age. *A priest's duty is to stay close to God and his parishioners*, he continuously repeated. *One cannot apprehend the divine without experiencing the profane.* After experimenting with various options, he ultimately found his second call to delve into Egypt's past of its sands and pursue hieroglyphic studies. Despite the harsh working conditions, the pernicious dust and the continual noise, he grew to enjoy helping his fellow labourers and wandering among the remnants of the ancient Kingdom of the Pharaohs. There was no contradiction in his mind between his religious beliefs and this. After all, according to the Gospel, the Holy Family sought refuge in the country to escape Herod's wrath. Each excavation team was a patchwork of disparate cultures and religions. Yet, all operated harmoniously with a single ambition: to discover more secrets, acquire more knowledge and promote tourism appeal. But Shenouda also wanted to learn and educate himself further about his past. As a Copt, eventually destined for the priesthood, understanding Egypt's first major civilisation was part of God's will.

Particularly in a region which witnessed the country's first attempt to affirm a monotheistic faith in a world dominated by polytheistic beliefs. And this, long before Christianity and Islam, and perhaps even Judaism, according to some controversial scholars.

"Reverend Deacon Wahba! Reverend Deacon Wahba!" The high-pitched voice jolted him out of his daydreaming. Anaghnostos Missael was hailing him.

"What is it, Missael?"

"The Right Reverend Bishop Athanasius sent me to inform you that he wishes to see you as soon as possible, at the very least today. It is rather important, he said." The younger man was panting, drawing irritating flies on his sweating forehead.

"Please respectfully tell Bishop Athanase that I am on my way to Tell el-Amarna. I committed to guiding the site's last tour on the final day of the digging season and, unfortunately, cannot afford to arrive late. But assure him I will attend his office first thing in the morning."

"He seemed anxious to see you, but I shall pass on your message." The novice bowed respectfully and proceeded to sprint away in the opposite direction.

"Anaghnostos Missael, one more thing!" The young man stopped abruptly. "Also, please inform him that I will most certainly be unable to attend vespers this evening."

Next, Shenouda exited through the gates and began running along the busy city streets toward the ferry dock. He did not want to miss the boat. He reached the pier twenty minutes later, covered in sweat, but, to his delight, at the exact moment the ship moored. *What does the old man want from me? Probably some widow or orphan to visit and console,* he thought. It can certainly wait till tomorrow. His deep blue eyes meandered around the dark, majestic waters of the Nile, gently moving on its bed. Across the horizon, behind the mountain range, mighty dark clouds were amassing, the sign of an impending storm. Over the last ten years, the country's climate has dramatically transformed. Humidity levels were rising with rainfall becoming more seasonal and abundant. The fertile lands were now expanding beyond the natural boundaries of the Nile for the delight of the fellahin. But it also significantly impacted the preservation of historical monuments not accustomed to increased atmospheric moisture after millennia of dry weather. And the political situation in certain parts of the world, directly affecting an Egyptian government already battling financial difficulties, added further pressure to preserve the country's heritage. Tourists were growing scarce. *Another reason for me to contribute to the survival of the site...*

"You're my best guide, Shenouda," Professor Walters told him a few days ago. "The final tour of the season is customarily the most significant and secures patrons and funds for the next one. The continuity of our research relies on its success."

"I will do my best, Professor, I promise. Do not forget this Sunday's worship is especially significant to our seminarians, our hierarchy and, above all, our community."

"That's why I programmed it for 6.00 pm. The group will convene several prominent donors and members of the board. They expect to be guided by a descendant of the ancient Egyptians. You know how much of an impact it makes. Please, I implore you." Professor Walter's voice was getting desperate.

"Again, I can only promise you I will try my best. Now, if you forgive me, I must return to my religious studies. As you are aware, God is a jealous master...."

The ferry was now sailing to the east bank, drifting peacefully on the serene waters amid a gentle breeze playing with the papyrus. *A descendant of the ancient Egyptians,* he thought. Yes, it was how the Coptic community was frequently referred to. Legend had it that the people of the Pharaohs converted to Christianity and later withstood Arab assimilation thanks to the strength of their faith. *But there is no evidence that I do belong to my community. I am merely a baby found abandoned on the steps of the Church of the Virgin Mary. I could be born into any other community.* However, the prospect effectively increased his popularity among tourists, resulting in considerable demand for his guided tours. And who could blame him when Father Zacharia constantly brought forth what he called "our heritage."

The young deacon finally reached the Amarna Dig House. *More than an hour and a half left before the tour.* That would give him enough time to wander the Southern suburb's excavation site where the remains of an unknown dignitary's family house had recently been uncovered. *Exciting!* He quickly gazed at the cliffs in the east, where the gloomy clouds grew increasingly menacing. The storm will break out this evening—

"Shenouda, my boy! You came!" Professor John Walter erupted, suddenly noticing the deacon. The Englishman was enjoying a cup of tea while seated at one of the outside tables. He rushed to the young man before hugging him tightly. "My God, I'm so delighted you're here!" The professor's bearded face was all smiles, his eyes sparkling joyfully and sneering like a five-year-old boy. Deep in his late fifties, the archaeologist was of a cheerful nature and always pleasant with everyone, even after five years of overseeing the mission. He wore an immaculate beige suit and polished black shoes.

"Do not be too excited, Professor; you want to produce a good impression on your guests," Shenouda chuckled. "Is it true the team has discovered a new dignitary's palace in the Southern City?"

"Indeed, indeed! Quite an exciting finding, I must say. However, your curiosity will have to wait for another day. Since you arrived in advance, I want to get to business immediately."

"But, Professor, you told me-"

"Please, please, please!" he begged with his hands. Our guests are already here, their boat is anchored at the Visitor Centre, and they look forward to it. This is how we proceed: I'll escort them to the Centre's conference room for a thirty-minute presentation of our most recent discoveries, budgetary report, and future needs. Then, you'll guide them on the usual tour, starting with the Centre's collection, followed by the Great Temple of Aten, the Great Palace and its surroundings, and ending with the Workshop of Tuthmosis. But this time, instead of continuing to the Royal Tombs, you'll lead them to the Stela S!" he said with an exalted voice.

"The stela S?" Shenouda replied with surprise.

"Absolutely! Its renovation was fully completed last week, thanks to the Ministry of Antiquities' last-minute assistance. It's the ideal opportunity to show our patrons how we use their donations and demonstrate our excellent relationships with the national authorities. You know how significant the Stelae Project is."

"I do, I do. But is it wise? The path to Stela S is arduous, and the forecast does not look optimistic." He pointed at the threatening sky in the east.

"It's a ten-minute drive, and the new stairs are also finished. We'll have just enough time, I can assure you. The storm isn't expected until later, I understand."

"All right, all right, I give up," Shenouda answered with a smile. "Just allow me fifteen minutes to freshen up."

"Of course, my boy, of course! Oh! This will be such a success!" He hugged him again before heading to the Visitor Centre, whistling. How could someone refuse such a candid person?

***

"… *As my father lives the living Ra-Horakhty rejoicing in what is Right,*
in his name as Shu which is in the sun-disk,
given life for ever and eternity,
as my heart is sweetened
over the king's wife, over her children,
that old age be granted to the great king's wife
Neferneferuaten Nefertiti granted life eternally,
in this million years,
while she is under the hand of Pharaoh may he live, prosper and be well,
and old age be granted to the king's daughter Meretaten
and the king's daughter Meketaten her children,
while they are under the hand of the king's wife

their mother for ever and eternity...."

"I will conclude our tour with this passage from King Akhenaten's pledge to the Aten. I sincerely hope you enjoyed it as much as I did guiding you today."

A frantic wave of applause and raucous cheers broke the silence. Shenuda modestly bowed and smiled at them in thanks. High above, on the cliff behind him, radiating in the dazzling sunset, the imposing carved image of King Akhenaten, Queen Nefertiti, and their four daughters were devoutly praying to the Sun God Aten, benevolently gracing them.

"Bravo! Bravo! Another round of applause for our outstanding guide, Shenouda. Professor Walters was cheering frenetically. "Wonderful, wonderful! No doubt you have a hundred more questions to ask this gorgeous young man. Let's all head back to the Centre for some refreshments and food. We'll be more comfortable to-"

The ominous iron sky suddenly burst into a brilliant flash of light, striking the top of the ridge. Then a deluge of water poured from the heavens, cascading over the nearby rocks. The small group rushed down the concrete steps to the safety of the minibus parked below. Despite desperate efforts to move, Shenouda's body remained frozen. The elements were raging around him in a flurry of lightning. An overwhelming impulse possessed the young priest with an irresistible urge to look at the stela, like a subconscious call. The whole carving was magically glittering in the brightness of the dying sun, surrounded by strobe lights, in a surreal manifestation of divine power. At that moment, the entire sculpted scene suddenly came to life. The Pharaoh, his wife and daughters extended their hands

21

higher towards the Aten, chanting loud prayers in hopes of receiving his magnanimous protection. In return, the Sun's all-powerful disk bestowed his everlasting blessings to its faithful worshippers. At some point, the image of Queen Nefertiti took form and moved slowly in Shenouda's direction. Light amidst light, beauty within beauty. A suave voice echoed through the commotion as her beautiful eyes peered deeply into the depths of his soul.

"Remember your oath, my son; remember your pledge to the Aten. Go north to the land of Khor. Find the sacred stone and fulfil your destiny."

The flamboyant Sun God behind her became larger and brighter. The Eye of Ra stared at him, magnificent, almighty, terrifying, before its aura scorched everything around in a massive burst of light. In the middle of the flare, Shenouda saw a large city burning to the ground. The vision was interrupted by another tremendous flash of light striking the top of the ridge for a second time, accompanied by a loud bang and a massive explosion of rocks. Only darkness remained in the end...

3

The sound of laughs echoed throughout the monastery's serene white streets. The three teenagers ran merrily through the deserted lanes of the residential quarters on their way to the main temple. The source of their euphoria was the special dispensation granted to them this afternoon, which they fully intended to enjoy.

"Come on Jamyang! We don't want to get late!"

"I'm coming; I'm coming, Kalsang! You know I can't get rushed. He was gasping for air while labouring to climb the steep staircase.

"It'd be easier for you if you were eating less momos!"

"It's not my fault if my mom keeps bringing them every time she visits me. She only wants me to remain strong and in good health."

His companion exclaimed, laughing. "You're not strong and healthy, Jamyang; you are FAT!"

"Kalsang, please! You should be more considerate of your brother and refrain from employing such language," said a third voice. "Where has your kindness gone?".

"Every patient carries their own doctor within him, Rinchen."

"But he who gives food gives longevity, pleasant complexion, happiness, stamina and intelligence," Jamyang retorted.

"Do not start, you two," commanded Rinchen, "this is not the time to debate right now. And we are almost there. Kalsang, next time, try to use a more compassionate word."

"Like?"

"Like… let's see… Like 'indulgence'! It is no secret that our brother Kalsang finds too much indulgence in the pleasures of food. We should pray to the Buddha to grant him strength in his daily struggle."

"Indulgence? Daily struggle? Really?"

The trio burst into laughter. Their teacher, the Venerable Kunchen Lama, nicknamed them the Inseparable.

Seventeen-year-old Rinchen was the eldest. Well-educated in the scriptures, his peers now addressed him as lama. He was born into an affluent family in Dharamshala. After serving the last Dalai Lama in his youth, his father became a prominent member of the Central Tibetan Administration. As the second son and following the family tradition, Rinchen was sent to the Tawang Monastery at seven to join the Sangha. Although his 'calling' initially started as an obligation, the young boy quickly embraced the monastic life, giving him a way to escape his older brother's relentless bullying. He also had a younger sister, but she was too little to recall him fully when he left. Nonetheless, she invariably included a few kind words in the letters sent by his mother. Physically, Rinchen was tall and slender, and his deep, black eyes emphasised his gaunt face. He was the wise one —studious, perceptive of all things and eager to learn.

Jamyang and Kalsang were his juniors by two years. They both arrived at the monastery on the same day, and Venerable Kunchen Lama tasked Rinchen to mind them. The three boys have shared the same cell ever since.

Jamyang was from Bomdila in the State of Arunachal Pradesh, farther to the south. After consulting the oracle, his parents agreed to make him a monk to improve the family's karma. They decided on Tawang over his hometown because of the monastery's greater reputation. He was the troublesome one —always on the move, possessed by inexhaustible energy, and rarely missing an opportunity to contradict his elders.

Kalsang was a native of Tawang. He has been obsessed with becoming a monk from a very young age. His mother would endlessly recount she regularly searched for him inside the monastery's grounds, where he constantly escaped. After observing his behaviour, the abbot, the Venerable Chophel Rinpoche, concluded this was no coincidence. It could only suggest Kalsang was the reincarnation of a former lama wanting to learn the Dharma further. Thus, after seeking his parents' permission, he joined the Sangha aged eight. Devoted to his studies and highly respectful of the sacred teachings, he was taciturn and constantly stood close to his two companions. He was the shy one —his eyes frequently expressed a peculiar, far-off melancholy.

"Hoy, you three, hurry over here!" It was the voice of Wangdue Lama, the cook. "Are you the ones who Kunchen Lama sent?" the robust man eyed them scornfully, his wrists crossed over his hips. Dirty grease stains were covering his shemdap and dhonka. However, the imposing monk was known for being unconcerned about those details. He was equally renowned for his rudeness. His sole source of pride was his cooking ability, and the Buddha knew how skilled he was.

"Yes, we are, Venerable Wangdue Lama", answered Rinchen, joining his hands together and bowing respectfully.

"Come along, then! See those six containers of leftover food here? Take them to the recycler."

"But that's the work of a young novice!" retorted Kalsang, defiantly.

"This is the task Venerable Kunchen Lama asked me to assign you! Therefore do it," he said with an ugly smirk. "Or go back to your studies and forget your afternoon off."

"We shall do it with reverence, Wangdue Lama," acknowledged Rinchen.

"But—"

"Kalsang, please. Happiness is not something ready-made. It results from your deeds. Let us perform this task with humility and then enjoy our afternoon."

They took the large containers and carried them to the recycling grounds a hundred metres away. Jamyang silently trailed his two companions before suddenly dropping his load. He was shaking, looking terrified.

"Jamyang, what is the matter?" gently inquired Rinchen.

"They're… there," he stammered. "You know… them…" His final word died in a whisper.

"Come on, Jamyang, you are fifteen years old!" Kalsang lectured him. "Don't tell me you are still scared of them?"

"You know we will both protect you, Jamyang," pledged Rinchen. "There is nothing you should be worried about. Let us get on with it."

They rapidly reached the recycling pad and began to dump the relish into the deep holes in the ground. Shortly after, loud squeaking sounds voiced over their heads. Sitting ungracefully on the edge of the wall, three fluffy creatures were peering at them with curiosity and greed. They belonged to the local group of macaques, whose territory included the landfill. Jamyang froze entirely, and his eyes well up with tears. A few years before, he had experienced a dreadful close encounter with one of the monkeys and was still distressed by the experience. One of the primates began to screech, and additional ones appeared within seconds. A bulky dominant male emerged along the wall and howled loudly while staring at them.

"Carry on with your task. Just ignore them. And most of all, do not stare at them. They will not become aggressive unless they see us as a threat. And, Kalsang?"

"Yes, Rinchen?"

"Do not toss any stone at them, as you frequently do. I am in no mood for a stand, and you know it is bad karma."

"Alright, alright, I won't…."

The three boys carefully took back the containers before slowly moving away. Then, as soon as they reached a safe distance, they started running frantically. The macaques behind them leapt down the wall and dashed for the relish while yelling and fighting. Jamyang flew ahead as if he possessed invisible wings while the other two were excitedly laughing at him. Gasping but merry, they finally made it to the kitchen. The stern cook was waiting there with their teacher, Venerable Kunchen Lama. The trio bowed respectfully at the wizened face grinning benevolently at them before he courteously returned the gesture.

"Ah! And here are our Inseparable! Have you completed the task I assigned you?"

"We have, Venerable Kunchen Lama," answered Rinchen.

"How about you, young Jamyang?"

"I did what was asked of me, Venerable Kunchen Lama." He was looking at the ground, still shaken.

"He was utterly brave and confronted his fear honourably!" Kalsang continued in a proud voice.

"Very good, Jamyang", said Venerable Kunchen Lama in a silky voice. "*Know well what leads you forward and what holds you back, and choose the path that leads to wisdom.* Very well, a promise is a promise. You three can go and wander wherever your hearts want. I expect you back for dinner at seven."

"Yeah!"

The older man turned to Rinchen. "Rinchen Lama."

"Yes, Venerable Kunchen Lama?"

"You will see me in the abbot's office tomorrow at noon, after lunch. There are important matters the Abbot and I need to discuss with you." He looked at Kalsang and Jamyang. "You may both accompany him."

They bowed simultaneously. "We are grateful, Venerable Kunchen Lama."

"Alright, off you go! Hurry, before I have a change of heart!" he commanded them, his eyes filled with malice.

They ran away without looking back until reaching the monastery's gates.

"Where should we go?" questioned Kalsang.

"Let's go to the lake!" answered Jamyang. He was behaving like a child now that the dread had left his mind.

"I'll ask my brother to drive us there; then we can walk back."

***

Lake Pang Teng Tso was quiet and deserted, if not for the singing birds flying around. The calm, crystal-clear waters glistened in the midst of the sky's radiant sun. The temperature was already relatively mild for March. Mount Kangto was majestically observing the surroundings in the distance, its last winter snowfall holding helplessly on its slopes before melting in the upcoming weeks. It has been a decade since the mountain range was completely blanketed with snow all year round. Rinchen observed the natural mirror with contemplation and admiration, awed by the peaceful setting.

"Rinchen? What do you think Venerable Kunchen Lama wishes to discuss with you?" Kalsang was lying lazily on the soft moss, wearing his shemdap, and drying in the sun after a vigorous dip in the chilly waters. His zhen and dhonka were folded on a rock beside him.

"I honestly have no idea, Jamyang. I presume I will know more tomorrow."

"Well, it must be important if Abbot Chophel Rinpoche is there too."

Rinchen allowed his thoughts to drift. He enjoyed today's morning prayers and meditation. As often, they helped him find some inner serenity. The last few nights had been troubled by the same recurring vivid dream. He stood in a foreign land, far away from India. A cold and wet place covered by brownish, round mountains. Then a moment later, he sat in a cell, two shadowy silhouettes beside him. One wept slowly while the other asked him in a distressed voice, "What am I meant to do, Rinchen? This goes against the Buddha's teachings." Each time, he woke up before he could answer. I should tell Venerable Kunshen Lama about this dream, he thought. He took three deep breaths and calmly emptied his mind.

"What a beautiful and quiet day," he then said. "An appropriate occasion to meditate."

"What?!" yelled Kalsang." But we already practised meditation this morning."

"To Meditate among our brothers in the temple is one part of the practice. To do it in communion with the creation is another one. The Lord Buddha reached awakening by meditating under a tree. We ought to follow his example. Then, I suggest we stop at Jamyang's house on our way back to the monastery. I am sure his mother prepared some delicious momos for us to enjoy while sipping tea. What do you think?"

Kalsang joined his hands and bowed reverently with a broad grin. "Venerable Rinchen Lama, you have once more spoken with wisdom..."

The three monks touched each other foreheads before sitting side by side in the lotus posture. They straightened their back, resting their hands on their legs. Then they closed their eyes, gradually relaxing their muscles from head to foot, allowing their body to settle and reach balance. They felt the soft, warm ground underneath gently supporting their brittle physical envelope. Simultaneously, the maelstrom of thoughts began to echo inside their minds. Their eyelids opened slightly, gazing at the vastness. Calm, slow breathing. The inner storm subsides, recedes, and floats away. Steady, slow breathing. The words of their teacher flooded their heads. Emptiness.

The air flows in and out, a comforting and soothing noise. Awareness. Awareness of the mind, the body as a whole and billions of cells bound into one entity. Awareness expands. Notice your surroundings. Feel the ground, the soft touch of moisture, the sun's warmth. Pay attention to the sounds of living creatures, the breeze delicately stroking the water's surface, joyfully playing with the grass, and the fragrant aroma of the blooming flowers. Expand further. Allow your consciousness to detach from its mortal sheath. Ascend over the mountains to the depth of space. Now, contemplate the Earth. This radiant blue sphere, gracefully floating in the void, elegantly dancing with its sisters around our blazing yellow star. Allow your life force to dance with them for a while before travelling further. Watch the Sun slowly shrinking, becoming smaller and smaller, until it becomes a bright tiny glittering light among countless other bright tiny glittering lights. Observe them gathering in the vast swirling cloud of our galaxy. Now, gaze at the whole Universe, constantly shifting and evolving in perpetual metamorphosis. Witness impermanence, 'mi rtag pa'—the eternal cycle of life and death. Finally, open your inner eye and stare deep inside your soul. Feel the touch of your consciousness. Embrace the light glowing in its centre. You are the light, and the light is you, a perfect symbiosis, a sheer harmony...

4

"Dear passengers, we have arrived at Edinburgh Waverley Station, where this train terminates. Please, make sure to take all your belongings with you. Scottish National Railways wishes you an enjoyable day...."

Giancarlo took the large suitcase, backpack, and pet carrier and headed to the carriage exit door. Finally there! He thought. A timid 'meow' came out of the basket.

"A little more patience Myst, we're almost there. I know; it's been a long journey for me too." A cheerier meow greeted his words. He checked his watch; it was 14:00. One could rely on the trains' punctuality.

Indeed, it had been an extensive journey. He left Milan for London late the night before on a fast train, followed by another fast train to Edinburgh. At least the first class was extremely comfortable, and he managed to get some sleep. Having just turned thirty, this new job was a fantastic opportunity for the recently graduated researcher he was. Born in Naples, the young man had spent his whole life in Italy, except for a six-month internship in California. Giancarlo looked forward to discovering a different way of life but also total independence from the intrusiveness of his family. His holophone rang. It was his mother.

"Si, pronto?... Si Mamma, sono arrivato a Edimburgo… Va tutto bene. Sono alla stazione dei treni… Devo andare all'appartamento. Ti chiamo più tardi… Ti amo Mamma."[*] He hanged up with a sigh.

The young man walked along the platform. His appearance was not typically Mediterranean with his medium-sized body, short auburn hair, and angelic face with wide-set brown eyes. Only his accent revealed his origins. Proceeding through the crowd, he eventually reached the platform's gate before noticing someone holding a sign with his name. He approached the slightly corpulent middle-aged bearded man wearing a beautiful tweed costume with a bright violet tie.

"Hi?"

"Doctor Caracciolo?"

"Si. Hem, yes." *Doctor…* thought Giancarlo, *I'm still not used to it.*

"How lovely to finally meet you in person!" A broad smile lit up the man's face. "Welcome, welcome!" He shook his hand vigorously. "I am Iain McEwan, Administrator of the research centre. Welcome to Edinburgh!"

"Thank you very much, Mr McEwan. It's a pleasure to be here."

"Please, please, call me Iain. Oh! And who is this?"

"This is Myst, my little cat." Myst meowed confidently. "She's eager to go to the flat, I believe."

---

[*]*Hello? Yes, mum, I have arrived in Edinburgh… Everything is fine. I am at the train station… I need to go to the flat. I will call you later… I love you, mum.*

"Of course, of course! This way, please, an executive car is waiting for us. Allow me to help you."

He took the suitcase, and they drove off the station five minutes later.

"How was your journey to Scotland?" McEwan enquired.

"A bit long to my taste, but still reasonable.

Fortunately, the fast trains make things less tiring. And I wish to thank you for upgrading me to first class."

"Not at all, not at all! Given that you did not want to fly, that was the least we could do. However, may I inquire about the reason for this decision?"

"Well, you see, it was much simpler with my cat. It's quite difficult to fly directly into England and Scotland with a pet."

"I understand, I understand. A wise decision. Well, the team is eager to meet you. I must say, your impressive CV and well-developed Thesis have made a huge impression among them already. I am confident we made the right choice by choosing you."

"I hope so. That's very kind of you to say. I'll do my best to keep up with your expectations—Wooow!" Giancarlo suddenly exclaimed, pointing to the left, "What's this impressive monument over there? Is it a tribute to a monarch or some politician? It's rather… big."

"Oh, this? It is the Scott Monument, a memorial to one of Scotland's most illustrious authors, Sir Walter Scott. He wrote several history-based novels, like Ivanhoe. Perhaps you are familiar with it or have seen one of its adaptations at the cinema."

"Sorry, I'm afraid I've not."

"Oh, do not worry. Regrettably, most young Scots are also unfamiliar with him… Look, we are now entering Edinburgh's district called New Town. At the top of the hill on your left, you can see Edinburgh Castle. And to your right, this massive mountain overlooking the town is called Arthur's Seat."

"Arthur's Seat? Is it related to King Arthur?" Giancarlo asked candidly.

"Ha, ha, ha! Well, my friend, some people will try to make you believe so. However, do not listen to them; it is a complete fib. The mount is just an ancient volcano. No need to panic; it has been extinct for millions of years, unlike the one close to your native city. But disregard my rambling, and do not concern yourself with those specifics. I arranged a private tour with a member of your team tomorrow morning to help you get acquainted with the city. Edinburgh may not be as big as Naples, but it has plenty of hidden gems. You will soon realise we take great pride in the history of our capital."

"Thank you, that's very generous of you."

"Not at all, not at all!"

Twenty minutes later, they finally reached the gates of the research facility. On the left, a sign said *Newhaven Lighthouse Park Research Centre. A Division of Pharma Cybernetics Corp.* This project is financed with the help of the European and Scottish Governments. After passing security, the vehicle rolled down the main road. The complex was more significant than Giancarlo had expected.

"It's a big place."

"We own two-thirds of the peninsula, courtesy of the Scottish Government. You can see the two primary research facilities to your right. The Biogeneric Unit, where your talents will be put to use, and further down the Cybernetic Department. The living quarters of our resident researchers are situated on your left. Given that you will be devoting extended hours in the laboratory, we thought it would be easier to assign you to one of the available accommodations there. It is a charming duplex villa at the edge of the complex with a nice sea view and a private garden which I am certain your little furry friend will enjoy."

"That's truly kind of you. I had such bad experiences finding accommodation in Milan and Rome, you know."

Their vehicle stopped in front of the villa. As mentioned, the building appeared both sophisticated and contemporary, wholly secluded and directly overlooking the sea. McEwan unlocked the front door.

"There you are! Come in, come in! Here are your two sets of keys and your temporary access badge. Security will issue the permanent one tomorrow. The house is completely furnished with all necessities. You will find a sizable living room, a kitchen with a dining area, and an office on the ground floor. There are two bedrooms on the top floor, each with a bathroom and many wardrobes." He sounded like a real estate agent. "A cleaner comes twice a week for your convenience. Just avoid leaving around any sensitive material. Use the safe situated in the office. Not that we do not trust our cleaning team, but one can never be too cautious."

"Understood."

"In here", he showed a sizable file, "is all the information concerning the villa, the various buildings and facilities of the complex. It is updated weekly. We have almost everything on site since we know how valuable our residents' time is. If necessary, goods can be ordered online and delivered from outside the compound. Just make sure to notify security as anything or anyone entering the complex must be vetted. Please get in touch with Ms Boswell, my secretary, if you require any additional home furnishings, technology, or conveniences. She will arrange everything for you. Oh, by the way, do you have a suit?"

"Yes…"

"Excellent! I am aware you might be a little tired. But tonight, we are throwing a little celebration to mark the Centre's fifth anniversary. Please come. It will allow me to introduce you to your future colleagues in a more relaxed environment."

"That's alright. I'll be there."

"Wonderful! I am certain you will enjoy yourself. Right! I will allow you to adjust to your new surroundings and see you in the auditorium at 19:00 sharp. You will find its location by looking at the map in the folder. Remember to bring your badge. And make sure to wear an extra layer on you as nights in March can still be rather chilly." Then he walked out. The place became suddenly silent, except for a tiny critter scratching her carrier bag.

"Myst! I didn't forget about you. Come here and let's see what we can find for you."

He took the purring furball out of the carrier and held her before exploring the surroundings.

***

The auditorium was conveniently positioned in the centre of the complex. Giancarlo entered one of the two wide doors and was met by a large gathering of people chatting and drinking. The hall was a broad, versatile circular room, convertible at will as a theatre or a functional space. *'A little celebration'*, *he said*. About a hundred people had gathered here, primarily scientists, technical staff and some officials. A loud voice hailed him.

"Giancarlo, Giancarlo! Come here, come here!" McEwan was waving at him next to a small group dominated by a dark figure with Asian features. The man, dressed in black, stared right into his eyes. Giancarlo recognised him right away. He was Professor Owen Yang, the Head of the Bio-genetic Unit, his boss.

"Allow me to introduce you to your colleagues." McEwan continued. "Here, of course, we have our great genius, Professor Yang!"

"It's a great honour to meet you and have this opportunity to work with you, Professor," said Giancarlo.

"Indeed", answered Yang in an obnoxious and arrogant tone. "Indeed."

"Good, good!" went on McEwan. "And over here are your co-workers: Doctor Colin Forsythe, who will accompany you around the city tomorrow, Doctor Ranveer Singh, Doctor Rebecca Schultz, Doctor Emilie Delariviere and Doctor Natalia Ipatievna. An ambitious international team, as you can see! I will enable them to introduce you individually to their area of expertise. It is far too confusing for me. Now, if you would excuse me, I have a speech to deliver."

He walked over to the stand at the back. A waiter came across with champagne flutes.

"Would you like a glass?" inquired a voice with an acute Eastern European accent. It was Doctor Natalia Ipatievna.

"Of course, gladly," replied Giancarlo courteously.

The young woman elegantly offered him one of the elongated flutes. She was petite but well proportioned, with a fair, complexioned face and long light blond hair. She stared at him with her deep grey eyes, smiling. An extremely attractive woman, visibly aware of her charms.

"I hope you will quickly adjust to our little troupe. If there's anything I can help you with—"

"Hem!" Professor Yang rudely interrupted her and gave them a stern look. At that moment, the sound of a microphone screeched in the background.

"Please, if I may have a few minutes of your attention," McEwan began. "Prime Minister, Mr Mayor, dear colleagues and friends. Allow me to thank you all for coming tonight to commemorate the fifth anniversary of our tremendous adventure. Five years and so many accomplishments! Looking back, who would have predicted that..."

Giancarlo stared at Professor Yang. The man displayed a sombre, shuttered tone. One could hardly interpret the emotions on his face.

"Don't pay attention to the old raven," murmured a voice with a pronounced Scottish accent in his ear. It was Doctor Colin Forsythe. "He may not be the most pleasant fellow, but he is fair and undeniably gifted. You'll get used to him. It's his way of handling newbies and asserting command over his domain if you like.

"I must say, it's quite effective," Giancarlo whispered with an embarrassed smile.

He looked back at the stage. McEwan now listed the discoveries made at the Centre since it first opened and the promising applications that might come as a result. As an introvert, Giancarlo was not an ardent fan of speeches, even more delivering one. He looked at the gathered crowd. People seemed to focus on the master of ceremonies, with one exception. A forty-year-old black woman was staring directly at him. She was slender and tall, with short hair, a delicate face, and a purple crayon dress accentuating her athletic figure. She walked slightly towards him in a gracious feline move and slowly raised her glass to catch his attention. He looked at Colin.

"Who is that woman over there on the right?" he asked. "The one in the purple dress."

"Ah ha! That's Professor Liz Edwards," answered Colin. "She's the head of the Cybernetic Department. Beware, she's a smooth operator", he went on with a wink.

5

Monika and Pierre-Antoine sat alone in one of the European Parliament's private lounges to share some quiet before the big event. They could contemplate the beautiful Zen Garden bordering the Canal de la Marne au Rhin through the large bay windows. On the other side of the water stood the brand-new government building, an intriguing blend of neoclassicism and modern style. Its height was deliberately ten metres lower than the parliament building to remind that, unlike the non-elected body, the directly elected assembly was supreme in legislative decisions.

"How are you Pierre-Antoine?" asked Monika. "I want to apologise for what happened earlier."

"There is no need to apologise, Monika. After all, my police are still maintaining order in Strasbourg for a few more days. And we always anticipate certain radical elements to attempt to cross the tight net. Fortunately, unharmed this time."

"Nonetheless, I find it suspicious how easily this guy managed to approach your limo. And also, how he and his accomplices escaped the strict verification by which each private agent is supposed to pass,' she grunted.

"You are a suspicious woman by nature, Monika", he chuckled. She gave him a disapproving glance. "Alright, alright. I will talk to Jorge, if it makes you feel any better."

"The police and the armed forces are not yet under your brother's command."

"Come on, we all take office tomorrow. And Jorge has been liaising with all senior officers for the last six months. I believe he is the best suited to conduct enquiries."

"Very well, I will stop bothering you with this." She grasped his right hand. "And what about…."

"Everything is fine. The surgery is scheduled here for Monday, discreetly. No one will notice my absence that day with all the movements accompanying the power-taking."

"That day?" she asked with a gentle alarmed voice. "Pierre-Antoine, you might want to take it a little easier. You have been pushing yourself too much recently."

"Indeed. Nevertheless, it is essential to create an illusion of business as usual. A few years will pass until things settle down and routine becomes the norm. I do not want to cause tension right at the start. In any case, the doctors have all been reassuring. The procedure will last less than an hour because it is still in its early stages. I promise to go easy after the surgery. The only unknown factor to be concerned about is a potential relapse in the future."

"I am glad to hear that. I will come by later to make sure you are alright." She kept holding his hand.

They had been close friends for almost two decades. They met on the benches of the Strasbourg University of

Politics. He was starting his fourth year of studies, and she was participating in an Erasmus exchange programme through the University of Hamburg. They connected immediately, and despite the burden of their political careers, their friendship never faltered through the years. But none of them would have predicted twenty years ago that they would one day hold the highest office in their respective nation and actively contribute to today's achievement.

"I am grateful, Monika. I sincerely appreciate your support. It means a lot."

"How is Franck doing? How are you two doing?"

"Not good, I'm afraid. He finds it more and more difficult to accept all this. I believe he likely assumed that I would give up my political ambitions once everything was in place. Yet, you know me..." he added, shrugging his shoulders.

"Well, let me know how things turn out."

"I shall, I promise. Alright, I believe we misused our time together. Let us enter the lions' den before they think we are drafting a new treaty..."

At that exact moment, someone knocked on the door. "Madam Chancellor, Mr president? Everyone is waiting for you."

"See?" he said, grinning.

***

The transition ceremony was to be broadcast live around the world from the Parliament's hemicycle, where the newly elected Members of the European Parliament, representatives of the national parliaments, members of the press, guests and, of course, the thirty-six political heads of state and government of the Union had gathered. Each of the latter will take on the roles of High Commissioners and Commissioners of the new government body as a reward for graciously relinquishing their country's last regal powers for the common good. This compromise was agreed upon to facilitate a smoother transition. Then, after the next parliamentary elections, organised in four years, the members of the European Federal Commission will be selected from among the MEPs. Finally, the European President will be appointed among the Commissioners by a simple majority, followed by a vote of confidence by the Parliament. This time, however, Austrian Prime Minister, Andrea Strauss, a humanist and Nobel Peace Prize laureate, had already been designated president after receiving unanimous approval.

Each head of state was expected to deliver a five-minute oath speech. But everyone anticipated that it would take longer. As host, France was scheduled to speak last.

Monika and Pierre-Antoine arrived together. The French President reassured the delegates rushing to him to inquire about his "dreadful" experience before his half-brother took him aside.

"Hermano, how are you?"

"I am alright, brother. It takes more than some paint and yelling to intimidate me."

"Indeed. I was more preoccupied with... you know?"

"Do not concern yourself with that. But, to get back to the main subject and ease Monika's concerns, I would greatly appreciate it if you could quietly investigate this morning's incident."

In retrospect, the two men were the intriguing result of an odd combination of circumstances. Pierre-Antoine's father died when he was only three years old. Two years later, his mother, Alexandra, married Felipe Sanchez, a Member of the Spanish Parliament. Jorge was born two years after. Coincidentally, the two brothers followed a political path that ultimately ended with one becoming President of France and the other Prime Minister of Spain, practically simultaneously. An unprecedented situation in the history of contemporary Europe.

"I promise I will. Bueno, I will see you at the reception after the ceremony. You look exquisite as usual, Monika," added Jorge kissing her hand.

"You are such a charmer, Jorge," she giggled, blushing.

Finally, the time for the final speech came after two interminable hours. The Master Usher came forward and solemnly announced, "His Excellency the President of France, Monsieur Pierre-Antoine Lascombes."

A roar of applause greeted Pierre-Antoine as he stood up and entered the stage.

"Ahem.

Madam President, Mister President of the Parliament, honourable Heads of State and Government, estimated Members of the Commission and the Parliament, citizens of Europe.

Allow me to join my colleagues and friends in reaffirming that today is no ordinary day. No, today is an unprecedented day in the history of this continent. Our continent. We all gather in this remarkable building, the symbol of our democratic institutions, to celebrate. To celebrate something that Europe has never experienced in the past, a union of wills, not a union of constraints.

For centuries, each of our nations bluntly walked the paths of discord, hatred, domination, and betrayal, blinded by the assertion of our righteousness. Despite numerous genuine attempts to strengthen our ties and hold on to a common goal, our old demons kept returning to lure us. Consequently, centuries elapsed with millions of innocent souls sacrificed as insignificant accessories. As current leaders, we are the unwilling custodians of this senseless, horrendous legacy of blood and tears. But we can no longer be complicit and accept hiding our heads in the sand.

Today, the time has finally come to redeem ourselves and to offer future generations the hopes so long denied to their forebears. It is our sacred duty to consider this endless list of past mistakes and ensure that, from now on, we will undertake every step, every action to protect and defend the fundamental rights every individual under our care is entitled to. Especially now, more than ever, as we collectively face an uncertain future. When our freedom and universal values are threatened on our doorstep. When across the Atlantic, the nation that was once the beacon of democracy and freedom is confronted with its worst identity crisis since 1861, plunging entire regions of the globe into political turmoil and uncertainty. When certain religious and factional groups try to dictate how we should live. And finally, when the very essence of life on this planet and our own existence as a species are at stake.

Therefore, as elected President of France, along with the approval of my national Parliament, I pledge my country to the service of our new Federation. As such, I officially surrender our regal power and swear allegiance to its Constitution ad Perpetuum.

But not only. We, your representatives, make this solemn vow in this new dawn. We cannot, and shall not, remain silent witnesses as the world slowly descends into madness. To quote Maurice Schumann, one hundred years ago, '*World peace cannot be safeguarded without the making of creative efforts proportionate to the dangers which threaten it. The contribution which an organised and living Europe can bring to civilisation is indispensable to the maintenance of peaceful relations.*'

My fellow citizens, let us send a message across continents: do not lose faith; Europe stands by your side! And that's what today's accomplishment is all about. Humanity is experiencing a crucial moment in its history. By seizing this opportunity to join forces and sever the ties that bind us, this Union shows the path to a more stable world by speaking with a single voice. On the day India became independent, Prime Minister Jawaharlal Nehru told his nation: '*Yet the turning point is past, and history begins anew for us, the history which we shall live and act, and others will write about.*' That wisdom should become ours.

Right now, the nations of the Earth are staring at us, some in praise, some in fear. To the former, we say, 'We are honoured by your trust.' To the latter, we say, 'We are not your enemies, respect us, and we will equally respect you.' Yes, I agree; those are substantive words with elevated expectations. This coming administration holds a moral obligation to set them into action. We make this pledge right before you. Mindful that failure to do so will irreversibly bring the clock back to the point of no return. This is the pivotal moment where we reject our old demons, once and for all, and commit ourselves to secure the stability and prosperity of those to whom we are now accountable.

Allow me to conclude with a quote from a former British Prime Minister. In 2002, she wrote the European Union was a *"classic utopian project, a monument to the vanity of intellectuals, a program whose inevitable destiny is failure."* Let me to tell you loud and clear: on this day, 25 March 2057, she is proven wrong. The European Union has not failed! It has not failed because we are determined to achieve the impossible.

Long live the United Federation of Europe! Thank you!"

A full standing ovation accompanied a new roar of applause, more intense than the first one, while cheers erupted outside the hemicycle. Thirty-six nations had surrendered their sovereign independence to further a higher purpose. It is done, Pierre-Antoine thought, relieved. Then his belly started to ache, signalling he needed to take his treatment soon.

***

The reception was in full swing in the Great Hall. In a raucous concert of laughter and boisterous voices, guests enjoyed the various food, beverages, and entertainment at their disposal. As a precaution, Jorge had increased security inside and outside the building, easing Monika's worries. The English ambassador approached Pierre-Antoine.

"Mister President."

"Your Excellency."

"Allow me to express my congratulations on this wonderful day and the outstanding speech you gave us earlier. It will undoubtedly go down in history as your finest accomplishment."

"I shall reassure Your Excellency by saying there will be more."

"Nonetheless, His Majesty's Government is pleased to see France finally put aside its long-standing stance for 'influence' against a humbler and more cooperative attitude. A decision which I hope will result in a stronger partnership with our country."

"Your Excellency knows His Majesty's Government is always welcome to rejoin our great family at any time. I am certain Scotland will be more than delighted to sponsor your return."

"But under the terms of the Federation, I presume."

"Needless to say…." Pierre-Antoine's attention suddenly shifted to a man in uniform mingling amongst the guests. "If your Excellency would pardon me, I need to talk to my brother about an urgent issue which just occurred."

"Nothing serious, I hope?" asked the ambassador suspiciously.

"No, no, nothing of concern. Please, keep on enjoying the festivities."

The French President swiftly sought his brother, who was talking to his Italian counterpart.

"My apologies Emilio, but I need to talk to my brother urgently if you do not mind." He gripped Jorge to the side.

"I believe that snobby Conservative roast meat did not appreciate your answer to Mother Thatcher. Even less, the quote from Nehru." He clearly was tipsy.

"Jorge, it is important. Who is that man in uniform on the right? The one next to the second pillar in the centre."

"Which one? I cannot see him."

"Put your heads together, please! Right there!"

"Ah! That one! He's part of the additional squad I ordered after your solicitation."

"Do you know him?"

"Of course not! Do you think I personally know every single police officer? I am not even High Commissioner yet. Colonel François handled those additional measures. Why?"

"There is something odd about him. Observe how he stands by himself, lying firmly against the pillar. And if you look closely, he appears to speak to himself, like praying. I also noticed he sweated profusely."

"Madre de Dios Pierre-Antoine!" burst Jorge, "You are becoming worse than Monika! The guy is most likely simply reporting to central command. And have you considered he might have sweating issues? If Colonel François assigned him there, he must be beyond reproach."

"You are worthless at times, Jorge!" sighed President Lascombes before waving at Barnabé, standing near one of the access doors. His collaborator rushed immediately to his side. "Barnabé, I need you to look at something right away."

"Monsieur le Président?"

"Do you see that policeman right there next to the pillar?"

"Absolutely."

"Something is wrong; I found his behaviour suspicious. Please, could you check with him? Quietly."

"Of course, at once, Monsieur le Président." He spoke into his microphone. "Security? Barnabé here. Could you come over and check on an individual, roger? Just leave it to me, Monsieur le Président."

Barnabé moved toward the suspect. At the same moment, the suspicious policeman began to get more agitated. His lips were moving frenetically. Barnabé was only five metres from him when the man extended his hand. He was holding a detonator!

"The Eternal Judgment is upon you!" he yelled. "*And I saw a woman sit upon a scarlet-coloured beast, full of names of blasphemy, having seven heads and ten horns. And the woman was arrayed in purple and scarlet colour, and decked with gold and precious stones and pearls, having a golden cup in her hand full of abominations and filthiness of her fornication. And upon her forehead was a name written, MYSTERY, BABYLON THE GREAT, THE MOTHER OF HARLOTS AND ABOMINATIONS OF THE EARTH.* Death to the beast, death to the Prostitute!"

"Everyone down!" someone shouted. Then, a sharp flash illuminated the hall, followed by a thunderous thud. Portions of the pillar and ceiling collapsed with a thundering sound. People started screaming, coughing, and running before the police barged in. Amid the chaos, between the debris, dust and scattered bodies, Pierre-Antoine noticed Barnabé's crushed corpse. The birth of the new Europe had been baptised with blood.

6

"No, no, and no! This is unacceptable!" Bishop Anastasius' voice was thundering in the corridor. "You just endangered his life for your deeds!"

"Please, Reverend Bishop. I swear it was completely unintentional. Nobody could have foreseen that a storm of this magnitude would occur in that location. It was an unfortunate combination of circumstances—"

"Which could have been partly averted if your team hadn't employed building tricks!" Bishop Anastasius violently slammed the ground with his walking stick. His bearded face wore a mask of rage while waving the silver rod, his dark cassock floating in the air like a whimsical magician about to cast a terrible spell.

Professor Walters raised his hand to stop the cleric. "I won't allow you to spread unfounded accusations against my team or me. The restoration was decided and carried out by the Ministry of Antiquities, as you are completely aware! I will not take the blame for the shoddy work of YOUR people!"

"They are not MY people! And none of this would have happened if you hadn't encouraged him to join your Luna Park. That… That blasphemy!"

"How dare you say that! It is one of your priests who first encouraged him. And calling our diggings "blasphemy" is rather rich coming from a religious leader who claims the Virgin Mary appears at every corner of his church—"

The chief nurse suddenly interrupted them, "Gentlemen! I need to ask you to lower your voice. You are disturbing the patients and visitors from the entire floor. I can no longer tolerate it. You either calm down or go outside to finish your argument. This is a hospital, not a debating forum."

"My sincere apologies, Chief Nurse, for raising our voices," replied Professor Walters. "I guess we are terribly concerned about the state of your patient." Bishop Anastasius muttered and nodded beside him. "How is he?" carried on the archaeologist. "Do you have any updates?"

"Dr Abbas is completing his evaluation; it shouldn't take long," she answered.

Shenuda was resting in his bed while the physician was examining him. The night before, he was rushed from Tell El Amarna to the Dayr Mawas central hospital minutes after the incident. He had awakened just an hour ago, and his vision was still foggy by unsettling light flashes rapidly dissipating. "Are my eyes alright?" he inquired.

"Nothing to be concerned. The sporadic flashes you are experiencing are just the result of the bright lightning you were exposed to during the storm. Your vision should return to normal in a matter of hours. Your general physical condition is excellent. I will release you in around an hour."

"Thank you, doctor." He stared at his bed. *Go north, to the Land of Khor…* The voice still echoed in his head.

"I would suggest a short therapy, though," the doctor went on. "I'll give you a referral if you'd like, but that's entirely up to you. Just let me know. I think your friends outside are quite eager to see you. Nurse, you can let the two gentlemen in now."

"Yes, doctor."

The two aged men entered the bedroom a minute later, looking first at Shenouda and then at the doctor.

"Mister Wahba is in perfect health," the physician started. "Fortunately, for him, despite the incident's intensity, no injuries are to report, if not for a bruise or two. He still suffers from physical trauma, like visual sequels and hearing issues. But nothing significant. I intend to discharge him within the hour. Once back home, I advise a complete twenty-four hours' rest, with little physical activity." He stared at the bishop. "I should recommend three or four therapy sessions, but I know your congregation's sensitivity to this issue. I'll leave him in your caring hands now, gentlemen. Please, don't overwhelm him; as I said, he needs rest." He walked out of the room, accompanied by the nurse.

"Shenouda, my boy, how are you? I am truly sorry for the tremendous burden I placed on your shoulders."

"I am alright, professor; stop worrying, please. You heard the doctor." He then addressed the abbot. "My apologies, Reverend Bishop; I recall you wanted to speak with me today about some important matters."

"It is alright, my son; do not bother yourself with that. We will talk later after recovering in your quarters. There is nothing you should apologise for."

54

"Yes, yes, he is right; you should not apologise," Professor Walters continued. "I am the one who should apologise for putting all of us at risk, even unintentionally. I will pass on a formal complaint to the Ministry of Antiquities. Such cheap work will no longer be tolerated in the future."

"The stela?"

"Destroyed, I'm afraid. Smashed to a hundred pieces. It will take ages to restore it, provided it is even achievable. These fools used an iron bar to reinforce the structure which was struck directly by lightning. Despicable! Luckily, our sponsors have been very understanding because of your outstanding performance. I am immensely grateful."

"Reverend Bishop…"

"Yes, my son?"

"Reverend Bishop... during the storm..." he stared intensely at the clergyman. "There was that intense light, and… and… I saw… her, she looked at me… she..."

The bishop dropped to his knees, elevating his hands and head towards the ceiling. "Holy Son of God! Once again, you bestow to us the honour of your grace in sending your Blessed Mother among us. Praised be Thee." He went back on his feet. "What glorious news, my son!" This is the confirmation sign that all of us have been waiting for. I knew from the day we discovered you that you were a godsend.

"Oh please, not again…" Professor Walters was rolling his eyes. "Haven't you done enough, three weeks ago during the church's vigil, with your fake pictures?"

The priest looked at the archaeologist with killer eyes. "How dare you challenge the will of God and the miracles he sends to his flock!" He turned to the young man. "My son, forgive me for abandoning you now, but something so significant must be promptly reported to His Holiness in Alexandria. I will see you later in the afternoon in my office. Blessed be my son, blessed thousands of times!" He ran outside, shouting in praise.

"But...", said Shenuda.

"Shenouda, my boy, do not listen to this man," interrupted the professor. He is but an old crazy priest. You are far more reasonable than granting any credit to these fables."

"Professor, I did not mean our Blessed Mother; I meant Her, the Queen Neferneferuaten. She talked to me!" he said in a mystic voice.

"Oh, my boy, my poor boy! What have I done? I feel so terrible. I will never forgive myself for the hardship I inflicted on you."

"No, Professor, it really happened! I swear!"

"Shush now. You are mistaken. You heard the doctor; you are still in shock, confused. It was only a thunderstorm. The explosion... you were so close when it happened. Your mind has been tricked. You have to rest... Yes, rest. And in a few days, everything will be better, only an unpleasant memory. But promise me—"

"Promise you what, Professor?"

"I implore you; no more talking about this story to Father Anastasius or anyone else. You are the rising star of your community. You are undoubtedly destined for tremendous achievements in this life. I can foresee it. So, please, do not jeopardise that future for some trick of the mind. Listen to me carefully. You saw nothing; you heard nothing. I would hate myself forever if you ended up revoked for some hallucinations. And I still need you on-site for the upcoming excavation season. Please, promise me!" He was in tears, a heartbreaking vision.

"For the love of God, Professor, do not cry. I promise. I will keep it between the two of us."

***

Shenouda was back in his room at the church dorm. Being in a familiar environment provided comfort and appeasement after all that had happened in the past twenty-four hours. Missael had treated him with devotion, bringing him tea and food. Maybe even a bit too considerate as he checked on him almost every half an hour. But allowing oneself a little self-gratification was no sin, was it? He imagined some of his colleagues nagging about his sudden rise to grace. *I implore you, no more talking about this story to Father Anastasius or anyone else.* Professor Walters was right. It would be unwise to bring those visions to the Bishop again. The church and his faith were all he possessed in that life; he had no luxury of turning to the warmth of a proper family. Not to mention archaeology, this other gift from God. Yes, his mind definitely deceived him; there was no Egyptian Queen, no mystical quest of any sort. Father Zacharia had been his surrogate father for as long as he could remember. And he did not want to cause any grief to the poor dying old man… Someone knocked on the door. *Missael, I suppose.*

"Reverend Deacon Wahba?"

"I am fine, Missael. I do not need anything, thank you. You may resume your duties."

"I apologise, Reverend Deacon; it is about something else. Reverend Bishop Anastasius wants to know if you can see him now.

"Certainly. Tell him I will be about five minutes."

The bishop's office was chilly, as usual. The cleric liked putting his air conditioning on at low temperatures, even on the cooler days of the year. He was sitting at his large mahogany desk on a wide armchair. Behind him stood a portrait of His Holiness, Demetrius IV, the current Pope of Alexandria, next to a painting of Christ emerging from his tomb on the third day after his crucifixion. A slight smell of incense was floating in the air. Bishop Anastasius wore a dark cassock and a large gold cross hanging around his neck. He was reading some papers, lost in deep concentration and did not notice Shenouda's presence.

"My apologies, Reverend Bishop. You wanted to see me?"

"Reverend Deacon! Take a seat, please! Indeed, we have some relevant matters to discuss. But most importantly, how are you feeling?"

"Much better, Reverend Bishop. The dizziness and flashes have practically disappeared, thank you."

"Not at all. We all owe you so much. So, first, tremendous news! His Holiness will visit us in three days. Two miracles within a month, isn't that marvellous? Praise the Lord and the benevolence he has bestowed upon our small community. This will improve the morale of our parishioners, particularly in these uncertain times. The government will no longer be able to ignore us." His face was shining.

"That is good news indeed. However, I do not want to cause any stir, Reverend Bishop. My vision was not clear, and it happened in particular circumstances. I may have overreacted at the hospital, you know..."

"Nonsense, Shenouda! God works in mysterious ways and at the most unexpected times. His Holiness and I agreed this was not merely a coincidence. We see it as a unique occasion to support our requests to the authorities and a welcomed opportunity to reassert the essential place of our religious centre in the Governorate of Menia. Therefore, you will meet our leader when he comes and adhere to your side of the story."

"As you wish, Reverend Bishop," replied Shenuda with reverence.

"Now, to the primary subject of your presence here. His Holiness would have preferred presenting you with the news on the day he arrived, but I think you should be informed immediately. Reverend Deacon, you have been our most dedicated and faithful student over the years since we have embraced you to this church."

"I owe you a lot, as well as Father Zacharias. And I seize any opportunity to express my gratitude."

"And you have, you definitely have. Attaining the rank of deacon so quickly is the explicit reward of our recognition of your accomplishments. But I believe, and so does His Holiness, that the time has come for you to deepen your studies before moving to greater responsibilities. Therefore, with His Holiness's approval and His Eminence Metropolitan Archbishop Tawadros' blessing, we have decided to send you to Jerusalem to perfect your religious education."

59

"Jerusalem!?" squealed Shenouda with surprise. Simultaneously, a voice echoed again in his mind: *Go North, to the Land of Khor.*" He was in shock.

"Yes, Jerusalem! And with what happened to you yesterday, this decision is all the more logical. You will be close to the tomb of the Holy Mother of Christ! How blessed you are!"

"It... I am deeply honoured by your trust and the opportunity you provide me, Reverend Bishop. But what about the people in my care here? And my charitable work?"

"You shall be dearly missed, no doubt. But we have enough clergymen to compensate your loss. And, before you mention it, you will also be able to carry on devoting yourself to your dear archaeological pastime. As you may know, the Holy City is now directly governed by the Council of the Revealed Faiths, which oversees historic excavations among its important missions. I have taken the liberty to talk to the Archbishop's secretary, Father Nazeer Atta, and he will be delighted to introduce you to some of the local people in charge. Although I do not completely endorse your extra curriculum, I still appreciate its importance to your personal development and faith. It would be unjustified to deny you such a 'distraction'."

"Reverend Bishop, I am humbly grateful for your solicitude."

"Do not mention it, my son. We all acknowledge the great expectations you are showing. And, most likely, when in the future you reach responsibilities similar to mine in the future, you will encounter another bright young man to whom you will certainly reciprocate. Now, go on, Deacon Shenouda. You will leave in ten days. It should give you enough time to put all your affairs in order and say your farewells, especially to a dear old priest. I discharge you from all religious duties and services as of this day."

"Thank you, Reverend Bishop; God bless you."

***

Following a long and busy week, Shenouda was two days away from his departure to Jerusalem, to the Holy City. He spent the previous day at the Tell El Amarna excavation site with Professor Walters, helping him to record and classify the latest discoveries. Later, the whole team threw a farewell party at the Amarna Dig House, where his fellow workers exchanged stories, memories, laughter and food. Then came the time for tears and farewell. Walters hugged his young protégé for a long moment.

"I am going to miss you so much, my boy," he said in a sad voice. "Your invaluable work during the past five years will not be forgotten. Thank you, thank you."

"No, Professor, thank YOU. You have been my second mentor and taught me a great deal, and I have learned so much. I will cherish these memories as long as I live, regardless of my future."

"Only good things, no doubt. And if you ever come back, make sure to come and visit your old professor."

"I will, I promise. But we will remain in touch. And You must report everything about the future excavations, or we will no longer be friends."

"Assuredly, what do you believe? But it will be hard not to see you around next year and to find someone as talented as you to guide our tours."

"Nonsense! The young Slimane is very promising and has been trained by me all year long. He will make an excellent replacement."

"I will make you accountable if not!" he laughed. "Now, before we part, there are two gifts I would like to offer you. First this."

He gave him a small wooden box containing an amulet made of lapis lazuli and garnet, representing the sacred winged Egyptian scarab pushing the sun-god across the sky.

"It will provide you with hope and protection wherever you go."

"This is magnificent, Professor Walters; I am extremely touched."

"This amulet was found here while digging on the site of the Royal Palace. Maybe, it belonged to Queen Nefertiti, who knows. Unfortunately, It seems I neglected to list it in the stock. Therefore, no one will miss it; I presume," he said with a cheeky smile. "I asked a local jeweller to turn it into a pendant. It will allow you to wear it under your cross."

"Professor! This is too much. I cannot accept such a present. It feels like stealing," Shenouda replied, embarrassed, handling the precious gift back.

"Come on, Shenouda. This object was carved and crafted by the ancient Egyptians whom you descend from. I am just returning it to its rightful owner, somehow. Just make sure to conceal it when you depart from the country. You do not want to be accused of stealing a 'national treasure.' It will be deplorable for my reputation," he said with a wink.

"I will treasure it; I swear."

"The second thing I desired to give you is this." The professor handed him a business card. "I heard Bishop Anastasius arranged for you to be introduced to Jerusalem's Holy College for Antiquities. This is, by far, much better. It is the business card from my excellent friend, Professor Marc Degrenes. We worked together on several various sites in the past. He currently leads a small archaeological team in the Holy City and its surroundings, overseen by the Apostolic Nunciature. He mainly searches for clues and artefacts of the presence of ancient Egypt in the region. A little wasteful, if you ask me, but the Church seems extremely eager to find evidence of the mysterious biblical Pharaoh Shishak, for reasons beyond my comprehension. Regardless, I have already reached out to Marc about you, and he eagerly looks forward to your arrival to join his team. In your spare time, of course."

"Professor, I do not know how to thank you."

"Then do not. Simple. All right, it is time for us to say goodbye." He hugged him once more. "I hope to see you again, my boy."

"I am convinced we will, Professor…"

Shenouda was presently sitting in a chair in an obscure corridor of Dayr Awas Central Hospital. But, this time, he was not the patient. He had come saying a last farewell to his old master and tutor, Father Zacharias. Aged ninety-six, the elderly priest was gradually but surely, fading away. No doubt this would be their last encounter. A nurse approached him.

"He is ready for you. You can come now."

"Thank you."

Father Zacharias was peacefully lying on his bed. He was on respiratory assistance, the heart rate monitor steadily beeping in the background. The old priest was not suffering from any specific illness. No, his life was simply coming to its natural end, like a candle reaching the end of its thread. He turned his head to the young deacon sitting next to him.

"Shenouda, my son," the clergyman said in a frail voice. "How nice of you to visit your old master before going to the Holy Land."

"I could not leave without saying goodbye, Father. You mean so much to me."

"Goodbye? More of a farewell, I would say," he chuckled. "Let us not deceive each other; this is our last meeting. Look at you! So young and full of promise. I thank God for enabling me to live long enough to see how much of a fine man you have become. Bishop Anastasius delivered me the good news a few days ago. You make me immensely proud."

"Do not say that, Father; you have been like a father to me. I owe you a tremendous amount of gratitude."

"My only last request is that you confidently follow the path I have put you on all these years and remain faithful to yourself and God."

"I will, Father, I promise..." Shenouda suddenly sobbed. "It is just... just that it makes me so sad to think I will never see you again, even when..."

"Do not be saddened, my dear Shenouda. I am leaving for a better world. Whether you are with me or not does not make any difference. God gifted you to illuminate the final years of my life and guide you. Now He shall guide you himself. Listen to his voice. Seek his advice in difficult moments. Never doubt his infinite love."

"I shall do as you wish." The young cleric stood up and started to walk away, but the priest stopped him with a movement of his right hand.

"Hold on, Shenouda. Before we separate in this life, there's one last thing you need to know. Go to my satchel on the table." Shenouda complied. "Open it. You will find a little package wrapped in paper. Take it."

"What is it?"

"It is a secret that I have preserved for a long time. God forgives me. Listen carefully. When I discovered you, abandoned by the gates of our church, I also recovered two objects in your basket. One, you were draped in. And the other one… I'll let you find out. It was most certainly from your parents or, at least, from a member of your biological family. I cannot be certain; there was no note left. I have carefully concealed them to this day. Nobody knows of their existence but me. I was anxious it might be misinterpreted. Forgive me for concealing them for so long, but I was waiting for the proper time. It has come now. I am confident you will use these items well and, maybe, shed some light on your origins. Please, do not open the packet here. Wait to be back in your quarters; it will be more prudent. Keep them hidden afterwards. For your sake."

"I will", replied Shenouda, intrigued.

"It is time that I bid you farewell, my son. May God preserve you, and may his wisdom be with you all your life, which I hope will be long and prosperous. Bless you, my child."

"Bless you, Reverend Father."

When he entered his room, Shenouda tore the wrapper anxiously. It contained a folded blanket made of traditional local weaving. He gasped after unfolding it. The inside bore a representation of the Aten. What is this? He thought. At the exact moment, a glowing object dropped and rolled onto the floor. He picked it up and froze in a stupor. It was a gold signet ring engraved with the Eye of Ra.

7

Rinchen was praying in the main temple of the Tawang monastery, repeatedly chanting today's mantra, the Shakyamuni Mantra. Dozens of other monks accompanied him in a monotonous and hypnotising litany. *Om Muni Muni Mahamuni Shakyamuniye Svaha* was solemnly echoed around the large Dukhang Assembly Hall decorated with exquisite carvings, murals, and painted scenes of various bodhisattvas and deities. At the back, looking benevolently at his disciples, the five-metre-high golden statue of the Lord Buddha, seated in a lotus position, bountifully bestowed his compassion throughout the universe. Resting at its feet was a portrait of Tenzin Gyatso, the last Dalaï Lama, who had left this world twenty years ago. The throat chanting was intense, mesmerising, floating in the air saturated with incense, punctuated by the steady sound of bells and gongs. Each monk called upon Siddhartha Gautama to bring forth the Buddha nature residing in all living beings. The deeper tone of their voice produced a resonant wave that travelled around the world, enabling every living consciousness to vibrate in harmony with the cosmos. The abbot had specially instructed this prayer as, today, several significant events were affecting the planet, with potential consequences for the well-being of most of humanity. They had to appeal to the compassion of the Buddha to soothe the myriad of unfortunate breathing minds, living, for most of them, in suffering, anxiety and dissatisfaction.

Several young monks were softly moving around along the aisles, offering their elders butter tea and porridge. One silently approached Rinchen to propose a bowl of the beverage. The young lama dismissed him with a gesture, unwilling to interrupt his prayer. He could feel his heart chakra harmoniously synchronising with the universe in a moment of plenitude where space and time had no meaning.

Jamyang and Kalsang were not with him. They were studying the scriptures and preparing for their spring examination at the library. The noon bell suddenly rang. All monks stopped chanting simultaneously. After a moment of silence to allow the body and mind to settle, each began moving randomly. Rinchen peacefully walked through the main gilded doors to the courtyard. The fierce sun was shining high in the sky. It was even milder than the day before. Some weather reports predicted water would be scarce this year, with another prolonged drought possibly affecting the city's inhabitants. There were even rumours among the lamas that if the situation continued for several years, the number of monks would have to be reduced for the monastery to remain sustainable. *Lord Siddhartha, grant us light and wisdom to prevent this adversity.*

"Rinchen!" Kalsang was running toward him, with Jamyang painstakingly following him.

"Kalsang, Jamyang, have you finished studying the scriptures?"

"We have", answered Jamyang, breathless but happy.

"Should we go see Venerable Chophel Rinpoche now?" asked Kalsang.

"No, we shall eat first. And, Kalsang, remember I am the one meeting with the Venerable Abbot and our teacher. You two are supposed to humbly wait outside until being called."

"What is the point for us to be there, then?" he replied, shrugging his shoulders.

"Well, I am not in the confidence of our two masters. If your attendance is required, there must be a valid reason. Everything shall be revealed in due time. Meanwhile, we must show patience and understanding."

"*The practice of patience guards us against losing our presence of mind,*" Jamyang replied, quoting the last Dalai Lama.

"Exactly, Jamyang. And what better practice than enjoying our lunch? Let's go."

The refectory was busy but silent. Only Wangdue Lama's bold voice could be heard in the background, yelling out his instructions to the other cooks. As soon as they sat, the three companions received a bowl of rice, stir-fried vegetables and a cup of butter tea. They started eating and drinking slowly, as required.

"There is no porridge", moaned Kalsang in a whisper as they were supposed to stay silent during meals.

"I heard water had started to be rationed, to some extent. They fear a third big drought. It seems the Arunachal Pradesh Government is struggling to manage water reserves," Rinchen answered. "Anyway, why are you complaining? It is usually Jamyang's role to moan about food. Didn't you get breakfast?"

"I am just a bit hungry, that's all. We had a long walk yesterday. I am not complaining. Just thinking about my health."

"*Health is not just about what you are eating. It is also about what you are thinking and saying.*"

"Hooo, hear our wise Jamyang Lama today! Someone enjoyed his teaching this morning, didn't he?" retorted Kalsang sarcastically. "And what about *keeping the body in good health is a duty; otherwise, we should be unable to keep our mind strong and clear.* Meditate on this!"

"Kalsang!", Rinchen interrupted. "Stop the attitude. You forget the teachings of the Five Precepts. Apologise to your brother."

"Do you three need any help with anything?" They blenched on their bench. Wangdue Lama was standing right behind them, firm as a mountain, his fists on his hips. "Because otherwise, I need help washing the dishes."

"No, no, Venerable Wangdue Lama", said Rinchen. "We sincerely apologise for causing disturbance to our brothers' lunch."

"Regardless, you cannot solicit us. We have an audience with Venerable Chophel Rinpoche right afterwards. No doubt he will be displeased if you have us late," added Kalsang, defiant. His companions turned to him with reproval.

"Well, guess what? You have just been granted an 'audience' with my dirty dishes after dinner tonight. And like Venerable Chophel Rinpoche, something tells me they will also be quite displeased if you arrive late. Now, eat in silence!" the cook yelled before returning to the kitchen.

"Well done, Karlang," Jamyang muttered.

"In silence, I said!"

***

"Come in Rinchen!"

The young monk silently stepped into Venerable Chophel Rinpoche's office. The Abbot was sitting at his short-legged desk on a big round pillow made of silk and brocade. A large fresco of a Green Tara meditating peacefully amidst pastoral scenes stood on the wall behind him. The wooden floor was covered with delicately woven rugs while incense sticks were burning on one side. Venerable Kunchen Lama was next to him, smiling benevolently.

Rinchen quickly walked toward the abbot, joined his hands, and bowed respectfully before prostrating three times with reverence.

"You wanted to see me, Reverend Chophel Rinpoche?"

"Indeed. Please, sit down, Rinchen Lama. Kunchen Lama and I have a matter of considerable importance to discuss with you."

"Rinchen", continued Kunchen Lama, "three days ago, we received an official letter from your father, Deputy Speaker Lobsang Gyaltsen. It contains some dire news for you and our community." Rinchen remained silent. "It appears that your older brother suffered a serious car accident that left him in a coma. As a result of his severe head injuries, his diagnosis is uncertain, if not unfavourable.

71

Your father requests our Venerable Abbot to send you back to Dharamshala as soon as possible."

"I understand, my teacher. I will make quick arrangements to visit my family if that is your desire."

"You are misunderstanding the content of your father's summon, Rinchen", said the Abbot. "He is not asking you to visit; he wants you to move back to Dharamshala."

"What? I... I do not understand."

"It looks like your father has lost all hope in your brother's recovery. Therefore, he expects you to take your rightful place at his side as the future head of your family," said Kunchen Lama.

"But... but... I am... a simple monk. I love being a monk. Living in the promise of the Buddha's enlightenment is all I want in this life. My only wish is to serve the Sangha."

"We fully know your commitment, Rinchen, and strongly support your pledge. However, I mentioned the letter was official. This is no mere petition made by a father about his son. It is a formal petition made by the Deputy Speaker to our Abbot, as leader of our monastery. In other words, a command."

"Rinchen Lama," the Abbot went on, "your father is putting our brotherhood in a very delicate situation. I cannot urge or even force you to renounce your vows. It is against our principles. Only you can make such a decision. But, since the death of the 14th Dalai Lama, the fate of our community, of most Tibetan Buddhist communities, has been precarious. Our people are torn between Tenzin Gyatso's last message, claiming the time of a reincarnated Dalai Lamas had ended, and the 15th Dalai Lama, placed on the throne of the Potala by the Chinese Government.

Half of our income depends on the subsidies the Central Tibetan Administration provides. Losing that income would persuade some members of the Sangha to seek money from China. It would lead to a devastating schism that would be fatal to our fragile institutions. To the delight of China."

"I understand your dilemma Venerable Chophel Rinpoche. But, respectfully, I am a Buddhist monk. I live in the serene contemplation of the Buddha and the teachings of the Dharma. My sole ambition is to become a teacher, like Kunchen Lama, and pass on what I have learned to others. I have no desire to live a civilian life, let alone comply with my father's wishes. And if this is only about his lineage, he has a grandson by my brother who can take over his name."

"Yes, you are right. However, your brother is too young to offer any prospects."

Rinchen's face showed a profound sadness and hopelessness. "You are asking me to forfeit myself, Venerable Abbot. My only options are to submit or bring shame to the monastery."

"Well, maybe not. There might be a third option," the Abbot said with cunning eyes. "But it relies exclusively on you. Kunchen Lama?"

"My dear Rinchen, we have a compromise to suggest if you are prepared to accept it. Yesterday, I contacted His Holiness Jampa Rinpoche in Dharamshala. He has enthusiastically agreed to welcome you to his community at the Thekchen Chöling temple complex. He wishes to offer you the position of one of his secretaries. Serving in the holy place of our beloved 14th Dalai Lama will confer us all a tremendous honour. By consenting to this compromise, the monastery will appear to submit to the Deputy Speaker's official request without renouncing your vows. By acknowledging this solution, you will fulfil your filial obligations to your father as a Buddhist monk until your nephew comes of age. No doubt this will displease your father, but he will not openly oppose it. I am conscious of the considerable sacrifice we require of you. But we must first consider our community's interests before its individuals' personal needs. It is a survival issue for all of us, especially in those uncertain times. But know that whatever decision you make, rest assured that we will stand by you, regardless of the consequences."

"I fully understand the situation, Venerable Abbot. I cannot allow my desires to—"

"Hold a moment, Rinchen," interrupted Venerable Chopel Rinpoche. "We have something else to propose to you."

"I am listening."

"We do not wish this situation to end like some punishment. While this is not completely in accordance with the rules of this monastery, we know how close you are to Kalsang and Jamyang, and reciprocally. Therefore, Thekchen Chöling Temple has also agreed to accept them in their community, giving you a unique opportunity to pursue your studies together. At the condition they accept, of course."

"I am beyond gratitude Venerable Chopel Rinpoche. I do not know how to thank you."

"First, wait to know their reaction. Kunchen Lama, if you will."

The Lama opened the door. "Kalsang, Jamyang, come in, please."

The two monks entered the chamber reverently. They looked at the Abbot, then at their friend, with a mix of fear and intense curiosity.

The Abbot addressed them. "Kalsang, Jamyang, we have a matter of considerable importance to discuss with you…"

***

Later that night, the young men were back in their quarters. The abbot had given them all night to consider their decision thoroughly. No matter their choice, it will irrevocably alter their future.

Kalsang was enthusiastic, jumping around, chanting, "we are going to Dharamshala, we are going to Dharamshala!" Deep down, he still resented his family's decision to send him to Tawang forcibly. He saw the prospect of moving to the Thekchen Chöling Temple as freeing himself from them and the oracle. Jamyang, however, was in a gloomy mood. He had lived in the city all his life. The idea of moving far away from his family and leaving the security of the temple, his second home, frightened him.

"I enjoy it here," he said. "The city, the mountains, my family, even the monkeys. This is a lot to demand," he said.

"Come on, Jamyang! Where is your spirit of adventure? Think about it; we are talking about the Central Government of Tibet. Who can ever dream of such an honour? Be sensible. And, as Buddhist monks, aren't we bound to anitya and detachment—"

"Kalsang, please," gently interrupted Rinchen. "This is not about honours but about each of our lives. Jamyang has completely understandable reasons for being hesitant." He stared at his friend. "Jamyang, you realise that though the Reverend Abbot has offered me a choice, there is none. I have no option but to accept Venerable Chopel Rinpoche's proposal. He is right; this is the best compromise for me and this monastery. Kalsang and I will be extremely pleased if you come with us. However, we have no right to force you. That will be your decision and your decision alone. Of course, we will miss you dearly if you choose not to come with us, but this is the foundation of one's life, anitya."

"But you two are my second family... I don't know, Rinchen. It's too confusing in my mind."

"I understand. Let's stop here, sleep, and pray to the Buddha to guide our hearts.

***

At noon the following day, Rinchen and Kalsang were back in the abbot's office.

"Venerable Chophel Rinpoche, after much consideration, I have decided to follow your wise suggestion. Therefore, I humbly request to be transferred to Thekchen Chöling Temple. I do this in the interest of our monastery, our Sangha, and to show my father the devotion owed by a son," Rinchen solemnly declared. "Kalsang Lama here has also agreed to accompany me and is extremely grateful for the honour he has been granted." The other monk bowed respectfully before the abbot.

"My dear Rinchen Lama, I wish to thank you on behalf of our community. I understand how difficult this decision is. Rest assured that I am personally indebted to you. Should you require any favour in the future, do not hesitate to consult me. We are also very grateful, Kalsang Lama, for choosing to accompany our dear Rinchen on his new adventure. May the Buddha grant you his blessings and his infinite wisdom. But… I do not see Jamyang Lama…"

"He is not with us, Venerable Chophel Rinpoche," replied Kalsang. "We haven't seen him since breakfast, nor has he spoken to us."

"Well, he must follow his own path, I presume. Right!" said the abbot clapping his hands. "Let's organise your trip. The monastery will cover all expenses associated with your journey. You will first travel by bus to Bomdila, allowing Kalsang to say goodbye to his family; if he so desires. Then the train for Delhi and, finally, Dharamshala. It will be quite an extended trip, so I will have Wangdue Lama prepare enough food and water. Our intendant will provide you with some spare money to cover unexpected expenses. Make sure you conceal it well while travelling. You haven't experienced the outside world for quite a while. Although most of the population regard monks with much respect, there are still careless individuals, willing to cause problems at the prospect of easily catching a few rupees."

"Thank you, Venerable Chophel Rinpoche, we are most grateful."

"I will message your father and his Holiness to inform them of the time of your arrival as soon as your tickets are ready and have someone greeting you at the train station. That is the least they can do, particularly the Deputy Leader… Now, go on, and resume your studies and daily tasks. We will meet again before your departure to bid you farewell."

The two monks bowed to the abbot, ready to leave, when Jamyang opened the door abruptly, sweating and gasping. He prostrated himself directly before the holy man's feet.

"Venerable Chopel Rinpoche, Venerable Chopel Rinpoche! Please, forgive my sudden intrusion. I am going too!"

8

"I am delighted you joined us, Dr Caracciolo. However, to be frank, you were not my first choice. But you should be a reasonable choice. I am confident you will fit in just fine with the rest of the team. One recommendation, though."

"Yes, Professor?"

"Work with me, abide by my instructions, and we shall be best mates. However, attempt to be a little rising star or act like a free electron, and I can assure you that we will be on the worst possible terms. I trust this is understood."

"That is quite clear, Professor Yang."

Best mates? Giancarlo was sitting in Professor Yang's office for his first face-to-face with the Nobel Laureate. The whole morning just went by like a dream. Colin took him for a long walk through the Old City of Edinburgh, New Town and Newhaven. He was fascinated by the apparent architectural harmony prevailing in the city's various districts. It contrasted sharply with the chaotic mixture of rich heritage and modern features at home.

Things here seemed so peaceful and balanced. And the people were amicable as well. Colin was very talkative — practically worse than an Italian, he reckoned— and had a thorough knowledge of his native town, its mysteries and anecdotes. Scotland's capital city was vibrant with culture and vitality. However, Edinburgers seemed to appreciate doing things at their own pace. This was a welcome change compared to the frenzy in Milan. The whole tour gave Giancarlo a reassuring sense of confidence about his drastic decision to move north. *I only need to get accustomed to the weather now, I suppose.*

"That will be all for now. I will let you get acquainted with your colleagues and our research this afternoon. You will start proper work tomorrow morning."

"Thank you, Professor." Giancarlo left the office and saw Colin waiting in the corridor.

"So? How did it go?"

"Is he always this way, full of himself?"

"Aye! Sometimes even worse. And full of vices as well: the man does not smoke, does not drink, eats only vegan food, and goes to bed precisely at 10.30 pm. A total twat!"

"A what?"

"Booooring!" And he laughed. "Come on, let's go to the lab."

The "lab" was a vast open space with every single state-of-the-art equipment a geneticist would dream of: cell cycle analysers, automated cell culture systems, chromatographs, versatile microscopes, etc. You just had to name it. Pharma Cybernetics Corp. was evidently investing a great deal of money in its research on experimental forms of cancer treatments while only seeking affordability. It was this ethical spirit that persuaded Giancarlo to accept their offer.

Ethics were essential to him, and Pharma Cybernetics Corp. was renowned internationally for putting investments above profits.

"Hi, fellow mad hatters!" Colin said. "Look whom I rescued from the dragon's den!"

"Hi Giancarlo", said Natalia, "welcome back."

"I believe Ranveer will briefly introduce you to our work," continued Colin. "He is the last surviving member of Yang's initial team and, therefore, the best-suited person for the job."

"Thank you, Colin. I feel somehow important now," Ranveer replied, gracefully bowing at his fellow researcher.

"At your service", responded Colin, bowing back.

"Cancers' treatments are this facility's core research. I insist on saying 'cancers' and not 'cancer.' But not any sort of treatments. Our goal is to seek a universal way to eradicate cancer cells independently of the organ they affect. To develop such a treatment, first, we collect and cultivate cells of various types of cancer. This is Emily and Colin's job. Then we proceed to extract the DNA from the cells and chart it. That is Rebecca and Natalia's job. Finally, we analyse the charts for common DNA features and sequence them. This is where you and I get involved. We are investigating a specific genome sequence common to all cancer cells. It is what Professor Yang calls Phase One. But, among us, we call it the Golden Egg. We are extremely close to completing this phase and, with your help, hope to achieve it in the upcoming weeks. Once Phase One is complete, we will move into Phase Two. What is Phase Two? Simply genetically engineering a treatment explicitly targeting the common cancer's genome and mass-produced it at an affordable price. Et voila! Thank you all for your attention." He bowed again with pride as his colleagues gave frantic applause.

"Wow!" uttered Giancarlo. "Several teams are working on such a project; some have been for decades. All of them have failed so far. I spent six months with one of them in California."

"That's because they haven't managed to hire the Dream Team!" said Colin, placing his right arm around Giancarlo's shoulders.

"As Ranveer rightly said, we are very close to a breakthrough on Phase One," continued Emily. "We should be there already if your predecessor did not leave unexpectedly. Or better said, had a *divergence of view* with Professor Yang before finding more *flexibility* with the competition."

"What we hope, now," continued Rebecca, "is that, as a newbie, you will look at our work with a fresh eye and help us beat the competition in the race."

"That's your predecessor's team," Colin whispered. He went down to his knees. "Help us, Obi-Wan Kenobi; you are our only hope."

"And let's not forget that Professor Yang desperately dreams of a second Nobel Prize," said Natalia. "So, no pressure, but…"

"Pressure!" the others burst out in unison, followed by laughter.

Giancarlo was staring at them. He was not simply witnessing teamwork. There was genuine complicity between them, a friendship he had not experienced before. At first glance, they seemed more like eccentric students than dedicated scientists willing to cure one of humanity's most significant plagues. And he liked it. The apprehension he was experiencing after leaving Professor Yang's austere office was at present gone.

"OK, guys, it's five o'clock, and it's Thursday," Colin proclaimed. "And who can tell our new friend here what happens on Thursdays?"

"The Storm!" they all replied.

"The storm?" asked Giancarlo.

"It's a pub, you silly. It's just over the road when you leave the Centre. 7.30 pm sharp! And no excuse!"

"Ok, I'll be there."

"And don't worry, no twat allowed", he winked.

***

It was already dark when Giancarlo reached the pub. The rumbling of an approaching thunderstorm could be heard in the distance. *It was a dark and stormy night...* Edward Bulwer-Lytton's words conjured up his mind. *And I'm about to walk into a pub named 'The Storm'.* He smiled at the thought. The public house was busy. The inside looked dated, with its walls decorated with shiny patterned wood panels and old photos of regatta scenes. A crackling fire was burning in a broad fireplace, adding some cosiness. He moved along the bar and through the crowd till he saw his team packed together.

"There he is!" shouted Colin. "You are late, Mister."

"My mother called just as I was leaving. I had to answer."

"I said no excuse." He placed his finger on Giancarlo's lips. He was already tipsy. "You're good this time, but just this one. Beer?"

"Si."

"Good!" The Scot returned a moment later, holding a tall glass full of the amber beverage. "Guys, guys!" he told the others. Let's raise our glasses to our new addition, Dottore Giancarlo Caracciolo, dragon-slayer! Hip, hip…"

"Hooray!"

"I couldn't hear you! Hip, hip…"

"Hooray!"

"Well, well, well. Isn't that the five musketeers?"

Giancarlo blenched. Professor Liz Edwards emerged from the shadows, dressed elegantly, before standing at his side.

"And who do you happen to be?" she went on, "I do not think we have been properly introduced. Are you the new d'Artagnan of this crazy bunch?"

"Liiiiz" Rebecca screamed, "you're here!" She rushed to hug her.

"Of course, darling. I told you I was coming, didn't I?"

"Beware," Colin whispered, "the vampires are out tonight…" Right at that moment, lightning stroked closely. Giancarlo blenched a second time.

"Well, Mister, you nonetheless didn't mention your name." Liz Edwards looked at him like a big cat ready to toy with its prey.

"I… I am Giancarlo Caracciolo. I just joined Professor Yang's research team. It is a pleasure to meet you, Professor Edwards. Your reputation precedes you, if I may say."

"And you heard only half of it," she said in a purring voice. "Caracciolo… Caracciolo? Any relationship with Prince Andrea Caracciolo, the distinguished philanthropist?"

"He is a distant cousin. I am from a cadet branch, the Caracciolo del Sole. My brother, Gianfranco, is the incumbent Prince of Capua and head of our family."

"I see. Pure Neapolitan aristocratic blood. I can easily spot a gemstone..."

"No? Really?" interrupted Colin. "Hey, fellas! Did you hear?" Newbie, here, is not only a dragon-slayer but also an authentic Prince!" He went on his knees, taking a supplicant stand. "Your Highness, forgive my audacity, but would it be too much to ask thee to buy another glass for the miserable thirsty worm I am?"

"Of course, I will buy you a drink, Colin, and to the others too. But please, stop calling me your Highness; it is embarrassing."

"Jings, his magnificence called me Colin!"

"Beer for everyone, I presume. What about you, Professor Edwards?"

"Liz, would you? I am more of a cocktail girl. Get me a Pink Panty Dropper, please. Don't panic; they know it here. Make sure they use Polish rather than Russian vodka."

"What is wrong with Russian vodka?" Natalia asked.

Liz softly pinched Natalia's chin with her right hand. "Let's say it lacks a bit of extra zing, sweetie."

Five minutes later, Giancarlo returned with everybody's drinks.

"There's your cocktail, Liz. Or should I say 'mixture'? It sounds rather intriguing. Do you mind if I have a taste?"

"I am afraid it is definitely not for young boys. But I am prepared to make an exception if you promise to visit my department first thing tomorrow. I will ensure you have a 'personalised' tour. And do not concern yourself with Owen; he is very understandable when it comes to me."

"Deal, then!"

***

Visiting Liz Edwards' research department turned into a fascinating experience. The place was equipped with state-of-the-art instruments, experimental robotic limbs, and a supercomputer capable of analysing trillions of data in microseconds. There was also a section dedicated to creating synthetic skin and blood.

"This is a very impressive lab, Liz," Giancarlo said. "I never imagined we had progressed so much in robotics."

"Well, to be fair, those represent mere little toys, experimental gadgets. They would be considered simple automatons if we lived two hundred years ago."

She had been the perfect host the whole morning while behaving differently than in private. He admired the extent of her intelligence and the composure she was exposing every detail. It was like being in the presence of Dr Jekyll right after meeting Mr Hyde.

"Mere automatons? You are far too modest! Everything I encounter this morning was deemed science fiction as recently as fifteen years ago."

"One cannot be overly modest," she replied. "I personally find this work tedious but unfortunately indispensable. Our motto is if you cannot mend or repair it, replace it. So, in a sense, we pick up when your division fails. No offence."

"None taken."

"You see, we work on two main projects. One is to reconstruct the human body parts that no longer function properly. We perform this by experimenting with two possibilities: cyborgs or robotics. On the one hand, we simply replace the defaulting parts of a limb while keeping the viable organic tissue intact. On the other hand, we substitute the whole limb and make it more 'human' looking by using prosthetic skin. We are still uncertain about the most efficient option."

"But could you imagine creating a fully synthetic body?" Giancarlo asked.

"That is what the second project is about. We first aim at downloading the whole human mind with its distinct personality and consciousness as data processing. Then, in a second phase, have this data transferred to a miniaturised computer with enough capacity to store such an enormous amount of information. We are considerably advanced in the process but are currently stuck with a two-thirds capability."

"Two-third! But it's nearly double what Professor Hendricks was able to accomplish!"

"Don't mention that cheat. His research has only one purpose: siphoning from the Russians all the money he can no longer drain from the Americans. I know a great deal about it as I was one of his assistants for five years. Fools! Naturally, all you have just heard and seen is strictly confidential, and I trust you will keep it inside the Centre's walls."

"Assuredly."

"Good. Alright, I do not want to take any more of your time, and there is an experiment I must attend in five minutes."

"Thank you for your time, Liz. It was an enlightening visit. I am extremely grateful."

"Well, I expect a dinner as payment. I'll be in touch. Enjoy the rest of your day."

***

Giancarlo spent the afternoon analysing the genetic data the team had gathered. The process was rather tedious and highly laborious. His colleagues had collected so many genomes to detect a possible marker that the task seemed endless. He could appreciate why Ranveer was grateful for his arrival. One pair of brains was hardly enough for the evaluation. Fortunately, an EXcite 1500S, the latest computerised analysis technology, assisted him in his task. Its performances were significantly superior to the one he had been working on in California.

The results were gradually turning up, one by one. But, so far, nothing significant. Some DNA sequences were determined as suitable candidates periodically but only to be dismissed after a closer examination. After two hours of hopeless study, Giancarlo discerned a small detail coming out on the screen. *Something doesn't feel right*, he thought.

"Ranveer?"

"Yes, Giancarlo?"

"What kind of algorithm have you been operating to analyse the data?"

"The one I worked out with your predecessor, Virgil. He was considerably talented at it, and we achieved significant progress. But since his departure, we have been going in circles."

"Is there any way for me to access the algorithm's root?"

"Of course, and fairly easily. Just type 'access source'. But I have reviewed it several times already and detected no discrepancy with what Virgil and I had originally programmed."

"Thank you Ranveer. Let me take a look to get a better understanding. If you do not mind."

"Go ahead. And, please, if you make any modifications, keep them local. I would like to avoid resetting the whole system and re-run today's work."

Giancarlo accessed the algorithm's long command chain and began a comprehensive analysis. Once, twice, thrice. Indeed, nothing obvious, he thought. Then, a fourth and fifth times. Still nothing. *Unless…* A sixth and seventh time. A chain of command seemed oddly jolting with each check, precisely at the same spot. *There is something here.* He did an eight reading and stopped the sequence right on the anomaly. By all accounts, the specific chain seemed completely normal except for a single variation. He gave it a closer look. *A hidden encryption!* Its access was prevented, but one with sufficient knowledge could easily subvert it—*time to practice those extra curriculum studies.* Within minutes, an entire chain of command materialised on the screen. *Jesus! It completely distorts the results and instructs the computer to disregard them. Simple but deadly effective. It seems Virgil did not just simply leave; he also made sure to slow down his ex-team to allow him enough time to catch up with them.* Giancarlo deleted the sequence and restarted the algorithm. Three hours later, it was still running, but with no results. *Perhaps I was wrong. If we are to discover something, it has to be in that data collection.* A fourth hour went by. He was about to give up for the day. His colleagues were already leaving. Then all of a sudden, he heard a faint alarm. DNA sequences began to overlap on the screen, one after the other. Ten minutes later, it was still going on.

"Guys?"

"What is it Giancarlo?" Rebecca asked.

"I appreciate I only have been here for just a day, but has anyone of you seen this sequence?"

9

Pierre-Antoine was reading the fifty-page report on the March bombing sent to him by his half-brother a few hours ago. *All those months of investigative work just for that?* He contemplated the Zen Garden through the window of his office. It was a relaxing view with its mixture of Japanese maple essences, gravel river flowing among tall mountain-like rocks, and charming narrow brook surrounded by a delicate carpet of bright green moss. At intervals, he could detect the faint sound of chimes or observe some frail birds gracefully fluttering around the Koi Pond. The idyllic picture of a sheer westernised Japanese fantasy in a perfectly balanced ecosystem. But the reality was radically different.

Everywhere, the planet was undergoing severe changes. Temperatures in most of Europe were still soaring to a dreadful 42 degrees Celsius, setting a new record for this time of the year. The summer witnessed some of the severest droughts registered in the countries of Southern and Central Europe. Water supply was promptly becoming a recurring seasonal issue, even though canal networks had doubled over the past decade. The European government now relied thoroughly on Scottish and Scandinavian reserves for the hot months. *And it is only Europe!* he thought. In some parts of the globe, deserts were turning oddly greener. But in other regions, fertile lands were slowly getting barren or irremediably flooded by rising sea levels. *Ecosystems are under considerable stress and are struggling to adapt to these rapid changes that intensify the ever-increasing pressure from the human population. Our planet is mutating too rapidly, if not starting to die slowly. A part of the scientific community naively perpetuates a complete fallacy. There is no way back. We have exceeded the point of no return! The balance in which our species' survival holds has become too precarious. Drastic new solutions need to be implemented rapidly if we are to survive.*

His desk phone buzzed.

"Yes, Isabelle?"

"Everyone has gathered in the conference room, High Commissioner."

"Thank you, Isabelle. I will be just five minutes."

Isabelle Marchand, his Personal Assistant, was the last remnant of his previous team following Barnabé's tragic death last March. Pierre-Antoine carried on reading the report. According to its content, two members of an obscure apocalyptic religious group managed to infiltrate one of the private security companies hired for the event. However, how they obtained and smuggled the explosives into the parliament remained unclear. *Good.* Miraculously, apart from some injuries, none of the members of the incoming government lost their lives. However, the rest of the guests paid a severe price, with twelve dead and twenty-seven severely injured. Among them, dear Barnabé. *An unfortunate loss.* Altogether, the damage was more emotional and political. New Europe was attacked on the first day it came into existence.

I should get going; my collaborators are waiting. Following the compromise, he was now European High Commissioner for Science and Technology. Not an overly exciting job at first glance, but it suited his ambitions. *For now.* He walked into the conference room, where everyone stood up as soon as he entered.

"Good afternoon to you all. Please sit down. I apologize for being a little late. I will ensure this will not happen again in the future, except in unforeseen circumstances. Catherine, we will start with you."

"With pleasure, High Commissioner. I have received several requests from different research centres for additional funding. They cover multiple..."

The discussions focused on different topics, mostly issues and concerns raised by the first two directors of his administration. The matter was swiftly expedited. Followed the turn of the Director for the Space Program.

"Gerrit, what is the news from our operations on the Moon?", Pierre-Antoine asked.

"The second phase of development has only just started, High Commissioner. The size of the European moonbase is about to be doubled to increase the settlement's capacity. Workers, engineers, scientists, and their families will soon be able to move into a more spacious and sheltered environment. We are also building new state-of-the-art facilities to expand mining exploration and scientific experimentation."

"And when should we expect this *soon* to become a reality?"

"Within three to five years, Commissioner—"

"Three to five years?! How can this be? The whole project began a decade ago! While President of France, I personally oversaw a significant budget increase to finance those operations. What happened to all this money?"

"… It… it is just that, apparently, there have been some delays over the last two years. As you know, we have adopted the stance to construct our base completely underground, unlike what the Americans, the Russians and the Chinese have done. In burrowing our facilities, the further protection we gain against space radiation for the colonists compared to a surface dome also means higher excavation costs. As a result, this report discloses we are under-resourced in the short term." He pointed to a dense file.

"And what about the orbital space station?"

"The European sector is meant to be completed. But in his last report, Colonel Rasmussen, the governor of our moonbase, stresses that he is experiencing serious technical difficulties in completing work due, once again, to a shortage of personnel and funds. He requests more money."

"That man is incompetent! And he has always been. His methods of executing the entire operation have been disastrous since the beginning. I sometimes question his motives. I believe the time has come for the good Colonel to contemplate a well-deserved retirement. Isabelle, set up a meeting with my brother at the earliest opportunity."

"At once, High Commissioner."

"Now, listen to me attentively", Pierre-Antoine went on. "I have received a specific directive from our President. Space colonisation is now one of the three top priorities of the present European Administration. The years of negotiations, hesitation and interminable committee reviews have ended. That this administration received a considerably larger envelope than the defence budget is no coincidence. We do not know how long this planet can sustain its current population or, worse, survive. We have five years to achieve success and significant results, or taxpayers will rightly consider we have wasted public money, as I have experienced it in the past. We have already lost six valuable months after this regrettable incident last March. We cannot waste any more time. Therefore, Gerrit, I want you to contact the European Lunar Base supervising board directly and request them to issue a report on spending priorities and personnel needs covering both the moonbase and the orbital station. I also want a survey on ways to shorten the current delays. Three to five years is way too long. Do not bother informing Colonel Rasmussen; I will deal with him. You have one week."

"Very well, Commissioner."

"Catherine, in the meantime, I require you to list the research centres that focus on anything to do with space travel and colonisation, including agriculture and water storage. If you receive any grievances from our State Department of Agriculture colleagues, forward them to me directly."

"I shall, High Commissioner."

"As your Direction will be the least solicited, Francis, I want you to provide all necessary assistance to your two colleagues this week. I will leave the details to you."

"It will be done, High Commissioner."

"Excellent! Let us stop here for today and get down to business tomorrow. Thank you all."

10

Six months already! I barely believe it, Shenouda thought. Living in the Holy City has been a dream come true. However, it was a completely different experience from Egypt; some days, he missed the beauty of the majestic Nile River. But there were compensations too. The priest had met and mixed with people from different countries and cultures on more intellectual grounds than with the tourist groups he was used to in Tell El Amarna. Jerusalem had become a melting pot of religious congregations, directly ruled by the Council of the Revealed Faiths. In the months following the conflict in the Middle East between 2045 and 2046, it became manifest that the States of Israel and Palestine would never resolve the status of Jerusalem. Therefore, the permanent members of the United Nations Security Council adopted a unanimous motion agreeing to give the Holy City the international status of a Free City inside a territory of 5 km around its walls. Its administration was transferred to a representative body composed equally of the three revealed main religions: Judaism, Christianity and Islam. It was tasked with maintaining peace and security, and ensuring the management of the holy sites within Jerusalem's boundaries. Under the established agreement, the two neighbouring states had to abandon their claims over the city and formally settle Tel Aviv and Ramallah as their official capitals. Sorting out the differences between the various religious communities within the three main faiths was no easy chore initially. But after several years, a balance emerged, ultimately promoting a more effective religious dialogue than the past political or nationalistic divisions did.

Shenouda occupied one of the cells of St Antony Monastery, generously offered free of charge by the Coptic Patriarchate. In return, he only had to participate in the shifts inside the Church of the Holy Sepulchre. A task similar to his former guiding activities, allowing him a great deal of spare time. His room was modest but comfortable enough. The young man spent most of his mornings praying and studying with the other resident monks. The afternoons were essentially free while remaining at the disposal of the Patriarch.

Shenouda was walking in the Muslim Quarter, wandering the streets of the old Arabic Market. The stalls were filled with an abundance of goods, food and intoxicating colourful spices. A decade of peace and stability ensured prosperity and riches to the city, and religious taxes enriched religious officials. He was looking at exotic fruits when his holophone rang. That was Professor Degrenes.

"Yes, Professor?"

"Marc, please. I told you to call me Marc a couple of times. Listen, Shenouda, I am organising a private meeting with some of my archaeologist's colleagues this evening. I would greatly appreciate it if you could join us and shed some light on the Tell-el-Amarna period."

"I should be delighted, of course."

"Wonderful! I'll be expecting you at 7.00 pm. Beverages and food are included. See you at my place." He hung up.

That was the second significant benefit of moving here. Thanks to the introduction by Professor Walter and Professor Degrenes' connections, he met several scholars and broadened his knowledge of archaeology. His phone rang again. It was Father Atta, the Patriarch's secretary this time.

"Yes, Father?"

"Deacon Wahba, I need you to come to the Patriarchal office. His Beatitude wishes to see you at once."

"Nothing serious, I hope?"

"I am afraid, I do not have the liberty to discuss this with you over the phone."

"I'll be there in no time."

He hastened to the Church of the Holy Sepulchre, the Coptic Patriarchate of Jerusalem seat. Despite arriving panting and sweating, Father Atta escorted him directly to the office of the head of the Coptic church before quickly closing the door behind him. Metropolitan Tawadros was not alone. He was quietly debating with two other persons. Looking at their clothing, one was a Catholic hierarch, and the other one a member of the Jewish faith.

"Your Beatitude," Shenouda said respectfully.

"Ah! Deacon Wahba, welcome. Please, have a seat. Allow me to introduce my esteemed colleagues and friends.

This is His Eminence Cardinal Paolo del Pietro, Apostolic Nuncio in Jerusalem, and here Chief Rabbi Yitzchak Eliyahu. We were also expecting His Eminence the Grand Mufti of Jerusalem, Suleiman Amin al-Sabri, but he is being held, unfortunately, to a serious last-minute issue. But rest assured, we speak on his behalf too. All right, we would like to discuss a matter of utmost importance with you. But, before, I must confess something to you, my son."

"I am listening, Your Beatitude."

"Well, you see, my son, your transfer to the Holy Land was no mere coincidence. In a way, you can thank your close friend, Professor John Walters, back in Egypt. Your friendship and active relationship represented the primary reasons we selected you. With His Holiness' consent at Alexandria, needless to say.

"Your Beatitude, I do not understand. You have me all confused." Shenouda looked at the three men, disoriented.

"What His Beatitude is trying to explain to you, young man, is that you are a wretched petty pawn in the hands of higher powers," bluntly replied Cardinal del Pietro. The Roman Catholic cleric was a tall man in his mid-fifties, dressed in a dark cassock, a traditional scarlet fascia tied around his belt, and a large silver cross hanging at his neck. His eyes were filled with wickedness. It was a startling contrast to the third religious man showing a more compassionate face behind his long grey beard and wearing a simple traditional black Orthodox Jewish long suit.

"My child", said the Chief Rabbi, "do not give too much credence to the coarse words of His Eminence. Regard yourself more as a gift of God than a pawn. We have no desire to hurt you or anyone. Rather, we are desperate for your help."

"My son," resumed the patriarch, "you are a man of faith. For the past six months, I have observed you meticulously. There are no doubts, in my mind, how dedicated you are to the service of God and our Holy Church. But, I wish to know if, given the opportunity, you will be willing to move farther in that dedication and protect the Glory of our Almighty Father who reigns in Heaven.

"I certainly will, Your Beatitude. But not at the cost of the damnation of my soul."

"Ah, ha, ha! Please do not misunderstand, Deacon Wahba; we are not urging you to commit an unpardonable crime. No, what is expected of you is a small favour. You see, we seriously believe that Professor Degrenes' archaeological work conceals a darker scheme. Something that could, potentially, severely undermine the foundations of our sacred beliefs."

"But I thought the Apostolic Nunciature financed his work. I guess his Eminence here is perfectly in control of the situation. Surely—"

"*Who he walks in the shadows, fears the light,*" the Cardinal interrupted.

"What our friend the Cardinal is trying to say is we seriously suspect the man to wear a mask and only to give us only what we want to hear. His true motives are deeply embedded. I am afraid I cannot go into much detail; the less you know, the better.

"Well, if so much is involved, Your Beatitude," replied Shenouda. "I am prepared to sever all ties with Professor Degrenes, at this point if that is what you desire from me."

"On the contrary, my son!" the cardinal responded. "We expect you to get even closer to him. We require you to nurture his friendship, gain his complete trust and become his confidant. As it happens, we are aware of the invitation you received to join a meeting this evening with several of his colleagues. We expressly want you to attend it. Go there, forge contacts, and be known by everyone. Remember, all this is for God's greatest glory."

"To state things more clearly, my child", concluded the Chief Rabbi, "we need you to operate as God's spy."

11

"That is all, Rinchen Lama. Kindly deliver this message to your father with my blessing. I suggest you use the opportunity to spend the night with your family to warm their hearts. I shall see you tomorrow."

"As you wish, Your Holiness." Rinchen bowed respectfully and promptly left what used to be the former residence of the Dalai Lama in Dharamshala. He found Kalsang and Jamyang awaiting him outside.

"What news?" the former asked.

"His Holiness is sending me on a mission to my father. A rather unpleasant one, I am afraid. He also requested I stay overnight at my family's house. That means I will not be joining you tonight."

"Is it serious?" Jamyang asked with a sorrowful voice.

"*Serious* would be a bold word, Jamyang. But, knowing my father, I anticipate a few words of resentment. Tensions between His Holiness' office and the Tibetan administration in exile have grown steadily recently. And my brother's death has not helped much."

"We will pray for the Buddha's compassion to enlighten your father's mind, Rinchen," Kalsang said. "Take these khatags with you as offerings."

"Thank you both; that is extremely thoughtful. Now, if you will excuse me, I need to haste to my father."

He stepped away and headed out of the compound through the main gate. He was nervous. A feeling inconsistent with his teachings. But it was the typical way his father affected his emotions. To set his mind at rest, he decided to walk down to his parent's house by the forest path. The air in Dharamshala was cooler than in Tawang but more polluted. In the background, the lofty mountains of the Himalayan range dominated the city, their summits covered with snow. Misty clouds hung from their cliffs, making them float in the sky. Outside Jampa Rinpoche's residence, he followed through a series of woodlands and small temples. Rinchen enjoyed walking along this trail. It allowed him to communion with his spirituality and the surrounding nature. Adjusting back to his hometown over the last six months had been more challenging than he thought. It made him realise that his Buddhist teaching and eleven years of separation had created a complex void to fill with a family more involved in political affairs. After months in a coma, the recent passing of his brother had made the situation worse, especially with his father. He could feel both loss and resentment in his behaviour, which his mother tried to temper as much as she could. She had persistently been the religious one in their couple, and Richen had inherited most of his disposition from her.

The monk reached a little white stupa on his left, covered with lung ta prayer flags, and rolled its colourful prayer wheels aligned along the wall. A dog, lying on its edge, looked amused at him. Rinchen smiled back before resuming his journey.

After another fifteen-minute walk, the young man finally reached his family home situated in the direct vicinity of the Tibetan Central Administration area. It was a spacious building made from whitewashed concrete walls and wood-frame windows. He walked directly towards the private garden at the bottom. He could hear the babbling of his nephew, Dache, likely playing with his sister-in-law.

"Dear Boshay, how is my nephew's mood today?"

"Rather cheerful, I have to say," she answered, standing up. "Rinchen Lama, what a pleasant surprise!"

He joined his hands and put one of the khatags, hanging on his left arm, around her neck. "May the Buddha's blessings protect you and your child."

She bowed back, accepting the gift. "And to what do we owe this unexpected visit?" she said, smiling.

"Official matters, I am afraid. But I will be staying for the night."

"That is wonderful!" she cheered, turning toward the house. "Mother Shenden, please, come quickly! Rinchen has come for the night!"

"Rinchen!" His mother rushed out with a joyous face. "I am so fortunate!" The monk put another khatag around her neck. "You honour me, as usual," she said. "How is it that the Temple has allowed you to come and stay all night?" Her face was glowing. However, Rinchen noticed fine lines around her deep eyes, betraying sleepless nights. Her long ebony hair, plaited with coloured pearls, rested on her white mourning dress.

"Official matters, mother, official matters. His Holiness thought spending time with my family would help ease some unpleasant news."

"His Holiness is wise as always. I will make your room ready immediately, and I will also inform your father."

"Is Penden home?"

"Not yet. Your sister is still at school but will be delighted to see you." She exited just as quickly as she appeared. A few minutes later, his father showed up on the doorstep wearing a traditional white chuba. He stood up and looked at him with his austere manner, amplified by his impeccably trimmed beard.

"Noble father, it brings me joy to see you in good health," Rinchen declared, holding a khatag with both hands. "May the Buddha provide you with long life and prosperity."

"I believe you came up with an answer," he replied adamantly. "Follow me into my office."

***

"That is unacceptable! Jampa Rinpoche seems to forget who placed him on the throne of the Dalai Lama. The very people he refuses to support!" Lobsang Gyaltsen was storming. He threw the message on the floor with rage. "If the government had listened to me twenty years ago, we would have preserved the tradition and prevented the current situation."

"But, Noble Father, the government has merely followed the will of the 14th Dalai Lama."

"The will of the 14th Dalai Lama was that his successor was elected as 15th Dalai Lama, not as Custodian! Rinchen Lama's current stance undermines the entire Tibetan administration."

"He simply uses his wisdom to protect our monasteries in Tibet and our religious communities across the world," Rinchen tried to appease.

"By remaining neutral and refusing to take the mantle he inherited, he only strengthens the Chinese puppet of Lhasa and spreads confusion in the ranks of the diaspora! You, above all, should understand that." He pointed his index at the monk.

"I am merely a messenger and a simple monk. It is not for me to take sides."

"Your place is here, with me, as my rightful successor, and not in these... these..." he stared at Rinchen's robes with disgust.

"Noble Father, I want to remind you that you put me into these robes, as the tradition you just invoked required. And you also have a successor. He is outside and is your grandson, Dache. You seem to forget."

"The situation has evolved."

"Evolved?"

"I am about to be appointed First Minister..."

12

"... a momentum, a significant step forward which brings hope to every human being today. I can officially announce that, under my supervision, my team will work on the second phase after this extraordinary breakthrough." Professor Owen Yang was standing in front of an audience of journalists, his whole body glittering in the crackling of the flashes, Ian McEwan by his side.

"Professor?" a journalist asked, "how long do you expect the process of developing a universal cure to take?"

"Well, we only just discovered the common denominator, you see. We now require to consider suitable candidates and determine relevant protocols. But, without being excessively optimistic, I would say to you, right here, within five to ten years, maximum. Cancer will represent a threat from the past, a minor illness treated by a simple injection or even an innocent tablet! In the meantime, this discovery will help secure new treatments for various cancer diseases. This is a tremendous step forward."

"What about Doctor Cunningham's research team?" asked another journalist.

"My good friend Virgil is welcome to consult our findings at his convenience. We are, of course, ready to collaborate in any way we can."

"Professor Yang, one last question! What do you think are your chances to be awarded a second Nobel Prize after such a discovery?"

"I certainly will not presume the decisions of the Nobel Committee. Now, if you will excuse me, I have to return to my collaborators, who desperately expect my return. Thank you all for coming today."

"What a blatant ass!" Colin exploded. "*I will not presume... My dear friend Virgil...*" He looked up. "I'm telling ya; he gives me the boke!" The whole team was watching the conference on television in the main lab.

"Take it easy, Colin," said Ranveer. "We are all aware of how he behaves. Swearing at him will not make much of a difference."

"This should not stop His Magnificence from mentioning his appreciation for his *collaborators'* work. And what about Giancarlo? He is the one who made the breakthrough, who discovered the little gift his *dear friend* left us!"

"It is ok, Colin. Ranveer is right," declared Giancarlo.

"No need to be too humble, Giancarlo." That was Emilie. "Colin is right; we owe you a lot. Before your arrival, we spent six months turning in circles. Then less than twenty-four hours into joining the team and *pouf!* Everything was resolved. You deserve as much acclaim as Professor Yang."

"Yes, but this is also your achievement. It is a collaborative effort; I am just a link in the chain. And it is incredibly inspiring working with you."

Professor Yang entered abruptly and walked directly to the young man.

"Dr Caracciolo, in my office now, if you please."

"Yes, Professor."

He followed the austere man to the secluded room.

"Close the door behind you and sit down. We need to discuss certain matters."

"I am listening, Professor."

"As you likely heard me saying a few minutes ago, we will promptly enter the second phase. I want it to start tomorrow and require you to supervise the team."

Giancarlo stared at him with astonishment.

"Your confidence flatters me, Professor, but I only joined the team six months ago. Ranveer is our team leader. He is the one that should continue to monitor us—"

"Ranveer is an excellent fellow researcher. But he is too complacent and short-sighted. Evidence is his inability to detect Dr Cunningham's alteration of our algorithm, despite working on his elaboration. This is unacceptable, and I cannot turn a blind eye to the incident. That is why I am placing you in charge and will ask Ranveer to assist you from now on."

"Again, Professor, I respectfully object to this sudden change in our organisation. Ranveer has an experience with this project I do not possess yet. At least keep him as my equal rather than my subordinate. This is a solid team, and we risk causing tensions between us."

"How very noble of you, and your objections are duly noted. But my mind is made up. You will take command of our research team, and Ranveer will be your second. You are popular with your colleagues, perhaps a bit too much, so there is no reason why they should oppose this change. And as far as I can recall, I am in charge. I will make certain they understand."

So, this is what it is all about… Giancarlo thought. *He is more perverse than I initially thought. He intentionally places me in an uncomfortable position, hoping to undermine our strong bond. Once again, Colin is right about him.* "I will do as you ask, then, Professor Yang."

"That is exactly what I expect of you, as I mentioned the day you began. In addition, I instruct you to ensure that, in the future, any new developments you may come across are reported directly to me before any of your colleagues. Is it understood?"

"Perfectly understood, Professor."

"Very well. Now, if you wish, ask Ranveer to come. I shall see you in the morning."

Giancarlo walked back to the lab, where his co-workers were nervously waiting. They instantly noticed his sinister face.

"What happened in there, Giancarlo?", Natalia asked.

The Italian only looked at Ranveer.

"The professor wants to speak to you right now."

Then he took off without a word. *I need to see Liz tonight.*

PART TWO
Awakening

13

"My father has confirmed Prime Minister Banerjee will travel to Dharamshala on Thursday to investigate the situation, Your Holiness. After a public session with the Cabinet and a speech to our Parliament, there will be a private meeting in my father's office, which he insists you attend. To quote him, *It is of the utmost importance that His Holiness is present with us, especially given how directly this issue affects our religious affairs.*"

"I see... And what would you do if you were in my position, Rinchen Rinpoche?" Jampa Rinpoche stared directly into his eyes as if he could penetrate his thoughts.

"Your Holiness, I cannot presume..."

"Venerable Rinchen Rinpoche, after seven years by my side, you are at present my first and most trusted advisor. Furthermore, should anything happen to my person, on a probable path to succeed me. Therefore, I ask you again. What would you do?"

"Well, as leader of our religious communities, I would find it difficult to reject my father's *offer*, even though it looks more like a summons. Doing otherwise would be unwise to preserve my position."

"Assuredly. And that is exactly what our secular leader expects. I believe he is finally tired of our little game of hide and seek and has decided to involve me directly in his affairs. Which I have successfully managed to prevent. Until now…"

Remarkable! This is precisely what father said! thought Rinchen.

"Any news from Tawang?"

"No, Your Holiness. However, Venerable Chopel Rinpoche mentioned that he would consult all of his brother monks before replying."

"It has now been three days. Contact him again. They must decide by tonight. The Indian Prime Minister will be here in two days, and I cannot wait much longer."

"As you wish, Your Holiness."

"Alright, you may leave me now. And please, I do not want to be interrupted for the next few hours, except for any new developments on the matter we discussed."

Rinchen bowed respectfully and returned to his office on the residence's first floor. Jamyang and Kalsang, now his private secretaries, were waiting for him.

"How did it go?" inquired Kalsang.

"Rather badly, I'm afraid. While touched by the blessings of the Bhudda, His Holiness does not like to be caught up in politics. But the whole situation smells like a tortuous trap. I feel that whatever choice we make will have dire consequences for us all."

"Is it that bad?" asked Jamyang.

"Terribly," answered Rinchen. "The 15th Dalai Lama's unexpected request for an official visit could not have come at the worst moment. The Indian Government's authority is weakened right now. The governing coalition in Parliament is hanging by a thread, and tensions are mounting with Pakistan. Prime Minister Banerjee's visit on Thursday indicates a likely sign that his cabinet is prepared to negotiate with the Chinese president, Deng Xue. My father is roaring at the prospect. He wants the entire Tibetan community in exile to close ranks behind the Tibetan administration, including the religious ones. And Tawang Monastery is his primary concern because of the symbol it represents. The Chinese are clearly engaging in a calculated game. But for which purpose?"

"Speaking about Tawang," said Kalsang, "an urgent message arrived from Venerable Chopel Rinpoche while you were with His Holiness."

"Give it to me right away! It is most likely the response we expected."

Kalsang handled the missive bearing the seal of the Abbot of Tawang Monastery to Rinchen. It was brief.

My dear Rinchen Riponche,

After carefully examining our situation and a long discussion with our brothers, we have concluded a visit from the alleged 15th Dalai Lama to our monastery is far too sensitive to hold solely in the hands of our modest community.

Therefore, while we recommend caution, we believe it relies on our spiritual leader to guide us in the proper direction.

In his infinite wisdom, I am confident the Buddha will inspire His Holiness with the most auspicious decision, which we will follow unquestionably.

May the Buddha guide your path and protect you on your ongoing journey.

Venerable Abbot Chopel Rinpoche.

***

"After being trapped by your father, I find myself alone in determining the fate of our exiled community. I did not anticipate an explicit opinion from the abbot. But, looking at what holds in the balance, some insight from the leader of one of our most revered places of worship would have been most welcome." Rampa Rinpoche had just finished reading the message Rinchen hastily brought to his attention. "How dares he! After all, I have done for him!"

"Your Holiness…"

"My apologies, Rinchen. I'm afraid I have let my emotions get in the way."

"But, to a certain extent, is he not right? Should you not exploit this opportunity to assess your leadership during these delicate times?"

"It is a delicate question, Rinchen, even for me." He sat on the wide golden chair behind his desk. "As you remember, I was extremely devoted to Tenzin Gyatso, our 14th Dalai Lama. I revered him wholeheartedly. My sole purpose in life was to follow his path to wisdom. He spent the last decades of his life distancing himself from the secular power he was handled in Tibet in 1950 to focus solely on his religious obligations. With the promulgation of the 1963 constitution, he created the Tibetan Central Administration and Parliament-in-Exile. Next, he transferred his political powers to the Kashag, presently led by a First Minister, at my request. The most powerful man in Tibet once said, *I always consider myself as a simple Buddhist monk. I feel that is the real me. I feel that the Dalai Lama as a temporal ruler is a man-made institution."* This transformation inspired my decision to refuse to accept the title of Dalai Lama after my election. Instead, I chose to be addressed as The Custodian. Like my teacher, being a monk is anchored deep inside me. My only aspiration is to serve the Buddha and pass on his teaching with the promise of enhancing human consciousness. I am not a politician and possess no ambition of becoming one or playing political games. This is not my path."

"I understand."

"But, sometimes, one must accept the inevitability of his obligations, notwithstanding his wishes. It seems that it is up to me to decide the fate of both our exiled community and the one across the Himalayas. I cannot hide any longer. Very well. Rinchen, take note of my response to Venerable Abbot Chopel Rinpoche. Inform him that Tawang Monastery is not authorised under any circumstances to allow the alleged Dalai Lama to enter its premises. Even if the Indian government directly petitions it. Ensure this message is dispatched safely, with instruction to the abbot not to mention any of its contents publicly. Would he not follow that directive, inform him that the government and I will ensure he resigns his seat. In addition, please confirm to your father that I will attend the meeting. But do not stipulate my decision regarding Tawang. The matter will be discussed in more detail on Thursday. I first want to know what the Indians' intentions are."

"It shall be done as you instruct, Your Holiness."

"Now, leave me. I shall retire and meditate on my loss of temper later. I am a simple monk but also a feeble human being...."

14

The view was breathtaking. Giancarlo looked down at the valley lying far below, with its two stretched lakes —or lochs as they were called here— glittering in the sun and surrounded by dense forests. The horizon was carved by mountain slopes, wrapped in large patches of brown and purple heather, like a cosy quilt laid by nature to keep them warm during the cold nights. The Italian gazed at the surroundings. The deep azure sky of this gorgeous day allowed him to see afar, offering a breathtaking view of the Central Highlands. It was worth the three-hour trek to the summit. Evidently, less spectacular in comparison to the majesty of the Italian Alps. Especially Lake Como's region, which he often wandered while studying in Milan. No, this was distinct. One word kept entering his mind, *magical.* Yes, that was it, magical. Bits of rocky earth suddenly rolled under his right foot, unbalancing him briefly.

"Beware not to fall; you are still worth something to me," laughed Liz. Her two arms softly wrapped his waist in a tender hold.

"I have been hiking all my life," Giancarlo replied. "These are smooth slopes. I would not have fallen very far and, at worst, end up with just a few scratches."

"Well, you never know. And a local legend says the entrance to the underworld hides somewhere around. It would be a shame to have you trapped in there..." she said with her familiar purring voice.

"Ah, ha, ha! Come on, you know I do not believe that kind of nonsense. I had my share of fairy tales in Italy."

"Watch out for thoughtless words. This is Mount Schiehallion, also named the Fairy Mound of the Caledonians. We do not want to anger the little fairies, do we?" She twitched her nose, mocking him.

"There is definitely magic around here, I admit. But it is nature's magic. Look!" He pointed to an eagle slowly circling above their heads. "You see, this is what I consider magic. No need for little winged creatures." He gently kissed her on her lips. "Thank you for taking me here. I needed this break. I feel stuck with this wasteful work."

"Let's walk back to the car and think about dinner."

They slowly made their way down the rocky path.

"You are avoiding the discussion again," Giancarlo declared after several metres.

"I am not avoiding any discussion. I know perfectly what you are about to say. And that is why we are here. To clear our heads and distance ourselves from work."

"Come on, Liz. Put yourself in my shoes. A consequent breakthrough seven years ago, and the team has been running around in circles without much success since. If only to make little progress."

"It is the accumulation of small advances which leads to a larger one. You are a geneticist. What do you expect?

Miracles? What are you anxious about, anyway? Losing your job? You are way too involved in the research and, as such, have become extremely valuable to the company. They would think twice before considering letting you go to the competition. Even Owen is too preoccupied with gambling on the prospect of claiming a third Nobel. Maybe he is the one who should be sacked. After all, what does he do besides conduct interviews and sit idly behind his desk while you do all the dirty work?"

"If not for his fame, Pharma Cybernetics Corp. would have pulled the plug by now. We are generating much less profit than your department—"

"Are you kidding me, Giancarlo? Less profit! How dare you speak of profit? Where have your ethics and morality gone? And since when does the company have profits as its primary objective? That discovery seven years ago radically changed medicine. Look at all the fatal diseases which now belong to the past or are under control. Malaria, Ebola, Coronaviruses, HIV, you name it. A small tablet or a quick shot, and hop! Ciao Bello! And when a new viral infection appears, a cure is found within one month, at worst. One month, Giancarlo! The last threatening pandemic on this planet dates back to 2054. You have fortuitously saved hundreds of millions of lives. What the hell profit has to do with this!?"

"Several cancers are still eluding us! Whenever we develop a promising therapy, they find a way out..."

He stopped to sit on a large chunk of rock, staring at the nearby moors. They seemed so peaceful and serene. He saw little birds fluttering by while bees industriously buzzed on the nearby wildflowers.

"They still have native bees here. Did you know? None of these bioengineered ones."

She embraced him. "Forgive me. I forgot about your mother. I was not trying to be hurtful. I know how much you miss her and how traumatic it was feeling powerless to save her. But it has been three years now. And we're all destined to die somewhere down the line."

"Not this way! Not by enduring that physical deterioration and agony. She was such a kind-hearted person, so innocent, so caring. She did not deserve to end like that, to… rot alive. And that priest during her last moments. That so-called servant of God, with his sweet words of comfort. *God moves in mysterious ways. Or God is calling you back to him. Rejoice, Margarita, because you will soon embrace his everlasting love and be comforted by his benevolence.* If God exists, he is a thief, and Death is an offence to life! Are you listening up there? I will deprive you of this death you so much indulge in by every possible means. Hear me!" He faced the sky with a defiant fist.

"Calm down, Giancarlo. You are frightening me now. All these emotions are ungood for you. I knew we should not have gotten into that conversation. Come on, let's get back to the cottage. I will prepare you a nice relaxing bath, and then we will have a pleasant dinner in this old inn you fancied yesterday."

She took his hand, and they continued walking in the warm sun among the busy bees.

Two days later, Giancarlo was back at the laboratory. His good old team, persistently working enthusiastically against the odds and, when needed, devotedly closing ranks behind him. Yes, the whole old gang. Despite the substantial change imposed by Professor Yans in 2057, they had all remained with him all these years. Even Ranveer. *I never had any particular disposition for leadership, to be honest*, he declared back then. The animosity focused primarily on Professor Yang and his lack of empathy in addressing the matter. Then things settled down after a while, evolving into a status quo that eventually benefited both parties. *But we are still at a standstill, achieving no progress.*

"How was Schiehallion? Did you and Liz manage to loosen things up?" Ranveer asked.

"The area is breathtaking. You were right, and I should have gone there earlier. Standing at the top feels like dominating the world around you. It was a great break. As for the rest… it's still complicated."

"No worries, man. You know I am not looking for specifics. What only matters is that you both enjoyed yourselves and put this…" he circled his right arm around, "… away for a few days. But, if I may ask, how are the two of you still not fully involved after all these years?"

"That, too, is complicated, Ranveer. Anyway, what results regarding experiment 317?"

"Like the sixteen previous ones since we started phase three. It works on fish and amphibians but is a complete failure once we get into mammals. Every subject ends up developing uncontrollable mutations and has to be put down. And I am barely talking about mice here. We did two tests on more evolved animals, and the result was identical."

"I do not get it. What makes mammals respond so differently to a modified virus than lower creatures? I mean, we found a DNA protein common to every distinct type of cancer cell. A deactivated oncolytic virus is modified by including the protein. The resulting chimeric virus is used to induce a reaction from T regulatory cells. Finally, it activates an immune response against the body's cancer cells, even the dormant ones. It is bloody simple! Now, what are we missing? We have been looking into this for four years. And whenever we find a solution, it only works for a few weeks until some types of cancer adapt. But why solely with mammals? It does not make sense."

"What can I tell you, Giancarlo? Perhaps we should revisit our initial findings. Maybe we missed another DNA sequence as important as the one we focus on?"

"By doing so, we will delay our research by many years. I don't know how long Pharma Cybernetics Corp. will accept to keep funding our research. Not indefinitely, for sure, if we persist in presenting them with no significant results. I just imagine the faces of the board when telling them. *Sorry, thank you for financing us all those years, but we just realised we went in the wrong direction and need to start again.* And Yang will never accept it. He will accuse us of attempting to sabotage his credibility. No, there has to be another alternative."

"Well, you are probably right. But whatever solution exists, I doubt we will uncover it tonight. If you did not notice, we are the only two left. So, if you will excuse me, I am heading back to my wife and children. Are you coming? Sanjita has cooked her fabulous Rogan Josh. You are welcome to join us."

"Thank you, Ranveer, but I will do a few extras tonight. I will look at those results you gave me earlier on."

"As you wish. See you tomorrow. Try not to overstretch yourself."

Much later, Giancarlo was still working in the lab. He was looking at a project he submitted a little over three years ago out of desperation because of his mother's condition. Professor Yang had categorically dismissed it. He still recalled the fiery argument.

"Are you completely out of your mind, Giancarlo?! I know how upset you are about your mother. As much as I share your sorrow, I will never authorise such an experiment."

"This is no experiment, Professor. Please take a look at the results; they are conclusive. It works like wonders!"

"My answer is still no! We are scientists here, not sorcerer's apprentices. We can adjust the rules occasionally, hiding behind the better good. But this monstrosity is sacrilege. It exceeds all acceptable ethical, moral, or even religious boundaries."

"Religion has nothing to do with our work nor its merchants of lies. This is about saving lives, Professor, valuable lives."

"Enough of that! Your personal motives are obviously interfering with your reason. Don't you ever dare to suggest this to me or anyone else again. I will forget this conversation did happen. Always remember we are bound to a code of practice, and I expect you to comply with it, like all your colleagues. The timing is not appropriate for your suggestion."

Well, Professor, I believe the timing is definitely appropriate. He went to the airlock, put on his protection suit, and walked into the biohazard storage room. He had a long night ahead of him.

15

"This is Fortress Europe! We are forsaking the very ideals for which we have created this Federation for one's little indulgence!" Monika thundered. She could not believe what she had just heard during the cabinet meeting.

"Monika, please be reasonable..."

"Reasonable? *Reasonable*, Mister President? How come? You are asking this Cabinet to approve the closure of all our borders to almost the entire world! And on what account? Because election time is fourteen months away? I honestly fail to underst—"

"Monika, if you please!" President Kowalczyk pitched his voice in exasperation. "This Administration is the first to have been directly chosen by the Parliament. Even though most of you are survivors of the previous one, mostly because of their excellent performance, we are now directly accountable to Parliament and the people. Therefore, indeed, we must consider the next election now, look at the polls and act accordingly if we want to pursue our action collectively. The recent results of the state parliamentary elections in Austria, Italy and Greece, clearly demonstrate we must change course on this particular issue if we stand any chance of re-election. I want to remind you that one of those ideals we have vowed to uphold remains the eradication, once and for all, the cancer represented by nationalist and extremist political movements. We must avoid risking ending up with a divided and weak Federal Parliament. The situations in North America, the Middle East, and the Indian subcontinent are increasingly unstable. People are getting concerned, if not scared. They want protection and security. If it means tightening our borders, then we tighten them. The African Union has already implemented identical measures, and the Central and South American Union is about to adopt similar ones. Unlike Russia, we do not have the luxury of a massive nuclear arsenal to threaten others. This thanks to my predecessor who halved the arsenal we inherited from France with her grand delusion of 'Peace, Love and Prosperity'."

"So, we are just going to wall ourselves in, hoping the storm will pass over our heads and do nothing to attempt to prevent it?"

"We have been trying for over six years. This endless civil war in America and the vacuum it created in the rest of the world has enabled powers like China and Russia to act with impunity—"

"Even though we were supposed to address that gap and assert ourselves."

Lord! She really is on the offensive today! thought Pierre-Antoine.

"Again, blame my predecessor, Monika. As her High Commissioner for Foreign Affairs at the time, I need not remind you that you blindly supported some of her decisions without questioning."

"Because I am loyal to the Administration I serve, Mister President. If you have concerns about my loyalty, you can still ask for my—"

"Mister President, if I may?" Pierre-Antoine interrupted. The President nodded in approval. "I believe this sterile debate has heated up enough. Everyone's position has been heard, and the matter should be resolved collectively before expressing words we will deeply regret afterwards. I suggest we submit the question to a vote. Don't you agree?"

A cold silence followed.

"As usual, the voice of reason, Pierre-Antoine," finally replied President Kowalczyk. "You are right; let's call the question."

The motion was adopted unanimously, with one abstention from High Commissioner Monika Richter.

"This brings the matter to a close," concluded the European President. "Jorge, I want you to reinforce and increase our defensive capability by any measures you deem necessary. We must show our potential adversaries that we mean business when it comes to any possible threat. Clearly, nuclear options are excluded from those measures. It goes against our ideals, and we do not want to start a new nuclear race." Monika grunted. "I also want you to collaborate with Pierre-Antoine to increase our military capacities on both our moonbase and orbital station. But with extreme discretion. Let us not be too conspicuous. As Monika relevantly pointed out earlier, China and Russia have overtly begun to increase theirs. Although worrisome, we do not wish to appear influenced by their strategic positions. All the investments made over the last seven years are starting to bear fruit. We must not risk having our rivals harvest them instead should a conflict, unfortunately, occur in the near future."

"Understood, Mister President," Jorge answered.

"Keep me both updated directly. Monika, I want you to contact the Secretary of State of the Eastern States Federation and assure him of our full support and assistance in their negotiations for a general cease-fire. If at least, we could achieve a status quo for a year, this would partly ease international pressure. Meanwhile, I want your team to work with the Department of External Affairs to probe our contacts within the Chinese government. This recent request from the 15th Dalai Lama does not feel right. The People's Republic of China is obviously hiding something."

"As you wish, Mister President," she murmured.

"Thank you all. That will be it for today."

***

Monika was back in her office, lying in her armchair. She was still fuming about the Cabinet session, and her right hand was shaking. I need to calm down. She took a few deep breaths and poured herbal tea into her mug. After a few sips, the warm beverage started to soothe and clear her mind. I almost did it this time. Detachment, detachment, always detachment.

"Always!" she shouted. 'As if…"

The intercom buzzed.

"Yes, Alessandra?"

130

"*High Commissioner, I apologise for disturbing you. High Commissioner Lascombes is here and would like to see you.*"

"Let him in, please."

She rose from her seat while Pierre-Antoine came in. He looked a bit pale. She hugged him and kissed him on the cheeks.

"My saviour, once more."

They sat on one of the sofas.

"*Monika, quelle mouche t'a piquée ?*[(*)]" He looked at her with a reprimand.

"I know, I know. I lost my self-control and should not have. I set a terrible example as the head of the European diplomacy. But that man is such a lousy politician."

"That man is doing his best to correct the wrong done by President Strauss. This idealistic woman was not fit for the job she was appointed for."

"And all because of the absurd outcome of the 2052 American presidential election and that populist candidate challenging its results. But who would have thought that, unlike 2020, he would succeed in his bid and start the Second American Civil War? Managing to engulf Canada with it and produce long-lasting global chaos on top of it?"

"I am pleased to see you returned to your senses!" he laughed.

"That does not excuse the man. With him, every decision is a step forward and two steps backwards. We are expanding our tactical capability to better bury our heads in the sand. We are strengthening our currency, but only to appease the markets. We have achieved a 95% result in green energy. Still, we ignore the pollution and destruction affecting what is left of this planet. And the list goes on. No, Kowalczyk only objective is his re-election. He does

not care about us, despite what he said earlier. The man is just trying to mislead [*] *What's got into you?*
voters into believing their small comfort will remain intact. We had an incredible historic opportunity to return to the centre of international politics, and he squandered it. He is a slug!"

"Calm down, Monika. Anger will not improve the situation and could only cause you harm."

"You know what? I think you should stand for office after the next parliamentary election. The way you handled the Cabinet session today was laudable."

"Me!?" He laughed before choking and displaying a painful grin while holding his belly.

"Great lord, Pierre-Antoine! Are you alright?" She started to panic and ran to the table. "Do you want something to drink? A glass of water? I have some herbal infusion here."

"It is alright, Monika, I assure you. This is partly the reason why I came here. I just received a call from the oncologist. They found two new tumours."

"Two more!" Monika was in shock. 'But that will be the—"

"The third time in eighteen months, I know. It is recurring quicker now. I was warned of that possible development when they found my first sarcoma seven years ago, if you remember."

"I thought they said the latest treatment was effective. What are the doctors saying about your outcomes?"

"They give me a year, perhaps two. The recurrence is undeniably accelerating now. Not a jolly thought, I know. The President is advised. It is the reason he requested Jorge to assist me with our moon program. My brother has been tasked with preparing for the transition. The Defence will ultimately absorb Science and Technology."

"Oh my God, Pierre-Antoine. It's such bad news; I did not expect the prognosis to turn out so bad."

"Well, I guess we all die at some point."

"How dare you say this? That is not you!" She stared at him with a reprimand.

"What can I say, Monika? I have exhausted all possibilities."

"Well, maybe not..." She walked to her desk and talked on the intercom. "Alessandra?"

"*Yes, High Commissioner?*"

"Could you come here for five minutes, please?"

"*Right away, High Commissioner.*"

Monika's personal assistant walked into her office within seconds.

"Alessandra, I need you to tell Pierre-Antoine about your cousin."

"Certainly, High Commissioner." She turned to Pierre-Antoine. "Well, you see, High Commissioner, I have this cousin… Doctor Giancarlo Caracciolo. He is the assistant head researcher at Edinburgh's Newhaven Lighthouse Park Research Centre. He works under Professor Owen Yang, the two-time Nobel Prize laureate. Maybe you have heard of him?"

"I have not heard of your cousin, but I am familiar with Professor Yang and his research centre. We give them significant funding every year."

"Great. So, they made this breakthrough in cancer research seven years ago. And since then, they have been working on a universal treatment for cancer or something like that. Sorry, science was not my best subject. Anyway.

Apparently, the treatment is quite advanced now. My cousin told me last week that their lab results were most encouraging. They have recently started seeking volunteers to begin human testing. But they experience difficulties in finding suitable candidates—"

Monika stopped her. "Thank you, Alessandra. You may leave us now. I will take it from there."

"As you wish, High Commissioner."

After her assistant left, Monika faced Pierre-Antoine. "You see, there is always another possibility! What do you make of this? I think it is worth trying because you have nothing to lose."

"Another painful treatment, not to mention being a guinea pig. Not something to consider lightly."

"Hope is hope, even thin. How can you be so hesitant? After all you accomplished in your life! Everything we achieved, you, your brother and I! I never expected you to quit so easily. I want you to carry on fighting against all odds. And Jorge and I will support you in your struggle!"

"Alright, alright. I give up. My operation is due next month. Then, I promise, I will contact this Doctor Caracciolo and see what he has to offer."

16

April was exceptionally hot, and the air conditioning struggled to keep up. Shenouda had called maintenance, but they were already busy and asked him to wait a little longer. The monk was desperately trying to cool himself off with an old fashion pedestal fan he had found abandoned in a storage. The gentle flow provided some relief. But he was still sweating in the muggy hot air, spoiling the comfort of his modest office above the Church of the Holy Sepulchre. He was, at present, Archdeacon and first advisor to the Metropolitan Archbishop. Although based primarily on the value of his abilities and religious education, this promotion resulted partly from his extracurricular activities. He had been mandated to increase the confidence level within Professor Degrenes' circle and eventually did. His rise into the local religious authority ranks helped consolidate his image as a liberal independent cleric supporting the cause of archaeology, unlike most of his more conservative colleagues. It was a constant delicate game to balance the thirst for historical knowledge with the will of God.

He looked through the open window. The sky was deep blue, flawless. Overlooking the Old City, the golden Dome of the Rock shone radiantly in the afternoon sun, a proud beacon of the Islamic faith. Shenouda heard the call to the afternoon prayer, Salât al-Aṣr. *Maybe I should go and pray, too,* he thought. He left his office, walked past Nazeer looking as uncomfortable as he was, and descended the stairs before heading directly for St Helena's Church. Originally built as an underground cistern, the small church was a haven of freshness when temperatures were soaring compared to the rest of the building. It was empty. The soaring heat seemed to have deterred even the most faithful pilgrims. He sat on one of the front benches opposite the iconostasis. A heavy purple curtain embroidered with a representation of St Helena maternally holding the cross of Christ she miraculously found seventeen centuries ago covered its door. Shenouda quietly began reciting the Lord's Prayer: *Our Father Who art in heaven; hallowed be Thy name. Thy kingdom come. Thy will be done on earth as it is in heaven...* While his mind wandered away, his subconscious mechanically took over the recitation, as in a state of meditation. Seven years! Throughout that time, he had followed the mission given by the High Council of the Free City of Jerusalem with devotion, hiding his true motives from people whom he also loved very much, and who, in turn, entrusted him. *Lord Jesus, have mercy on my miserable soul and give me the strength to carry out the difficult task you have bestowed on me.* Feelings of guilt overcame him from time to time. Without the moral support of the Coptic Metropolitan, he would have simply failed.

Never forget, my son, that you are fulfilling God's will, His Holiness gently reminded him regularly. *There is no sin in carrying out His purpose and serving His eternal glory.*

Nevertheless, the task was arduous. *And for which purpose?* All these years, Professor Degrenes only acted as the passionate and enthusiastic archaeologist he was, like most of his colleagues. At times, he expressed his frustrations with the Religious Office for Antiquities and their despotic control over each excavation. However, he was not the only one to react this way. As formalised in 1949, the Status Quo had been extended to the Jewish and Muslim faiths with the City's new status to the satisfaction of all religious groups. But this further complicated the administrative procedures. And Pharaoh Shishak's —or Shoshenq I as it was commonly accepted— visible presence in Jerusalem still eluded the archaeologist and his team. Paradoxically, the Holy Nunciature seemed unconcerned, and Cardinal del Pietro kept actively funding the professor's work with explicit support from the other members of the High Council. Despite repeated attempts to gather information, none of the clerics was willing to provide Shenouda with any specific justification for this unending encouragement to pursue a primarily futile task.

Everything comes to those who wait, my son, the Apostolic Nuncio told him once. *We have absolute confidence in Professor Degrenes' capacity to achieve the breakthrough we hope for. It is God's will. As said from the start, your task only consists in informing us of any development, regardless of how insignificant it may seem."*

At least, this game of cat and mouse enabled Shenouda to discover the hidden treasures of the Holy City. The average tourist or pilgrim had no slightest idea of the wonders carefully preserved beneath its surface, rivalling the beauties of Egypt for some.

A scream interrupted his thoughts and the serenity of the place. A child ran along the church benches directly to the iconostasis with the manifest intention to check behind.

"I am sorry child; no one is allowed to go through," Shenouda said placidly. The little one froze and watched the ghostly presence with fear and frustration.

"Matthew! Get back here! You are disturbing the priest," yelled a pronounced American voice—the mother, most likely.

"My apologies, ma'am, but as written at the entrance, it is a place of prayer and quietness. I invite you to respect the simple rules of these sacred grounds," he continued.

"My apologies, Father. We did not see you. We will leave you in peace. Come Matthew! We are clearly unwelcome here!"

Tourists! No ounce of respect. He felt his holophone vibrating softly. It was Professor Degrenes. He walked outside before answering.

"Yes, Marc?"

"Shenouda! You need to come to my place immediately! I have a surprise for you. And it comes with a breakthrough. We found it, my friend. We found it!"

***

Professor Degrenes' residence stood in the Muslim quarter, near Herod's Gate. It was a vast apartment on the top floor of an old, elegant two-storey building accessed through a luxury garden. The interior was elegantly decorated with oriental furniture and Ancient Egyptian and Israeli artefacts. The archaeologist greeted the monk with unconditional warmth.

"Shenouda! Welcome! I am so glad you managed to come quickly. Please, have a glass of water; it is so hot outside," he said, pointing to a tray displaying several glasses.

"Thank you, Marc. I am always happy to enjoy the freshness my office does not provide at this time of the day." He grasped one of the glasses. The cold beverage cheered him up. "What is it you found requiring my immediate attention?"

"Something extraordinary! But before, I have a surprise for you. John? A corpulent man dressed in a sand-coloured costume emerged from the back room.

"Professor Walters! Oh my god!" cried out Shenouda. "You are here! What a wonderful surprise!" He rushed into the old man's arms.

"Shenouda, my boy. It is so nice to see you again after all this time. Look at you! All grown up now. What a fine-looking priest you are."

"Not yet, Professor. I still haven't taken the vows. I wish to wait a bit longer before entering the full service of God. But look at you as well. Egypt seems to treat you well."

"I am just becoming a little older and a little less wise, my boy," he laughed.

"You should have told me you were coming. I would have prepared something."

"That is why it is called a surprise, Shenouda," went on Professor Degrenes. "Right! Before remembering the good old days, let us discuss why I asked you here. John, if you please."

139

"Right away, Marc. My dear boy, as you know, after each end of our digging campaign in April, I go to Cairo to report on our discoveries to the Ministry of Antiquities. Next, I indulge myself in wandering the basements of the Grand Egyptian Museum's dusty storage rooms, searching for forgotten artefacts that could help our research. While looking at the Amarna letters collection, an unusual object abandoned at the bottom of a drawer caught my eye. It was a clay tablet similar to the others except unexpectedly written in hieroglyphics. As you know, the Amarna letters are all written in the cuneiform alphabet. I examined this atypical relic more closely. To my surprise, it bore the seal of Osorkon I, son of Shoshenq I!"

"No doubt a misplaced object, Professor. The Amarna tablets are quite well catalogued. This tablet likely belonged to the artefacts of the 22nd dynasty and was inadvertently brought there."

"Wait, wait, this is where it becomes crucial." He showed Shenouda a large photograph of a clay tablet carved with hieroglyphs. "Look at the text. Pharaoh Orsokon mentions his father's campaign in Jerusalem! This is the first text ever to mention the city among the conquests of Shoshenq. And it is explicitly addressed to Abijah, King of Judah. King Jeroboam's son! Look, Shenouda, an archaeological relic mentioning King Solomon's grandson! Something generations of archaeologists have been digging for. And there's more! In this section, Orsokon writes: *"Thy noble father was shown the hidden place, the cursed one, by his humble servant, Jeroboam. It lies underneath the Holy of Holies, defying beloved Amun. The curse manifested itself before it could be destroyed. My Noble Lord ordered the heretical room to be sealed and forgotten for eternity, on the life of his servant, your faithful father, so as the*

140

curse would never more pervert the ka of men. You are to renew that oath to us, for you and all your descendants." Of course, this is an approximative translation done by me. I admit some inaccuracies."

"Wow! This is… incredible!"

"Yes, Shenouda! An extraordinary discovery!" Professor Degrenes said. "We finally possess tangible proof that Pharaoh Shoshenq did enter Jerusalem and did not just to claim a tribute from his vassal. And more importantly, his son declares that whatever hides there was sealed, not destroyed. It means that under Solomon's Temple foundations exists an undiscovered room containing something feared by pharaoh Shoshenq and his successors. Imagine its significance, the ultimate proof of the authenticity of the biblical texts! Suppose the name of Jeroboam appears there, too, as it does on the tablet. In that case, we shall have indisputable evidence of his existence and, therefore, of King Solomon and King David. It will be the most remarkable archaeological discovery of the twenty-first century!" He was in a transcendental state.

"It is indeed a truly tantalizing prospect. But the First Temple's location lies just underneath Temple Mount. Excavations will never be permitted there. You know how sensitive the area is, even today."

"This explains my presence here, Shenouda", Professor Walters replied. "If I am unmistaken, a recent earthquake damaged some sections of the Dome of the Rock, compromising parts of its integrity. And an extensive restoration and consolidation of its structure have been commissioned, starting in two weeks."

"You are not mistaken, Professor. The High Council gave its consent four days ago."

"Exactly. And we need you to convince the High Council to allow Marc to approve excavations during the restoration work."

17

"Good morning. My name is Leif Forsberg. I have an appointment with Isabelle Veyre?"

"Naturally. Please, take a seat in the lounge behind you. I will inform Mrs Veyre right away."

"Many thanks."

Five minutes later, a stylish, heavily pregnant woman walked confidently down the stairs, her long, curly hair bouncing off at every step.

"Mister Forsberg, how nice to meet you. I am Isabelle Veyre, Personal Assistant to High Commissioner Lascombes. Follow me, please. We will take the lift; it will be quicker and easier."

"Right after you."

"I must say, you look dashing," she said with a smile.

"Oh! Thank you", answered Lief, embarrassed, wondering whether it was a compliment.

They swiftly reached the fifth floor and entered a bright, comfortable, and spacious office with exquisite wood panels and custom-made storage cabinets, overlooking the canal and the European Parliament.

"Please sit down." She sat behind a broad mahogany desk and directly talked through the intercom.

"*Yes, Isabelle?*" a voice answered.

"High Commissioner, Mister Forsberg is here and may see you as soon as you are available."

"*Please, bring him in.*"

She turned to Lief. "Mister Forsberg, High Commissioner Lascombes will see you for fifteen minutes now."

"Now? But I thought it was an initial contact with you."

"If you are going to work here, Mister Forsberg, you need to get used to last-minute schedule changes. Do not worry; you are smart enough," she winked.

When the door opened, Pierre-Antoine was clearing up his desk by arranging his papers in order. Isabelle introduced a young man wearing a dark blue three-piece suit, enhanced with a bright red tie and flawless Italian-made shoes. *Tall, blond hair, blue eyes, a real stereotype,* he thought, amused. He rose and shook the candidate's hand before inviting him to sit down.

"Mister Forsberg, nice meeting you. May I get you a coffee?"

"No, thank you. High Commissioner, this is an unexpected honour. If I was told—"

"Unexpected, unfortunately, seems to become a motto in our prestigious institution, Mr Forsberg. Just relax; this is purely informal. Let's see. You are thirty-five years old—"

"Thirty-six since yesterday..." he politely corrected.

"Happy birthday, then!" The High Commissioner began reading a sheet of paper. "So... thirty-six, Swedish, graduated from Cambridge in economics and a year exchange at Yale. Then a year of sabbatical in Kenya, volunteering at an endangered species protection centre. Finally, three years in financial banking at Shamble & Drumond in Berlin. That is a remarkable CV. Now, explain the reasons for this sudden career shift by applying for a temporary job as a personal assistant....."

Isabelle Veyre prepared two coffees and a glass of water. She checked her watch. *Fifteen minutes in three, two, one...* The door behind her opened suddenly, showing the High Commissioner shaking Lief's hand vigorously.

"Thank you for coming. I leave you in the skilful hands of my assistant, who will accompany you to the way out. Pleasure."

The door closed behind Leif. Isabelle immediately noticed that he was a bit overcome by the interview.

"Please, Mister Forsberg, take a seat for a few minutes. I have prepared you a coffee and a glass of water."

"Thank you," he answered with relief. "Is he always this way?"

"Mostly, but not always. You easily get used to it and quickly learn he is fair and mindful. He just loathes being bothered with pointless details. One needs to be extremely concise in his presence."

"Are you expecting soon?' he asked, trying to take his mind away.

"I am due in two months. It's a girl. I will go on maternity leave next month. Just enough time to instruct the successful candidate."

"Well, I sincerely doubt whether I'll have that pleasure. Forgive me for saying this, but it was one hell of an interview. The High Commissioner was quite blunt and made it clear that I did not fit the profile for the position. It was worth a shot, I guess."

"Never abandon hope, Mister Forsberg. Life is full of pleasant surprises, not just bad ones," she replied, placing a large cup of coffee in front of him. "Milk? Sugar?"

"Both, please."

An email popped up on her computer screen. It was a message from Pierre-Antoine consisting of just one word: *Approved.*

"May I call you Leif?" she asked, pouring milk.

***

Monika was reviewing the latest report from the embassy in Beijing. *It is a hollow shell without anything substantive,* she thought, *making it even more worrisome. I refuse to believe that nothing is happening or our Embassy in China withholds information. If not being compromised.* She switched on her intercom.

"Alessandra?"

"*Yes, High Commissioner?*"

"Has Director Pavlović arrived?"

"*Just now, High Commissioner.*"

"Send him in."

"*Certainly. May I also mention that Ambassador Tian arrived five minutes ago?*"

"Offer her some tea and invent some excuse to make her wait a little longer." *Let her steam a bit in her juice.*

"I shall, high commissioner."

Her office door opened to a tall, dark-haired man in his thirties with a rugged face as if carved with a knife. Rebuking but very efficient. And devotedly loyal.

"Ah, Fabijan. Please come and sit down. Thank you for seeing me on such short notice."

"Any time, High Commissioner."

"Fabijan, I have a problem requiring your eagle eyes and sharp judgement."

"I am listening."

"Earlier on, I received a report from our Embassy in China regarding this intriguing request made by the 15th Dalai Lama to the Indian Government, seeking permission to visit their country officially. Our President rightly suspects some manoeuvre orchestrated by President Xue, as this move is inconsistent with the stance the alleged religious leader of Tibet has taken so far. As you know, we do not formally recognise the legitimacy of this Dalai Lama, blatantly enthroned with the blessing of the Chinese Communist Party. We continue to convey our unanimous support to the Tibetan government in exile, and the Indian government fully ensures its protection. However, the latter has been experiencing significant internal problems lately due to a series of corruption cases, such as the recent Nagpur scandal. Consequently, the governing coalition is severely weakened and could collapse anytime. Add several Indian states refusing to comply with the federal state and threatening to rebel unless new elections are held. We have all the ingredients for an explosive scenario. The Chinese regard it as an opportunity to gain back influence after decades of Hindu supremacy in the region. Prime Minister Banerjee will unlikely oppose the visit to prevent losing control of the situation. He will attempt to mitigate the strong opposition of the exiled Tibetan administration to the visit. After all, it has not gained its nickname Surrender without reason. We should work effortlessly to avoid a disastrous repetition of the American scenario."

"Assuredly"

"In short, I instructed our embassy in Beijing to dig into what could be behind the 15th Dalai Lama's move, calling on our local contacts. The report I received this morning is full of banalities and familiar facts. Nothing significant."

"So, you smell a rat."

"Exactly! I suspect, not to say I am convinced, that our informants' ring has been infiltrated or compromised. Therefore, as Director of the Foreign Affairs General Inspectorate, I want you to arrange a surprise inspection at our embassy to check on some internal issues with the local staff. Unofficially, you know the reason. Take with you someone you rely on in the Department of External Affairs to investigate our sources."

"I will ask Colonel Schwartz. He is cautious and reliable."

"I leave the details to you. My only concern is we get information in a timely fashion before the visit begins."

"I will do my utmost."

"Very good. Make arrangements to travel today."

"Right away!" He rose and swiftly made his way to the door.

"And Fabijan?"

"Yes, High Commissioner?"

"You report directly to me. Exclusively."

"Understood."

Monika took a minute after the door closed. *Efficient and reliable, she thought. If not for his face... But that is what intimidates people and produces results!* She switched on the intercom.

"Alessandra?"

"*Yes, High Commissioner?*"

"Please, invite Ambassador Tian in."

"*At once.*"

Her assistant entered, accompanied by an elegant Chinese woman dressed in green with her dark hair impeccably rolled in the back. *A spider in the body of a doll,* Monika thought, heading towards her with a charming smile.

"Ambassador Tian, thank you for coming so quickly. It is always a pleasure to see you," she said with a honey voice. "Please accept my apologies for keeping you waiting. I had something urgent to take care of. But please, have a seat."

"High Commissioner Richter, the pleasure is mine," she replied with a dazzling smile. Her perfect white teeth sparkled like a toothpaste commercial.

"Indeed, indeed. But first, may I offer you some tea or drink?"

"Tea will be marvellous, preferably Lapsang Souchong, if you have."

"Of course I do. Alessandra?"

"I have already brewed some. A few seconds later, she returned with a pot and two cups, leaving the two women alone.

"You mentioned the matter was important," enquired the Ambassador while delicately drinking the beverage.

Straight to the point, Monika thought.

"To some extent. But let me assure you, this meeting is purely informal. You see, President Kowalczyk has asked me to pass on to your government his preoccupation concerning the request made by the 15th Dalai Lama to visit some parts of India officially. A sensitive subject to the Tibetan community in exile and of significant interest to us. We want to ensure all precautions are taken to prevent potential friction."

"My dear High Commissioner, you can reassure President Kowalczyk and the Government of the United Federation of Europe that the People's Republic of China is giving this matter the utmost attention. On many occasions in the past, His Holiness has expressed to the Chinese government his profound desire to walk in the steps of the Buddha Gautama and those of his predecessor in India. Furthermore, it represents an opportunity to meet his people settled there. The unfortunate international misunderstanding that followed his enthronement had always prompted our government to recommend prudence to His Holiness. However, we are convinced the time has finally come to promote reconciliation between the divided communities. We are confident this peaceful visit will allow the alleged Tibetan government in exile to realise how wrong their perception of His Holiness has been over the years and that his intentions are genuine."

"This is an excellent initiative, I concur. And we are prepared to offer our full support to this initiative. My government, however, has reservations regarding the suggested visit to the Tawang Monastery. We all know how delicate this issue is. Maybe we can agree on some arrangements regarding this specific question."

"As the successor of the 14th Dalai Lama, it seems reasonable for His Holiness to stop at the premises where his predecessor started his voluntary exile. Against the goodwill and intentions of the People's Republic of China, which is still genuinely saddened by this decision, I must point out. And I do not need to remind you that His Holiness, the 15th Dalai Lama, has officially been recognised as the legitimate reincarnation of Tenzin Gyatso by the religious authorities in Tibet. As such, it is understandable that His Holiness would be willing to return to the prominent places of his previous life. And my government fully supports this approach."

"Allow me to convey my admiration for the People's Republic of China's sudden enthusiasm for religious affairs," said Monika.

"High Commissioner, more than a century has gone since the War of Liberation. China is different today, modern, open to the world and attentive to preserving its millenary culture in all its expressions. The well-being of all its citizens is one of its most pressing concerns, including the people of Tibet. Let us turn the page on all the resentments that have unfortunately ruined our well-intentioned relations with the 14th Dalai Lama. We have entered a new age, like Europe, and we merely seek peace and harmony among the communities of our great country."

"I see… A very enlightening affirmation. Very well, I will not take any more of your valuable time. I will ensure to pass on your assurances to President Kowalczyk. Thank you for coming. I will accompany you back to your car."

"It was a heavenly pleasure, as usual, High Commissioner. And congratulations to your assistant; she truly mastered the art of Chinese tea."

"She will be delighted to hear it."

A moment later, Monika observed the diplomatic vehicle driving away. The entire conversation had a bittersweet taste. *Fabijan is right, I smell a rat...*

18

"First Minister, your Holiness, um, I completely appreciate your position, but you must acknowledge mine. My government, um, is in an extremely precarious position. A small, um, opening towards China's request will be a sign of goodwill. It will appease the tensions we are experiencing with Pakistan at this moment..."

Prime Minister Banerjee was walking in circles in First Minister Gyaltsen's office. The tension was palpable throughout the whole room. Rinchen sat in a corner, holding his mala in his left hand and silently praying, each bead moving from one to another after each mantra. He was enjoined to observe while remaining silent. His father sat at his desk with an exasperated face. His Holiness was standing opposite, his eyes slightly closed as if meditating. But Rinchen knew it was just an act. Everything went smoothly in the morning. Before all the Tibetan Parliament-in-Exile, the Indian Prime Minister renewed his honourable intentions and the indefectible protection his government would continue to provide to the exiled community. The official luncheon was a success, and each participant left assured that India was beside them. However, once behind closed doors, the message changed.

"A little opening'? Do you hear yourself, Prime Minister? This *small opening* could cause the irreversible fracture of our already badly divided community. It would have already fractured if not for His Holiness's continued efforts. You are allowing China to mingle directly in our internal affairs. As for your government's situation, this is purely Indian politics. We have never interfered with them and do not intend to start any time soon. When the 14th Dalai Lama, blessed be his light, departed this life, your government gave us explicit assurances that it will never back China's puppet."

"That was, um, with the predecessor of my predecessor, my dear First Minister. Things have, um, evolved since, and a lot of water has flowed under the bridge. Isn't, um, anitya one of the main principles of Buddhism? I am persuaded, um, it should ease your dilemma."

"Therefore, instead of being your guests, we are at present your hostages? If you expect me to silently bow to the Chinese government, you are being delusional, Surinder," the First Minister's voice rose up.

"My dear Lobsang, um, do not misunderstand me. The Tibetan diaspora has constantly been, and will remain, the welcome guests of the Indian Government. I will never ask any of you to, um, go against their principles. That does not mean we cannot seek slight gestures from you, um, from time to time. Naturally, the situation would be different if Venerable Jampa Rinpoche had accepted the title of Dalai Lama, as he was expected to. He instead took the one of the *Custodian* while still agreeing to be addressed as His

154

Holiness. You realise how confusing this is and the limitations to my actions it creates."

"This is no slight gesture! Must I lose face in front of my people to serve your desperate attempt to save your coalition doomed to failure? And do not involve His Holiness in this matter. He made a decision upon his ascent, and despite my personal concerns, I respect it, as do the rest of our people."

"Come on, First Minister, we are merely urging you to offer us, um, a little token of your gratitude. I can assure you, um, that we will handsomely reward you in exchange. Maybe some additional schools and one or two more monasteries. I do not doubt we can find common ground and, um, offer mutually beneficial concessions."

Here enters the leader of a government irreversibly corrupted at its core, thought Rinchen.

"The sole concession I am willing to offer is about the Hemis Monastery," His Holiness suddenly interrupted. "But Tawang? I will not permit it. And Dharamshala even less."

"See, First Minister, concessions can be made when one becomes reasonable. Given the current circumstances, I have, um, already respectfully informed the 15th Dalai Lama of the unfortunate impossibility concerning Dharamshala. But I am confident he will be delighted to hear about Hemis when, um, I greet him later this afternoon."

Rinchen dropped his mala on the floor.

"What!? What do you mean by *when you greet him later this afternoon?* He is supposed to arrive in five days!" erupted his father.

"My apologies, First Minister. I neglected to mention there was, um, a last-minute change in his schedule and that, following the approval of the Chinese authorities, he arrived in the country this morning. He crossed the border with the State of Arunachal Pradesh only two hours ago."

"Are you insane, Surinder!? By the Buddha, are you even aware of what you have done? You've been... manipulating us all that time! You are a vile snake! I shall never forget this betrayal!" A loud bang at the door interrupted them. "What!?"

"I apologise for disturbing you, First Minister," a voice answered, "but it is urgent. You need to turn the news on quickly. Something serious is happening."

Rinchen's father swiftly tuned in to the news channel. It showed some chaotic pictures.

"... *I am back live at Tawang Monastery, where the situation is escalating. Half an hour ago, the 15th Dalai Lama, who apparently began an official visit today, not reported to the mainstream media, presented himself at the entrance of the Tawang Monastery in the state of Arunachal Pradesh. His representative asked for an audience with the Abbot, the Venerable Chopel Rinpoche. In response, the Abbot ordered the monks to lock the gates and informed the 15th Dalai Lama that he was not welcome and owed his allegiance only to the Custodian in Dharamshala. Following this reply, a group of monks among the 15th Dalai Lama's delegation tried to forcefully open the gates, vigorously opposed by monks from within the monastery. The Indian state police have intervened in an attempt to break the feud. However, the situation is still extremely confused there. ...*"

Images showed monks disorderly pushing one another through the iron gates among rows of insults. Rinchen recognised Wangdue Lama as leading the charge on the Tawang's side. But the most concerning was that the opposing monks, in their majority, were undoubtedly Chinese and not Tibetan.

"Surinder, look what you have done! It is a tragedy! How could you allow yourself to get involved in this?"

"My dear Lobsang, um, I am persuaded it is some misunderstanding. I shall, naturally, intervene promptly and protest vehemently to the Chinese government..."

The news was still on, and the anchor was back on the screen.

"... *Thank you, Bilal, for this dreadful live showing the considerable confusion that reigns at Tawang. Do not hesitate to come back to us if any new developments occur. Now for today's other big news. The Times of India published a few minutes ago a very concerning article that, if confirmed, will seriously damage the fragile coalition in power. According to their sources, Jenya Banerjee, the wife of Prime Minister Surinder Banerjee, is heavily involved in a network of lawyers selling orphaned children to the highest bidders. Their investigation reveals that some of these children seem to have fallen into the hands of organ traffickers. If those horrific facts were corroborated, it would dramatically end Mr Banerjee's political career and seriously jeopardise his party's chances in the next election, which now seems inevitable...*"

The Indian Prime Minister's face got livid.

"Lobsang, turn it off," the Custodian ordered abruptly. "My dear Prime Minister, I believe you are undergoing a significant crisis that requires your urgent attention in Delhi. Rinchen, provide His Excellency with all necessary assistance to arrange his rapid departure."

"At once, Your Holiness."

"Surinder, despite this sinister news, which I am certain is only a misunderstanding and a pure invention of the press, I nonetheless expect you or a member of your

Cabinet to resolve the situation in Tawang. I will not accept that this usurper, evidently accompanied by Chinese communist agents, seizes the monastery by force. If you still possess any self-esteem, you will undertake whatever necessary steps to restore order in your country."

"Of course, of course…" he whispered.

***

Rinchen returned to his father's office after accompanying the Prime Minister of India's delegation to their helicopter half an hour ago. The two men there were watching the news and openly evaluating the situation.

"The Chinese have completely manipulated this imbecile from the start. Worse, he ignored us! And now, this!"

The holoTV was displaying new images of the events in Tawang, when a 'Breaking News' logo suddenly appeared.

"*We are interrupting the current program to go to Beijing, where President Xue is addressing the nation about the current events. Let's hear President Xue.*"

The image of the Chinese leader dressed in a black Mao collar suit appeared.

"*This afternoon, at the invitation of the Government of India, His Holiness, the 15th Dalai Lama, accompanied by a delegation of Tibetan monks, crossed the Indian border in the state of Arunachal Pradesh. His Holiness' motive was to peacefully follow the path taken by his predecessor, the beloved Tenzin Gyatso, more than a hundred years ago. His journey first took him to the Tawang Monastery, where he intended to pray with its community and advocate for reconciliation. This was a peaceful move. To our surprise, His Holiness was refused access by the local religious leader who, instead, sent a gang of violent thugs dressed as monks with the express intention of attempting on his life. His beloved Holiness narrowly escaped the treacherous attack on his sacred person and, thanks to his followers, was safely repatriated to the security of our nation. We possess evidence that this dreadful action was meticulously planned and organized by the so-called illegitimate Tibetan Government in Exile, with the blessing of the Indian government. The People's Republic of China will not allow this conspiracy to go unpunished and will examine all available options to bring the perpetrators before its impartial tribunals. China's government holds Prime Minister Banerjee personally accountable for delivering justice to our glorious nation!'* The image returned to the network studio.

"That was President Xue's statement, live on national television," said the presenter. "We are now back in Delhi, where…" First Minister Gyaltsen switched off the holoTV.

"This is devastating. I expected a reaction from Beijing, but not something of this magnitude, nor so rapidly." Gendün, what should we do?" It was the first time Rinchen heard his father address His Holiness with his first name.

"We have no option, Lobsang. We must act swiftly to protect our government, our nation and our religious independence. We need to move on to the contingency plan, which we reviewed recently. The situation is visibly escalating by the hour."

"Your Holiness, forgive my interruption," said Rinchen, "but what plan are you referring to?"

"My dear Rinchen, from day one of his arrival in India, our beloved 14th Dalai Lama had to anticipate the possibility of having to flee again. At the time, the tensions between China and India were significant, with the prospect of a general conflict between the two countries. Therefore, we established a procedure to ensure our institutions survive such a scenario. Our community will divide into two groups in the hope that one will outlast the other. This is why, while we wait to ascertain how the situation evolves, I want you to move to Chennai, accompanied by a few monks of my choosing, as early as tomorrow morning."

"But…"

"I have no time to argue with you, Rinchen. You will proceed as instructed. Our survival depends on it. I will prepare several items this evening that you will also take with you. And Kalsang and Jamyang will accompany you. No discussion."

"For my part," his father said, "half of the government and the elected assembly will join you. Minister Dhargyal will preside over this second executive. You have worked with him on several occasions, which will facilitate your task. And you will also take your sister and my grandson with you, out of caution. I called your mother and sister-in-law earlier, and they have decided to stay by my side. You will now look after your siblings."

"Surely, father, aren't you both overreacting? China's reaction is rather conventional. They repeatedly put on a big show of words to—"

"Your Excellency, your Excellency!" A man suddenly rushed to the office.

"Yes, Rahul. What is it?"

"Your Excellency, I am terribly sorry to interrupt you, but a Cabinet representative in Delhi has just contacted us."

"What is it about?"

"It is the Prime Minister, Your Excellency! He seized a gun from one of his security guards and committed suicide in his helicopter, Sir!"

19

The five clergymen sat in a circle around an elegantly carved wood table covered with a delicate white tablecloth embroidered with a large Star of David. On their left stood an alcove containing a wide menorah made of pure silver, surrounded by wooden panels adorned by the ten commandments in Hebrew. Several centuries ago, the room was used as a small synagogue and a sanctuary when the visibility of Judaism was restricted. They were the guests of Chief Rabbi Yitzchak Eliyahu. His residence in the centre of the Jewish Quarter in Jerusalem ensured discretion and safety in discussing matters. To see the leaders of the major monotheistic religions chatting and eating together out of apparent animosity would seem quite surreal in other parts of the world. But nothing was surprising any more since the creation of the Free City of Jerusalem. And the situation was critical, requiring a unanimous agreement.

"Thank you, Sarah. My dear wife, your dinner was exceptional, as always. I am certain all my honoured guests will agree with me." A row of approval ensued. "You may leave us now. We have a pressing issue to discuss. Ensure the door is carefully closed and no one disturbs us."

As soon as she left, the rabbi turned to Nicodemus II, the Greek Orthodox Patriarch of Jerusalem.

"Your Beatitude, I leave you the honour to start this meeting."

"Thank you, Chief Rabbi, and once again, thank you for your generous invitation and this superb dinner you and your wife have offered us."

"By all means."

"My dear friends," the Patriarch continued, stroking his bushy grizzled beard, "we have gathered this evening at the demand of His Eminence Cardinal del Pietro to reach a decision on Professor Degrenes' request. For my part, I believe the outcome to be straightforward. The Greek Orthodox Church will not approve these excavations, if only as a mark of respect for our venerable colleague, Grand Mufti Amin al-Sabri, here. I remain a firm believer in the Status Quo. We do not want to give rise to needless tensions between our pacified communities."

"Thank you, Your Beatitude, for your consideration," replied the Grand Mufti. "My assumption, also. We have managed to establish a stable harmony between our various confessions. Let us preserve the relative peace that has prevailed in this city for decades instead of triggering unrest for obscure archaeological reasons. The Temple Mount, the Dome of the Rock, and the Temple of Herod remnants remain volatile places. We should not risk inadvertently offering a voice to certain extremist religious fringes."

"If I may," interrupted Rabbi Eliyahu, "we should perhaps first listen to what His Eminence has to say before adopting a final decision." He turned to the Cardinal. "For instance, I have always been puzzled as to why Your Eminence insists on keeping a close eye on this Professor Degrenes. After all, his work is funded by your nunciature under the oversight of the Holy See. If he represents any particular threat, why not simply transfer him to another country? Or even sack him?"

"Thank you, Chief Rabbi, for raising these points," the cardinal answered. "I am afraid the situation is not as simple as you all seem to believe. At the Vatican, we have closely monitored Professor Degrenes since he became affiliated with another eminent archaeologist and Egyptologist, Professor John Walters. From the first day those two scholars became acquainted, they became keenly interested in the Amarna period, especially the Aten heresy. In addition to proving the presence of biblical Pharaoh Shishak, who most scholars now regard as Shoshenq I, in Jerusalem. This weird fixation turned into an obsession a decade ago that soon raised concerns in Rome. While actively seeking it, we believe those two have found a dangerous artefact with severe religious implications. We also believe they are members of a Freemasonic lodge aiming to undermine the predominance of revealed confessions. Following this unclear discovery, they appear to have divided their efforts. Professor Degrenes lodged an unexpected application to manage our archaeological mission in Jerusalem. The Vatican eventually approved it to keep a closer eye on their intentions. However, after a few months, it became apparent the man acted cautiously in our presence. Therefore, I decided, seven years ago, to urge the members of the High Council to allow recruiting an individual tasked with befriending Degrenes and gathering more accurate information. That was when Shenouda entered the stage, thanks to the kind assistance of His Eminence, Metropolitan Archbishop Tawadros II, here at my side."

"Respectfully, Your Eminence, we are all aware of the circumstances," declared Patriarch Nicodemus. "But, as you just mentioned, it has been seven years, and this mole of yours has been inefficient so far. And, in my opinion, this whole story is purely based on unsubstantiated suspicions. If the Vatican still wishes to support it, the matter only concerns your hierarchy. Not the rest of us. However, the reason for our gathering tonight goes beyond this little game of conjecture you seem so fond of. My distinguished colleagues and I harbour deep reservations about approving something that could jeopardise the delicate balance that has substantially benefited us all these years."

"And I would have been as reserved as you are, Your Beatitude, if not for this." He placed on the table a small clay object inscribed with hieroglyphs.

"What is it?" asked the Patriarch.

"If I am not mistaken," declared the Chief Rabbi, "it is one of those correspondence clay tablets used during Antiquity, mainly by the Sumerians and the Babylonians. But it's oddly written in Egyptian hieroglyphs. An extremely uncommon artefact, I must say. Where did you obtain it?"

"One of our agents in Cairo saw Professor Walters photographing it at the Grand Egyptian Museum before attempting to conceal it carefully. We decided to *borrow* it to investigate its content."

"And?"

"It mentions Pharaoh Shoshenq I and the existence of a secret chamber sealed under Solomon's Temple. It additionally employs words like *cursed* and *heretical*. I should note that this tablet was discovered among other clay tablets stored in the Tel-El-Amarna artefacts section."

A faint murmur swept through the other members of the Council.

"And what assurance do you have that this artefact is authentic?" asked the Grand Mufti.

"One hundred per cent, Your Eminence."

"I see. However, the relevance between the biased beliefs of a pagan ruler and the established truth of our noble religions eludes me."

"Because this is not what the tablet has to be associated with." He exhibited an ancient parchment meticulously protected with tissue paper and written in Latin. "This is a letter from the Grand Master of the Knights Templar, Bernard de Tremelay, addressed to Pope Eugene III and dated from June 1152. It records the excavations ordered by the Knights within Temple Mount after the collapse of a well. It mentions the discovery of a long tunnel sealed at its end by a wall engraved with strange images and symbols. They believed them to be some witchcraft or demonic incantations. Several scared workers decided to destroy it, but when they began hammering it, much of the ceiling collapsed, killing most of them. Believing a curse caused it, the remaining workers filled the tunnel with the collapsed rock and sealed its entrance to ensure nobody could ever look at this *abomination* again. In addition, the Vatican possesses a confession from Jacques of Molay, the last Grand Master, obtained during his interrogation following his arrest by the French Crown. He, too, speaks of the existence of a hidden place below Solomon's Temple containing a terrible secret, threatening to reveal it unless the Church assists the Templars. Pope Clement V believed the threat authentic enough to petition the King of France to place the accused under the Holy See's jurisdiction. The similarities of the stories detailed in these three artefacts cannot be ignored. The Vatican and I are utterly convinced that the location of this secret room is behind Professor Degrenes' excavation request. Oh! Did I mention that Professor Walters showed up in Jerusalem five days ago?"

"Let's go no further," Patriarch Nicodemus interrupted. "I admit all your little trinkets and stories are quite entertaining. And indeed, Professor Walters's unexpected presence may seem quite suspicious. But let's all be realistic. Those fairy tales bear no substantial significance."

"Allow me to dispute your assertion, Your Beatitude. We have before us tangible evidence of the existence of a mysterious room hidden beneath Temple Mount. While its contents remain unknown, its presence is alarming enough to generate three similar accounts at distinct periods. We must ensure that whatever lies there do not fall into the wrong hands."

"Well, there is only one course of action that is appropriate. We deny the application and evict these two ranters from the Holy City."

"This would indeed be the perfect resolution to the matter, Your Beatitude. But only to a certain extent. My primary concern is we possess no indication of the geographic location of this hidden room. What if it was inadvertently discovered during the renovation of the Dome of the Rock? The survey clearly specifies its foundations are severely weakened. As a result, a significant part of the work consists in stabilising and reinforcing them to avoid endangering the safety of the pilgrims and visitors.

What will happen if a team of workers discovers this hidden space in plain sight and its contents prove detrimental? Remember that to help finance the cost of the works, we have allowed a crew of National Geographics to be present. Would it not be wiser to keep any crucial potential discoveries under control by securing our own archaeological team?"

"Indeed, Your Eminence, this is a valid argument that has not entered my mind and deserves thoughtful consideration. However, to approve this scheme of yours, the Council needs to consider a subterfuge to validate our endorsement."

***

Shenouda sat with his two friends on the luxuriant patio behind Professor Degrenes' residence, drinking a hot mint tea. The sun was declining on the horizon, allowing the outside temperature to cool rapidly.

"Still no news from the High Council?" Professor Degrenes asked the priest.

"I am afraid not, Marc."

"Well, not to be overly optimistic, Mark," declared Walters, "it has been three days. We would have already received a response if they wanted to reject it. So, let us keep our hopes high. Shenouda, my friend, if you are free tomorrow, perhaps you can take me to the site of Herod's Palace in Caesarea. It is a place I never had a chance to visit. I am not fond of Roman remains, but I am told it is situated in a breathtaking location. And it will be a splendid opportunity to reconnect."

"With pleasure, Professor. I have no plans for tomorrow. I will make arrangements with my usual guide. He is as passionate as I was back in Egypt. I think you will enjoy his company."

"Very good, very good. It is a deal, then. I am convinced we will enjoy ourselves."

Shenouda's phone rang.

"If you will forgive me." The monk walked to the front house before answering. "Yes, Your Beatitude?"

"…"

"I see…"

"…"

"I understand… Yes, I am listening and memorising."

"…"

"That is perfectly clear. I will make sure Professor Degrenes understands—"

"…"

"I will, Your Beatitude. Thank you."

He returned to his friends.

"Gentlemen, I received good news for you. The High Council has conveyed today and has unanimously accepted to grant your request."

"Oh my god!" burst Professor Degrenes, "I cannot believe it! This is indeed fantastic news. Oh my God, John, we are so close to proving our theory."

"Indeed, indeed!"

"Do not make haste, gentlemen. There are conditions attached, and they are extremely restrictive. You must accept them with no reservations."

"We are listening," Degrenes replied.

"Excavations will only be allowed if a substantial underground discovery occurs during the renovation work.

168

They can only start after validation by the High Council. For each permission, a license will be issued for a specified number of days. Their added total cannot exceed sixty days out of the two hundred and thirty days the works are expected to last. Each member of your team will require clearance by the High Council's administration. Two members of the religious police will be allowed continuous access on-site. You are not allowed to work on or tamper with the Western Wall. And finally, I will oversee all your investigations. In return, you will be granted exclusive archaeological rights without any potential interference from the National Geographic team. Such are the conditions imposed by the High Council and, I quote, *take it or leave it.*"

Professor Degrenes grasped the archdeacon's right hand before shaking it and saying with a broad smile: "It is far too valuable for us. Welcome on board, Shenouda!"

20

"The security link should be activated in a minute, Mister President."

Monika was in a secured meeting room with President Kowalczyk and the Army Chief of Staff, General Esteban de Soverosa. Initially scheduled as a simple debriefing, the President insisted on being present, with his Chief of Staff, following the events in North-East India and the unexpected death of Prime Minister Banerjee. A red light flickered on the wall next to them.

"I believe we are connected now. Fabijan, can you hear me?"

"I can hear you, Monika..." The hollow image of the Director of the D.E.A. appeared in front of them. "... and see you, now. Mister President, General."

"Fabijan, I apologise for coming back to you so quickly, but I am sure you understand that, after the last developments, the President wanted to be briefed immediately."

"I perfectly understand, Monika. It is part of the job."

"So, what can you tell us?"

"Although Colonel Schwartz and I are still looking for the source, I can confirm that our network of informants here in Beijing has been compromised. I have taken the necessary steps to secure further infiltration until the agent involved is uncovered. However, beforehand, one matter needs to be resolved swiftly. It first requires your approval, Monika. My authority is limited on that issue."

"What is it?"

"I believe Ambassador Valchev and the embassy's second secretary must be recalled to Strasbourg within the next twenty-four hours."

"Why, Fabijan? Are their lives in danger?" asked Monika nervously.

"Simply put, Monika, they have unfortunately placed themselves in a troublesome position here and become a liability threatening their lives. I recommend exfiltrating them quickly before anything scandalous becomes public. Though I am not quite convinced we might be spared the latter."

"Director Pavlović," interrupted the President, "are you saying that the Chinese intelligence compromised our Ambassador and second secretary?"

"That is my conclusion, I am afraid, Mister President."

"This is an outrage! They will have serious justifications to answer for!"

"Mister President," continued Monika, "we certainly can discuss this later. Let us return to the main topic of this video conference. Fabijan, what have you learned regarding the Chinese?"

"Only puzzling facts. Several of my contacts report that three PLAAF brigades have been mobilised and are undergoing intensive training within the Western Theatre Command Area —basically Tibet—. Moreover, the 6th Fighter Division and the 36th Bomber Division have been on alert for two weeks. On the other hand, I found no indication of preparation for the Ground Force and the Navy—"

"I apologise for interrupting you, Director Pavlović," General de Soverosa said. " Correct me if I'm wrong, but aren't three PLAAF brigades regrouping half of these military elements?"

"Apologies, but what are the PLAAF?" asked the President.

"Their paratroopers, Mister President," the Director answered. "Affirmative, General, you are correct; that is half of their units."

"It is extremely concerning. What are they exercising for?"

"What concerns me, Monika," Fabjian went on, " is that The Chinese do not appear to be trying to cover any of these activities. They parade them in plain sight as though they were intentionally trying to get everyone's attention. A simple satellite search will confirm this information. But there are other areas of concern."

"Tell us, Fabijan."

"Monika, Mister President, some of my intel are reporting a high diplomatic activity with another country. Just one. It seems to have started six months ago at the most elevated levels of government. However, I am unable to determine the identity of that country."

"Russia?"

"Definitely not, Monika. My sources are positive. And they are more reliable than China. I fear we must prepare for something of considerable importance."

"I think you're a little too dramatic, Director Pavlović," said the President. "While somewhat alarming, it is most probably theatre and gesticulation on the part of the Chinese government to exert more pressure on the Indian government. We faced this scenario several times in the past, and each time the mountain roared, it brought a mouse. Would you concur with that, General?"

"I need to consult my sources, Mister President, before giving you an affirmative answer."

"Very well, then. This is how we should proceed. Verify your sources, General. Director Pavlović, I want you to focus on finding the mysterious country that China has come into contact with and report any new developments to Monika. We need to learn more about the situation before considering any decision. In the meantime, we should remain vigilant. I will immediately call Acting Prime Minister Patel in India to see if he has any insights which might enlighten us."

"As you wish, Mister President. Pavlović out."

After a week on the job, Leif Forsberg was getting used to his new working environment. Isabelle was on a break, and he was filling out documents. As expected, High Commissioner Lascombes was hard work, with everything having to be brief and concise. *Wasted words are a waste of energy*, he repeated constantly. But Isabelle was right; despite his rough skin, the man was decent and mindful of his staff's needs. *If you are not happy, then I am not. And two unhappy people make a lot of noise* —another quote from his collection. But his mind was remarkably sharp and fast to act.

"Excuse me?" interrupted a voice. He looked up. A vaguely familiar woman stood facing his desk.

"Yes, can I help you?" Leif asked.

"I am sure you can. Are you new here? Where is Isabelle?" the woman asked in an obnoxious voice.

"She is having a short break, Madam. She should be back in a few minutes. I am Leif Forsberg, the new temp. I will replace her in three weeks while she is on maternity leave. Maybe I can be of any assistance before she comes back."

"If that is not too much to ask, I would like to see High Commissioner Lascombes. Now."

"I am afraid you need to make an appointment beforehand. Allow me to take a look… His agenda is, unfortunately, full today. However, I might have some possibilities tomorrow…" *What an unpleasant person*, he thought.

"Young man, know I never require an appointment. Simply notify him of my presence, and he will receive me immediately."

"And you are, Madam, if I may ask?"

"You may indeed. I am Monika Richter, High Commissioner for Foreign Affairs."

Leif's face turned livid. Isabelle's instructions popped into his mind. *Unless he is in a meeting, High Commissioner Lascombes will always find time for both High Commissioner Richter*

174

and High Commissioner Sanchez. You should make sure you recognise them.

"My sincere apologies, High Commissioner. I am still unaccustomed to everyone's faces. Naturally, I will inform High Commissioner Lascombes immediately." He pressed the intercom.

"Yes, Isabelle?"

"It is Leif, Sir. I apologise for disturbing you, but High Commissioner Richter is here to see you."

"By all means, let her in."

"Thank you, young man," said Monika before proceeding directly into Pierre-Antoine's office.

"Monika! How are you?"

"I am fine Pierre-Antoine." She sat on the couch and smiled. "I have just given your new assistant his baptism of fire. It was very entertaining. They are so impressionable when they start. Like we were a few years ago. He seems quite efficient, though. And... he is very handsome!" she said in a silky voice.

"He is pleasant to look at, I admit, but that is not why he was hired. I am glad you approve, though. He adapts very quickly and effectively, which is deeply comforting. Coffee?" He pressed the intercom.

"I do need one."

"Isabelle?"

"It is still Leif, High Commissioner."

"Leif, bring us two coffees, please. One black, no sugar, and one with milk and one sugar."

"At once, High Commissioner."

"What news?"

"I am just out of a meeting with the President. We had a holo-conference with Director Pav—"

175

Leif knocked on the door before entering the room with two cups on a tray, which he placed on the coffee table.

"Thank you, Leif."

"My pleasure, High Commissioner." He left as quickly as he came in.

"Here is your coffee, Monika."

"Thank you, Pierre-Antoine. So, as I was about to say, I just had a meeting with the President, his Chief of Staff and Fabijan, via a link with Beijing. The situation is quite odd. Movements of troops in Tibet, in full view, and mysterious contacts with an unknown country. We are still investigating. But, as usual, President Kowalczyk is standing still, despite the incidents in northern India."

"Caution is always advisable when it comes to China. I will not blame him."

"Still, I can smell a rat when it stinks. Though, maybe you are right. How about you?"

"Apart from my surgery in a couple of days, nothing really. It is scheduled at ten, and I will be back the following day. That is the one good news."

"And regarding…"

"I have carefully considered our last conversation, and you will be happy to hear I have decided to see this Doctor Caracciolo after all. We scheduled an appointment in two months in Edinburgh. As Alessandra informed us, his research Centre has recently developed a new treatment that, in his opinion, is very promising. He wants to meet with me for an evaluation and, if successful, allow me to participate in the test campaign. Given my more than limited prospects, I have nothing to lose. If I decide to accept, I will be on leave for two weeks, which is the time required for the first proceeding."

"This is marvellous news, Pierre-Antoine. I am so thrilled you made the decision! I doubt I will be able to accompany you for the duration of your stay, but I am certain I can escape for a few days to visit you."

"Honestly, Monika, there is no need for—"

"Pierre-Antoine! If I can come, I will! No need to argue. And let me organise your accommodation. I want to make sure you feel comfortable and relaxed."

"As usual, you are acting like a big sister," he said, grinning.

"That is what true friends are for—"

The intercom buzzed suddenly.

"Yes, Leif?"

"*It is Isabelle, High Commissioner,*" she giggled. "*I apologise for interrupting you, but the Office of the President tried to contact you directly without success. High Commissioner Richter must report immediately to the President's Office. It is extremely urgent.*"

"She will leave at once."

Monika rushed down the corridor towards the lift. A minute later, she entered the President's office. Jorge and his Chief of Staff were with him. *This must be serious.*

"Ah, Monika, thank you for coming so promptly." He appeared pale and distressed. "It is devastating news! I was talking to Acting Prime Minister Patel when all of a sudden, our communication was interrupted... Monika! Two Pakistan Army battalions crossed the border into Kashmir. They are marching towards Srinagar and Jammu without opposition at this very moment. The Indian Government has just called for a general mobilisation of its army."

21

Venerable Kunchen slowly exited Tawang's temple after an hour of meditation. An exercise that he was still particularly fond of despite his old age. Assisted by his walking stick, he moved toward the courtyard. The weather was warm and clear today, and he thought teaching in the open air would be appropriate. It will also provide an excuse to warm up his tired body plagued with arthritis. A small group of young monks, wearing red and saffron robes, were already sitting on the floor, waiting for him. The old monk sat on a prepared chair, assisted by one acolyte.

"Thank you, Jampa. How very kind of you. Good morning young ones."

"Good morning, Venerable Kunchen Lama", they answered in unison while respectfully bowing to him.

"Before we start studying the noble teachings of the Buddha, I know some of you have raised questions about the ongoing situation. I will be delighted to answer them to the best of my knowledge. Who wants to go first?""

"Do we have two Dalai Lamas now?" asked one.

"Well, Lunghup, it is a complicated matter. Our community does not recognise the one who lives in Lhasa. We believe he was not chosen according to our traditions."

"But there is one in Dharamshala too now, no?" asked another.

"Yes, there is one there as well, Tsering."

"How can he only be Dalai Lama now when he is so old?"

"Ha, ha, ha! He is not that old, Tsering. Let's say he was supposed to be the Dalai Lama from the beginning. But, because he was very attached to our beloved 14th Dalai Lama, he thought accepting it was too much of an honour. He has now changed his mind and decided to take on his responsibilities fully, as we all should."

"But, the other Dalai Lama who came a few days ago, was he evil? Was he a demon? And the ones with him too? Is this why they were not allowed in?"

"Ha ha ha! No young Lunghup, they were not demons. Our Venerable Abbot simply could not let them in for reasons you are yet too young to understand."

"Our older brothers were fighting against them. It was frightening," said a fourth.

"I know, Tsewang, it was frightening, indeed. And our brothers had to atone for their violent behaviour. But, when our community is in danger, it is allowed to defend itself, as long as no life is harmed."

"So, the Indians soldiers outside, they are defending us now?"

"Somehow, Tsering. But, also, because there is a war in the west."

"Why is there a war?"

"The threads of existence are like the sky above us, Tsering. On some occasions, it is bright and blue, pleasant. Then, on other occasions, it is gloomy and wet, unpleasant. And sometimes, it becomes dark and threatening, like Indra when he is angry. But this is what the Bhavachakra teaches us. Like the sky, always in motion is the future. Today, we are blessed with a beautiful sky, so we should take a minute to enjoy this gift of beauty."

They all stared at the heavens. They were perfectly blue, flawless. High above, Venerable Kunchen observed an eagle gliding. Then another, then many others. Except, their trajectory was unusual, like flying in a straight line instead of circles. Suddenly, tiny dark spots appeared around them. A few at the start. Then a multitude shortly afterwards. They rapidly increased in size. These are not eagles!

"Young ones, I am afraid we have to shorten our session. I want each of you to calmly return to your dormitories and follow the instructions of your elder brothers. Stay indoors, no matter what you see and hear."

"But…"

"Right now, Lunghup. No questions. Come on!" He turned to the monk to his left. "Tseten Lama, you must alert our brothers and prepare defensive measures. We need to protect the abbot. Quick!"

***

"I want mummy!" Dache had been causing a commotion for the past ten minutes. Rinchen's sister, Penden, was doing her best to console him. Still, the eight-year-old struggled to comprehend the whole situation. *And who may blame him?* thought Rinchen. Along with the executive and assembly members, some accompanied by their families, the refugees were staying in a large villa near Puzhal Lake, east of Chennai, courtesy of a wealthy Indian businessman. Because of the monsoon season, the warmth and humidity were oppressive. Despite the available space, the small community was getting crowded, and tents had to be erected in the gardens. The lake's proximity brought swarms of irritating mosquitoes every night, adding to the general discomfort. But they were managing. Kalsang and Jamyang had been remarkably helpful and thoughtful in overseeing everyone's needs, allowing a daily routine to settle in.

Rinchen walked to the lakeshore and sat on a large rock to escape the noise momentarily. He gazed at the calm waters spoiled by human waste, thinking of the latest events. *As if the friction with China was not enough, we are now in the middle of a war with Pakistan. And this happened on the same day His Holiness finally agreed to take the title of the 15th Dalai Lama. Bad omen. As expected, it immediately infuriated the Chinese government even more, promising swift retaliation. When would people stop fighting over trivial things? Religion is about preparing one's soul for the afterlife, not politics or nationalism.* Before leaving Dharamshala, His Holiness gave him a large golden wooden casket carved with Buddhist symbols and sealed with his personal crest. *Do not open it, he said. Not unless something happens to me. It holds the future of our nation. Do you understand?*

"I do…"

"Venerable Rinchen Gyaltsen?" He flinched at the unexpected voice coming from behind. "My apologies, Venerable Gyaltsen; I did not mean to startle you."

"My apologies, too, Venerable Pema Lama. I was deep in my thoughts. How can I be of service?"

"The Deputy Premier asked me to bring you back. There is news that calls for your urgent attention."

"I am coming."

They walked back to the mansion. Rinchen crossed the main hall and headed to what used to be the living room, now the Deputy First Minister's office. He and his four other government colleagues stood before a large holo-screen, watching the news. It displayed confusing images of Chinese army men among what seemed frightened Tibetan monks running in all directions. There was tear gas' smoke everywhere. All of a sudden, the screen showed the colourful gates of a temple. *Tawang!* They opened violently, and a familiar face appeared, accompanied by five Chinese soldiers. *Venerable Chopel Rinpoche!*

"Deputy First Minister, what is happening?"

"Venerable Rinchen Lama! It is a tragedy!" he was in tears. "An entire brigade of Chinese paratroopers parachuted to Tawang Monastery half an hour ago. After neutralising the Indian troops, they began detaining the monks. They are all being transferred to transport helicopters as we speak. These are images transmitted live by the Chinese High Command via their national network. Look! They have taken the Venerable Abbot. And most of the Indian army is concentrated in Kashmir, unable to help. What should we do?"

"Well, first of all, we need to stay calm, Deputy First Minister. I share your emotion. But you and I are the leaders of our little community here. It is our duty to present a resolute face. Then, we need to wait for my father's instructions. I trust he will react soon."

The images on the screen switched to paratroopers jumping out of a plane before showing the ground below quickly getting closer. Rinchen gasped when he realised what the goal was. *Great Buddha! I's Dharamshala!* The broadcast suddenly cut, and the Indian anchor appeared.

"We interrupt this transmission to deliver further dire news. Chinese paratroops are jumping on Dharamshala at this precise moment. President Xue issued the following declaration a few minutes ago."

The Chinese leader appeared, vociferating from a podium.

"...the time has come to terminate the existence of the illegitimate so-called Tibetan Government in Exile, led by the false 15th Dalai Lama. Their terrorist actions that have repeatedly threatened China's integrity for so many decades will end today. They will all be arrested and repatriated to our glorious land before being transferred to Vocational Education and Training Centres, where they will learn to reintegrate our grand society peacefully. While seeking justice, we also know how to be merciful..."

The anchor appeared back on the screen.

"As the events accelerate, we return to Dharamshala, where First Minister Lobsang Gyaltsen is about to make a statement. First, a warning to our sensitive viewers. It seems some Tibetan refugees have armed themselves and are courageously resisting the Chinese offensive, helped by the few Indian troops stationed in the city. Expect to see combat footage and injuries."

Rinchen's father appeared on the screen, dressed in his black chuba, with his wife, sister-in-law and Gendün Drubpa by his side with the rest of the Cabinet. They were all grouped inside the Parliament Chamber.

"Citizens of free Tibet, nations of the world. Today is proof the relentless determination of the People's Republic of China to erase the

183

entitlement of our people to live according to our values and beliefs knows no limits. As I speak, our brave forces, joined by the dedicated local Indian soldiers, are heroically resisting this illegitimate transgression of the inviolability of the Indian territory. I will use the extra time their bravery allows me to address our people all over the world. From this point forward, all executive and parliamentary powers are transferred to Deputy First Minister Jheshong Dhargyal and the members of our government and parliament safely located in Southern India. They will act as de facto First Minister, executive and parliamentary bodies. And this, until they see fit to organise free democratic elections. Furthermore, His Holiness Venerable Gendün Drubpa, the legitimate 15th Dalai Lama, has offered his resignation from his official position and renounced all his religious duties and responsibilities. In application of the terms of our constitution, the sieging members of the Cabinet and Parliament have accepted it and unanimously designated Venerable Rinchen Gyaltsen Lama as the 16th Dalai Lama. We are convinced he represents the best-suited choice to perpetuate our traditions and religious faith and guide our people towards a prosperous future. I urge all the nations of the world to respect our decision and provide every possible assistance to His Holiness and his government wherever they seek it. Long live free Tibet, long live His Holiness the 16th Dalai Lama—"

A sudden explosion interrupted the First Minister's speech, followed by screams of panic. Then the video broadcast went dead. Rinchen was in shock; thoughts and emotions overwhelmed his mind. He closed his eyes and started breathing exercises to calm the maelstrom. When he reopened them, he realised he was surrounded by dozens of people respectfully bowing down to him.

"Long live the 16th Dalai Lama."

***

A few hours later, Rinchen was in his bedroom, meditating. He requested these minutes of silence and self-isolation. Kalsang and Jamyang stood on the other side of the door, preserving his privacy. Within an hour of the announcement, a whole battalion of Indian infantry encircled the entire villa before a swarm of journalists and cameramen arrived. Acting Prime Minister Patel ordered the deployment and called Acting First Minister Dhargyal to assure him that the *mistake* of Dharamshala would not be repeated in Chennai. There was no further news from the people up north. The Chinese forces had evacuated the region with their bounty as quickly as they came before the Indian army had the time to respond. It was the perfect abduction operation.

Rinchen looked at the golden casket sitting in front. Despite the emotions trying to take over his mind, he had a duty to perform. *It holds the future of our nation.* He broke the seal and opened the box. Inside, he retrieved some personal objects belonging to the 14th Dalai Lama, including his singing bowl, his prayer wheel and mala, and two envelopes. One from His Holiness and one from his father. He opened the first one.

My Dear Rinchen,

If you read these lines, it means the time has come for you to face a new path in your life, whereas mine is fading. I know how demanding this task appears at first, for I have faced it before you. I am convinced you will successfully assume the responsibilities that await you. You possess all the qualities and mind required to make a dedicated Dalai Lama. It is also the belief of our whole Government. From the beginning, I recognised similarities between you and our late Tenzin Gyatso. You both retain a distinct vision of the future, which I sadly lacked. Nurture it with the help of Kalsang Lama and Jamyang Lama. Their friendship is your greatest strength; keep that in mind.

Please do not commit the mistake I made and tried to correct too late in the end. Accept the honour vested in you. You are now officially the 16th Dalai Lama, the spiritual leader of our nation. Unlike you, my friendship with my old master was my weakness. I realise it now.

Your father left instructions for you in his letter. Follow them. Your survival and the one of our people in exile depend on them. I can assure you that, behind his apparent harshness and coldness, your father loves you and is proud of your accomplishments. He just never learned how to express it.

I doubt I will ever again gaze upon our sacred Potala or beloved land. And, probably, neither will you. But the Buddha teaches us about impermanence. Our faith in him does not reside inside a palace elevated above the lands of the Tibetan plateau. Or within the line of beautifully adorned fragile manuscripts. No, it lives inside our hearts and soul as a priceless gem embedded in the Universe.

Farewell, my dear Rinchen. My prayers shall be with you to my end, when and wherever it comes. May our lights encounter each other in our next lives.

Jampa Choegyal
15th Dalai Lama

He opened the second letter.

My son,

Do not be overwhelmed by the burden our Government has chosen to place on you. Guided by the wisdom of His Holiness, our Parliament and Cabinet unanimously approved your appointment as the 16th legitimate Dalai Lama. I believe, we believe, that you possess all the qualities necessary to fulfil the noble destiny that awaits you. After all, you are a Gyaltsen. You come from a long line of Imperial Preceptors, Kings, and even a Panchen Lama. I do not doubt you will preserve this heritage and pass it on to my grandson.

Attached to this letter is a list of instructions to follow in order to preserve whatever is left and secure our future. The villa's owner, Mister Krishna Chowdhury, is a very old friend from the university. You can fully trust him. When you are ready, he will arrange for you all to be transported out of India by boat. With the current situation, your trip will be safer than by air. Your destination will be revealed once out of the Indian territorial waters. The Cabinet and I have concluded that this country is no longer safe for our people, at least for the time being. Do not bother with the details; Jheshong will arrange everything.

Your mother asks me to tell you that she loves you very much and will keep you and your sister in her prayers. Boshay is confident you will care for her son. She asks you to tell him how much she loves him and how much she regrets no longer being with him. I trust you will find a way to explain everything and to understand once he is mature enough.

I wish some words would assist you along the way. But there are none. This is the burden attached to power and on those who hold it. Only know I have been proud to serve our people all those long years, and I am convinced you will find the same pride in serving them.

Be strong, my son, and may the Lord Buddha give you his wisdom and blessings.

Your father

He placed the letters back in the box.

"Kalsang?" he asked.

"Yes, Your Holiness?"

"Kalsang, please inform Acting First Minister Dhargyal that I wish to talk to him immediately."

"At once, Your Holiness."

Your Holiness, Rinchen thought. A minute later, Jheshong Dhargyal entered the room.

"You want to talk to me, Your Holiness?"

"Yes, Acting First Minister." He handled the note from his father. "These are my father's instructions for our departure from India to some unknown destination."

"Unknown, Your Holiness?"

"Yes. Apparently, it has all been arranged with our host, Mister Chowdhury and revealed when we are safely out of this country. I did not take the time to read my father's instructions, but I rely entirely on his judgment and ask you to follow them strictly. As for my enthronisation, which you mentioned earlier, I believe it can wait until we reach a safer haven. Until then, it is not our priority; we must travel incognito. Just keep me informed. Thank you, Acting First Minister; I wish you good night."

"I shall start preparations for our departure at once, Your Holiness."

The door closed behind him. Rinchen stared back at the golden casket and began to cry.

22

"Forty days, Shenouda, it has been forty days! Yet, nothing!"

"Calm yourself, Professor, there are still one hundred and ninety days left..."

The two friends were sitting comfortably at the terrace of the Pontifical Institute of Notre Dame de Jerusalem Centre, enjoying coffee and sweet oriental delicacies. A gentle rain was drizzling over the Holy City, cooling down what would otherwise have been a hot summer day. In his eagerness, Professor Walters was losing his legendary patience, like a toddler longing for a new toy. It was sweet for someone his age but quite tiring after a while. This was not the reasonable man Shenouda was accustomed to.

"... and do not forget that, so far, your deductions rely on fragile historical elements. I should advise caution before rushing to conclusions."

"You speak like them, like the members of the High Council."

"Because I first serve and represent them, and they have assigned me an extremely delicate task. This is not just about archaeology, Professor. While the Status Quo has provided stability, we cannot risk the tiniest religious incident. Even for the sake of historical research. This is not Egypt."

"I hear you, Shenouda. I apologise for my impatience. And, as usual, you are reasonable. A single piece of writing cannot categorically prove what it refers to still exists after almost three thousand years. Even if we find just one little clue, I will still see it as an accomplishment."

"At least, if nothing comes of it, you will have the satisfaction of returning to Tell-el-Amarna."

"A meagre solace, I am afraid."

A waiter approached them.

"Do you, gentlemen, want another coffee?" he asked.

"With pleasure. Professor?" The old scholar nodded unconcernedly, his mind wandering in his thoughts. "Two more black coffees, then. Mine with milk, this time."

"Absolutely," the waiter acknowledged.

He returned two minutes later with the hot beverages. The rain had stopped, but gloomy clouds still shrouded the sky. It seemed they would not clear out before the night. A little freshness is more than welcome, Shenouda thought while enjoying his drink.

His holophone beeped. It was the Archbishop's secretary.

"Yes, Nazeer?"

"..."

"I see.... Tell his Beatitude I am on my way. My apologies, Professor, but it's urgent. I must go."

"Nothing serious, I hope?"

"Hopefully not."

***

It took Shenouda about twenty minutes to reach the esplanade of the Al-Aqsa Mosque on Temple Mount. Two guards of the Religious Police accompanied him. The large stairs to the Dome of the Rock were just before him, still wet from the earlier rain. The place was silent as worshippers and visitors were allowed only at specific hours and days while the renovations were carried on. Behind him, he could hear the gentle dripping of the Al Kas Fountain. Two of the contractors walked down the stairs to approach him.

"As-salaam alaykum", he said respectfully. "Gentlemen, it is a pleasure to meet you again."

"Waʿalaykum Salaam," replied the eldest, Mohammed al-Husayni. "It is a delight to meet you, too, Archdeacon Wahba."

"Inform His Eminence the Grand Mufti that we are all present," he instructed one of the guards, who hastily left toward the mosque. Then, he looked back to the contractor. "So, Master al-Husayni, the message from the Archbishopric said you needed to see me urgently. Have you discovered anything that calls for my attention? I hope it is not another empty cistern like five days ago. I start to believe our Ancients were more concerned about storing as much water as they could than worshipping God."

"Well, Archdeacon, it may look that way at first, but there's also something else that I believe is significant. It is better if we show you."

Shenouda heard footsteps going in his direction. That was the guard returning with the Grand Mufti.

"Good evening, Your Eminence. My apologies for bothering you right after the evening prayer."

"Good evening to you all. Do not apologise, Archdeacon Wahba," the cleric answered, "I am persuaded these gentlemen have a legitimate reason to request our presence."

"I hope so, Your Eminence. Mister al-Husayni, here, thinks they have stumbled upon something significant. How would you like to accompany us and see what it might be?"

"With pleasure, it will be a welcome break from my obligations."

"Mister al-Husayni, should we head back to the Dome?"

"Actually, Archdeacon, we need to go through El-Marwani Mosque."

"Lead the way, then."

They walked to their right, then down a stairway until they reached a vast underground enclosure filled with rows of stone arches and tall pillars. The small group moved through lines of red wool prayer carpets to a back door displaying a No Entrance sign heading to a long hallway.

"This corridor leads to two cisterns just beneath the Dome, if I am not mistaken," Shenouda said. "We were there a couple of weeks ago, as I recall."

"Indeed, Archdeacon," replied al-Husayni. It is one of the two locations severely affected by the earthquake. Because the upper structure rests on these cisterns, the damages weaken the eastern base of the Dome. We are actively repairing and consolidating the section."

They finally reached a vast rectangular vaulted space used as a water reservoir in antiquity. The ceiling presented several cracks recently renovated. Several workers were lying casually on the floor, and all work seemed to have halted.

"This way, please."

They walked towards the right side of one of the walls perforated in its centre.

"Very well, Master al-Husayni," said Shenouda, "what brings us here?"

"You see, archdeacon, the cistern surrounding you has been carved directly in the rock. Yet we were surprised to detect a crack in this wall. It seemed worrisome since we initially thought it meant an entire section of the retaining rock was compromised. As we examined it, this section here collapsed. To our astonishment, we rapidly realised that the pieces of rock that came out of it were in fact large cut stones. Once we removed several of them, a void space appeared. Using a light, we looked inside and discovered a long corridor heading down to staircases. It does not appear on any of our plans. At this point, we decided to call you."

Shenouda turned to the Grand Mufti.

"What do you think, Your Eminence? Is it worth our friends' attention? To their credit, it seems very suspicious to have a stairway descending from what used to be a cistern. A single tunnel would suffice if its goal was to transport water and should come from the surface."

"This is why we rely on you, Archdeacon," the imam replied. So far, you have dismissed all previous findings as insignificant. I trust your expertise to assess their relevance. You have my permission to call Professor Degrenes. It could not have happened at a more appropriate time since praying is currently not permitted at night. And I spotted the National Geographics team heading home about half an hour ago. Hence, it will remain perfectly inconspicuous. I will head back to my office and notify the other members of the High Council. I am confident they will support my decision."

***

By the time Professor Degrenes arrived, the workers had widened the hole on Shenouda's instructions. The archaeologist was breathless, but the excitement was visible on his face.

"Oh my goodness, it is so thrilling! A tunnel with stairs, you said?"

"Look for yourself, Marc," said Shenouda while handing him a large torch.

"Let me see... Yes! I see low-slope stairs going down a few metres. This is remarkable! Has anyone been down there? You, perhaps?"

"No. Professor. I wanted you to have the honour of being the first one to explore the section. I hope you did not inform Professor Walters, as I requested. Despite its appearance, it might merely be a path leading to another cistern or even nothing. I did not want him to experience another disappointment."

"I promise I did not, Shenouda. Come on, let's go inside."

"After you, Professor."

They entered the dark corridor cautiously, progressing steadily and aided by their torches. The passage was high enough for an average man to stand up fully beneath his vaulted ceiling. The archaeologist stopped right before the first steps, looking closely at distinctive marks patterning the walls.

"Observe these lines, Shenouda. They are characteristic of those left by carving tools. This tunnel was dug directly on the rock."

"Like most of the tunnels we have found, so far, Professor."

"Indeed, but look here." He directed the light towards the ground. "The stairs have also been carved in the rock. Building this passageway took a great deal of time and effort. This is not the type of work you do for a simple reservoir. And can you smell the air?"

"I don't smell anything specific apart from the scent of ancient stones."

"Precisely! There is no moisture, and the walls show no signs of dampness. This place was never used to convey water. Let's keep going."

They moved down the stairs. Although very large at first, they gradually narrowed and, after several meters, spiralled down at right angles.

"No time or technology to curve them, which is understandable. Note how the limestone becomes harder here." He raised his eyes as if they could see through the rock all the way up. I believe we are underneath the dome, probably just below the foundation stone. This is getting so exciting."

Their descent lasted approximately five minutes until they reached what appeared to be the end of the staircase and the start of another tunnel. Professor Degrenes froze suddenly. In the opposite direction, directly sculpted in the rock, stood an arch created by two winged mythological creatures facing each other. They were wearing typical Israelite robes, and holding what seemed to be oil lamps.

"Oh, my goodness! Oh, my goodness! Look at this, Shenouda!" the archaeologist cried out. "Cherubim! The servants of God! Like those mentioned in the Bible when describing the interior of Solomon's Temple. I cannot believe it! It goes beyond all my expectations. This may be connected to the Ark of the Covenant. What if we were on the verge of discovering its secret cache?" His entire body was shivering.

"Marc… I am speechless. If you are accurate, that might be the most significant discovery of the century. And think of the ramifications for all monotheistic religions. But let's not draw conclusions too fast. Let's keep going first."

"Look!" Degrenes pointed out another carving on the ceiling above the angels. "The Knights Templar Cross! They were here! They must have discovered the place while they were occupying the Mount. If only…"

He started running before Shenouda could stop him.

"Marc, wait! You do not know what is ahead, it could be dangerous. Please, wait for me!"

He heard the steps echoing ahead until they abruptly stopped. Then a long cry of despair broke in the shadows.

"Nooooo!"

"Professor. I am right behind you, hold on!" Shenouda hastened carefully until he reached his friend. The scholar was on his knees, sobbing. In front of him, the tunnel ended abruptly, blocked by large chunks of rock that had collapsed from the ceiling.

23

"… This is the current situation after forty days, Mister President." General de Soverosa was reporting to the entire Cabinet in an extraordinary meeting. "The warring factions are still at a standstill. The front has stabilised on a line about fifty kilometres south of the Islamabad-Srinagar's axis. Two weeks ago, the Indian army managed to recapture most of the Indian-administered zone in Kashmir, except for the capital of the state and the northwest territory normally under their control. During this counterattack, their forces also succeeded in breaking the eastern front towards the Pakistani capital. But, as I mentioned earlier, their advance was stopped fifty kilometres away. Half of the rest of the armies of both countries are massively concentrated on their respective borders. The military commands show no signs of willingness to extend the conflict there. Both factions have presently reached a standstill. Furthermore, there are no indications that either country is preparing for a nuclear strike. But I believe High

Commissioner Richter possesses more information in that regard."

"Thank you, General", said President Kowalczyk. "Monika?"

"Mister President, I had active and productive talks with Acting Prime Minister Patel of India and Prime Minister Aziz of Pakistan. As stated by General de Soverosa, neither of the two leaders is considering the nuclear option. It would be legitimate to say they finally realised China had duped them. Especially Pakistan, which, according to my sources, had been promised military support in its campaign.A promise which never took form."

"We have all been deceived," interrupted the President. "The Chinese have cleverly manipulated everyone, even us. My apologies, please, carry on."

"Thank you. We are now facing the fact that none of the parties seeks to undertake the first step leading to reciprocal withdrawal. Either side justifies this as national pride. On one side, Acting Prime Minister Patel is expected to ask the Indian President to dissolve Parliament once the crisis ends. But he does not want to jeopardise his gains in the polls after the successful counterattack campaign if he withdraws his troops too early. On the other side, in taking the first steps, Prime Minister Aziz fears being viewed by his people as the puppet of foreign powers. Even though his reputation is substantially tarnished, he is unwilling to lose the last piece of credit he still holds. On our side, we do not want to see either country destabilised politically by allowing more interference from their neighbours."

"Hence I suppose we should gather everybody around a table and hold a peace conference?"

"Precisely, Mister President. And to offer more credit to its outcome, I suggest inviting another major player to participate."

"Another major player? An uneasy task, Monika. We cannot ask China. It will be disastrous and most certainly rejected by both belligerents. Neither can we involve any of the three American states. The two others will perceive this as a provocation. Not forgetting their influence is completely irrelevant, as is the Pacific Alliance. By principle, the African Union refuses to get involved in diplomatic talks unless it directly concerns its security. And the Central and South American Union has unanimously condemned both parties for, I quote, *breaching World accord*. As if..." he shrugged up. The rest of the cabinet chuckled. "Hold on, Monika; you are not suggesting…"

"… Russia. Yes, I am, Mister President."

A rumble spread through the Cabinet members. "Unacceptable!" erupted one. "Outrageous!" yelled another. The fiercest voice came from the High Commissioner for European Integration.

"How can you suggest such a thing, Monika? You are asking our President and this Cabinet to drop our pants and leave 'Catherine the Threat', that animal, to use our asses as she pleases. Was no lesson learned eleven years ago? It took us years of effort to finally muzzle this criminal state. You advocate a radical change to our stance by restoring Russia's international voice to serve our foreign policy."

"My dear colleague," replied Monika, "I do acknowledge your position, especially as a Ukrainian national. But I want to stress that the events you are referring to happened eleven years ago, and President Alexeyevna was not in power then."

"We are talking about the daughter of Grigory Alexeyev, the *Butcher of Kiev*, for God's sake! And we have gathered ample evidence of her plausible implication during the final assault. Why do you think most of us nickname her *Catherine the Threat*!?"

"Those are mere speculations. And the sins of the father should not fall onto the daughter."

"Realpolitik cannot justify everything, Monika. You are—"

"Very well, Yurij. You have made your point," interrupted the President. "Monika, I assume you realise how sensitive this subject is. I presume you have a perfectly valid argument to support this initiative."

"I indeed have several, Mister President. First and foremost, Russia's good diplomatic relations with India and Pakistan. Primarily given that, it remained neutral towards both states for once. Even calling for an immediate ceasefire while condemning China. In my opinion, this was a wasted opportunity. Next, the country currently possesses the largest nuclear arsenal while remaining politically stable. Notwithstanding its notorious lack of democratic reforms and the threat it still represents, Russia's participation will attach more weight to an initiative for peace. After polling them, I should finally add that both Acting Prime Minister Patel and Prime Minister Aziz have confirmed they would consent to have President Alexeyevna join the negotiation table."

"Providing she wants to," said President Kowalczyk.

"Well, Mister President, Russia has been under diplomatic quarantine for the last ten years. Undoubtedly, its government will be more than interested in rejoining the exclusive club of diplomatic influencers. But I agree we cannot allow her *to use our asses as she pleases*, to quote my esteemed colleague. President Alexeyevna will participate in the United Nations Climate Conference in Geneva as an observer. This will be the first time her country will be permitted to attend such a prominent international event since the institution of permanent members was abolished. I suggest meeting with her at some point during the session. Beforehand, I will contact the Russian Minister of Foreign Affairs, Ivan Kozyrev. The peace initiative should appear as coming from them. However, we will insist the conference takes place in Vienna to stay in control. I am confident she will accept the proposal if she sees it as an opportunity to improve her image internationally and at home. I am convinced her decision to remain neutral towards the Indo-Pakistani crisis was a calculated move. We should reach out with one hand while keeping the other one ready to respond."

"Alright. It is a risky game, but I think it is worth it." He looked at all the Cabinet members. "I appreciate some of you have justified reluctance about this, me included, rest assured. However, we must not forget we keep paying the price for the destabilisation of the United States. We do not want the chaos it has sparked to spread any further than it already has, especially by ignoring two of our closest allies. Therefore, I am asking for your support on the promise that I will remain vigilant and not compromise the roots of our ideals while keeping the beast on a leash. We will do everything in our power to prevent that disastrous Chinese interference. Let us vote."

The motion was approved with two abstentions.

✶✶✶

"Monika, that was a bit far-fetched but well done! I would have been unable to persuade the majority of the Cabinet without your help," said President Kowalczyk. They were both in his office relaxing over a coffee. "Did you see how Yurij reacted? I never expected it to be this rough."

"It was no surprise. And I understand why. I would have responded the same way if I were in his shoes. Let's not forget he and his sister survived the horrific massacre of civilians in Kyiv. A tragedy which could have been avoided by a stronger and unified response from the countries of Western Europe then. Instead, we hid our heads in the sand, focusing too much on salvaging a lost cause on the other side of the Atlantic."

"Yes, you are right. Dire moments indeed. But we cannot keep looking at the past, and there comes a time when old resentment must give way to new perspectives. You do not take on greater political responsibilities holding a personal grudge. Had I proposed this, some High Commissioners would have been too happy to jump on the opportunity to destabilise me before the entire Cabinet by voting against it. Thank you again for supporting me in this. I will not forget it."

They heard a knock on the door.

"Yes?" It was High Commissioner Jorge Sanchez. "Ah, Jorge. Please come in."

"You wanted to see me, Mister President?"

"Indeed. Please, sit next to Monika. I wished to consult you both on a topic I did not want to discuss with the

203

others. This skirmish between India and Pakistan has eluded another one equally important. Can anyone advise me on what happened to the 16th Dalai Lama and half of the Tibetan Government in Exile? Monika?"

"Well, Mister President, I wish I had a straight answer for you. The last we heard of them was in some obscure suburbs of the City of Chennai, under the close protection of the Indian armed forces. But one night, everyone simply vanished. And right under the noses of those meant to guard them. The Indian Government denies any involvement, and according to Director Pavlović, the Chinese are as clueless as we are. We received reports that their intelligence services are actively searching for them all over the subcontinent and surrounding countries."

"Would it not be an attempt by the People's Republic of China to conceal a covert operation?"

"That sounds extremely unlikely, Mister President. They invested too much effort into openly capturing prominent Tibetan figures, live on all global networks, to suddenly operate covertly. I genuinely believe they are as puzzled as we are."

"It means they could reappear anywhere, as far as we are concerned."

"Absolutely, Mister President."

"Alright. Jorge, this is the reason I asked you to join us."

"I am listening, Mister President."

"I want our entire border watch on high alert. Every coast guard, customs officer, police at the border, etc. You know what I mean. If the 16th Dalai Lama or any other representative of his government were to turn up on our soil, I want them to be secured right away, with the utmost discretion and protection. No publicity, nothing. Transfer them to an undisclosed location until we can bring them into the spotlight. Moreover, if this happens in the next couple of months. We must avoid any unwanted publicity that could compromise the prospects for the future peace conference and further escalation with China. I hope I can rely on you."

"You can, Mister President. I will give the necessary instructions at once."

***

It was practically 7.00 pm. Inspector Principal Philippe Martin, Custom Officer at Marseille-Fos Port, had almost finished his day shift. He was on his way to Pier 117 in East Harbour, accompanied by Customs Comptroller Julien Lagrange. They were about to inspect the Indonesian cargo ship Dewi Sri, which arrived an hour before in transit to Norway. The two men reached the medium-sized vessel, laden with dozens of containers, and approached her captain, who was waiting for them on the footbridge.

"Good evening, Captain Sharma. I am Inspector Principal Martin, and this is Custom Comptroller Lagrange. Permission to come on board to inspect your ship, Sir."

"Permission granted, Inspector Principal. Please follow me. My Second in command, Ensign Singh, will show Mister Lagrange around if you don't mind."

"My pleasure, Captain."

The customs officers made the usual rounds. Since they inspected the vessel several times in the past, it was an easy way to finish the day. After half an hour, having completed the inspection, the Inspector Principal was on the bridge with the captain checking the different paperwork.

"Everything appears to be in order, Captain, as usual."

"Thank you, Inspector."

"I'll wait for my colleague's return, and you'll be on your way." His walkie-talkie crackled.

"Philippe, can you hear me? Over."

"Yes, Julien, I hear you loud and clear. Over."

"I need you to come to hold five quickly, please. Over."

"On my way. Philippe out. Captain, would you mind taking me there?"

"Of course, Inspector. Follow me."

They proceeded to the main deck before reaching their destination. His colleague was waiting with the Second in command a few meters from a large container strangely isolated from the rest of the load.

"What is the matter?" asked Inspector Martin.

"I was completing my tour when I saw this container oddly stored on its own. According to the bill of lading, it contains furniture. But I'd swear I heard some noise inside earlier. All seems silent now. Could you check? I do not want to embarrass us by making wrong assumptions."

"If you have any doubts about anything, you have the authority to request an opening. No need to ask for my prior approval."

The Inspector approached the large mass of metal and placed his right ear on one of its sides. After several seconds, he heard muffled sounds and stifled movements. He inadvertently bumped his foot onto the panel. All noise ceased except for some murmurs.

"Captain, I am sorry, but I must ask you to immediately open that container for inspection."

After a moment of hesitation, the captain nervously walked towards the container's door and unlocked it.

"Let me out, let me out!" shouted a voice suddenly.

"Dache, No!" yelled a female voice.

Looking inside, a crowded group of people appeared to Inspector Principal Martin's bemusement. He stared at the ship officer with a rebuke.

"Captain, what is this about?"

At this point, one of the individuals, dressed in a large red and saffron robe, rose and approached him.

"Good evening, Sir. Pleased to make your acquaintance. My name is Rinchen Gyaltsen, and I am the 16th Dalai Lama. I kindly request asylum for myself and all my travel companions."

24

Monika has done wonders, as usual, Pierre-Antoine thought. Once again, he was delighted to have placed his trust in his friend to arrange accommodation in Edinburgh. The two-storey apartment was spacious and comfortable. Open bay windows provided plenty of light during the day, while the interior design gave a feeling of cosiness at night. A glass veranda on the top floor provided a direct view of the Firth of Forth. And the location was only a fifteen-minute walk to the Research Centre. While his appointment was in half an hour, and despite the wind and rainy weather, he decided a little stroll would do his legs good after yesterday's flight. He took a comfy jacket and wandered the surrounding streets on his way to the Centre. The neighbourhood was quiet. People were going about their business simply and uncomplicatedly, some nodding as he passed by. The area was predominantly residential, with typical brown and grey stone houses and buildings no more than four-storey high. The capital of Scotland seemed wrapped in calm and friendly love. A striking contrast with the frenzy of the grand metropolis he lived in. Strasbourg had lost its charm in evolving and extending its size to fulfil its new status as a capital. But here, things seemed untouched, with time moving gracefully slowly. Pierre-Antoine followed the moderately steep road — a prevalent feature in the city— in the direction of the research centre. While walking, his belly started to ache acutely. *Not now, please,* he admonished his body. Just over a month had passed since his last surgery, but he could not determine whether the pain was caused by a new growth or his recent scar. The rain stopped, and the clouds broke away, allowing a mild sun to appear. Subsequently, the ache calmed down, and he accelerated his pace. He finally reached the boundaries of the Newhaven Lighthouse Park Research Centre, surrounded by tall, imposing concrete walls, like a forbidden city jealous of its secrets. *They have made several significant discoveries here, and we have authorised substantial investments in their research programs. The complex is classified as 'sensitive'.Who can blame them for being secretive?* After passing security, he walked to a receptionist who smiled at him.

"Good afternoon. How may I help you?"

"Good afternoon. I am Mister Pierre-Antoine Lascombes. I have an appointment with Doctor Giancarlo Caracciolo."

"Certainly. Please take a seat. Doctor Caracciolo will be with you shortly."

A moment later, a tall, dark-haired man approached him.

"Mister Lascombes?" he asked with a distinctive Italian accent. "I am Doctor Caracciolo. How nice to meet you."

"Nice to meet you too."

"Please follow me to one of our interview rooms. This way, please."

They walked through a long corridor before entering a sober, windowless cubicle with just a long table and three chairs. A woman in a white coat was waiting there.

"Please, take a seat, Mister Lascombes. This is Doctor Ipatevna, one of my associates. She will assist me during this meeting. I apologise for not giving you a tour, but due to the Centre's strict visitor policy, we do not allow prospective patients in our secured areas."

"I understand."

"Alright! First question, how familiar are you with our research?"

"Somewhat, given my field of work. But honestly, I do not read every memo forwarded to my department before approving funding."

"Naturally. I can appreciate how busy you must be. Aren't we all? Right, I examined the chart your surgeon communicated us. You appear to have advanced soft tissue sarcoma, primarily in the abdominal area."

"Exact. Although it hasn't progressed to the metastatic stage, doctors detected traces of cancer cells in one of the lymphatic nodes. Tumours seem to grow only in my abdominal tissues so far."

"Indeed, you are still at a stage we call T3 N1 M0. Forgive my scientific jargon. With the current range of treatments, you can expect survival for up to five years."

"Well, my surgeon is more pessimistic than you, Doctor. He believes the tumour resurgence is accelerating. My last surgery was a month ago, whereas the previous one was three months earlier. I used to have only one surgery once every two years, just two years ago. And I have had six of them since. The standard treatments seem to become less and less effective, and they are starting to take a toll on me."

"Indeed, not encouraging. Well, we are here to help you, Mister Lascombes, and hopefully to cure you. My colleague will now give you a brief introduction to our experimental therapy. Natalia, if you please."

"Thank you, Giancarlo. Mister. Lascombes, you may be familiar with T-cell therapy. Its principle is simple. We collect T cells from a blood sample and some patient cancer cells by biopsy. Next, we extract the receptor from the cancer antigen and, using a chimeric virus, we add that antigen to the T cells to train them to fight cancer. Those trained cells are then multiplied and reinjected into the patient. Ultimately, the immune system takes over and eliminates tumours. The main side effect is typically an immune response causing symptoms similar to those associated with normal vaccination. Except the former usually last more than a few weeks instead of a few days for the latter. This method has been successfully developed and implemented in the past twenty years. It could be employed on you as soon as the next tumour appears, saving you from continuous surgeries and chemotherapy. And for most patients, that is our recommendation. But you would not require us, then. These procedures are easily available in most hospitals offering a cancer treatment ward."

"What makes me different?"

"Well," she continued, "this treatment has several flaws. First, it is strictly patient-oriented. This means we must carry out this laborious process for every patient and cancer. It is time-consuming and not cost-effective. Next, it is a race against the clock when it comes to extremely aggressive cancers. Finally, and it concerns you directly, while the treatment successfully eliminates the tumours, it is ineffective in detecting and fighting hibernating cancerous cells. After some time, the body naturally eliminates modified T-cells as they cannot reproduce. After a while, cancer returns, the tumours come back, and we are back to square one. A scenario extremely familiar with cancers like yours. Furthermore, when a patient reaches stage N, which you have, it gets even more complicated. If cancer manages to affect another organ, a new therapy has to be implemented, and so on. That represents several different therapies under my scenario. I said earlier the side effects were not excessive, but only in the case of a single treatment. Having a patient undergoing several different therapies at once can be life-threatening. And treating only one cancer each time gives others a chance to develop up to the point of no return or compromise a patient's physiology. You see the dilemma, especially when a person is at an advanced stage."

"I do."

"This is where we step in. Giancarlo?"

"Thank you, Natalia, for that exhaustive presentation. Mister Lascombes, as you know, this research centre had a major breakthrough seven years ago. We succeeded in isolating not an antigen but a DNA sequence present in each known cancer, but not in healthy cells. A shared mutation, if you prefer. Some scientists have nicknamed it the Devil's sequence. Allegedly because of its ability to alter the so-called perfection of 'God's creation'. Rest assured, you will not hear this type of metaphysical nonsense here. Anyway, this discovery represents the long result of a decade spent sequencing healthy and cancer cells. We were the first lab to achieve a breakthrough. It has resulted in the development of a broad range of treatments for widespread and emerging viral diseases. The fact this sequence was found in each type of cancer might also imply it exists in a dormant stage in every individual. The next step of research is where it hides and what triggers its activation. I'll leave that for now, as our current primary focus is a cure. Our solution is to implement antigenic treatment to DNA using mRNA therapy. In short, we are developing a cancer vaccine. Upon success, and we will succeed, people will ultimately only require a small annual injection, as with common viruses. Presumably, even less as the technique improves. Imagine! A future with no cancer, no suffering, and no painful therapy. Except for some unknown reason, our trials, although successful with less evolved vertebrates, have all failed when tested on mammals. The cause of that failure has escaped us so far. However, two months ago, an unexpected development occurred. Its implications extend beyond our expectations. We have successfully tested a treatment on rats and apes, which, besides being universal, seems to eradicate cancer after a single injection completely. This may be the second breakthrough awaited for so long."

"Truly amazing," said Pierre-Antoine. "But if this discovery was made two months ago, how can you be certain it will work long-term?"

"Well, I cannot at this stage of development for apparent reasons. It is too soon to tell. And this is why I have to rely on volunteers like you for our human trials. You are in your fifties, suffering from a life-threatening condition, or at least with a reduced lifespan. You represent an ideal candidate because your cancer develops in soft tissues, not vital organs. It is what we are considering for our initial trials. I will not lie to you, Mister Lascombes. I am offering you an experimental treatment which could take at least five years to confirm its effectiveness. And it will be quite challenging physically because we will need to extract some of your stem cells from your bone marrow. I can't even warn you of the potential side effects you may experience. I am essentially asking you to be a guinea pig. But I also offer you a unique and reasonable prospect to keep enjoying your productive life, particularly your successful political career, for decades to come."

"You speak as astutely as a politician, Doctor Caracciolo."

"Let's say I am desperate to find suitable candidates. Whatever the outcome, having a high-profile figure like you among my first patients will certainly boost those prospects."

"I see... you understand I have to give it some thought."

"Of course! I would have been extremely surprised if you had agreed instantly. At least, it is not a no, though?"

"That would be preposterous of me, Doctor."

"Excellent!" He placed a white envelope on the table. "This envelope contains more specific information and data about what we have just discussed and a detailed description of the different procedures. Please take the time to consult them carefully and examine them. Any questions you seek answers to, just contact Doctor Ipatevna directly. Her details are included in the documents. And I wish to stress the sensitivity of their content. I trust I can rely on your discretion."

"Naturally, Doctor."

***

Pierre-Antoine was returning to the flat, torn between scepticism and hope. *That would change everything. It opens up new perspectives and an opportunity to achieve what I have already initiated.* Or to accelerate the inevitable end... He decided to stop thinking about it and leave the issue until the following day. His mind wandered to the other reason for his presence here, of a more diplomatic nature. He recalled the meeting with President Kowalczyk, Monika and Jorge five days before in Strasbourg.

"Pierre-Antoine! Please join us," said the President, pointing to the seat next to Monika.

"How can I assist you, Mister President?"

"Pierre-Antoine, you are travelling to Edinburgh in five days, right?"

"Indeed. I have informed you of the reasons for this trip; I bel—"

"Absolutely, no need to evoke them. I sincerely hope for the best with this new treatment. We would be extremely saddened if you were to abandon us *permanently*. However, that is not why I asked you to join us. No, I wish to take advantage of this unofficial trip to Edinburgh to ask whether you would be willing to conduct a confidential diplomatic mission."

"A diplomatic mission, Mister President?"

"Pierre-Antoine," interrupted Monika, "know I expressed a strong reservation about this. And so has Jorge. Haven't you, Jorge?" Pierre-Antoine's half-brother nodded timidly. "Your health is your priority."

"This is why we are all here to discuss it calmly, Monika," replied the President.

"It's alright, Monika. I am listening, Mister President."

"What I am about to mention now is known only to Monika, Jorge, General de Soverosa, Director Pavlović and a few others. The rest of the Cabinet is uninformed. Secrecy is essential. Undermining it could endanger the lives of many prominent individuals and jeopardise the Peace Conference that begins this Friday."

"Endanger the lives of many individuals? What is happening?"

"Three weeks ago, a cargo ship from Singapore stopped at Marseilles en route to Bergen. During the routine inspection, fifty-eight people were discovered hiding in a container and immediately apprehended."

"A terrorist group? This sounds like an extensive operation."

"In fact, I would classify them as a kind of clandestine immigrants. I am talking about the 16th Dalai Lama, his entourage, his Prime Minister, the Tibetan Cabinet and Parliament members, and part of their families."

"The 16th Dalai Lama is in Marseille! But the whole world is looking for him. And how come it has not made the headlines yet?"

"Well… let us say that the timing of his arrival could not have been worse as we had just started negotiations with Russia to organise the Indo-Pakistani Peace Conference. Making this public would have risked undermining the whole process. We could not afford this."

"Where is His Holiness then?"

"Fortunately, thanks to Jorge, our borders were on high alert to anticipate his possible arrival. Once apprehended, the entire party was quietly exfiltrated to Scotland. They are currently safely housed in a Buddhist monastery about ninety kilometres south of Edinburgh. Which one Jorge?"

"The Kagyu Samye Ling Monastery, Mister President."

"Precisely. I had to pressure the Scottish Prime Minister a little, but she is always cooperative. However, she was not briefed on the exact identity of her guests. Only that they were Tibetan refugees holding vital interests to this government. Lorna is no fool, of course, but the situation will remain unchanged until we resolve the crisis in the Indian subcontinent."

"I'll be damned," swore Pierre-Antoine. "This is so unexpected. But what do you want from me?"

"I do not need to stress how sensitive the situation is. Although I fear His Holiness is probably wondering why he ended there, as we acted hastily without giving him any details or reassurance except to remain indoors. It also means that I cannot authorise direct surveillance and protection or send an official delegation without risking attracting the Chinese' attention or, worse, the press. Any leak could have a tragic outcome. However, what if a prominent member of the Cabinet happened to be in the region for, say, personal health reasons? And what if this same member of the Cabinet discreetly conveyed a message to His Holiness in the name of the European Government? I believe I made myself quite clear."

"You should refuse, Pierre-Antoine."

"Why should I, Monika? So far, I am only going to Edinburgh for a medical appointment, not some other surgery or tiresome treatment. And it will aid me to focus on something else."

"Expect to be followed by Chinese agents," the President added. "But Jorge will set up a surveillance network to cover you."

"This sounds fun. You can count on me, Mister President…"

And here he was, playing both a patient and secret emissary. The sole issue was how to complete his mission.

25

"The High Council of the Free City of Jerusalem is now in session. We are eager to hear your report, Archdeacon," Patriarch Nicodemus II solemnly stated.

The five leaders of the religious government of the Holy City had gathered to hear an update on the progress of the excavations on Temple Mount. The clerics were sitting in a semicircle on wooden chairs resembling thrones. Shenouda stood before holding several pages of notes.

"Thank you, Your Beatitude. Let me begin by briefly reminding the honourable members of the High Council of the reasons for today's meeting. Twenty days ago, while repairs were carried out on an ancient cistern below Temple Mount, an unregistered tunnel was discovered by a team of workers. In accordance with the agreement between the two parties involved, the High Council of the Free City of Jerusalem and the excavation team, I conducted an initial investigation along with Professor Marc Degrenes. After examining some of the excavated ancient passage, we determined that it dates back to the early 10th century B.C.

This hypothesis is based on the existence, towards the end of the accessible section, of a sculpted arch representing two cherubim wearing typical Israelite clothing."

"So, around the time of Kings David or Solomon?" asked Cardinal del Pietro.

"Indeed, Your Eminence. However, as I just said, the hypothesis must be confirmed. We suspect the structure itself to be much older. Still, we are waiting for the sample analysis results to get back to us. The investigation had to stop a hundred metres away due to large boulders obstructing the end of the passage. Most certainly resulting from the collapse of the ceiling, possibly due to a violent earthquake. What is the current situation twenty days later? The obstructing boulders are being removed while the ceiling is carefully consolidated. We have excavated about three tonnes of stones and cleared five more metres of passage."

"Five metres in twenty days? That is not much."

"Indeed, Chief Rabbi. It is Professor Degrenes' opinion as well. But I am sure you understand the need for caution to ensure nobody is injured accidentally, or worse, in another collapse that might compromise the above rock structure. Especially as several human remains were found on the last two excavated metres, causing some apprehension among the local workers. The analysis of these remains and their equipment indicates that they belonged to Christian labourers or artisans from the period of the Kingdom of Jerusalem. Most likely mid-12th century BC. It would indicate the tunnel was probably used, or at least rediscovered, during the Templar occupation of Temple Mount. This theory is supported by a carved

Templar cross above a cherubim's arch adorning the tunnel."

A rumbling passed through the council chamber.

"It also appears that the wall located between the tunnel and the cistern was built around the same period. No other artefacts or inscriptions have been found to help determine what lies ahead beyond the rubble. However, Professor Degrenes brought up the hypothesis, based on the presence of the Cherubim and the geographical situation of the tunnel —situated right under where Solomon and Herod's temples used to stand— that the passage might lead to an underground chamber containing or which used to contain or conceal, the Ark of the Covenant."

The rumbling increased in level.

"I must say I am rather sceptical about this hypothesis, especially looking at the absence of wall decoration expected to be found in such a place."

"Anything else, Archdeacon?" asked the Patriarch.

"Nothing relevant, your Beatitude. We believe to be approaching the end of the removal of the rubbles. This morning, what appeared to be a wall showed up at the top. According to the overseer's calculation, clearing the site completely should take another five to seven days."

"Very well. Thank you for your clarifications on the situation. You may leave us now."

"As you wish, Your Beatitude."

Shenuda bowed respectfully before them and left. After he left, Cardinal del Pietro started to speak.

"Gentlemen, I guess you all heard well? The Templars were there. Hard to say this is a coincidence. It is consistent with the evidence I presented you a couple of weeks ago."

"The Ark of the Covenant…" thought aloud the Patriarch. "Can you imagine its impact on the rest of the world? Its discovery would be a formidable blow to all these heathens and atheists! The ultimate proof of the existence of our glorious God!" He raised his hands towards the heavens.

"Thousands of pilgrims flocking to the Holy City, bringing more richness," praised the Metropolitan Archbishop.

"The Jewish faith acknowledged as the mother of all monotheisms," added the Chief Rabbi.

"Purified and perfected by our Lord Jesus Christ and his Holy Church," concluded the Patriarch.

"What do you suggest by *purified*, Your Beatitude? Does anything in your eyes stain my faith?"

"Christ did not die an old man, didn't he?"

"I cannot believe I am hearing this from someone so erudite and respectful. This is disgraceful."

"I am certain that his Beatitude meant no harm, Chief Rabbi," declared the Metropolitan Archbishop. "After all, it was God's plan all along. Your people could merely follow the path laid out for them by the Creator."

"Are those words meant to comfort me, Your Eminence?"

"Gentlemen, please!" interrupted the Cardinal. "Now is not the time to quarrel with one another and revive ancient religious grievances." He looked at the Grand Mufti who appeared lost in thoughts. "Your silence surprises me, Your Eminence."

"Well, my dear Cardinal del Pietro, I recalled our discussion at this pleasant dinner not too long ago. I clearly remember that the two artefacts you presented us

222

contained warnings. They employed words like *cursed*, *evil*, and *terrible secret*. Those words do not conform with what one would use for something as sacred as the Ark of the Covenant. Undoubtedly, the Templars would have benefited from such a discovery, especially in the middle of the crusade period. Instead, they buried it and described it as an abomination. I apologise, dear colleagues, but something is not right in this story. Whatever lie there might be more consequential than we initially thought."

The council chamber fell into a frozen silence as if all hope had vanished until broken by Cardinal del Pietro.

"You are right, your Eminence. Something feels amiss. Our expectations are blinding us. We could be on the verge of inadvertently excavating Pandora's Box."

"That's how I perceive it. It would be a mistake to lower our guard. Instead, I recommend increasing surveillance as a precautionary measure."

Shenouda was walking down the tunnel. Lights have been fitted throughout, allowing him to walk faster than during his first visit. On the way, he passed several workers carrying-up loads of stones. The clergyman stopped by the arch, as he had done several times. There was an enticing sensation of being in the cherubim's presence. *Why only there?* he thought. *Their conventional purpose was to decorate places of worship. The passage is almost a kilometre and a half long, but there is no evidence of other religious artefacts. What is your purpose?* He could now hear Degrenes and Walters' voices coming from the end. They were arguing with excitement.

"I am telling you! This is it. We found it!" was saying the latter.

"How can you be certain?"

"Look at this! It is undeniable proof! Whatever we find there will shake their..."

Shenouda emerged from behind.

"Good evening, gentlemen. What is happ—" He stopped abruptly. The end of the tunnel was almost completely cleared, exposing a wall engraved with lines of Egyptian hieroglyphs. "How can it be? As you reported, I informed the Council that completing the work would take another five or seven days."

"We have something to confess, Shenouda," Professor Walters said, looking embarrassed. "We... lied to you. Only a little..."

"Professor! What about our friendship and collaboration? Do I not deserve your trust?"

"I know, my boy, and believe me, I am truly sorry. But it was for the better good. We meant no malice. Look, look at the inscribing on the wall! It mentions the same things as on the tablet, except that these are the words of Pharaoh Shoshenq. And over here is a quote from the Egyptian Book of the Dead. Listen!

'Ra, who opens the gates of the horizon straightway on thy appearance,

Apep hath sunk helpless under thy gashing.

I have performed thy will, Oh Ra, I have performed thy will.

I have done that which is fair, I have done that which is fair,

I have laboured for the peace of Ra.

I have made to advance thy fetters, Oh Ra, and Apep hath fallen through thy drawing them tight. The gods of the south and of the *north, of the west and of the east have fastened chains upon him, and they have fettered him with fetters;*

The god Rekes hath overthrown him, and the god Hertit hath put him in chains.

Ra setteth, Ra setteth; Ra is strong at his setting.

Apep hath has fallen, Apep, the enemy of Ra, departeth'.

"This is a common invocation to repel evil, Shenouda. Whatever stands beyond that wall scared Pharaoh."

"And look at this," continued Professor Degrenes, showing small colourful objects. "Amulets of the Eye of Ra, commonly used in Egyptian tombs to ward off evil. They were meticulously attached to the wall. Whatever secret lies behind needed to remain trapped. No doubt we are at the edge of a great discovery."

"Alright, just calm down. We must return immediately to the High Council to inform them and ask their permission to cut that wall."

Professor Walters grasped the cleric's left hand.

"Please, Shenouda, could you delay this for twenty-four hours, or at least until the morning?"

"I apologise, professor, but you know the terms of our agreement. I must notify the High Council of any new developments. I am the guarantor of those terms and am bound to my hierarchy by an oath of trust."

"I am not asking you to deceive anybody. Just this one time, please allow an old man the satisfaction of realising his dream by looking at treasures away from a crowd of workers and officials before he departs this world. Do you remember what Howard Carter wrote when he discovered Tutankhamun's tomb? Give me the pleasure of being Carter once in this life. I promise you; we will make a hole just big enough for a glimpse, then close it."

225

"What if the workers see us? What about the National Geographics team?"

"We sent them home for the night," said Degrenes. "It shall be only the three of us. And I just switched off the lights to prevent arousing suspicion." Shenouda looked back and realised the tunnel was completely dark. "I have a hammer and chisel here. We will make a little opening on the right, just enough to pass that small drone connected to my holotablet. No one will ever notice it tomorrow. Look at those marks, there and there. Someone has evidently tried penetrating the wall in the past, unsuccessfully. We only need to declare it was done at the same period."

"I am unsure. It does not seem right. You both know how I feel about this."

"Please, my boy, this is my last chance. Just the three of us. Forgot your pledge for only a couple of hours. What harm could it possibly do to anyone?"

"Alright, professor, I yield. I only hope I will not regret it. Proceed, Marc, but with caution."

"Wonderful! I am so excited!"

The archaeologist picked up the tools and slowly began to hammer the wall. It was not as strong as it looked at first glance, but still relatively thick. Interminable minutes passed as stone fragments were painstakingly removed one by one. Nothing but the echoing chisel could be heard in the dark tunnel.

"I believe I am nearly there. I'm getting less resistance..."

Suddenly, a big lump of rock fell to the other side. At the same moment, they felt a rumble, and the ground started shaking under their feet for several seconds. Then it completely stopped.

"Earthquake," murmured Shenouda. "Let's wait a few minutes to make sure it was just an isolated tremor… Watch out!" he shouted, pulling them back as the entire wall collapsed in the blink of an eye, accompanied by a thick cloud of irritating dust. "Is everyone alright?" the monk asked, coughing.

"I'm fine," replied Professor Walters.

"Me too," said Degrenes.

After a few minutes, the cloud began dissipating, revealing a large opening.

"Well, I suppose no one can stop us from looking inside now. I shall record this." He switched on his holophone's camera.

"Hold on!" shouted Degrenes. "Let me turn the spotlight on."

As soon as the light went on, the three men gasped. Right before their eyes stood a vast square room decorated with Egyptian and Canaanite carvings and paintings. At each corner were monumental statues of cherubs holding the painted ceiling depicting a large sun radiating in all directions. But what really captured their attention was the imposing object carved into the room's eastern wall. It was a stela, identical to the ones in Tell-el-Amarna. It represented the adoration of the Aten by Akhenaten and Nefertiti. But instead of their daughters at their sides, there was a group of people wearing Canaanite clothes worshipping the Sun-God. One was standing at the Pharaoh's right, in a prominent position. A hieroglyphic inscription accompanied it. Shenouda began reading it and froze with consternation before falling to his knees.

"Joseph, son of Jacob, son of Isaac, son of Abraham, may he live and prosper in the benevolent light of the Aten…"

His voice was still echoing when they heard rapid footsteps from the tunnel. It was the Religious Police.

"In the name of the High Council, you are all under arrest!"

26

My third guided tour… sighed Pierre-Antoine. It is becoming tedious, but no other option. He was using an alias and had not shaved in three days to make himself less recognisable. His position as High Commissioner for Science and Technology was relatively low-profile, and most people had likely forgotten the face of France's last president. Despite this, he could not avoid the occasional *you look vaguely familiar* remark. Being a solo traveller on guided tours was not exactly his thing. It typically meant engaging in trivial conversations with people who wanted to socialize or introduce him to their own lone travelling companion. But, in the end, joining these tours seemed the most logical way to deceive any possible surveillance from the Chinese agents. *If there even was such a thing. My 'protectors' have not spotted anyone so far. No doubt they are likely roaming the world in more prominent locations than southern Scotland.*

"Ok folks, our coach is currently approaching the Kagyu Samye Ling Monastery," their guide said. "We'll stop at the car park and walk to the main complex. From there, two

229

options are available, guys. You can remain with me for a guided tour, with the opportunity to attend an exclusive Buddhist prayer session followed by a guided meditation. And that's included in your tour! For those who feel less religious, you can wander freely. Don't miss the monastery grounds with its statues and water features. And, of course, the beautiful temple. I expect you all to respect the monks' daily routine. Do not wander into the sections closed to the public, which are clearly displayed. It's 10:15. We'll stay here for about two to two hours and a half, lunch included. Next, we'll head north to Melrose Abbey. A tremendous day to connect with your spiritual side! Okay, here we are. Please follow me."

They got off the bus and walked together to the complex.

"Are you joining the guided tour Herve?" asked a woman.

"I am afraid not, Rachel," answered Pierre-Antoine. "I think I am going to wander by myself and hope to gather more inspiration for my book."

"Sure, I forgot about your book. Well, Evelyn and I will. We are quite excited about the prospect of the guided meditation," she said, giggling.

"Enjoy yourselves, then. I will see you back at the bus."

Besides himself and one other person, the rest of the group went together. Pierre-Antoine strolled through the gardens for a while, passing by the white stupa along the ponds decorated with auspicious symbols and prayer flags. He looked around without detecting any suspicious activity before heading towards the main building. The temple mixed Tibetan and local architecture. Its exterior did not possess the charms of an ancient Himalayan monastery but nevertheless created a vibe of peace and well-being. He entered the inner courtyard and began to think of the most effective strategy for achieving his mission. *The inner temple is not an option. Too crowded, like the library.* A monk in a traditional red and saffron robe came through.

"My apologies, Venerable Lama. May I interrupt you for a minute?"

"Of course. How may I assist you?"

"Well, my solicitation will seem rather unusual at first glance, but I need to speak to the abbot of this monastery about a significant matter. And, before you ask, I have no appointment."

"I do apologise, but our Venerable Abbot does not grant random audiences. But you are fortunate. As his personal assistant, I could set up an appointment for you in the upcoming days, depending on the relevance of your request."

"You are his personal assistant? I am in luck, indeed. Well, you see... I came here to deliver a message to the abbot that is of the utmost importance on behalf of the European government. I can provide official credentials. It is about a certain person who recently arrived here, whom you are probably familiar with if that helps. I am afraid I can only stay for two hours to avoid arousing suspicion. So, I would appreciate it if this meeting could be held immediately."

"I see... Please, follow me. We will be more comfortable discussing this in my office."

It took Pierre-Antoine precious minutes to justify his official position and the importance of his mission. The monk's prudence was completely understandable. He waited patiently in the office, expecting the police to debark anytime to apprehend this 'madman'. The monk returned after twenty minutes.

"Please follow me. Our Abbot, the Venerable Thekchen Rinpoche, will see you now."

They crossed a long hallway before reaching a rear door heading to the main outside road. They entered a large white house with painted red, deep blue and green window frames a minute later. The assistant led him into a spacious, Tibetan-styled room and asked him to sit before departing. Pierre-Antoine looked at the dark wooden walls covered with colourful thangkas and decorated with shelves containing small golden statues of Buddhas and Taras in various postures. At the far end stood a large desk with an impressively carved chair. The Abbot's main office, most certainly. A narrow door on the right opened, allowing a jovial man in his thirties wearing a saffron and red robe to enter.

"Good morning. I am Lama Thekchen Rinpoche, the Abbot of this monastery."

Pierre-Antoine joined his two hands and bowed to the monk.

"Venerable Thekchen, thank you for accepting to receive me on such short notice."

"Not at all. I beg you, remain seated. I would like to apologise for keeping you waiting. Still, you must understand we had to observe some precautions, especially in light of the circumstances."

"Understandable. Please, no need to apologise. I could have been anyone and was bound to act with discretion to maintain things as low profile as possible."

"We have not been properly introduced, though."

"My sincere apologies. My name is Pierre-Antoine Lascombes, High Commissioner for Science and Technology. President Stanisław Kowalczyk sent me here to deliver a message to His Holiness the 16th Dalai Lama. I would be grateful if you could forward it to him."

"It would be better done in person," he said with a broad grin. The little door opened again to a familiar Tibetan monk.

"Your Holiness, it is a rare honour," said Pierre-Antoine as he rose. "Forgive my attire, but I must avoid attracting attention."

"Please remain seated, High Commissioner," replied the Dalai Lama, smiling, "let us keep the formalities out for now."

"I will leave you alone," said the abbot. "My presence is required in the Temple. I will do my best to entertain your group a little longer to allow you more time. Someone will fetch you some tea. It was good meeting you, High Commissioner."

"Likewise, Venerable Abbot."

The Dalai Lama put a white khatang scarf around Pierre-Antoine's neck.

"Please, accept this offering as a gesture of friendship, and may the Buddha bless your path. I hear you have a message for me, Mister Lascombes?

"Indeed, Your Holiness. President Kowalczyk sends his regards and wishes to apologise for the secrecy in which he had to confine Your Holiness since your arrival. It has been made necessary by recent events and the preliminary stages of the peace process. He wants to reassure you that this is a temporary arrangement. As soon as the Indo-Pakistani Peace Conference is concluded — a matter of days now—

we will officially inform the rest of the world of your presence here. My government also wishes to confirm its intention to grant the protection and privileges associated with your person and your entourage."

"How generous of you." Please tell him my government and I appreciate all the care we have received so far. And I send my blessings for the peace process to reach a favourable conclusion. We did not contemplate the decision to leave India lightly, and we are appreciative of this warm welcome."

"I am certain he will be delighted to hear it, Your Holiness."

"I am just surprised he sent a cabinet member to forward this message. You undoubtedly have more important things to carry out than play the messenger."

"Well, Your Holiness, I happen to be here for personal reasons. And my position gives more credence to my mission than a modest emissary."

"May I ask what these personal reasons are, if not intruding?"

"Not at all. You see, I was diagnosed with a terminal illness. At most, I most likely barely have two more years to live, as all existing treatments have failed. I travelled here to try a new one on trial in Edinburgh. This is, somehow, my last chance, I suppose. I am scheduled to start the procedure tomorrow afternoon."

"We are unfortunate to hear this, High Commissioner. I will ask the Buddha to bestow upon you strength and serenity to assist you through this ordeal."

"Thank you, Your Holiness."

Someone knocked, and a reserved-looking monk appeared carrying a tray holding two teacups and a bronze teapot.

"Ah, tea! Excellent! Please, Jamyang, place it on the table. Have you ever had butter tea before, Mister Lascombes?" asked the Dalai Lama, presenting him with a cup.

"I had, Your Holiness. It was during my last official visit to India. I met your predecessor while president of France. I am quite fond of it, I must say."

"That is a splendid omen, Mister Lascombes, a splendid omen, indeed."

***

It was later in the night. Rinchen was in the abbot's office, and the two men were having tea together before retiring for the night.

"Well, it appears we will not disturb the serenity of your kind community for much longer, Venerable Thekchen. High Commissioner Lascombes seemed convinced that an agreement should be announced in the next few days. Once our presence becomes official, our little group will be able to move to a more convenient location and leave you to your responsibilities. The First Minister and I will be eternally grateful for your hospitality."

"You are welcome to stay here for whatever time it takes, Your Holiness. You are no disturbance to us."

"That is kind of you, Thekchen." He took a sip of the warm beverage. "But I am thinking of your authority as abbot. It will become embarrassing for me to remain here

235

for too long. And obviously, the members of the Government and Parliament cannot extend their stay either. You will ultimately be constantly disturbed by official delegations and stringent security measures. Believe me, it is quite unpleasant, and I have no right to impose this on all of you. No, we should leave at some point. High Commissioner Lascombes pressed that Norway was not convenient, and President Kowalczyk insisted that we remain in Scotland. But he was also preoccupied with the monastery being too exposed and close to the border with England. They are still discussing a more appropriate location with the Scottish government."

"With your permission, Your Holiness, I might offer you a solution."

"Of course."

"As a result of several extremely generous donations, we recently purchased a modest property surrounded by land on the outskirts of Edinburgh. We intend to transform it into a Buddhist cultural and religious centre. Rather, allow me to lend it to you and the government for a nominal amount. You can all move right away. It offers multiple possibilities to accommodate a monastery, a temple, and our Administration's offices. I know several benefactors who would be thrilled to fund it."

"This is a highly generous and thoughtful offer. But I cannot deprive you of your initial plans. It would be unreasonable.

"Quite the opposite, I insist. Consider this my gift for your forthcoming ascension, which must occur as soon as your presence is formally announced. The First Minister is right. It would be best if you consolidated your legitimacy in the eyes of the diaspora as soon as possible. And I am confident you will still find a little corner big enough to host my cultural centre. I am also thinking about the benefits and aura your presence will bring to our small community. Please, I insist."

"All right, I accept."

"Good! I will promptly begin organising your move."

27

"We placed our trust in you, Archdeacon," admonished the Patriarch. "Look how you rewarded us back. Betrayal!"

Shenouda had spent four days being interrogated about his role in the whole affair while being detained in one of the main police building's cells. But he experienced no guilt at all.

"I fail to see what in this whole affair qualifies as a betrayal."

"You allowed these men enter that... place without notifying us. Do you realise the consequences?"

"I did nothing. The wall collapsed due to the earthquake, entitling Professor Walters and Professor Degrenes to enter the room freely. What else am I supposed to declare? That it was God's deed?"

"God's deed?! This infamy has nothing to do with God if not the Devil himself! Do you realise the terrible ramifications if that ominous... thing was revealed to the outside world? It could cast doubt on millennia of beliefs or spark religious strife. Luckily for us, it has all the signs of a preposterous fake. A conspicuous plot initiated by these two evil henchmen desperately trying to discredit the faiths of billions to justify their atheism. Make no mistake; we uncovered hidden documents indicating without a doubt their association with an atheist organisation dedicated to crippling religious influence in civil society. And you were their accomplice the whole time!"

"I was no such thing!"

"Then your naivety enabled them to manipulate you, which is an even greater offence."

"How dare you throw such accusations at me, Your Beatitude? I have been a devoted servant of God and the Holy Church my whole life. And just so you know, the contents of this room can't have been created recently. I saw the inscriptions on the wall and the artefacts found there. Such work would require weeks to complete, employing highly trained craftsmen. This chamber is located in one of the most scrutinised places on Earth, with a single access. There is no way anyone could have planted it without being detected. Unless you suspect the Grand Mufti to be complicit too?"

"Do not insult my intelligence, Archdeacon."

"Then the only conclusion is that everything there is simply genuine! Your denial is a dismay of the clear truth."

"The clear truth? What truth are you referring to, Archdeacon? Please, indulge me…" He was looking at him malevolently.

"The truth, Your Beatitude, is quite manifest from what I have seen. The Israelite tribes settled in Egypt much later than most scholars believed. Most likely towards the end of the reign of Amenhotep III. After his death, under Joseph's leadership, they adopted the cult of Aten and supported

Akhenaten's religious changes. In their eyes, the Pharaoh's conversion could have only been initiated by the God of Abraham embodied by the Solar Disc. It was their revelation. Imagine! Semites, Canaanites, and Egyptians together, bound in their faith in one God as they constructed the new capital of Egypt, Akhet-Aten. A city dedicated to universal acceptance and the service of God. The beacon of a new hope. But when Akhenaten died, the old priesthood succeeded in regaining control and, as a result, destroyed what they considered heretical and enslaved them all. Till Moses came along. Can't you see it? It looks so indisputable. This is the genesis of the Nation of Israel. The servitude, the Exodus, and the Temple in Jerusalem are all connected with the Amarna period. Erecting that stela under the precise spot where God asked Abraham to sacrifice Joseph's grandfather was no coincidence. It was a statement to future generations. But, ultimately, it ended in the shadows. They had to hide this testament of their faith under the command of Pharaoh Shoshenq I. The true face of God was to become invisible so that their beliefs would survive and its glory would embrace the world. Think of this. The words of the Great Hymn to Aten are encountered in the three Revealed Scriptures. Altered in their formulation, assuredly. Yet alive in their meaning. It is a reminder that God and the Aten are a single entity!"

"Heresy! Blasphemy! A fairy tale created by your illusory mind to justify your actions and cover your betrayal. You are forsaking your faith, our faith."

"A faith that is deeply entangled in lies. Look at the evidence again, Your Beatitude. The presence of the cherubim in the tunnel is a clear manifesto that the

240

chamber was still used as a place of worship in the days of Solomon. David and Solomon lived alongside the Aten! But we have nothing to fear; God's message is still there, don't you see? This is the long-awaited opportunity to set our religious differences aside, to end millennia of senseless theological conflicts."

"How valuable is the message of our Lord Jesus Christ if it comes from the demented son of a heathen divinity? How worthy is the message of Mohammed if the Archangel Gabriel is no more than the delusion of a fasting man? And how worth are the Prophets' words if their forefathers were lunatics who blindly worshipped an Egyptian divinity under the direction of a schizophrenic pharaoh? Enlighten me, Archdeacon. How do you intend to explain to billions of devout souls that they have been following an aberration for generations? Explain me!"

"Repentance."

The patriarch's face turned colourless.

"Repentance? Repentance! Have you gone insane? Are you suffering from a concussion caused by a stone falling on your head during this earthquake? Or under the influence of some drugs? Do you want to be the cause of the largest religious conflagration ever seen in the history of mankind?"

"No, Your Eminence. God has finally revealed himself to me, to us. He has been guiding my path since Egypt. I thought I was delusional, but I was just blind and refusing to accept the truth. I accept it now, and so can anybody. Let us proclaim the evidence while expiating our past mistakes and misguidance as men of God."

"... I fear we lost him completely. I do not believe he is performing an act. Whatever happened in that room that night has completely altered his reason."

Patriarch Nicodemus II finished reporting Shenouda's condition to the rest of the High Council. He stopped walking in circles and faced his colleagues. Their faces displayed a mixture of scepticism and discomfort. They were all assembled at the Metropolitan's office of the Coptic Orthodox Patriarchate.

"Fortunately," said Cardinal del Pietro, "we kept him low-profiled. His disappearance will scarcely be noticed."

"His disappearance, Your Eminence?" asked Metropolitan Tawadros. "What disappearance are you referring to?" The prelate stared at him suspiciously.

"You do not expect us to allow a ranked cleric of the Eastern Church to roam the streets of Jerusalem, preaching his paranoid theories, do you?"

"Neither do I expect him to disappear, Your Eminence. He is still a servant of God, for Christ's sake!"

"Which God?"

"It would be wise to set aside your Christian rabble for now," interrupted the Grand Mufti. "We have to concentrate on more important issues. The two archaeologists, for instance."

"They will be expeditiously tried and sentenced to twenty-five years in solitary confinement under religious section 43," answered the Patriarch. "No public proceedings. At the end of their sentence, their existence and their work would be completely forgotten. We will make sure of it."

"But, what about the stela?" asked the Chief Rabbi. "This is unquestionably a crucial issue."

"It must be rapidly destroyed, and all traces of its existence with it!" urged the Metropolitan. "We should take no unconsidered risk."

"To destroy it is to risk creating more witnesses than we already have," declared the Grand Mufti while sitting down. "We need to consider this option carefully. Unless some of you feel physically strong enough to execute the task themselves. For my part, I am too old for this, not to mention lacking such skills."

"Witnesses can be eliminated."

"Disappear, eliminated. Cardinal del Pietro, does Your Eminence always resort to extreme solutions to resolve complex issues?" asked the Metropolitan.

"They possess the merit to be radical, Your Beatitude. It would not be the first artefact to conveniently vanish from world history."

"And here we go again—"

"Alright, this debate is turning sterile," interrupted the Patriarch with a clap of his hands. "To begin, I suggest sealing the room and the tunnel again, which seemed the most effective solution the Egyptians and Templars could find. Then, when the other issues are sorted, settled, and calm is restored, we will think of the most appropriate strategy to adopt regarding the stela. Things are more manageable when the storm is gone—"

He stopped at the sound of someone banging on the door. It was the Metropolitan's personal assistant.

"Your Beatitude, Your Beatitude! I apologise for interrupting the High Council, but there is something you urgently need to see!"

"Come in, Nazeer," said the Metropolitan.

Nazeer was deeply agitated, holding a holotablet in his hands.

"Your Beatitudes, Your Eminences, you must watch this. This video appeared on social media half an hour ago and has already reached more than twenty thousand viewers on this site alone."

They watched the holo-video and instantly panicked. At first, it showed nothing but a large cloud of dust. People could be heard coughing in the background. *Is everyone alright?* asked a voice, followed by undistinctive answers. Then, after several seconds and more inaudible words, a glaring light revealed the hidden chamber. The front carving and the two cherubs at the back were plainly visible. *Shenouda, can you read it?* Then the Archdeacon appeared on the screen, looking petrified before falling to his knees and saying: *Joseph, son of Jacob, son of Isaac, son of Abraham, may he live and prosper in the benevolent light of the Aten.* Finally, at the end of the video, a voice shouted, *In the name of the High Council, you are all under arrest!*

"Holy Mother of God!" yelled the Metropolitan, falling from his chair. "This is a disaster. We are all doomed!"

"How on earth did this video reach social media?!" asked the Grand Mufti. "I thought it had been intercepted and destroyed. Is there a traitor among us?"

"Please, Your Eminence," said the Cardinal calmly. "Why would any of us want to make public such heresy at the risk of undermining its church? And our Police units are beyond suspicion. No, it has to come from some other concealed device. The National Geographics' team? We need to trace it."

"I agree. However, the video is now public. We must act promptly to have it removed or alter its authenticity before too many people watch it and the situation escapes us. Particularly since it involves us directly."

"You are right, as always, Chief Rabbi," said the Patriarch. "We need to issue a unified official denial and declare this video a fake made by anarchist extremists trying to destabilise our institutions or something like that. We will release it as soon as the media starts talking about it, which should not be long. Acting before will arouse suspicion. When done, we consider the incident closed and no longer comment on the matter further to avoid controversy. Once we take over the situation, this incident will die as soon as it is out. You know how flighty people's minds are."

"What about Archdeacon Shenouda?" asked Cardinal del Pietro. "He is perfectly recognisable on the video, and his name is clearly audible—"

"I was coming to that. The archdeacon must disappear from the public eye." He heard a gasp. "Do not worry, Tawadros, not the way the Cardinal suggested. No, we need to discreetly exfiltrate him out of Jerusalem, no later than tonight, to a secure location. And I know a perfect one."

28

Pierre-Antoine slowly opened his eyes. His vision was distorted. He was feeling giddy and slightly nauseous. His left pelvic bone was sore. Before the procedure, the surgeon informed him of the possible side effects but told him they would eventually recede within forty-eight hours. One week in observation, and he would be free to leave.

His eyesight was gradually coming back. He was lying on a slightly reclined bed with blood transfusion and fluids perfusion tubes on his right arm. The regular beep of the heart monitor resonated in the background. Voices were echoing around him. One of them was Monika's. The successful conclusion of the Peace Conference a few days ago enabled her to be present for the procedure. She was whispering to someone who responded with an Italian accent. *Doctor Caracciolo, of course.* His vision had nearly returned to normal, and he could discern them sitting beside each other, wearing face masks. Pierre-Antoine started to move a bit and grunted. The sound captured Monika's attention.

"Look, Doctor, he is conscious."

The scientist approached his bed.

"Mister Lascombes, do you hear me?"

"Loud and clear, Doctor," Pierre-Antoine answered with a cracking voice.

"How do you feel right now?"

"Groggy, somewhat nauseous. My pelvis is kind of sore."

"This is quite normal, as you were informed earlier. We are administering you a moderate dose of morphine today, just to facilitate things, until tomorrow. Then, normal painkillers. The ache should wear off within a couple of days. You may find sitting for a long time or climbing stairs uncomfortable for a week."

"I see."

"Right. You'll be glad to hear the procedure went very well. As I explained a week ago, a dose of the genetically modified virus compound we have created in the lab has been injected directly into your pelvic bone. The remaining solution is being transfused directly into your bloodstream. We will keep you on observation for a week, and then you will be free to leave! Next, we wait and see. But I am very optimistic. I can see your lips are slightly dry. I will ask the nurse to give you some beverages in addition to the fluids you are receiving."

"Thank you, Doctor."

"Very good! I leave you now in the caring hands of Mrs Richter and will see you again in two days for a few tests. In the meantime, rest."

Giancarlo walked out with a satisfied look on his face. Monika moved her chair next to Pierre-Antoine.

"I am pleased you managed to come, Monika. I told you several times not to, but now I am glad you did not listen to me."

"I am pleased to see you too, Pierre-Antoine. Of course, I had to come! We have been close friends for so long. I needed to make sure everything was fine. Doctor Caracciolo sounds like a competent young man. I feel safe with you under his care."

"Yes, he is. How are things in Strasbourg?"

"They are fine. The conference proved a prodigious success. Your suggestion to involve the Russians was a clever move. And we used the outcome to minimise the announcement of the Dalai Lama's presence in Scotland. India and Pakistan have both given their support, and the African and South American unions their assurances. The other countries remained neutral. We have successfully isolated China diplomatically! At least temporarily."

"It was my idea, but to you goes all the credit to convincing our President to accept it. There is a reason you are in charge of our diplomacy, Monika."

She flushed.

"The trick is always to make them believe the idea comes from them. Especially those with an oversized ego. I never forgot that lesson of yours when we were at university. How was your meeting with the new Dalai Lama?"

"We got surprisingly close. He is a brilliant man, gifted with wisdom. He reminds me very much of the 14th Dalai Lama. Their various shared characteristics have almost convinced me of reincarnation. The whole group of refugees has moved to a massive estate called Craig House in Edinburgh's southwest suburbs. It belongs to the Kagyu Samye Ling Monastery, which recently acquired it. I believe through some pretty substantial donations. You should see the size of the building! His Holiness immediately complained that it was too vast for his needs and that he did not require a second Potala Palace. However, Jorge and Fabjian unanimously approved the location, built on a small hill and surrounded by a spacious park. Great for ensuring effective protection, they say. Combined with the pressure from the exiled Tibetan Government and Parliament members, His Holiness eventually gave in."

A nurse entered the room, carrying a glass of water and a small cup filled with multicoloured tablets.

"Alright, Pierre-Antoine, get some rest. I will go back to the apartment and return tomorrow. I will call Jorge tonight to let him know the good news. See you tomorrow."

"Thank you again for calling on me, Monika. Enjoy your night. I do recommend the restaurant down Newhaven Road. I left a note in the kitchen."

***

Monika removed some books from her bag that she intended to read aloud to Pierre-Antoine, as she had done in the past couple days. Doctor Caracciolo entered the hospital room with a beaming grin on his face.

"Good morning, Sir. Despite yesterday's little blood-sucking and CAT scan, I guess you are feeling better today."

"Good morning, Doctor. Indeed, I have improved significantly in the past twenty-four hours. I feel rejuvenated."

"Excellent! I am pleased to inform you that the test results are extremely encouraging. We are seeing a significant drop in the ratio of cancer cells in your blood. The scan shows a dramatic reduction of the two tumours on your cervical lymph nodes."

Pierre-Antoine eyes opened wide with surprise.

"My apologies for not mentioning this detail a week ago following your body scan. The good news is you appear to respond very well to the treatment, even above my expectations. And, at this point, you display no side effects, which is even more encouraging. Naturally, we should not get overly excited as this is an early stage in the treatment. But I am quite confident for our success."

Monika rushed to his side.

"Do you hear it, Pierre-Antoine! This is incredible news! I am so happy for you." She turned to the researcher and started to shake his hand. "Thank you so much, Doctor, for all you have done at this stage," her eyes were misty with joy. "It is clear in my mind now that my personal assistant being a cousin of yours was no coincidence. There must be a divine hand at work here—"

"Monika, come on!"

"Thank you, Mrs Richter. Well, as I said, let us remain cautious. Clearly, I will not dare to speculate on the possible existence of higher beings. Still, I am glad my cousin was a factor in this fortunate encounter. She gave me my first patient. On that encouraging note, if you forgive me, I must return to the lab. I will see you tomorrow." He walked away.

"Monika, what went through your mind to say something so ludicrous?"

"Pierre-Antoine, you know me; I was simply overcome by joy. I know you are not a religious person. But do not dare to criticise my beliefs in moments like these. It is no mystery to you that I am very attached to them, even though I have the courtesy of never expressing them publicly. Doctor Caracciolo was born into a traditional Italian aristocratic family. I am sure he did not mind. So, shush! And now, a bit of reading." She took a voluminous book in her right hand. "Look what I brought! That should keep us occupied."

"War and Peace? You want to finish me off! They have a holo-cinema here; I would not mind a good movie."

"Shush again, I know it is one of your favourites, and I am the one taking care of you. Therefore, I decide what is best." She sat comfortably and began to read.

"Book I: 1805, Chapter One,

Well, Prince, so Genoa and Lucca are now just family estates of the Buonapartes. But I warn you, if you don't tell me that this means war, if you still try to defend the infamies and horrors perpetrated by that Antichrist, I really believe he is Antichrist, I will have nothing more to do with you and you are no longer my friend…"

Monika's narration was quite soothing. Pierre-Antoine listened silently, enjoying the moment. After a few minutes, his left leg started to bother him a little, like a tingling sensation.

"… *Prince Vasili did not reply, though, with the quickness of memory and perception befitting a man of the world, he indicated by a movement of the head that he was considering this information…*"

The uncomfortable sensation now extended to his right leg, followed by the remainder of his lower body. His mouth became dry, and he felt his heartbeat quickening.

"… *Listen, dear Annette,' said the prince, suddenly taking Anna Pavlovna's hand and for some reason drawing it downwards. 'Arrange that affair for me and I shall always be your most devoted slave…*"

His breathing became difficult, and his right hand was shaking. He tried to speak, but his mouth refused to budge. A sudden feeling of panic overcame him.

"… *The highest Petersburg society was assembled there: people differing widely in age and character but alike in the social circle to which—*"

Monika stopped abruptly, alerted by the gurgling coming from her friend's bed. When she looked up, she saw Pierre-Antoine convulsing uncontrollably. His entire body contorted up and down as his arms and legs shifted erratically. His eyes were glazy, and he was gasping for air like a dying fish. She immediately pressed the alarm button.

"Nurse, nurse! Someone, please! I need help! My friend is dying!"

29

Like every late afternoon, Shenouda strolled along the monastery's cloister before dinner. It was the only time of the day his gaolers permitted him to leave his cell. Clearly neglected, the surrounding gardens painted a bleak picture. A tall palm tree was growing amid a series of iron arches covered by climbing roses struggling to thrive. The remnants of some broken antique marble columns completed the scene. It was a pathetic view. At least he could gaze at the azure sky and lush hills in the background. Sombre clouds were gathering on the horizon, heralding the arrival of another storm. The third in five days. Once a week, he was granted permission to walk on the east walls under close supervision; his hands clenched with handcuffs to slow down any escape attempt. *Like a petty criminal! And to escape where?* It, however, allowed him to stretch up to the leaning tower and gaze out over the blue waters of the Sea of Galilee. They brought back fond memories of the magnificent Nile River and his native country. *Will I see the land of my ancestors ever again, he thought. How long will I be trapped in this austere fortress?*

The night after his interrogation, he was hastily transferred to the Greek Orthodox monastery of the Twelve Apostles in Tiberias upon instruction from the patriarch. Only for his protection, they informed him. That was more than three weeks ago. *My protection? Protected I am, and quite well! And deprived of any freedom of movement. This is a prison. The only thing that it is protecting is them!*

The monastery was an ancient Crusader and Ottoman bastion transformed into a religious building in 1867. While it retained much of its distinctive military characteristics, the dark stones used for the renovation added a gloomy touch.

His only 'freedom zone' was in his cell. Even there, he suspected the presence of spying devices. The weeks had gone by in solitude, except for his warden, Brother Dimitri. A sinister Greek Orthodox monk who resembled a bouncer more than a cleric. On the day he arrived, he met the abbot, who advised him to pray every day for the salvation of his soul. His soul? It was split between his commitment to his faith and the incredible revelation he received. His right hand reached his upper chest. Beneath his cassock, he felt the engraved ring bearing the Eye of Ra clinging to a golden chain, invisible to all. He had become overly attached to it following the recent events, bringing him solace, unlike the Holy Cross tied next to it. The disappointing attitude of his alleged brothers in the faith had altered how he looked at them. They appeared more and more like strangers. However, there were times when he prayed for Christ's protection and the comfort of the Holy Mother. Or were they Akhenaten and Nefertiti? He did not know anymore. His mind was troubled, confused, shattered. *What am I meant to believe?* He fell to his knees and looked at the heavens in despair. *I need a sign. Please, give me a sign!*

"Archdeacon?" interrupted a deep voice. It was his 'carer'.

He rose to his feet.

"Yes, Brother Dimitri?"

"Archdeacon, you have visitors. Follow me into the refectory, please. I have to put them on," he added, handcuffing him.

The refectory was empty, except for three men sitting at the table. Shenouda instantly recognised Chief Rabbi Eliyahu, Great Mufti Amin al-Sabri and Cardinal del Pietro. As soon as he entered, the Chief Rabbi approached him.

"Shenouda, my boy. How nice to see you!" He noticed the handcuffs and addressed the orthodox monk. "Is that really necessary?"

"These are strict instructions from His Beatitude, Chief Rabbi," Brother Dimitri answered. "Archdeacon Wahba has to wear them whenever he leaves his cell."

"Unfortunate... Well, we do not want to displease His Beatitude, I suppose. Follow me, Archdeacon. Come and sit with us."

They walked to the table and sat while the other two men nodded.

"How are you, my boy? Are they treating you properly?"

"Chief Rabbi, thank you for your kind solicitude, but I doubt the purpose of your presence is to inquire about the conditions of my confinement. I have been cast away for the last three weeks without explanation, so what do you want from me? And where are Professor Walters and Professor Degrenes?"

"We understand your bitterness, Archdeacon, but we felt it necessary to remove you from the public eye temporarily," the Grand Mufti replied. "That video had quite a damaging impact, you see, and you were clearly recognisable. The sole purpose of all this secrecy is to protect you. We have received reports that certain extremist religious groups are actively seeking you, and we sincerely fear for your safety—"

"And these, Grand Mufti?" interrupted Shenouda, presenting his cuffed hands. "Are they for my protection as well? And what video are you speaking of?"

"Well, my boy," answered the Chief Rabbi, "the footage of the moments of your inopportune discovery has regrettably found its way into social media and the news network. We are still seeking its source."

"And as for your two acolytes, continued the cardinal, let's say they have been neutralised for the next decades from doing further harm."

"You... you murdered them?"

"Well, if it had been my call... But no, Archdeacon. You can rest assured no physical harm was done to them. We have simply implemented draconian measures to ensure they are quickly forgotten. The Sinai Peninsula is an ideal place to reflect and meditate on the wrongs of the past."

"And you profess to be servants of God. You are just pathetic schemers working together to secure your influence!"

"It is because we are servants of God that we have had to take action to preserve his message, Archdeacon," replied the Grand Mufti. "As a man of faith yourself, you certainly comprehend the forces involved."

"We must adopt all necessary measures to safeguard the delicate balance that has been forged throughout so many millennials," the Chief Rabbi added.

"Deus Vult," concluded the cardinal.

"Regrettably, your little plot seems to be compromised by this video, it seems," said Shenouda, sarcastically.

"You see! I told you it was him!" burst the Cardinal.

"Was it truly you, Archdeacon? Have you really perpetrated this sin?"

"I wish I had, Grand Mufti. I wish I had. But whoever did it has rendered a valuable service to humanity!"

"Apostate!" yelled the Cardinal, pounding its fists on the table.

Shenouda gave him a defiant look.

"If the reason for your visit is to obtain my confession, I am afraid you are heading for a great disappointment."

"As it happens, Archdeacon," declared the Chief Rabbi, "we are here for something else, yet still linked to this horrid video. You see, despite our united efforts to deny its genuineness, we found ourselves under pressure from certain religious fringes who believe the High Council should adopt a more prominent stance on the matter. Some suggested a public trial. But we object to the idea. We are concerned it would cause the opposite effect by drawing attention to the story and those behind it and granting them more credit. Others specifically demand that you appear publicly to clarify the rumours circulating about you. We are more inclined to consider this option. We—"

"Archdeacon," interrupted the Grand Mufti, "in short, we require you to refute this video and condemn its content publicly and completely. But also to resolutely reprove the exactions of those two archaeologists, those heathens, who clearly conspired to cast doubt on the beliefs of billions of faithful. Finally, you will exhort forgiveness for your lack of judgment in this whole affair and offer atonement for your sins."

"Atonement for my sins?! But what of yours, Your Eminences? Look at the three of you, the ultimate vision for religious harmony. Divided in faith, but united in crime." He gave them a disgusted look. Then a thought crossed his mind. "And supposing I accept your demands, what will I get in return? I guess you are not expecting me to consent as an act of good will?"

"At last, you finally come to your senses! I was confident we would come to an understanding," said the Chief Rabbi. "We have long discussed a substantive reward for this small sacrifice we ask of you. For the greater good, obviously. We want to offer you the position of Abbot of the St Catherine's Monastery on Mount Sinai. Although a Greek Orthodox monastery and you being Coptic, we have managed to overcome the slight reluctance raised among some members of the High Council..."

Aaah, that explains the absence of the other two...

"... This is a tremendous offer, and it would be unwise to reject it, especially looking at your current situation."

"And it will ensure my convenient removal from the public eye. While allowing me to follow in the footsteps of Moses for the next forty years, in search of God's Promised Land—"

"Excuse me for interrupting, but what are you holding with your hand?" asked Cardinal del Pietro.

Shenouda suddenly realised that he had unconsciously grasped his ring through his robes. He released it straight away.

"Nothing of interest, Eminence."

"On the contrary, it seems of great interest to me." Brother, please?"

Brother Dimitri, who had been waiting patiently beside the refectory door, barring the way, approached the Apostolic Nuncio.

"Hold this man, will you?"

The monk forcefully grabbed Shenouda by the shoulders while the cardinal searched him.

"Ah ha! What do we have here?" He picked up the shiny gold band attached to a chain and looked at it. Within seconds, his face blemished. "How did you come in possession of this? Answer me!" The prelate stared directly into the archdeacon's eyes. "How… No, that is impossible. You… You cannot be…"

The sound of a distant rumbling interrupted him.

"Give it back; it's mine!"

Shenouda ripped the ring from the cardinal, who fell to the ground and violently hit his head on the table's corner, splashing blood everywhere. Brother Dimitri rushed to help del Pietro while the other two clerics retreated in dismay. Taking advantage of the confusion, the archdeacon hurried outside, blockading the door behind him. *Where should I go? The alarm will be raised shortly.* The elements were raging around him. The sky was pitch-black, strewn with lightning, and pierced by thunderclaps. Heavy rain suddenly fell, rapidly soaking his garments. *The tower!* He swiftly climbed the staircases leading to the east wall. The Sea of Galilee was restless, tormented by strong wings violently crashing tall waves against the monastery's outer defences. Shenouda heard screams coming from behind. *They are here!* In haste, he reached the leaning tower assailed by the enraged waters. The voices were approaching.

"Shenouda!" shouted the Chief Rabbi, followed closely by the Grand Mufti. His damp hair was blowing around erratically in the wind. "Shenouda, stop for the love of God! Do not make any inconsiderate choices. Think about your everlasting soul!"

"For the love of God?" Shenouda yelled back. "Which God, Rabbi? Tell me!"

"Please, you are only confused. Come back, I implore you. We will take care of you." The religious leader closed in.

"Do not approach me further; I am warning you!" In a provocative gesture, the cleric raised his handcuffed hands towards the sky. "Look, Rabbi, look around you! Your God is speaking. Look at the Sea of Galilee, the Sea of Chinnereth, on whose bank the Messiah will rise again, where the Apostles saw Jesus walk on its surface. Behold the wrath of God, Rabbi! Fear his judgment! You will all be judged!" He stepped on the edge of the tower.

"Archdeacon! This is madness!" screamed the Grand Mufti. The howling of the wind was partially muffling his voice. "Step down!"

At that precise moment, a formidable lightning bolt struck the tip of the bell tower next to them in a thunderous cracking noise. The metal cross at the top caught fire and began melting in a viscous incandescent liquid. Shenouda stared at them with demented eyes.

"The sign! The sign!"

Then, a second lightning bolt struck Shenouda's handcuffs in an intense flash of light, shoving him into the waters below.

"Noooo!" The Rabbi screamed, running to the edge. At the bottom of the wall, the waves were dancing frantically. There was no sign of the Archdeacon. Brother Dimitri arrived, panting. "The Cardinal?" The monk shook his head. "Send word to our friends. I want an extensive search to be organised as soon as this storm is over. Find Archdeacon Shenouda, alive or dead!"

30

"His condition has remained unchanged for ten days now, Doctor. There has to be something that can be done!"

"I am sorry, Ma'am, we have explored all possibilities so far," the hospital's physician answered. "We placed him in a medically induced coma to halt his body gradually shutting down. He has now stabilised and responds favourably to all treatments. All I can say is something seems to be blocking his consciousness. Perhaps a protective instinctive reaction in response to the sudden aggression on his immune system. This has been reported multiple times in the past. His encephalogram shows clear, vivid brain activity. He is alive, physiologically speaking, but not present with us. I can merely reiterate what I have advised you these last few days. We must wait. It might be brief; it might be prolonged. Now, if you'll excuse me, I have other patients to attend to."

He left Monika alone. She began losing faith and being overwhelmed by a terrible sense of guilt. After all, she was the one who convinced Pierre-Antoine to go through this new cancer treatment, and now he was in a coma. The first two days following his unexpected reaction had been dreadful. Her lifelong friend had to be resuscitated three times. The second time took nearly an hour. Pierre-Antoine would have been pronounced dead if not for her insistence. His vital organs failed one after the other before miraculously functioning again. Finally, on the third day, his entire body stabilised and recovered. She observed him. He seemed peacefully asleep, breathing slowly, even smiling. Every now and then, his eyes rolled frantically under his eyelids. The only visible indication of brain activity. She sensed a presence at her side. It was Jorge, who had arrived the day before.

"Here is your coffee, Monika. You should have some rest; the nurses told me you barely slept for the last five days."

She looked at him in despair, with tears in her eyes.

"How can I sleep, Jorge? It is all my fault!"

"Come on, Monika. You perfectly know it is not your fault. You have been friend with Pierre-Antoine long enough to realise he is not the suggestible type. His decisions are always well thought through. He would have refused to participate in the experiment if he had the slightest doubt. So, keep the guilt away. It was his choice, his way of showing us that he wanted to fight the odds. And he continues to fight. Look at what the doctors are saying."

"But... I feel so... powerless."

"I think you should return to Strasbourg for a couple of days, catch up on your homework and relax. Also, the President is asking for you. I will look after him in your absence."

"No, I cannot go. I cannot leave him until he returns to us and improves. Just allow me two or three more days, and then I promise to take a break. And regarding the President, I will talk to him via video link this afternoon."

"Alright, but only two or three days. I shall see to it. Now drink your coffee before it gets cold," he told her with a gentle smile before sitting down.

Doctor Caracciolo entered in haste, making Monika jump from her chair.

"You! Where have you been for the past three days?! Look at him! You exploited him, and now he is no longer your concern!"

"If I may—" started Giancarlo.

"I do not need your apologies. You… you… sorcerer's apprentice!"

"Monika, please calm down," said Jorge, returning her to her seat. "Please, doctor, forgive her. She has barely slept for several days due to her anxiety."

"Do not worry, Mister Sanchez. Her anger is completely understandable. And I have effectively been missing for three days. But I needed to run a few more tests to confirm the recent results. At least, I am the bearer of astounding news. We performed a complete series of tests, again and again, as well as a full body scan yesterday. This is incredible! The cancer has just… gone!"

"What?" gasped Jorge.

"I am unable to explain it myself. And I do not mean remission. Nothing remains of it. And your brother appears to have developed an immune response to any recurrence. We exposed various types of cancer cells to his blood samples, and they were systematically eliminated. This is practically like… like a… miracle."

"My god! Are you hearing this, Monika?"

"Your miracle has left him in a coma, Doctor! A healed man in an unconscious state."

"Mrs Richter, I do understand how upset you are, but I never lied to him. Mister Lascombes fully understood that it was an innovative treatment and that side effects were part of the risk. However, there is no rational explanation for his condition. Physiologically, he is perfectly healthy—"

"Am I interrupting anything?" inquired a voice behind them. Three men wearing red and saffron robes were standing by the doorway.

"Your Holiness!" choked Jorge. "What an unexpected surprise! How come?"

"I was only informed about my good friend's condition yesterday evening. Otherwise, I would have come sooner. I hope this is not a bad time?"

"On the contrary, please come."

The 16th Dalai Lama entered the room whilst Kalsang and Jamyang remained outside. He quietly came near Pierre-Antoine's bed.

"What happened to him? I know he started this new treatment several days ago. It did not work?"

"I fear having bittersweet news, Your Holiness. Doctor Caracciolo has just informed us that my brother is apparently completely cured. However, he has been in this state for over a week since being out of an induced coma. According to the physicians, his general condition is excellent. Except he remains unable or unwilling to regain consciousness. It's beyond my comprehension."

Rinchen approached Pierre-Antoine and, to others' surprise, began to sniff his face before pressing his forehead to his.

"I see… Rather surprising, indeed."

"Is everything alright, Your Holiness?" asked Monika, wiping her tears with a tissue.

"Well, his condition reminds me of something remarkably similar I witnessed as a novice monk in Tawang Monastery. One of our senior lamas had a deep inclination for long solitary meditations. He was quite adept, I must say, and the most accomplished teacher in this field of practice. What was his name? … Oh yes! Venerable Tinley Lama. It means something like enlightened activity in my mother tongue. A quite well-suited name." He squeezed his chin. "Anyway. One day, our abbot was called in a hurry. Venerable Tinley was missing from his teaching session and found nowhere around the monastery. Due to his advanced age, the abbot rapidly organised a search. Our venerable teacher was eventually discovered in a deep meditative state at the foot of a banyan tree near the forest trail. You know, the type of tree under which our beloved Gautama Buddha achieved enlightenment. But after a few minutes, despite repeated efforts, no one could wake him up. The abbot concluded he was about to die by the sound of his weak breath. Therefore, his body was returned to the temple, and we began preparing the death rituals. Meanwhile, our brothers took turns chanting mantras seated around him. Two days later, Venerable Tinley was still barely breathing while showing no sign of being on death's doorstep. Then, suddenly, his eyes opened. He was quite surprised to find himself lying in the main temple surrounded by his brothers. Even more surprised when we told him he had been lying there for a couple of days. In his mind, he had barely left for a few hours. He told us he travelled throughout the universe, going from place to place until he

266

perceived the sound of our chanting mantras that eventually called him back. I'll spare you further details."

"Um, a fascinating story, Your Holiness, but I am not sure it has anything—"

"Silence, Jorge!" interrupted Monika. "I completely understand what His Holiness is suggesting. Please, proceed. I am that desperate, Jorge. And we have nothing to lose."

"I shall help in any way I can." Rinchen turned to the two monks standing by the door. "Kalsang, fetch some of our brothers here. We must start immediately."

The scene unfolding in front of the hospital staff was surreal. 'OM AH HUM VAJRA GURU PADMA SIDDHI HUM'. The Tibetan monks had been chanting the monotonous, deep litany in shifts for more than twelve hours. Despite minor concerns from the nurses, some personal touches were added to the room: a colourful thangka representing the five Tathagatas, a heavy incense burner, and a sizeable rug on which the monks prayed. The Dalai Lama was sitting in the lotus position on a separate carpet while reciting prayers, holding his mala bracelet in his right hand. And finally, Monika sat next to Pierre-Antoine's bed, stringing a rosary.

"Do you really approve of this?" Giancarlo asked Jorge.

"No more than any of the alternatives. And it seems to please Monika. What more can I ask for? And as a Spaniard, it's part of my DNA. Surely, being Italian, you understand."

"Let's say God and I are not on the best terms since my mother died."

"We all get to question our beliefs at one point in our life, Doctor. However, I long concluded that most human beings need to believe in something that gives them hope. It is in their genes. It may be religious, spiritual or otherwise. See Monika? Who would imagine that the ex-German Chancellor, High Commissioner for Foreign Affairs, the woman who showed so much assertiveness throughout her political career, is such a devout Catholic?"

"But are those two involved?"

"What do you mean? Romantically? Monika and Pierre-Antoine?" He laughed. "Don't be daft! My brother is openly gay. No, Doctor, the relationship between these two transcends sex or friendship. They share a deep connection that defies any rational explanation."

"But you seem very close to your brother and her."

"I am, but differently. I act more like a catalyser. I need them, and they need me. Our symbiosis is rather difficult to apprehend, believe me," he chuckled. "But, unlike them, I do not require their constant presence. If my wife were here, I am sure she would come up with a more rational explanation. She is an expert at this kind of thing..."

Monika was devotedly going through the beads of her rosary, one after one, her eyes closed. Ten Hail Mary followed by an Our Father, then again. Her mind was quiet, focusing on the words she was reciting in her head. The sound of the mantra surrounding her acted as a benevolent protective barrier. Her spirit was like floating in the air, liberated from its physical cage, in a sheer spiritual fusion. She suddenly felt someone grasping her hand. She flinched before opening her eyes. Pierre-Antoine was looking at her, confused.

"What on earth is everyone doing here? Is this some sort of spiritualistic session?" He looked around. "Your Holiness, why are you here? Am I dying or something?"

"Pierre-Antoine!" screamed Monika with joy.

They all rushed to his side.

31

Three weeks after his miraculous recovery, Pierre-Antoine was back in the comfort of his office in Strasbourg. He was completely cleared out by the hospital a week before. No sequels, nothing. The preliminary tests were confirmed after another round of examinations. It was as if his cancer had never happened, like a dreadful dream. He was feeling liberated and filled with hope, even stronger physically. Naturally, the risk of relapse remained, and he would need to be closely monitored for the next few years. But this long-lasting burden seemed to have been completely removed. He looked out the window. He smiled. The same sky, gardens, water features, and birds fluttering around. But he observed them with new eyes, those of someone who had been given a second chance. And he intended to use it with both hands. His intercom buzzed.

"Yes, Lief?"

"High Commissioner, High Commissioner Richter and High Commissioner Sanchez are here."

"Please, let them in."

"Right away."

Monika and Jorge walked in, staring at him anxiously.

"Monika, Jorge," he said, "how nice of you to visit me on the first day I return to work."

"Come on, brother. You are the one who called us in. And you mentioned it was important. Is everything alright?"

"Yes, Pierre-Antoine. Are you feeling OK? Don't say your cancer has returned. Or worse!"

"Of course not. What a ludicrous idea. I have not felt this good for years. Come on; you heard the results with me in the hospital one week ago."

"Well, it could have returned as quickly as it had vanished. We know virtually nothing of this cure that man provided you."

"Monika, Doctor Caracciolo saved my life; that is all I see. And you were among the firsts to praise him, initially."

"He saved your life after almost taking it away three times in a row..."

"Let us stop there for now. Sit down, both of you, and have some coffee. We must discuss more crucial issues."

"What do you desire to tell us, brother?"

"First, I am eager to know everything that happened here during my four-week absence. Especially as far as the President and Cabinet are concerned."

"Tensions are growing within the Cabinet, and divisions are more palpable," declared Jorge. "Despite the success of the Peace Conference, some members did not accept we involved Russia in the proceedings. They were quite content to continue isolating it diplomatically."

"Good."

271

"Others," went on Monika, "are increasingly concerned about his continued indecision regarding the situation in North America and the presence of dangerous nuclear weapons in the hands of unstable nations."

"I see…"

"Add in the current economic situation, the lack of decisions about global climate change, and the scandal at our embassy in Beijing, and you end up with a disastrous outlook for the general elections in a few months," Jorge continued. President Kowalczyk's position appears insecure. In turn, during Cabinet meetings, he becomes increasingly irascible and authoritarian. A stance that even its most vigorous supporters find difficult to accept."

"I should also point out that he has totally disregarded the recent events that occurred in the Free City of Jerusalem," Monika said. "Personally, I think the situation should be observed even if, officially, the authorities claim to have regained control. Fabijan has received several reports of increased activity by some local extremist religious groups, which have remained inactive since the implementation of the new Status Quo. The banned video, still circulating in the underground networks, is not as insignificant as our President would have us believe. Even I, as a Catholic, found this worrisome. For what reasons would anyone want to post such a prank?"

"Well, Monika, I agree with your suspicions," confirmed Pierre-Antoine. "And our President's bleak outlook does not bode well for our own prospects. We could be out of a job a few months from now. We must start acting now if we intend to remain in our seats and survive the impending crisis."

"We'll all retire at one point, Pierre-Antoine." You know that. It is our inevitable destiny as politicians in the game of democracy."

"You speak wisely, Monika. And I would have agreed one hundred per cent with you a few weeks ago. But now I think our perspectives have changed, and I feel like taking a little more risk."

"I hear you, my brother, but I struggle to think of someone close capable of undertaking leadership. And I do not see myself being a last-minute fervent supporter of our despicable leader of the opposition. Our best ticket is Stanislaw, who can still rally a sufficient majority to form a third cabinet. At worst, we will end up with a hung parliament."

"And this will weaken our institutions when they need to be strong. The crisis caused by China admirably illustrates the difficulties to come. And voters are more concerned with global stability if it threatens their comfort level. They are now getting used to the safety resulting from the vast assemblage we created seven years ago and the benefits it brings."

"What exactly do you suggest we do then?"

"Monika, I have given much thought to our conversation a few months back. As I mentioned earlier, I see things from a different perspective now that I have been healed. I believe the time has come to address the mounting incompetence of our President. Therefore, I wish to inform you that I will be running for President, and I hope you will both support me."

"You asked to see me, Professor?"

"Yes, Doctor. Please, take a seat."

Giancarlo entered Professor Yang's office. To his surprise, Ian McEwan was also present. The administrator seemed uneasy and nodded rapidly.

"What is the matter?"

"Doctor Caracciolo, there is a significant issue that Administrator McEwan and I must discuss with you now that the incident has ended."

"What incident are you referring to?"

"I am referring to your first trial at the hospital."

Giancarlo lifted his eyebrows.

"If this concerns Mr Lascombes' adverse reaction, I want to reassure you and the Board." He looked at McEwan. "The High Commissioner signed a complete waiver of his responsibilities, Ian. You can put the Board at ease. There will be no lawsuits, especially since the subject fully recovered and was declared cured. It is our first success and hopefully not our last."

"My apologies, Doctor. I believe I did not express myself correctly enough. I wasn't mentioning the patient; I was talking about the actual treatment."

"I fail to comprehend what you allege, Professor. I followed all your instructions, and you gave me your consent to use the chimeric candidate. Your insinuation seems misplaced."

"Does it? Well, let me tell you a wee story. When your patient's vitals shut down one by one, I took the liberty of analysing some of his blood samples and studying your little creation." He suddenly burst out in rage. "You deceived me, doctor! All of us! It is not the chimeric virus you

274

submitted to me. It is a monstrosity! Something worth Victor Frankenstein! You did not just break all the ethics we are supposed to follow; you altered nature itself. That is unacceptable! And we are fortunate the patient survived. Looking at his political standing, what would a post-mortem have revealed to the whole world? That this research facility is playing God! How dare you weigh the reputation of your colleagues, your friends, to pursue your own goals? What is it you are looking for? Fame? Profit? Answer me!"

"I saved this man's life, don't you see?! We have struggled to obtain the appropriate treatment for years. This combination seemed the most relevant, and I seized my chance. You did not approve it because you did not want to disrupt your little existence and self-satisfaction. My solution will take us to a new era of medicine, and I just opened its doors."

"At the cost of sacrificing all our principles in the process!"

"Sometimes, the end justifies the means."

"Administrator?" Professor Yang asked McEwan.

"Well, I am dreadfully sorry to hear these words in your mouth, Giancarlo. Ethics and principles are the pillars of this centre and its organisation. You implicitly adhered to them when you joined us. One of our members cannot conveniently discard them whenever they face a challenging equation. We would be no better than our competitors and eventually forfeit the confidence of our shareholders, benefactors, and government support. You cannot ask the Board and me to dismiss this as an innocent mistake. We are extremely fortunate indeed our first subject recovered without noticeable damage. However, we cannot foresee your terrible creation's possible long-term side effects. Therefore, all existing references and candidates related to this deviant research, I should say experiment, will completely be erased."

"I object. You cannot do that!"

"I am not finished," calmly continued McEwan. "In addition, I believe you acknowledge the need to assume the consequences of your devastating initiative. After consulting with the Board, I must inform you that this centre gives you twenty-four hours to resign and leave the facility. Please accept the decision and spare yourself the trouble of a long, painful lawsuit that will only jeopardise your future and tarnish your reputation. In exchange for your voluntary collaboration, Professor Yang and I have agreed to issue an extremely favourable letter of recommendation. A commendation written by a double Nobel Prize winner, as well as being his direct assistant for seven years, should offer you a broad range of promising new opportunities. You are a remarkable researcher, Giancarlo, with enormous potential and probably destined to accomplish wonders. But, sadly, not among us."

***

The sun had just set, leaving only a sliver of pale pink light on the horizon. A black limousine approached a heavy blue gate with the inscription Monastery of the Twelve Apostles Capernaum in Greek. The driver honked two times, and an orthodox monk emerged from a side door. He inspected the vehicle and nodded in approbation. He disappeared, and a few seconds later, the gate opened, giving access to the car. A small shadow emerged from the back seat as soon as it parked. The monk then signalled the visitor to follow him along a paved path. They walked through a colonnade edged by a colourful Mediterranean garden and rows of grenadiers, cheered by the throbbing sound of singing crickets resounding in the night. On the right stood a large white church with pink domes, resembling a giant frosted sponge cake. The shadows finally arrived at a dark grey and white brick structure with closed blue shutters. They swiftly entered and headed directly to the basement.

"This way, Your Beatitude," invited the monk, indicating a small room at the back.

The temperature was quite cool inside. In the centre was a table with what seemed to be a body covered by a white shroud. A man was waiting, wearing a black suit.

"Good evening, Your Beatitude. I hope your journey was uneventful."

"Spare me the civilities," replied the patriarch with a tense voice. "Is that the corpse you reported earlier?"

"Indeed, Your Beatitude. A fisherman discovered it washed up on the shores of Hof Sappirit Beach, not far from here.

"As anyone else seen it?"

"Not to my knowledge. This beach is often deserted, and the monks were alerted in minutes."

"Show me."

The man pulled the sheet downwards, revealing a half-putrefied, half-charred body. Patriarch Nicodemus II gasped at the sight. The unfortunate creature's arms were raised, and the remainder of its face was frozen in a terrified expression.

"Are we certain it is him?"

"Well, Your Beatitude. I can't be a hundred per cent sure, particularly since we possess few medical records for the archdeacon. As you can see, the body has spent quite a bit of time in the water. Several weeks, I would say. Coinciding with the time of the archdeacon's disappearance. Most teeth are missing, and the few remaining ones aren't enough for a positive jaw identification. It has severe burns on the upper body, undoubtedly caused by lightning. And we recovered bits of metal, possibly handcuffs, deeply melted into the wrist bones. I can't be totally affirmative, but it fits properly with the description we've been given."

"That's enough compelling evidence. It will do, Doctor. I want you to prepare a death certificate identifying Archdeacon Shenouda Wahba. For the cause of death, mention severe burns resulting from natural electrocution followed by drowning. And find someone to arrange the body, especially the face, as presentable as possible. It will need to be exposed to avoid suspicions or conspiracies."

"As you wish, Your Beatitude."

"Better a dead martyr than one alive," mumbled the Patriarch as he walked away.

PART THREE
Atonement

32

The day was about to end. Trapped in the tormented elements, a man walked alone, struggling through the deep layer of snow, only aided by its long coarse wooden rod cut from a large olive tree. The icy wind was howling furiously around him, like the voice of an angry god, blasting freezing snowflakes flogging his fragile body. Despite his exhausted muscles imploring him to stop and his weakened bones weeping for a moment of rest, he continued, determined, stubborn. Stopping meant death. Resting meant death. He had no intention of surrendering his immortal soul to the beyond. At least for now. No, he had to live, to fight the odds to the end. His purpose was all that mattered. God was testing his body and resolve. Once again. What little clothing he wore was nothing more than shredded rags. His extremities and face were crudely wrapped in strips of dirty fabric, with part of his hands and feet darkened by frostbite tormenting his limbs. The phantom could barely see more than a few steps before him, his vision blinded by the blizzard that tried to thwart his long, inexorable march. His thoughts were jumbled with memories of his confused past, the circumstances that prompted his long journey, and the places he had visited in the previous months. God had not mentioned his final destination, where his steps were supposed to take him. No, He had only commanded him to walk through the lands, the deserts, the fertile plains, the mountains. To wander the earth tirelessly until given a sign to stop, to finally rest. The darkness had now completely subdued the world, metamorphosing him into a shadow entering the realm of shadows. The temperature dropped rapidly, and the cold bit him with its sharp teeth while the wind laughed at the prospect of a hopeless night. Maybe God had finally decided to abandon him, look away from his doomed carcass, and cast him out into limbo.

Then another shadow emerged from the darkness, holding a storm lamp and accompanied by the baaing of a frustrated and anxious sheep tied to his shoulder. It was a shepherd defying the storm to rescue one of his animals separated from the herd. The young man initially flinched at the sight of what resembled a wandering demon searching for souls to devour. But he rapidly realised that the frail shade standing before him, shivering like a sickly bird, was no creature from the underworld. He approached him, fathomed his wretchedness, then, submerged by compassion, gestured to follow him, promising food and shelter, at least until the weather improved. The man accepted his invitation. At long last, God showed mercy. The pair walked for another half an hour, slowly, painfully, until they reached the footsteps of a towering cliff. Then they followed a long trail of steps to an opening cut in a thick stone wall through which they entered what appeared to be a fortified town. Both men continued down several streets before arriving at a massive blue door that led into a courtyard. The shepherd took the sheep to the sheepfold and invited the stranger in, where his wife anxiously awaited her husband's return. The couple sat the man by the warm crackling fire while wrapping him in woollen blankets. She offered him a cup of tea and some food. His lips were severely blistered after days of exposure to the bitter cold. Each slurp was a torment, immediately relieved by the comforting warmth of the beverage. The taste of the succulent stew made of mutton and vegetables comforted his greedy stomach, unfed for several days. The rescuers were modest people, living humbly but happy to share what little they had. They explained the local warlord demanded his share of the flock every year, leaving them just enough to replenish it for the following year. It was unfair, but, like most villagers, they had little choice but to ensure the protection of the town against other warlords. Despite trying for years, God had not blessed them with children, but at least they had each other. Later, they took the wanderer into one of the rooms upstairs. The shepherd brought him clothes belonging to his brother, long lost to the war. And, before leaving the stranger for the night, he told him he would accompany him to the hospital in the morning to treat his wounds. The bed was comfortable, the linens clean and the room cosy. The man enjoyed a dreamless resting night for the first time in weeks.

The following day, he was taken to the Sheikh and Elders after visiting the medical centre. He remained silent while clearly understanding the questions they asked him, responding only with gestures and signs from the head. The leaders concluded the traveller was mute and agreed to leave him under the shepherd's care until he was fit to go if he so chose. They were kind and compassionate people who had experienced adversity. His past or background did not matter to them. God always rewards those who help those in need. Thus, the stranger settled at his saviour's house, lovingly cared for during the following weeks. Then the first miracle took place. After years of infertility, the shepherd's wife became pregnant. The happy couple was overjoyed. In the spring, the ewes gave birth to an abundance of lambs not seen for many years, and the orchards blossomed abundantly, the promise of a bounty of fruit. A few months later, the shepherd became the proud father of a healthy son. People started talking. This could not be a mere coincidence. The unexpected arrival of the stranger had reversed the tides of the previous miserable years they had endured. They said he was a blessing from God, the answer to their prayers. The Sheikh and the Elders asked the wanderer to remain among them. He agreed. They mentioned this abandoned house near the Zoroastrian fire temple, where he could live independently. The townsfolks repaired it and refurbished it. It was modest but comfortable, with a small roof terrace where he could enjoy the warm summer nights.

A young man, an orphan, was sent to his service, fostering him, calming his wounds, and nourishing him. The neighbourhood brought food daily or humble offerings hoping the stranger would bless them with good fortune. And small miracles happened. The goldsmith, the butcher, the tanner's wife, the baker's son, and so on established his reputation as a holy man. The stranger rarely left the house except to join the offices at the mosque, the church and the temple, wearing a black and white robe. He did not directly participate but merely watched and observed the various rites, peacefully smiling at the faithful as if satisfied with their devotion. The community's core rested on an ancient tradition of harmonious religious coexistence. The Council of Elders led the townspeople, consisting of two elected representatives for each local faith, Muslims, Christians, and Zoroastrians, who appointed the sheikh yearly. Thus, they believed the stranger's silent approval was a sign of God's satisfaction.

The months passed quietly, placidly. But anything God gives, God can take. Winter came, and the townsfolks turned greedy, sharing less and less with the neighbouring villages, selfish of their new wealth. Consequently, words of discontent and jealousy began spreading throughout the region until reaching the ears of the local warlord. He travelled to the city with his warriors. He witnessed its prosperity and then demanded his share—more taxes in payment for his protection. The stranger was nowhere to be seen, confined in his home, withholding gifts from the people and sent away by his servant. He had forsaken them by betraying their pledge. God was displeased.

The city was defenceless, and its inhabitants practically unarmed. Who would fight, anyway? They were not soldiers. The people feeling helpless, submitted and paid the warlord. But three months later, he returned, asking more. And again three months after. The townsfolk's situation had become hopeless again.

During this time, the stranger's servant regularly visited the tailor and the silversmith. He requested something, but they had to keep it secret or face God's wrath. Another winter came, and the stranger remained in seclusion. Eventually, the city's gained abundance wavered like a dying stream in an arid desert.

Finally, the following spring, the foreigner reappeared on the roof terrace of his house. The trees blossomed again abundantly; the ewes gave birth to twins. Renewed hope filled the community's heart. Perhaps God had at last forgiven them; they thought, when the warlord and his soldiers returned. Someone had betrayed the community by revealing the stranger's existence. He ordered them to bring him. He declared that the man belonged to Qadesh and argued they did not deserve him. He should be his protector and bestowed by his miracles. Some folks rushed to the holy man's house, gathering before his door and kneeling to protect their benefactor. They were unarmed and frightened but resolved to protect him. The warlord approached, accompanied by his heavily armed men. He commanded the townsfolk to step aside. They remained still. He threatened to kill them all unless they moved away from his booty. They did not move. They prepared to die. Death was more merciful than hardship. They vowed to redistribute the city's wealth with the other villages but refused to hand over the stranger. They faced the radiant Sun, ready to sacrifice their life for the common good. The soldiers formed a line and armed their weapons, to the horror of the other inhabitants.

All seemed lost when a thundering noise erupted. The servant appeared on the rooftop, dominating the crowd. Behold, he shouted. The stranger emerged behind, except he was no longer the stranger. No, he was God's radiant messenger wearing a thick gown woven with gold threads, adorned by a large sun embroidered in the middle. A broad golden pectoral, crimped of multicoloured gemstones, encircled his neck, and a gilded mitre covered his head. His right hand held a long staff capped with a solar disk made of pure gold. His whole body glowed in the sun, like the sight of a celestial creature. Amid the gathered people, a voice shouted *Musharifin!*

The apparition stared at the dazzled crowd, both terrifying and magnificent, its eyes compelling respect and carrying fear. He fixed the warlord, the disc on his staff beaming the sunlight directly onto the man who commanded the stage just a moment ago. God saw him, scrutinised his soul, weighed it, and sentenced him. Defiant, the commander pointed his weapon at the mighty being, ready to fire and kill, when he suddenly screamed with dread. He dropped the gun and fell to his knees before collapsing dead on the ground. The crowd knelt in fear, followed by the warriors about to shoot them. After many months of silence, the stranger addressed them loudly and clearly.

"Behold the Messenger of God! Believe, and you shall be rewarded forever. Refute, and you will be cursed for all time. Follow his words, and you will live in his everlasting glory. Defy his commandments, and you shall suffer eternally. He is the Eternal Light, and I am his Bringer. I have come in His name to redeem your souls. Join me, and together we will subdue his enemies and make them bow before him. He speaks through my voice. I am the Prophet, the Servant of the Light!"

33

"Non, encore une fois, non!$^{(*)}$ I cannot approve this!" Pierre-Antoine was furious. "Since 2057, we have invested in the European Space Program with one objective: to provide the people of Earth a future amongst the stars and preserve what is salvageable on the planet. The lunar settlement represents a key element of this program. I will not slash its budget to embark on some Martian nonsense blindly!"

"But, Mister President, the mission to Mars venture has been approved by the Parliamentary Space Commission and will certainly be adopted by the Members of Parliament on Thursday."

"It is not a venture. It is a senseless adventure! Gabriel, we have a majority in this Parliament, don't we? So, let's use it!"

"It is not so simple, Pierre-Antoine, and you know it. You cannot command Parliament…"

"And why not, Monika? They owe me their survival and

$^{(*)}$ *No, once again, no!*

287

their fortified majority. Without me running two years ago, Kowalczyk would have caught us all in his downfall. And that idiot of Van Dijk would probably be sitting in my chair, still pondering how he ever made it. Yes, they do owe me! Instead, these ungrateful bastards are operating on my back!"

"They are only concerned, Mister President. Worried about the impact the Chinese and Russian success on Mars will have on the opinion if we do nothing. It is all over the news. The Indo-Pakistani mission will land in two weeks while we still wander around its surface with our two rovers. Try looking at the bigger picture. We should not make the same mistake as on the Moon and allow other space powers to control our future access to the Red Planet."

"At the risk of repeating myself, this is not an opportunity but a pending disaster. I have been following its development for eight years, Gabriel. I know the costs involved. Our most prominent scientists have predominantly concluded the colonisation of Mars is a fantasy created in the 2020s. The polar caps contain a more substantial proportion of carbon dioxide than was previously thought. The rest of the water is so deep underground that it requires huge resources to extract it. Assuming it is potable. This implies a restricted water supply and limited prospects for future colonisation. Not to mention terraforming. The Parliament is asking us to squander enormous sums of money and resources simply out of national pride. This Mars race is no different than the space race of the second half of the last century. It possesses the potential to weaken us, and the Russians and

Chinese are undoubtedly aware. I cannot approve this bill; it's not in our interest."

"You cannot veto it either, Pierre-Antoine. That would be politically disastrous in the middle of your first term. Especially if you are seeking a second one, as I suspect you are. Support for the bill extends well beyond our majority. If you disagree with its content, we will have to negotiate a compromise so that no side loses face."

"A compromise, Monika? With those backstabbing cowards?"

"Yes, those. I recall a time when you were more flexible and receptive to these issues."

"Perhaps because then no category five hurricane was heading for Western Europe and threatening to wreak havoc on the entire Atlantic coast and beyond. Maybe because I was not under pressure from several governors to evacuate millions of people or risk chaos. That crisis is my pressing financial concern, not the financing of the hunt for elusive little green men. Alright, enough of this. You want negotiations? We will negotiate. Gabriel, I am sending you as my envoy to the majority leader. Express my disappointment at not having been consulted about the bill. Then, tell him that I am ready to meet him with the other party leaders and discuss a compromise to reach a unanimous stance on the issue. Schedule a meeting for tomorrow morning at any time. I will cancel my other engagements on that day."

"Very well, Mister President. I will contact him right away."

Pierre-Antoine picked up his intercom.

"Lief?"

"Yes, Mister President?"

289

"High Commissioner Oliveira is leaving us. Have Jorge, Fabijan, and General de Soverosa arrived?"

"They have been waiting here for the last ten minutes."

"Take them in, please. And get the holoprojector I asked you to prepare. Also, cancel all my tomorrow's appointments. I shall meet with the leaders of Parliament."

"Right away, Mister President."

A moment later, they gathered at the conference table. Leif finished installing the projector before exiting.

"I hope you gentlemen are all well. I want to stress that the content of this meeting is strictly confidential and should not leave this room unless I state so."

"What… is this meeting about Pierre-Antoine? I received no memo."

"Monika, I fear I have deliberately left you out of our little intrigue. Not that I do not trust you. You have my full confidence. But because I needed Fabijan and General de Soverosa to gather information before involving you. Besides, I required you to concentrate on the American situation that demanded all your attention. Again, it is essential that what we are about to discuss remains out of the Cabinet's ears."

"I hear you."

The intercom buzzed.

"Mister President, the secure link you have requested is ready."

"Perfect. Put the communication through."

The holo-projector hummed, and a 3D holographic image materialised before them. Monika recognised Vince Johnson, the Administrator Principal of the European Lunar Base.

"Good afternoon, Vince. How are things going on our beautiful moon?"

"Very well, Mister President. We recently welcomed fifty new colonists, bringing our total population to seven hundred and twenty-five. If all goes well, we should expand our capacity to a thousand by the end of next month."

"This is undeniably good news. Well, if I'm unmistaken, there will be seven hundred and twenty-six shortly. How is Marisa?"

"Extremely well, Mister President. Two weeks till the big day. This will be the tenth birth since we authorised moon pregnancies."

"Excellent. Another Selenite. I suppose I can congratulate you personally when I visit the base in a month and a half."

"Indeed. The whole base is enthusiastically looking forward to your arrival. Our first-ever presidential visit. You can bet we will make it memorable."

"I definitely hope so, ha ha ha! Okay, let's move to business. Fabijan?"

"As you requested, Mr President, Esteban and I, with Vince's precious assistance, reviewed recent Chinese-Russian activities on the Moon and its orbital station. Our suspicions seem to be confirmed. In the past few weeks, there has indeed been another increase in military presence on both bases. We counted one hundred and sixty army-related personnel on the Russian base and two hundred and fifty on the Chinese one. For the record, Russia counts five hundred settlers and China seven hundred."

"This represents a third of the total population for each settlement if I add up right!"

"Precisely, Mister President. And you can add twenty-five Russians and Twenty-seven Chinese on the orbital station," said General Oliveira. "This is definitively a joint operation."

"But to what end?"

"Well, we can only speculate at this point," Fabijan continued, "but the most likely explanation is the control of the extraction of rare earth elements. As you know, those are becoming increasingly scarce and less accessible on Earth. There's an increased demand for space colonisation and new weapons technologies. That's officially the main reason behind the Martian race. But we all agree this is smoke and mirrors because the exploitation of the red planet is not economically viable in our current state of development. In contrast, although abounding fewer quantities than Earth, the Moon is closer and partially colonised. And most of the resources already identified are located on the surface or the upper crust. What if these two powers could take control of most of the known mining sites deploying their combined military forces? It would require weeks for a UN force to put together a contingent. And even though, what would it do once there? I do not see Chinese or Russian forces willingly withdrawing. The international community will be paralysed and limited to issuing empty official protests. No need to elaborate any further."

"But this is a terrible scenario!" Monika cried out.

"You now appreciate why our interests on the Moon are much more important than *Mission to Mars*, Monika. We must act swiftly; we cannot allow two of the greatest threats on this planet to take control of valuable resources.

Thankfully, my predecessor and I started forecasting this possible development two years ago. Didn't we, Jorge?"

"Yes, Pierre-Antoine. Seventy-five of our lunar residents are military as well. They are primarily engineers and miners but are all trained for potential space combat. They can respond when necessary. This is in addition to the twenty soldiers formally stationed there alternating between the orbital station and the base."

"But that is clearly not enough, looking at the current situation. Vince, I am afraid you will soon have to cope with more colonists. I want you to start working double shifts to increase your capacities to one thousand and five hundred colonists, instead of one thousand, as soon as possible."

"But how are we going to justify this to the UN and our Parliament?" asked Monika.

"Well, this is when the rabbit comes out of the hat. Vince, carry on."

"Sure, Mister President. I can confirm the information I provided to you some days ago. Our geologists have discovered a large pouch of Scandium and Yttrium, conveniently located a short distance from our base. As a reminder, both elements are essential for aerospace components and engines. This discovery was made during a digging initially designed to enlarge some of our underground facilities. We were unsure about its volume initially, but I can confirm it is substantial now. Several tons…"

"Several tons! When that information comes out, there will be a gold rush."

"Absolutely, Mister President. As a result, you understand I desperately need additional hands very

293

quickly. It is a convenient opportunity to solicit more settlers from Parliament without raising any red flags."

"You are reading my mind, especially as it will whet the appetite of our two competitors. Jorge, I want you to enlist more special troops as quickly as possible. We need to match the total of both our competitors."

"I have already made preparations as a precaution."

"Vince, we must also expand our water supply and storage capacity."

"I am working on it. However, I have a slight concern."

"Tell me."

"I hear a bill is being drafted to cut some of my funding to finance a human-crewed mission to Mars."

"Alas, you have heard very well."

"That is rather troublesome. Accommodating additional people here means additional resources to invest. I am able to handle food and water, but energy will be more of a problem, especially digging. Can you do nothing to prevent this or at least curtail it?"

"My hands are tied, Vince. I cannot cut the budgets of other departments to compensate. The constitution prohibits it. Parliament members see the Moon as less important than Mars for reasons that will take too long to explain. Monika and I will meet with the parliamentary leaders tomorrow to negotiate the extent of the cuts. What can you give me?"

"Well, not much, Mister President, as I just explained. There may be a plan B, though."

"Carry on."

"It is rather unconventional and hazardous. But if you agree, I can commit fifteen per cent of my budget."

"Shoot."

"Alright. You see, the abandoned American base lies nearby. It is stocked with unused materials, just at our reach. Maybe…"

"Vince, if I authorise such an operation, it will have to be done covertly. Our legislative body will never approve it, let alone the UN."

"Well, let's say I have done some 'forays' in the past. This fruit is too tempting and too close to leave to rot."

"What?" said Monika, jumping out of her seat. "Administrator, you do realise this is completely illegal and violates the Lunar International Convention. Had you been caught…"

"Respectfully, High Commissioner, there is no reason to panic. I have been extremely cautious and ensured that our neighbours notice nothing. We have only used reconnaissance missions to identify areas of interest. Mister President, I can assure you that our little 'raid' will be completely invisible because I know exactly where to strike. Naturally, if you can provide further support, just in case…"

"Very well, I agree. Initiate this as soon as possible. The sooner, the better, while everyone focuses on Mars. Gentlemen, I will let you arrange the details with Vince. Monika, we now have a fifteen per cent negotiating range on the budget. This is more than necessary, and I am counting on your talents to ensure a lower number tomorrow. At the same time, we need to reach out to President Wilson in America. I will arrange his support for the operation to cover any unforeseen incidents. We will present it as a temporary loan to assist us in overcoming pressing technical problems. I am certain he will understand the situation. In exchange, I stand prepared to vigorously support the recognition of the Eastern States Federation as the official successor state of the United States of America."

Monika's jaw dropped out.

"But we will break our neutral position in the conflict! They just signed a cease-fire."

"The fifth since the start of the civil war. That endless game has gone on long enough. The time has come to stop burying our heads in the sand and take a side. After all, this is the sole government still ensuring democratic representation on the continent. I have no inclination to the Western Dictatorship or the Southern Theocracy. Include it on tomorrow's agenda."

34

Father Luca Calleja had been waiting patiently for fifteen minutes in the hallway of the first floor of the General Curia of the Jesuits in Rome. He felt uneased in his black suit and shoes and his tab collar tight around his neck. The clergyman's appearance was not what most people would associate with a priest. In his late thirties, he resembled a character straight out of an Ian Fleming novel. His tall, athletic build, short black hair, handsome square face, and soft, round, dark blue eyes starkly contrasted his ecclesiastical status, associated with poverty, chastity and obedience. He flew from Valletta the night before, forced to shorten a few days' well-deserved break at his mother's following his recent mission in Peru. The pleasant home-cooked dinner was interrupted by a man carrying an urgent dispatch. *Come to Rome now – jet scheduled at 18.30 - meeting at 10.00 tomorrow.* Naturally, the fact he left after only three days upset his mother a little. The only excuse he could come up with was to remind her of his oath: *Servio ad voluntatem* —I serve at will. And because of this oath, he was now waiting beside the Father General's Office. *Ad Majorem Dei Gloriam* [*]. Father Calleja did not like being summoned to last-minute schedules. In his experience, this could only mean trouble. His last assignment in the Andes — chasing the resurrected Shining Path to persuade his leader to initiate negotiations— had been challenging, even hazardous at some points. He felt unprepared to confront a similar mission so quickly. The door across the hallway opened, revealing a slightly overweight, cheery little sexagenarian sporting a distinctive white moustache, black pants, and a black shirt with a tab collar.

"Welcome, welcome, Father Calleja. How nice to see you again. Please come inside. We have been expecting you."

The priest entered a room modestly furnished with a broad desk surrounded by three contemporary armchairs, a single bookshelf, and decorated with a few plants and an icon of a Madonna holding baby Jesus in the eastern style. Two other men were waiting. One he recognised instantly. It was Father Giovanni Puglisi, the Admonitor of the Jesuit Order. However, it was his first time meeting the other. The individual wore a black simar with scarlet piping and a scarlet sash at the waist. *A cardinal, no doubt.*

"Please, Father, take a seat," invited the Father General.

"Thank you, Very Reverend Father."

"Enable me to introduce you to our little gang. Father Puglisi, whom you already know. And allow me to present our newcomer, Cardinal Edvard Retz, Prefect of the Holy Office. He took his office less than two months ago, explaining why his face may seem unfamiliar to you."

[*] *For the Greater Glory of God (motto of the Society of Jesus)*

The Head of the Holy Office! This means involvement from the Pope himself...

"But first, I would like to congratulate you on the success of your mission in Peru. Dealing with the guerrilla was not an easy task. Still, you have brilliantly managed to bring both sides to the negotiating table. It is now up to the diplomats to secure the right compromise and hopefully end this needless violence. Well done!"

"Thank you, Very Reverend Father."

"All right, let us move on to the reason for your presence in our midst. I apologise for interrupting your well-earned break so suddenly. But certain recent events in the Middle East have caught the attention of the Pope, and you are the best qualified to handle them. Your Eminence, if you will."

"Thank you, Reverend Father. Father Calleja, you might remember three years ago, an incident occurred in the Free City of Jerusalem involving the members of the High Council. It resulted in the tragic death of Cardinal del Pietro, our brother in the faith."

"I vaguely recall, Your Eminence, to be honest. It did not make the headlines, and the Secretariat of State handled it as News of minor importance. Unless it was intentional."

"And indeed, it was. The death of a Cardinal in such a volatile zone was rather sensitive. The Church had no choice but to quickly limit its impact to prevent unnecessary scrutiny, despite the murky areas surrounding the circumstances of the accident. Having said that, are you aware of any video circulated on social media at that time, a few weeks before this unfortunate tragedy?"

"I am afraid not, Your Eminence. In my defence, I was on a mission in central Africa, quite cut off from the rest of the world."

"Well, I will ask my office to forward you a copy of the video quickly. Though brief, I must warn you that this is a rather disturbing video. It shows bothersome images of a stela linking biblical father figures to the ancient Egyptian cult of the Aten. Fortuitously, the religious authorities of the Holy City reacted promptly and denounced it as a deepfake made by some anti-religious secret society. It eventually got watered in the mass of similar conspiracy videos that social media are accustomed to producing in troubled times. It raised concerns in Rome at the time, although we could never confirm or refute its authenticity. Neither to uncover its origin."

"That is a most instructive story, Your Eminence. But where do I fit in?"

"I am getting there, Father. But first, allow me to carry on with more recent developments. Something has happened in recent weeks in a remote part of what was once Kurdish Iraq. The city of Amadiya recently witnessed the rise of a local religious leader who calls himself the Prophet and the Servant of the Light. He is preaching a new creed, claiming that all monotheistic faiths originate from a single and same dogma perverted through the centuries by religious leaders. According to information gathered from the local Assyrian priest, he advocates reconciliation between Judaism, Christianity and Islamic faith, regardless of their interpretation of the Gospel. Followers are urged to give up past mistakes by re-joining God's light or something like that. Honestly, the full concept is unclear, and that poor priest was useless.

Naturally, my office is accustomed to dealing with the apparition, here and there, of so-called prophets claiming to be sent by God, if not being messiahs. Their proportion has tended to multiply exponentially since the mid-twentieth century, keeping us very busy, I admit. Of course, all of them turn out to be crooks or lunatics. But here, the situation appears different. First, that 'prophet' has been credited with performing several miracles. This is not the first time a trickster challenges the established faiths, and most certainly not the last. Except, according to our contact, they appeared convincing enough to persuade much of the local community to join his vision. Including the Zoroastrian followers, who enjoyed quite a revival in the region in the last decade. More concerning is the apparent lack of opposition from the local religious leaders. But we are short of tangible facts, and the situation needs to be evaluated directly. Another concern comes from the location where this petty delusion is happening. Do you possess any knowledge of the city of Amadiya and its history, Father?"

"If I remember correctly from my religious studies when I was a seminarian, it is believed to have been the Biblical home of the Magi in addition to being a historic commercial centre. According to some Wiccans, it was there that men first learned to harness the power of magic."

"Correct." The cardinal came closer. "But other local legends might be more worrisome than our three benevolent magi or the birth of magicians. One is the existence of a Jewish tomb that the Kurds believe to be that of the prophet Ezekiel, just a few kilometres away. You would remember Ezechiel prophesied the destruction of Jerusalem and the restoration of the land of Israel. The book of Ezekiel is one of the foundations of the Jewish mystique. Our 'prophet' apparently made two public pilgrimages to that tomb, perceived positively by the local population, knowing the three local religions hold the site in the highest regard. Have you ever heard of David Alroy?"

"Honestly, no."

"Despite his very English-sounding name, David Alroy was a Jewish man born locally in the Twelfth Century. He spent the last years of his tame life claiming to be... the Messiah! The man caused quite a stir in the Seljuk Empire at the time, gathering many followers to liberate Jerusalem from Muslim domination, restore Solomon's Temple and pave the way for the coming of the Kingdom of God. In other words, the end of times. After years of unrest, he was eventually captured and promptly executed. But the story remains firmly rooted in the region."

He stopped to have some water.

"Looking at this accumulation of mythical manifestations, resurrected by this man from nowhere, and the local population's apparent support, several Curia members, including the Holy Father, are becoming extremely preoccupied with a possible evolution beyond our control. You are aware the main objective of this papacy is to re-establish the Church's foundations and gradually purge it of all the absurd liberal reforms promoted over the last sixty years. Only then should we regain the trust of our followers who have spent too long in the confusion of conflicting policies and deserted us. Despite secular resistance, this project is well underway now. We cannot afford to have it jeopardised by some fanatical lunatic who is not taken seriously enough. How the Islamic

State started its crimson adventure is still vividly embedded in our minds. However, before acting blindly, we need to obtain a more explicit picture of what is happening in this remote, destabilised part of the world and quickly determine whether it requires to be contained. And this is where you come in, Father Calleja. Very Reverend Father?"

"Gladly," replied the Father General before clearing his throat. "Luca, you are our best agents to deal with such issues. You know how to take the time to evaluate each situation and act accordingly, in addition to being our most valuable negotiator. I know you are not entirely accustomed to all the subtleties of the Middle East, having been there only once and for a short mission. But I am confident you are the most suitable man for the assignment we have in mind."

"You ought to be proud, Father," interrupted the Admonitor. "Our Holy Father himself has expressly asked for you. A tremendous honour bestowed again to our glorious congregation dedicated to the service of His Holiness's command. We all look to you to..."

"Thank you, Father Puglisi. I do not doubt Father Calleja is well aware of his obligations. So, if I may continue…"

"Naturally, Very Reverend Father. My apologies for this interruption."

"Luca, you leave tonight for Jerusalem. I set up a special ride for you. When you get there, I need you to contact our Apostolic Nuncio, Cardinal Elie Chehab, who will organise your transfer to northern Iraq. While longer, it is the most secure starting route since the Afghanization of the region. Baghdad is no longer safe, and we have no reliable contact there. The Curia will cover all your expenses, and Brother

Willem de Vries will assist you in your mission. He is a member of the Apostolic Mission in the Holy City who speaks fluent local languages, including Kurdish. You will find him quite helpful. But I believe you already know each other."

"Indeed, Very Reverend Father. We executed a short mission together in 2063 to recover an artefact from the Grand Egyptian Museum for the Vatican. It will be a pleasure to work with him again."

"Excellent! One last thing. I would like you to use Cardinal Chehab's position to set up a meeting with the other members of the High Council of Jerusalem. As we discussed before, the death of Cardinal del Pietro is obscured by numerous clouds. Try collecting additional information where possible. But remember, your primary target remains Amadiya, and time is of the essence. There is a mounting concern that things could be speeding up quite quickly. Remember that this is a reconnaissance mission with no purpose other than gathering valuable information. Unless otherwise instructed, you should never be personally involved. And you respond to me, and me alone."

"As you command, Very Reverend Father."

35

The three six-wheeled vehicles were moving slowly on the lunar surface, like giant beetles devoid of grace. Looking through the windows, Administrator Johnson contemplated the dusty greyish earth under a starry sky now his home. It had become a familiar vision which had lost the wow factor of the first months following his arrival. *I suppose I am turning into a real Selenite*, he thought. Right ahead appeared the slopes of the Shackleton Crater, their destination.

"We could have taken one of the shuttles, you know."

"Emile, we are not having this conversation again. The less attention we receive from our Chinese and Russian friends, the fewer complications we experience. And try to maintain a steady speed. We'll have to transport energy and solar cells back. Let's avoid any technical problems caused by an excess of lunar dust. Slow down a bit and look at the path; the ground can get treacherous."

"Aye, aye. Just saying. Personally, I'm quite enjoying the ride. Since you're visibly on one of your bad days, I figured you wanted us to hurry up."

Chief Engineer Emile Dubois was driving nonchalantly. He had been stationed on the moon six months ago and was still living his childhood dream. His boyish face was glowing with the excitement of his first real long escapade from the base. He looked into the rear-view mirror.

"Hey, Einar, everything alright back there?"

"It is Captain Hauksson when we are on assignment, Dubois. Keep the familiarities for when we are in private, please. My men need to follow the chain of command. I'll appreciate you respecting it in public," replied a voice in the shadows.

"Oh, la la! It's just the 3 of us here. You two are so tense today. This is a simple mission, no need to be that nervous."

"We have no idea what to expect there," replied Vince Johnson. "The base had remained inhabited for almost a decade. What will we find there? What if our neighbours had the same thought long before we did? That could compromise the entire plan. I already gave up ten per cent of my budget, and we need those extra resources."

"You're overthinking, Vince."

"That is the burden that comes with responsibilities. How far to go?"

"Twenty kilometres before reaching the rim of the crater."

"Good."

Twenty minutes later, the three vehicles arrived at the edge of the perfectly round remnant of a long-standing meteorite impact. Vince could see the outlines of the abandoned US lunar base in the shadows below. There was no evidence of human activity visible remotely.

"Okay, let's gear up."

"Sergeant Reid, get your men ready," ordered the captain into the com. "I want half of them armed, and the other half equipped to transport heavy loads. We're leaving the vehicles here until the facility is secure, Roger."

"*Roger that, Captain,*" responded a crackling voice.

The fifteen people cautiously walked down the crater before finally passing a batch of solar panels to their right. Emile ran in their direction to inspect them.

"Vince, they're in excellent condition if not for the accumulation of dust."

"Great, we will salvage them if necessary. But next time, do not separate from the group unless you're escorted by one of Captain Hauksson's guys. We must remain safe at this time."

"Okay. Sorry…"

A few minutes later, they finally entered the base's main enclosure. Everything seemed deserted and forgotten. No one had been there in ages. After the start of the Second Civil War, which divided the North American continent into three factions, none of their governments could sustain the installation. The European team repatriated the remaining personnel to Earth nine years ago.

Vince walked to the main building's entrance hatch. He activated several switches, but with no results.

"Emile, can you check the transformers over there, please? They probably shut them down when they abandon the base."

The chief engineer rushed to the large steel boxes on his right. Although built separately by each country, a

307

consensual collaboration was reached to adopt the same technology and materials in each base. It allowed all colonies to provide assistance and spare parts in case of severe damage until new components were shipped from Earth or directly manufactured on the Moon. The only differences were in the design, as the Europeans decided to bury their facility inside the Earth's crust while the other bases established on its surface.

The entire basin suddenly lit up, revealing the sight of a ghost town. There were four large warehouses, two hangars on the left, and a communication zone on the right, next to the transformers. The main building stood in the middle, adjacent to the living quarters.

"Emile, I need you here. The door is still not opening. Check whether you can overpass the security command. I want to save our oxygen supply by not breaking in."

"Right there."

Five minutes later, the first door of the airlock opened with a raucous hiss.

"Thank you, Emile. Captain, I want your guys to inspect the warehouses and identify their contents. Focus on power cells, which are our primary purpose. Also, inspect the transport vehicles. Get them charged if they appear functional. We will take them along for future use. I want anything of value brought back to the base. I doubt we'll get a second chance when our neighbours find out the precise purpose of our little getaway."

"Understood. Sarge, you remain with Administrator Johnson and Engineer Dubois. The rest of you come with me."

They left while Vince, Emile and the NCO entered the airlock, securing the exterior door behind them.

"Depressurisation sequence initiated. Please wait," said a computer voice. The surrounding temperature rose, and their movements became easier. *"Depressurisation sequence completed. Welcome. Oxygen levels at twenty-five per cent and rising."*

The second door unlocked in another hiss, and they moved inside an extended tunnel. The lights turned on automatically.

"I think we can remove our helmets now. The atmosphere should be fairly breathable," said Vince. "Let's leave them here."

"Great! The stuffing is the one thing I don't enjoy about these suits." Emile looked at the Sergeant. "Philippa, that's your first big adventure, too, right?"

"Yes," they answered. "I've done some outdoor training since I got here, but no proper mission. This is really exciting."

"Philippa and I arrived on the same shuttle," Emile explained to Vince. "That was a lot of fun!"

"Good to know. Now let us concentrate on what is nearby. Fortunately, this base is not significant. The Civil War abruptly suspended their plan for an extension. In the end, only twenty people lived permanently here. Emile, take a look at the living quarters for anything of value. Sergeant, check the mess hall for edible food. Not that we require anything in particular, but our colonists still appreciate some extras. I'm going to the command centre. Meet me there in half an hour."

He followed the corridor to his right and, after two turns, arrived in a vast room filled with various research equipment, a meeting table, some maps, and a large console. He removed his gloves, pressed a switch, and spoke out when the primary screen turned on.

"Computer, access main system."

"Main system available."

"Computer, display Commander Abrahams' personal logs."

"Logs available."

Vince reviewed the records. Most were banalities about the daily routine and work, nothing of interest. He was about to stop when a June 6, 2055 entry captured his attention. It was a comprehensive list of stored materials and goods received from Earth that day. Food, equipment, and parts. All meticulously recorded, except for Zone 2B, Area 4, 25. *Twenty-five what?*

"Computer, locate Zone 2B."

"That information is unavailable."

"Unavailable? Computer, identify Zone 2B."

"That information requires special authorisation Gamma Alpha C. Request denied."

"Okay, let's play otherwise. Computer, display lunar base chart maps."

"Complying."

A 3D view of the base appeared before him. Like the other bases on the Moon, it was divided into multiple zones using a grid. It helped to rapidly determine the location of technical problems to facilitate needed repairs. The American base was divided into six sectors, each comprising three subsections. 1A, 1B, 1C. 2A, 2C, 3A… *Where is 2B?*

Captain Hauksson was supervising the retrieval of the technical equipment and rechargeable batteries found in two warehouses. It was like finding Aladdin's cave. This additional equipment would allow the base to expand immediately without waiting for the next shipment from Earth in four months. They also discovered three heavy lunar transport vehicles in perfect working condition. They would be fully charged within the next twenty minutes. After fifteen years of active service on Earth, he appreciated that last assignment. Despite the risks involved, he volunteered for that three years assignment looking for a change of scenery. And what a change it was. *The Moon!* He no longer had a family and was not yet prepared to return to Iceland and take a well-deserved retirement. The command revived the excitement of his early years of armed service. He walked outside. Low gravity was slowing down his mesomorphic body. These spacesuits were the only things he detested due to their movement restrictions. *Maybe, I will not return to Earth. I love it here. So peaceful. And aside from the lack of water features and active volcanoes, it is similar to Iceland. Nothing compares to an earthrise—* A flashing yellow light on his left glove took him out of his daydream.

"Yes, Administrator?"

"Captain, I want you and two of your soldiers to walk to the section about twenty metres northeast of your present position. I am forwarding you the coordinates right now."

"Anything, in particular, you'd like me to look into, Administrator?"

"I will advise you as soon as you get there. And bring a ground scanner with you."

"Roger that. Mitchell, Kowalski, with me!"

Five minutes later, they reached the designated location.

"We are there, Administrator."

"What do you see?"

"Nothing. The whole area is unoccupied. No facility, no equipment. As flat as Holland."

"I want your men to inspect the ground. Something should be there, but without further investigation, I cannot state what."

"Received. Come on, guys, let's do it."

They wandered around, but nothing appeared suspicious except for some interference affecting the scanner. After a while, it appeared that the area held no particular interest.

"Shit!"

"What's happening, Kowalski?"

"Nothing, Captain. My right foot's just stuck on the ground. I forgot to disconnect my magnetic boots once more. Ok, done now."

"You've been with us for six months, Kowalski. In a hazardous situation that could screw your batteries... Wait, how can you get stuck on lunar soil? Stand where you are."

He walked towards the private, and his blue, round eyes examined the suspicious spot. The footprint was deep and clean on the ground. There was nothing apparent, only the usual layer of moondust.

"Mitchell, bring me that metal stick up there."

"Here you are, Captain."

Hauksson took the rod and began hitting the moon's thick dusty layer as deeply as possible. After a couple of seconds, he hit a hard surface.

"Okay, guys, there's definitely something here. Let's clear it out."

They went to their knees and started to remove the dirt. After a few minutes, they cleared a large square steel panel with a flat handle at one end. A hatch! He pulled the handle, and the hatch rose automatically, revealing a stairway.

"Is anybody ready for some adventure? Kowalski, ammo up, just in case."

312

They went down cautiously, step by step. It was about ten metres deep. A light suddenly went on at the end of the stairs, unveiling a vast storage room. But what awaited in the middle caught the three soldiers by surprise. Hauksson hit the transmitter button.

"Administrator, we found something. I believe you should come and see it right away."

"*On my way.*"

"Mitchell, go and fetch him."

Johnson headed back to the airlock in a rush.

"Emile, Sergeant, I am going outside. Wait for me at the Command Centre."

He put on his helmet and gloves and walked out of the building. After five minutes, he reached the suspected Zone 2B. Private Mitchell was waiting for him next to what appeared to be an underground entrance. He followed him down and found Hankssen and Kowalski examining their discovery. And what a discovery that was!

"No, they have not! That is in total violation of the Lunar Convention! I can't believe it. How many of them?"

"Twenty-five, fully operational and protected by a jamming system making our scanner inoperative. The previous owners hadn't even bothered destroying the slot cards before they left."

"Probably because the remaining personnel was unaware of its existence."

"*Vince?*"

"Yes, Emile. What is it?"

"*I just received a communication from our Central Command. They are detecting a vehicle coming from the Chinese base and heading our way. ETA fifty, fifty-five minutes.*"

"Thank you. We need moving. Emile, I want you and Sergeant Reid to bring our SEV here."

"*What about the food? Philippa found many goodies.*"

"Forget the food. We have a more important load to haul. We'll come back later if allowed. Captain, call your men. We will take everything with us. We leave in thirty-five minutes."

36

Sitting with his legs crossed over the edge of the cliff that had long served as a natural wall defending the city of Amadiya, the Prophet was serenely observing the sunrise on the horizon. A small altar of white stone carved with the symbols of the various religions associated with the city — the crescent of Islam, the cross of Christendom, the Atar of Zoroastrianism, and the star of David— stood behind him. The Golden Disc crowned its table, the emblem of God's benevolent light, the universal unifier of men's faiths. Ferhad, his devoted servant, patiently waited a few metres away, ensuring his master was not interrupted. The devout man was meditating with his eyes softly closed, clothed in his black and white robe, while the ascending light of the sun slowly warmed his frail body from the coolness of the night. He had spent the previous hour cultivating this discipline learned from a holy man he met during his protracted wandering in search of God's revelation. Over time, the ritual had developed into a vital instrument for contacting the Creator of all Life and requesting his guidance. But it also provided comfort when his mind was consumed by the commotion of his past traumatic experiences. He was now so skilled that, with just a few slow breaths, he could calm the ravenous storm inside in minutes. However, this morning, there was no chaos. God was finally in communion with him after three days of fasting, speaking to him, and his Servant was listening intently. The Light was pleased, and his Prophet was thankful. Then, he was alone again, at peace. The path ahead was clear. He could now feel the sun's heat gently warming his face. The venerable man opened his eyes. The celestial light shone fiercely above the horizon, bestowing his benevolence upon the world. He detected a presence behind him.

"Yes, Elend?"

"Forgive me for disrupting your prayer, Noble Mahd, but they have arrived."

"All of them?"

"Yes, Noble Mahd."

"And you did as I instructed?"

"Yes, Noble Mahd."

"You are a worthy servant of your Prophet and our God, Elend, and a loyal one. Do not apologize for disturbing me whenever it is necessary. God and I shall always hold you in high esteem as long as your heart is pure. Is your heart pure, Elend?"

His dark eyes gazed intensely at those of the first lieutenant of his personal guard, penetrating deeply into his soul.

"Always in your presence, Noble Basheer," he answered with a devout and fearful voice.

"A faithful man shall abound in blessings. Very well, let us meet your father the Sheikh, the Elders, and the religious representatives. God has spoken to me, and I must deliver his message. Help me, will you, Ferhad? I fear this long chilly night has stiffened my poor legs. And give me my staff too."

Assisted by the young servant, the Prophet slowly rose and started to walk. Elend stood still, looking at his uniform, his hands clasped behind his back.

"Is there anything else you would like to discuss with me, Elend?"

"Yes, Aleem." His youthful face sounded embarrassed. "I… I wish to understand something…"

"Speak your mind."

"There are still people in town who refuse to accept your guidance. They speak lowly of you, some calling you names. Some of my Peshmergas are deeply offended by their demeanour. They ask why these people are allowed to spread their filth without being punished or at least compelled to admit their wrongdoing and submit to conversion. They say we are showing weakness, and I feel as confused as them…"

"True strength lies in the presence of weakness and the acknowledgement of God. I am The Messenger of Good News, the Basheer, Elend. Not Iblis, the Dark Angel, the Bringer of Sorrows. There will always be doubtful souls, Kafirs or Dharis. Those who deny the Light will ultimately behold God's wonders and repent from the errors of their ways. God promise me success. This success will wipe the last clouds off their eyes. I came to liberate people's souls, not to bind them by force. I forbid intentional violence. It is loathsome. However, those who choose to use violence against us will face the full strength of God's wrath. Tell your peshmergas my orders are to disregard these people. Do I make myself clear?"

"Very clear, Noble Mahd." His voice was now trembling.

"And if a member of my guard has an issue with my precepts, he or she may discuss their grievances directly with me rather than bothering my first commander."

"I shall make them understand, Noble Hafeey."

"Very good. Do you know why I chose you as my commanding officer, Elend?"

"Because of my combat skills and also because my father is the Sheikh?" he answered ingenuously.

The Prophet laughed at him.

"Your combat skills are undeniable, and your father's support is equally valuable. But no. I chose you because your name means daybreak. You bear the light out of the darkness and clear the path to the Messenger of Life."

Elend knelt and cried with joy.

"I am grateful for your guidance, Noble Prophet. I shall ever faithfully honour your wisdom."

"Arise now, my child. Let us meet the others."

The city's dignitaries were all gathered in the courtyard of the Great Mosque, where the bushes of jasmine and tea roses subtly blended their fragrances around them, playing with their senses. They wore white clothes and modest sandals at their feet to show humility in the presence of the Prophet. Several guards stood by the entrance, silent and still like statues. Then the man they once called 'the stranger' entered through the main gate, accompanied by his two closest followers. His frail body was moving with difficulty. A sign that he never wholly recovered from the dreadful icy nights he faced before his rescue. But his apparent weakness was entirely compensated by the fire burning in his eyes and the reverent fear it engendered. He calmly invited everyone to sit down and asked for coffee to be served. Elend stood alone by the gate, a few steps away.

"You wanted to see us, Noble Prophet?" asked Sheikh Zoran Barzani. He was smoothing the silvery hair of his beard with his right hand —a habit the Prophet had rapidly identified as a sign of discomfort or perplexity.

"Yes, Sheikh Barzani. God spoke to me last night. He is displeased with the leaders of this city. While the rest of his people suffer and yearn for justice in his treasured Kurdistan, you revel in comfort and indulgence."

A murmur passed among them.

"Noble Prophet, surely, God cannot blame us for the gifts he bestowed upon us," replied the goldsmith.

"He does not blame you for accepting them, Elder. He blames you for cherishing them greedily rather than using them to expand his glory. You felt the sting of his discontent once. Be wary of feeling it again, even more strongly. I deliver his message to you once again. The time is ripe for action. Amadiya is the first spark of the fire, which will eventually cleanse the souls of this world. God has condoned your past sins and has resolved to designate you as his chosen ones. You must fulfil your promise of obedience several months ago and pay your debt. Your Honour demands this."

"You are right, as ever, Noble Prophet. Yet you must understand you are asking us to go to war. To send our children away while we finally live in peace and safety. Surely, God does not want any more martyrs."

"God does not ask anyone to die in martyrdom, Imam Hozan. But how long do you think this peace will last? How long will it take for another warlord to start looting the surrounding villages and demand a tribute from the city? How long?"

"But... you are the Messenger of God, and your presence protects us."

"Not if I leave. If you are not prepared to follow God's path, He will lead me to a place where others will."

"Noble Prophet! You cannot abandon us!" wailed the elders in unison.

"I have no desire to abandon you as long as you fulfil your oath of allegiance to the Light. And the first step to achieving this is to liberate our beloved Kurdistan. This land has lived in chaos for far too long, left to the mercy of powerful men who seek only their selfish gratification. The time has come for the Just to be seen and for the world to see Him."

"The Light, the Just. Who are you deceiving, *Noble Prophet*, or should I say, *Noble Charlatan*?"

The others turned to the Chaldean priest with dismay, some trembling with fear. The sheikh's son began moving slowly towards him.

"Stay right there, Eldin. I can handle it perfectly. Father Agrin, I am wounded by your unkind words. One would believe the prospect of my departure would delight your corrupt heart."

"There is no corruption in my heart. You ARE a charlatan, A FRAUD! Leave if you want. Good riddance! Your little tricks are no miracles; they are the work of an illusionist. You may have fooled most of the city's inhabitants with them, but you are not fooling me. You manipulate their fears and play on their hopes. You are the Devil in disguise!"

"Is that what you reported to the Apostolic Nuncio in Jerusalem, Father? The list of my tricks?"

The priest's face turned pale in shock.

"Yes, Father Agrin, I am familiar with your little game of spying and your eloquent correspondence with the envoy from Rome. You see, God speaks to me, has eyes and ears everywhere, and—"

"God does not speak to you, and he never did! You were in need. We gave you shelter and food with goodwill. And as a reward, you mislead everybody. You are just another opportunistic—"

"Silence, priest! How dare you interrupt the Servant of the Light and challenge its message? A single word from me and your insignificant little church will welcome only ghosts!"

He rose, pointing the finger at him. At the same moment, they heard a gunshot from the rooftop to their right. The Prophet collapsed as some Peshmergas rushed toward the fleeing sniper. The other ones ran to shield their leader and Ferhad, who hurried to his help. A scarlet stain marred the holy man's immaculate robe.

"Noble Prophet! Noble Prophet! Talk to me!"

"It is alright, Ferhad. It is just my leg." The Prophet's face was distorted by pain.

"Quick, guards, take him to the hospital."

A few hours later, almost all the city's population had gathered on the main esplanade following a call from their sheikh. Contradictory rumours claimed the Prophet had been shot, was seriously injured or even dead. The citizens of Amidaya were in shock; some were hugging each other or crying, and others begging God not to abandon them. A large podium was hastily erected at the end of the square, surrounded by Peshmerga fighters armed with Kalashnikovs. The Sheikh and the Elders assembled to the right, and the religious leaders to the left. The tension was palpable everywhere in anticipation of an upcoming announcement. Then the Prophet appeared, magnificent in his golden and brilliant attire, holding his sacred staff. He walked labouriously, limping on his right leg, helped by his first lieutenant and closely followed by his servant. He raised his hands toward the sky, silencing the crowd.

"My brothers and sisters! Today, someone attempted to deprive you of the presence of your Prophet. Today, someone tried to silence me!"

The whole square exploded with screams of rage.

"But this miserable conspiracy has failed! God protected me, and the perpetrator was apprehended!"

Two Peshmergas appeared, dragging a chained prisoner before forcing him to his knees at the podium's edge. Several voices demanded his death. Some people attempted to reach the man, giving him a menacing glare whilst being held by the warriors.

"My brothers and sisters, citizens of Amadiyah! I understand your wrath, and your thirst for justice humbles me. But this man is as much a victim as I am. He is innocent in his guilt, a wretched soul manipulated by an unscrupulous evil mind willing to destroy the Messenger of God. I spoke to this man. I saw his suffering lingering at the bottom of his soul. And I forgave him, as Abraham, Jesus, and Mohammed forgave the kafirs before me!"

The crowd erupted with loud cheers.

"Yes, my brothers and sisters! I forgave him because he acknowledged his sin and rejected the evil spirit who tried to pervert his eternal soul. I forgave him, for God is merciful and blesses the souls of those who repent! But God is also angry! He is angry at those who have sought to silence His voice, to silence yours!"

"Retribution!" shouted someone.

"Yes, retribution! God demands that this crime not remain unpunished. Because God rewards the faithful and chastises the heathens. God calls for your help. Be his avenging sword against his enemies."

"Show us the way, Noble Prophet! Be our guide!" called out someone else.

The Prophet grasped the hand of the chained man.

"This wretched creature revealed everything, and I have listened to his confession. He speaks of a dark shadow in the west plotting against our wealth, our families, and our peace. Hear me out! A new evil is in our midst, ready to sow chaos and destruction. This evil lurks in Qadesh!"

Elend stepped forward, facing the crowd, and raised his weapon above.

"To Qadesh!"

"To Qadesh!" they all answered.

37

The four heavy armoured vehicles moved at high speed in the middle of the chilli, bleak night, leaving behind heavy dust clouds. Before the Second American Civil War broke out and the entire region collapsed into chaos, the arid landscape surrounding them was formally known as the Kingdom of Jordan. They now fast-approached their destination, the city of Madaba. The convoy crossed the suburbs until it reached the gates of a sumptuous residence protected by high concrete walls, barbed wire, and a group of mercenaries. One of the heavily armed guards approached the leading car and allowed them in a moment later. The courtyard was lusciously planted with palm trees and exotic essences soothing the austere surroundings. The right rear door to the middle car opened, and a grim, hooded shadow emerged before rapidly entering the main building. The inside was lavishly decorated with mixed blue ceramic tiles on the walls, carved columns and patterned wood panels while furnished with elegant contemporary furniture. The owner of the house was deliberately flaunting his wealth. And wealth during those turbulent times could only come from cunning power or profitable smuggling. The ghostly figure was introduced into a private lounge where a man wearing a traditional keffiyeh and thobe waited for him. He was self-proclaimed Emir Abdul Al-khawaldeh, the Conqueror of Amman, one of the most powerful warlords in the Middle East with a dire reputation for greed and a taste for violence.

"The peace of God be upon you, Emir Al-khawaldeh," declared the hooded man whose only visible feature was his prominent grey beard.

"And upon you, Wali."

"Thank you for agreeing to this meeting, although I was not expecting such a fancy place."

"You insisted on the location being secure and discreet. My good friend Osman Tawil, owner of this house, suggested it. The place is safe and away from indiscreet eyes."

"Safe? How can we be certain he is not spying on us? Allow me to question the motives of the largest arms dealer of the region."

"For if he betrays me, my face will be the last thing his eyes will ever see in this life, Wali." The dark eyes of the emir fixed the shadow with displeasure. "Measure your words, Abd Allah. To insult my host is to insult me. At least he does not conceal his face before me."

"Pardon me, Emir; I meant no disrespect. Naturally, I have confidence in your judgment. And you are fully aware we cannot be sighted together, even in private."

"What is the situation in Jerusalem?"

"Moving slowly, too slowly. The High Council members are divided on how to respond to the situation in

Kurdistan. We may have to shake the complacent ones before it gets out of hand."

"May I remind you that you—"

"You do not need to remind me anything, Emir! I am well aware of the calculated risk I take by requesting your assistance. There's nothing left to argue. However, that assassination attempt on the so-called prophet was a mistake. It achieved the opposite of what we had agreed upon."

"That was not my doing. My contact believes there could be another faction at work. We need to be more careful down the road."

"Or the man is cleverer than we initially thought. That means he will be uneasy to control. A more worrisome thought. We can initiate our other plan in the worst case, provided your troops are ready."

"Five years of preparation, they are more than ready. I am more concerned about the possible response from the Israeli-Palestinian Federation. After all, they are the guarantors of the Treaty of Neutrality."

"Leave that to us. We dispose of well-positioned friends within their government. The Federation will not move until the deed is executed and your men are safely back behind the border. You will have plenty of time to destroy this monstrosity, as we should have done years ago."

"What about the two members of the High Council who are not part of our little arrangement?"

"One has declining health. He represents no threat and is easily manipulated. The other one is fully occupied with Kurdistan, thanks to the unexpected help of the Vatican. If necessary, I will feed these servants of Rome with more baits to lure them away from our affairs long enough. Once your part is achieved, we will make sure they acknowledge the benefits the loss of a few lives brings compared to what would happen if the abomination were revealed. As long as order is restored and the continuity of our faiths ensured, they will turn a blind eye to this small price."

"And you will recognise my claim?"

"As a reward for your services in delivering us from that sword of Damocles. We shall recognise your claim as Caliph and Protector of Jerusalem."

"Insha'Allah."

"Insha'Allah. Now, if you will excuse me, I shall return to my duties. I will keep you informed through the usual channel. Good night."

The shadow swiftly fled the mansion as discreetly as he arrived. However, as he went out, he failed to notice the presence of a black banner showing the Seal of Muhammad...

***

Father Calleja had just passed through the immigration gates and was carrying his small bag out of the international area. He was two days behind schedule. An unexpected severe storm had forced his private jet to land in Cyprus with no alternative but to wait for air traffic control to give the captain clearance. *Hopefully, nothing major had happened in the meantime*, he thought. The news was more focused on hurricane Konrad's devastations than the obscure situation in Kurdistan, which, in a way, was an auspicious sign. After passing through the rear gate, he exited to the arrival area. People gathered behind the metal fences, waiting impatiently for friends, relatives, or work colleagues when he recognised a familiar figure holding a sheet of paper with his name. It was arduous to forget that bold, cheerful face standing proudly on a stout, short body.

"Brother de Vries, how nice to see you again! Thank you so much for picking me up at the airport after that dreadful journey."

"My pleasure, Father. I'm so glad I was assigned a mission with you again. So many years have gone by since we last collaborated."

"I must admit you have not changed at all! The same bountiful man I recalled. You certainly seem to take advantage of the local delights and the climate."

"Absolutely! And I'm not embarrassed to confess it! While you got more grey hair."

"My last assignment in Peru has been more stressful than expected, my friend. Hopefully, this one will be more accommodating. Any news?"

"Nothing I'm allowed to divulge until you meet His Eminence. My orders are to accompany you directly to the nunciature. All I can say is you shouldn't be expecting good news. Things have taken a new turn in Kurdistan."

"Let's go, then!"

The diplomatic car took them through the only direct route connecting Ben Gurion - Arafat Airport to the Holy City. Remains of the concrete walls and miradors that separated the two states until the middle of the century bordered the highway. Some portions had been preserved in memory of a bygone era. Unexpectedly, after more than a hundred years of shed blood and tears, the collapse of the American power drove the long-standing enemies to open friendly talks, eventually leading to a single-state solution. A federation built on equal foundations among a Middle East disintegrating into multiple factions. They finally reached the Christian district, home to the apostolic nunciature in Jerusalem. Father Calleja went first to his room to freshen up before being escorted to the office of Cardinal Chehab where Brother de Vries was already waiting.

"Father Calleja, I am delighted to meet you. Your reputation at the Vatican precedes you. Welcome to Jerusalem. I cannot tell you how pleased I am to see you here. May I offer you a drink? I have quite a selection to choose from."

"Thank you, Your Eminence. A simple coffee, with milk and no sugar, will be wonderful."

The prelate took a thermos and poured the beverage himself before handing a cup to the priest.

"Please sit down. I heard you experienced an eventful journey on your way here."

"I have become familiar with the word 'eventful' quite often lately, Your Eminence."

"Well, I fear you'll still have to deal with it."

The cardinal's face turned into a more solemn gaze as he sat in his chair.

"Over the past three days, the situation in the Kurdish region has accelerated. We have received reports of a recent attempt on the life of the so-called prophet that sparked a regrettable chain reaction. The instigator seems to have been a local warlord based in the city of Qadesh, about ten kilometres west of Amidaya. Within a few hours, the Prophet's Peshmergas captured it with almost no resistance. The incident could have ended there if the Prophet, encouraged by his success, had not decided to pursue the adventure, launching a crusade to subject all the local warlords and unify the whole region. Brother de Vries, if you please."

The Jesuit Brother spread a large-scale map of what was once Northern Iraq on the table.

"Here is Amadiya," carried on the Cardinal while pointing out the place. "And here is Qadesh. The Prophet's forces subdued the entire area from the Turkish border to the Tigri in just two days, rallying more partisans and troops. They have now established their command headquarters in the city of Duhok, which holds the southern route to Mosul. I suspect this may be their next target. And from Mosul, they will most likely head for Ebril, the former capital of the province of Kurdistan. At this rate, if nothing stops them, they will control the whole country within a week. What happens after this? Hard to predict as we lack information. That's where you step in."

"And Turkey has not intervened?"

"Absolutely not! The Kurdish parliamentarians threaten to withhold their support to the coalition's government if it attempts to intervene in what they regard as a *liberation movement after ten years of suffering in the hands of the local warlords.* They also accuse the Turkish state of laissez-faire when those same warlords crossed the border to raid their lands. An attempt to initiate talks was unsuccessful."

"I see…"

"And to top it, the entire conquest has been achieved without bloodshed to this day."

"What do you mean by *without bloodshed?* There has been no fighting?"

"Except for some skirmishes, nothing! Every time the prophet's troops approach a village, a town, or a city, the same scenario occurs. The local population rebels and overthrows the leaders in place before surrendering them to the insurgents. All the deposed warlords have been imprisoned and are awaiting trial. The Prophet's orders are strict: no bloodbath, no self-righteousness. This whole thing is just baffling. We have yet to see if Mosul will follow a similar path."

Father Calleja sank into his seat bewildered. What he just heard made no sense. *A man who professes to be a prophet on a mission to unite Kurdistan peacefully? What is the catch?*

"Did the prophet make any claims or demands outside Kurdistan?"

"Nothing, so far, except for a few confused reports received by the High Council about bringing religions together under one dogma."

"I was forgetting the High Council. What is its response in that regard?"

"Very little. Not to my knowledge, anyway. Officially, my colleagues consider Kurdistan too remote to be of concern, despite my numerous calls for a more thorough investigation. They have been wallowing in their privileges and position for far too long. But Rome has a different perspective and sent new instructions for you. You must travel to Mosul and make contact with this self-proclaimed prophet."

"Contact?" Luca opened his eyes in surprise. "But we were only supposed to assess the situation from aside."

"Sadly, this was before the recent turn of events, Father." Now, the Holy See wants you to adopt a more direct stance and determine what potential threat this man could represent. You are granted the power to open negotiations if required. You have Carte Blanche from the

Vatican. I asked Brother de Vries to make all the necessary arrangements for the two of you to leave tomorrow morning at dawn."

"The sooner, the better, of course... There go my hopes for an ordinary, boring mission. Our Very Reverend Father entrusted me with another task before I left, but I suppose it will have to wait."

He looked at Brother de Vries.

"Well, Willem, I better get a good night's rest just in anticipation of forthcoming sleepless ones."

"Not before a proper dinner, my friend."

38

"Dear holo-viewers, thank you for joining us tonight." Gerhard Hoffmann, the star presenter of Words of Truth, the most popular political show on the European networks, fixed the cameras with his emerald eyes. "For forty-eight hours, our network has promised you an exceptional guest this evening. Trust me; you won't be disappointed. Although the most prominent politician in our country, he rarely appears on the holos. His devoted supporters will explain he's an extremely busy man, committed to working for the good of Europe. His critics accuse him of deliberately avoiding the media because he despises them. His election two years ago defied everyone's expectations. His resolve and courage to stand up for his political convictions while tackling his personal health issues have won over enough of our citizens to give him a comfortable majority in Parliament before securing the supreme office. On several occasions, I've tried vainly to invite him to participate in that program. It took the recent dreadful events for him to accept joining us finally. Tonight, he'll answer the carefully chosen questions from our secret random hollow-viewer panel and give you the answers YOU want. Arrrre you ready to hear his words of truth?"

"Yes!" replied the audience with enthusiasm.

"So, please give a warm welcome to Pierre-Antoine Lascombes, the President of the United Federation of Europe!"

Pierre-Antoine entered the stage under intense applause and a few hoots. After a vigorous handshake, both men took their seats.

"Mister President, it's a great honour to have you with us tonight on this special program that your team and I have worked on for the past few days. I want to thank you for accepting our invitation, despite the terrible circumstances that have affected our country since last Wednesday."

"You are welcome, Gerhard, and I would like to thank you for having me here tonight."

"So, before we address more personal topics, can you update the millions of people watching us on the situation as it is this Friday?"

"With pleasure." The President looked at the cameras and the audience, placing his feet firmly on the ground and interlacing his fingers. "My fellow citizens. I stand before you after spending the past twenty-four hours visiting various sites along the Atlantic coast to assess the damage caused by Hurricane Konrad. I have witnessed scenes of desolation and devastation. Hundreds of cities and villages have been ravaged, thousands of families have lost everything, and much of our Atlantic coast is in ruins. It is the first time in the history of our continent that we are confronted with the consequences of a level-five cyclone.

We all know the reasons so much damage took place. For decades, eminent scientists warned such a disaster would ultimately reach our shores and that Europe needed to adopt critical measures. Of course, successive governments allocated resources to develop and improve facilities to limit the impact of such a possible climate event. And without these investments, the devastation would most likely have been worse. But considering the devastations I saw, they were insufficient. When the sole strategy available is to evacuate thousands of square kilometres and put over fifty million people into shelters to wait for the storm to pass, you know our measures were insufficient. Fifty million people! And this is merely for our country!"

"How should the authorities respond, Mister President?"

"My primary concern is providing protection and care for the hundred thousand people left homeless. As such, I have ordered the deployment of multiple regiments from France, Italy, Spain and Germany, in each afflicted area, in cooperation with local police forces. As I speak, shelters and refuges are being erected on the mainland under the supervision of the High Commission for Defence, the High Commissioner for Domestic affairs, and the Commissioner for Industry and development. I also addressed Parliament to vote on a special resolution to immediately release, under the supervision of the European Central Bank, an emergency package of five billion euros to cover the cost of the immediate damages. Each affected person will receive a fifteen thousand euros subsidy for immediate expenses until insurances take over. The European Federation Solidarity Fund will ensure every claimant receives a just compensation. But I also want to take this opportunity of being live tonight to address you, my fellow compatriots."

Pierre-Antoine stared at the cameras with a solemn face.

"Citizens of Europe, tonight our country is facing a bleak time. Hundreds of thousands of individuals, families, children, and seniors are alone on our streets and need your help. I urge you to put our differences aside and show the rest of the world what we, Europeans, mean by solidarity. Demonstrate the reasons our Federation was created. Any initiative to alleviate the burdens of these people, even the smallest, will be a blessing to them. So get out, visit your neighbours, contact your national or local associations, volunteer with your local governments and administration. They expect your commitment; they expect you!"

"That's an intensely moving appeal, Mister President. Bravo!" A tear rolled down Gerhard's cheek. "Everyone watching tonight's show will answer it fervently. Will you?"

"YES!"

After a brief hiatus, he faced the cameras. "You heard the man, people, let's all work together. Show you care!"

The audience applauded enthusiastically.

"For those willing to help, a national emergency number displays at the bottom of your holoscreens. Operators are ready, do not disappoint them. With your permission, Mister President, I would like to return for a few minutes to the extent of this unfortunate catastrophe. You said earlier the measures implemented were insufficient and that more could have been done to minimize the impact of this tragedy. What more could we have done, in your view, and what prevented the implementation of these measures?"

"My dear Gerhard, thank you for allowing me to clarify the circumstances that led to this federal failure. Because, yes, our government institutions have collectively failed. And I want to apologise tonight to everyone who lost their house, possessions, or worse, a family member. We failed you. We have not failed you because of our incompetence. No, we have failed you because the institutions supposed to defend you are flawed. That program is called Words of Truth, so let's hear it. Since our unification ten years ago, successive federal administrations have been petitioning the different political parliamentary groups, seeking increased funding to implement solutions to the unstoppable decline of our planet resulting from global warming. Yes, I mean it, unstoppable. Continuing with the belief, as some people keep pretending, that we can turn back the clock is an illusion, a fantasy. We have long moved beyond the point of no return. In part because our world has become a playground for individualist nations that refuse to work together. This hurricane is the first major event of an established line of coming climate disasters, and we need to adapt our country to the challenges it faces. For instance, under President Kowalczyk, I proposed legislation to erect stronger coastal defences against tidal waves, tsunamis, and sea-level rise. What was our Parliament's response? To vote a mere mite and delay the adoption of the entire text because it did not consider it a priority, and the cost was exorbitant. But what is the cost of this inaction to our unfortunate citizens this evening? At the same time, local authorities were encouraged by some of our parliamentary leaders through a partisan decision to grant building permits in areas at risk. For which reason? To protect short-term profits and developments! As a result of this greedy behaviour, our government is currently experiencing a major disaster with substantial financial consequences. I have consistently advocated for launching a new class of weather satellites capable of partly regulating the weather. Naturally, they cannot stop hurricanes but can reduce their strength. In my last attempt to propose their commission, I was explained the time was not right. Well, I tell these politicians that the time is right for millions of homeless people tonight!"

He turned to the cameras.

"This will be my second appeal tonight. Heinrich Wagner, President of the European Parliament, where are you?! Will you answer my call? Will you finally accept the responsibilities for which the people have elected you? Will you give your full support to this administration and act in the interests of our citizens? The time for concerted action is now. Prove your courage and resolve rather than hiding behind your chair!"

A high pitch gasp burst backstage, immediately covered by the audience's boisterous cheers.

"This is a passionate plea, Mister President, with strong accusations. But President Wagner represents the majority which elected you. Without a doubt, your words will cause a stir."

"This majority elected me, thinking I would spend my time cutting ribbons. We are a presidential political system; we must work together and implement the agenda for which we were elected. I cannot leave our administration's actions on hold because *the time is not right*. The European people are judging us tonight. They want a display of unity, not of disagreements."

"Well, I'm confident that President Wagner will respond promptly to your call. Meanwhile, to illustrate the situation, let's watch a short report."

The lights went out, and on a big screen appeared disturbing images of people in tears before their houses and buildings in ruins, asking for help or wandering with a helpless, desperate look. The video swapped to religious groups of different confessions praying, invoking the mercy of God; some holding signs quoting the Book of Revelation or shouting warnings of the forthcoming apocalypse. The scene shifted to Saint Peter's Basilica, where Pope Urban IX was leading a joint prayer with the leaders of the major religions, imploring God's forgiveness for their sins. Then the light went back on.

"These are intensely moving images. How do you react to them, Mister President? One cannot blame expressing religious beliefs after seeing these images worthy of an apocalyptic scenario, right?"

"Though I have the utmost respect for all religious beliefs, which, I remind you, are protected by our Constitution, I feel uncomfortable looking at these pictures of prayers and calls to expiation. It seems that rather than helping directly and acting compassionately, religious leaders are again using the fear card. A propensity that has increased among various confessions in recent years."

"You are hardly religious, aren't you?"

"I have my own beliefs, like most people, I suppose. However, as a politician elected on secular principles, I refuse to allow those beliefs to interfere with my duties and my oath to act for the sole benefit of our nation's citizens. Over the past twenty years, religious lobbies have campaigned conspicuously to reverse some of the egalitarian policies and laws introduced by our administrations to protect the freedoms of each individual. On several occasions, Pope Urban IX, Berlin's Grand

Mufti, France's Chief Rabbi, or Kiev's Orthodox Patriarch, to mention the most active ones, have tried to interfere in our secular affairs, sometimes collectively. Fortunately, unsuccessfully. But I believe their influence may, under certain circumstances, threaten our institutions, particularly through radical religious groups. We should not forget that ten years ago, a member of an apocalyptic movement defiled the birthdate of our federation with the blood of innocent people, all in the name of God. Therefore, it is our duty to remain vigilant while preserving the freedom of expression of our spiritual ideologies. The present crisis should not serve as an excuse for these leaders to preach a message of fear. That is my message tonight."

The audience reacted with a mix of approval and whistles and boos. The host calmed everyone before continuing.

"We hear you, Mister President. On the other hand, you just mentioned egalitarian policies and freedom of expression. How about civil liberties and freedom of speech? They have lost ground over the last ten years. Some people and civil activists are accusing the government and parliament of trying to confine us to a police state. For instance, certain temporary measures appear to have become permanent. Don't these measures go against the statement you just made?"

"Well, Gerhard, let us not lose sight of the reality surrounding them. Since the beginning of the century, most governments have encountered significant challenges. To name a few, two major pandemics that, thanks to recent medical advances, are part of the past. The current Second American Civil War and its nuclear threat to the world. Not forgetting the Ukrainian crisis, the fall into anarchy in the

Middle East and, more recently, the Indo-Pakistani conflict that, fortunately, my government succeeded in ending in extremis. They remind us that our world is no longer as stable politically and geostrategically as it once was. Consequently, we had to put in place restrictive measures to ensure our citizens could continue their daily activities without being armed. And, yes, at the expense of losing a little of their freedom. Regrettably, some have had to be extended because the situation is still volatile. However, in my opinion, by renewing the legislative that approved these measures by a landslide, the majority of our citizens have shown they support our decisions."

"What about social media? They are presently virtually completely under control. This is presumably the most flagrant example of a breakdown in freedom of speech."

"Everyone knows I retain a specific position on the subject and must agree to disagree. The confusion and inaccuracies with which uncontrolled social media smeared over two decades could not continue unchecked. Their adverse consequences, like during the second pandemic and the last American election, had to be stopped before the inevitable happened. The resulting proliferation of conspiracies, often orchestrated by certain foreign powers, was eroding our institutions and the foundations of our modern societies. I refute acknowledging it as a *breakdown in freedom of speech*. We have established a controlled environment, validated unconditionally by the European Court of Human Rights, allowing individuals to enjoy freedom as long as they respect its boundaries. To those who scream *dictatorship*, I would recall they can still freely criticize our institutions without fear of being deported to a gulag or a re-education camp!"

A part of the audience burst into applause while others looted.

"Wise words, Mister President. Before concluding this interview and taking a break, I have one last question. We were talking a moment ago about religious groups and the Middle East. What's the Government's position regarding the extraordinary events in Kurdistan?"

"I can assure you that the Government is closely monitoring the development of the situation. Currently, we have no certainty about the insurgents' motives. Are they political, nationalist, or religious? So far, we do not possess any specific claims reports that could enlighten us. All I can affirm is they did not commit any acts of violence or crimes against civilians. Everything has taken place peacefully and with the consent of the local populations. We have long supported the Kurdish people and will back any effort to pacify the region, provided it is done democratically."

"Are you not concerned we might take too long to respond?"

"Sometimes, you have to gamble in politics, Gerhard."

"Mister President, thank you very much for this illuminating conclusion and for attending our show tonight. Dear holoviewers, we will take a fifteen-minute break before welcoming our second special night guest, retired porn actress Candy Galore, who will reveal all her innermost sexual secrets. A not-to-miss opportunity to spice up your most intimate moments, assuredly…"

Pierre-Antoine shook Gerhard's hand and went backstage, where Monika was waiting for him with an ominous expression. Five minutes later, they were en route to the official residence in the presidential limousine.

"I cannot believe you convinced me to attend this show! Exclusive interview of the President of the United Federation of Europe, followed by a retired pornstar! What a farce!"

"She was extremely popular until her recent retirement, Pierre-Antoine. The ideal opportunity to maximise the audience potential and address the average voter, rather than a boring national speech from your office."

"Well, no doubt they were not disappointed by my performance... What is it, Monika?"

She was staring at him with killing eyes.

"What has gotten into you there? Are you mad? Openly attacking the President of the Parliament in front of a hundred million viewers! He is our ally, for goodness' sake!"

"An ally who exploits every opportunity to undermine the government's decisions as long as it serves his interests. Who needs enemies with such allies? Not to mention his utter incompetence."

"Possibly, but he knows how to maintain the majority together if necessary."

"Exactly, *if necessary*. Earlier, I asked him to grant me the exceptional powers provided by section 46 to address the crisis. He refused! *The Parliament is supreme!*" Pierre-Antoine mimicked the man's voice. "Fair enough. Well, work it out now, ha! Let us not discuss it anymore. The deed is done and hopefully will force him to shake his ass."

Monika became silent in her seat, crossing her arms and expressing disapproval.

***

Pierre-Antoine sat at his desk, mentally exhausted by a busy morning. Heinrich Wagner, accompanied by the various leaders of the majority, had left a few minutes ago after a lively discussion. Despite the anger and harsh words, they had reached a compromise and agreed to the emergency package. Just before, he had to endure a call from the Vatican Secretary of State demanding an apology for last night's comments. One of these days, I suppose... Leif came in, bringing a coffee.

"How did it go?"

"Didn't you hear from outside?"

"Oh, I did, trust me. It does not mean I know what went on."

"They will vote the package unconditionally. Which is more than I expected after the clarification last night."

"Ah yes, last night. Honestly, what went through your mind?"

"Leif, Monika lectured me already. If possible, I would like to avoid justifying myself to everyone close."

"Alright, alright, I will say no more. Your appointment is here. She waited patiently, under the attentive care of your humble servant, of course."

"Thank you, you are a star, as always. I could have found no better replacement for Isabelle."

"Neither a closer one," he replied with a wink.

"Don't you dare start... Come on, take her in before I kick your butt out."

"Yes, Mister President. As Mister President wishes. Right away, Mister President..." he replied obsequiously.

Leif returned to the waiting lounge.

"Ms Edwards, President Lascombes is ready to see you. Could I offer you another coffee?"

"A glass of water will be fine, thank you."

Liz Edwards entered the President's office with her customary feline grace. She wore a long cobalt dress, matching shoes, and a large red garnet pendant around the neck.

"Miss Edwards, I am delighted to finally meet you in person. I heard a great deal about you and your work. And please, accept my sincere apologies for keeping you waiting this morning. Regrettably, sometimes the affairs of the State cannot wait. But please, have a seat."

"It is an honour to meet you too, Mister President. And no need to apologise; I understand completely. Please, call me Liz."

"Very well, Liz. But before we begin, please tell me about our mutual friend, Doctor Caracciolo."

"He is fine. He works in Geneva now, as the Head Scientist of a pharmaceutical group. He also serves as an expert for the UN. He is quite a busy man."

"That is good to hear. How unfortunate he had to leave Edinburgh and stop his research there. As far as I am concerned, his cure still works wonders. Almost three years on, and still no side effects or trace of cancer. I genuinely never felt this great since my condition was diagnosed."

"This is exciting news. I will make sure to pass the message along next time I see him."

"Hopefully, very soon, as I am about to present you with an opportunity that might place a bit of a distance between you two. If you accept it, of course."

"You have my undivided attention, Mister President."

"Well, Miss Edwards —pardon me— Liz, I've been following your work for some time. In fact, from the time I was High Commissioner. I must tell you that I find your robotic creations fascinating and inspirational."

"Thank you, Mister President. I'm honoured."

"I know you also have been working on android concepts and even mind uploading."

"You are quite well informed."

"It is one of the privileges of my position. But my sources tell me you recently found yourself —how to state it properly?— limited. Yes, limited in progressing with your experiments. Am I wrong?"

She gasped before regaining her composure.

"You are more than well informed, Mister President, which troubles me about our security protocols."

"Do not concern yourself. Your secrets are perfectly safe. Let's say it is easy to detect one's frustration, and I have excellent intel. I wish to know the reasons for this lack of progress with your permission. Rest assured that whatever you say will remain entirely confidential."

"Well, Mister President, without entering any specific details and violating the terms of my employment, I would say I lack access to certain types of resources, mainly rare ones, in addition to a specific working environment. And you are right; I find the situation rather frustrating. But why do I feel you are already familiar with my problems?"

"As I can see, it is difficult to deceive you. You prove your reputation. So let me be frank with you. I am aware of your concerns, and my government looks forward to resolving them. I also know money is not an incentive to you. Here is my offer. As you likely know, over the last decade, we have entered a space race to colonise the promising quadrants of our solar system. This race is now focussing on Mars. I do not believe in this planet's prospects as a colony for various reasons that I will not dwell on here. No, while everyone is engaged in rushing to the Red Planet, I decided to expand our presence on the Moon. I believe it provides a more reasonable value for money before planning to look beyond. To ensure a rapid expansion of our installations, I am convinced robotics is the key. Therefore, I require somebody with extensive experience in this field. You are, in my opinion, the most appropriate candidate for this critical and delicate task. That is why I invited you here to offer you the position of Chief of Robotics Engineering on our lunar base. It should provide all the resources and the environment you desperately seek with full government funding."

Liz's jaw fell off.

"Oh my god! This is so unexpected. I... I'm not sure what to say."

"Say nothing yet. In less than two weeks, I am going on an official visit to the Moon. What about joining the delegation and me? You could meet our Administrator Principal, Vince Johnson, and the scientific team. Then decide if the prospect interests you. I have already taken the liberty of asking your employer to grant you a special leave. Naturally, if you are interested."

"If I am interested? Are you mocking me, Mister President? I will be more than happy to accompany you. This is like a dream come true!"

"Welcome aboard then," he replied, shaking her hand.

39

"Ferhad, serve me more tea, will you?"

"Right away, Maraj."

The young man took the teapot and poured some of the hot beverage into a gilded tin cup while the Prophet looked at him. He had remained his faithful servant for nearly three years, relentlessly caring for him and the places they shared. Before being brought by the local villagers, Ferhad lived like a pariah, a child orphaned by the war, wandering the neighbourhood streets, begging, or offering up his skills in exchange for a few dinars. Whenever the authorities tried to place him in foster care, he escaped after a few weeks, returning to the streets and the small den he used as his home. Ferhad cherished the freedom a solitary life allowed him. But all suddenly changed with the arrival of the holy man. From the first moment he encountered him at the shepherd's house, he knew his life's purpose was to serve and tend him. When the Elders decided to settle the Prophet in his own house, he offered his services and has followed him ever since. The orphan never complained or expressed disapproval, seemingly happy about his condition. His master always allowed him to express his opinion freely or to dispense advice, which was highly valued. But most of the time, he remained silent. *Be my eyes and ears*, enjoined him the holy man. The religious leader never treated him as a servant but rather as an equal. In a way, the Prophet represented the father he had never had, the family he had desired, and it was comforting. He handed the warm cup to his master.

"Ferhad, did you ever desire your life to be different?"

The detached face looked at his master.

"No, Maraj, for my destiny has led me in your path. It is God's will."

"But don't you ever long for a wife, someone to seek after you and offer you a home, a family? I could give you all this if you wanted. You merely have to ask."

"I lost my family very young, Maraj. And the ones who looked after me never filled the void of my soul. I do not know how to care for someone or give love in exchange. How can I desire something I possess no knowledge of?"

"You do take care of me, and I believe, in your way, you hold me in your heart. Why wouldn't you feel the same for someone else?"

"This is different, Maraj. I serve God. And when God is happy, I am happy. When God is sad, I am sad."

"I am no God, Ferhad."

"You are his Voice, his incarnation. My sole purpose is to serve you."

"No matter what happens?"

"No matter, Maraj."

"Even if, for some reason, I choose to follow another path in the future?"

"Who am I to judge God's choices? I shall serve you till my last breath. If you ask me to die for you, I will. This is my fate."

Then the servant sat a few steps away and remained silent, signalling he was done talking. The Prophet sipped his tea slowly. From where he sat, he could see the light of the full moon reflected into the calm waters of the Tigris River. His commander had sheltered him in a vast villa on the eastern shores of the old city, away from the enthusiastic crowds eager to see and praise their saviour. All seemed peaceful around. He could perceive the sounds of crickets and frogs mingling with the lapping water and smell the delicate fragrance of the jasmine bushes lingering around the terrace. It was nearly the middle of the night, but most houses had lights on. A group of people emerged from one of the rooftops on the Western banks, laughing and dancing, shouting their gratitude to the Prophet in the clear starry sky. The city had been liberated for a week now. Still, people continued to celebrate the downfall of the tyrant Abdul Bakr. Then, the call to prayer broke in the night, and everything went silent again. The vibrations and aromas captured the holy man's senses, luring his spirit. It would be so easy to remain here and enjoy a gentle and peaceful life among his followers, to settle down once and for all. But it's not my destiny; God decided otherwise... He was pulled out of his thoughts by a voice behind him.

"…Mahd?"

"Yes, Elend?"

"I just received news from Erbil, Noble Mahd. The city has yielded."

"Any casualties?"

"Very few, Noble Mahd. Apart from the local emir and some of his warriors, there was hardly any resistance, like everywhere else. Unfortunately, we did not capture the emir. He died during the final assault."

"It was his fate."

"Insha'Allah," echoed Ferhad.

"We also captured a priest. A Jesuit who calls himself Father Calleja. He travelled with another man, a Brother, he said. They surrendered willingly. The priest asks to see you; he says he is an emissary of Rome. What are your instructions regarding our next moves, Noble Mahd?"

"I shall surprise you, Elend, but we shall stand our ground and wait. The nations of the world now have their eyes on us, aware of our achievements. And the presence of this priest is proof of it. Let's not disappoint them. They were so focused on our advance to Mosul that they did not anticipate us simultaneously dividing our forces and marching on Erbil. We liberated all of Iraqi Kurdistan. That pleases God, for now. I want you to liaise with Commander Kawani. The two of you must recruit skilled and influential people in the communities to form a temporary government, draft a constitution, and organise elections within the next six months. The last decade was the second time in this century that the soul of our nation has been violated. First and foremost, we must strengthen our achievements. We have a country to bring together, and I confer the responsibility for overseeing its reconstruction upon you. As for the priest and the brother, I want them detained and treated reverently. I will look into the matter later.

"But, I thought—"

"I have spoken."

"It shall be as you ask, Noble Haad. Forgive my impudence. I will contact Elfesya at dawn."

Elend humbly inclined his head and began to walk away.

"There is one last thing I require from you."

The commander froze.

"Tomorrow, I will address the people in the Grand Mosque and send a message to the world. I want you to arrange a team to record and forward it to the major global networks. They should use the video I gave you a few days ago for editing. Good night Elend. Ferhad, pour more of that tea, please."

***

At noon the following day, an immense crowd of people of all ages, religions, and backgrounds gathered around the imposing mosque in the city's northern part. Its seventeen gilded domes glowed majestically in the deep azure sky. Despite the heat, people crowded out as the inner building was already filled. The Prophet, the liberator of Kurdistan, was about to speak, something he had not done since his arrival in the city. They were eagerly waiting for his message. Inside the mosque, those who had come early enough were contained behind metallic fences around the minbar at a safe distance. Three holo-cameras pointed up the pulpit, ready to record this historic announcement. Local dignitaries and religious leaders had been allowed closer inside the circle, under the vigilant eyes of the peshmergas, to prevent a repetition of the incident in Amadiyah. Soon after the prayer, the Prophet appeared dressed in golden robes, holding his gilded staff, and wearing a large mitre that partially hid his bearded head. He ascended the stairs and stared at the multitude gathered at his feet. The entire building went silent.

"My brothers and sisters, today is a joyous day. Erbil pledged allegiance, and all Kurdistan is free from its distasteful tyrants!"

The people exploded with great rejoicing. Some started dancing, while others kissed each other or cried tears of joy.

"You are now free to fulfil your destiny, to rebuild what has been destroyed over so many decades. I have instructed my two commanders to gather your most trusted religious and civil representatives from every corner to form a provisional government and draft a constitution to lay the foundation for our nation's future executive and assembly. I will ensure this process is conducted in a democratic, transparent way. I have no intention whatsoever of accepting the role of supreme leader, now or ever, or of founding a religious state. No. No religion or dogma will be granted predominance in state affairs, and your representatives will be elected out of their influence. I give you my solemn oath today!"

The second round of cheers was even louder than the first one.

"I will now address the nations of the Earth. People of the world, I come to you as the humble servant of the universal light, the messenger of the one God. Do not fear me, do not fear my people. We mean you no harm. We only seek to enjoy the freedom we have been deprived of for so long. I am the bearer of a message of hope and unity. For ages, your religious leaders have misled you, divided your faiths, coerced you against each other, and used fear to better control you. God is neither Jewish, Christian, nor

353

Muslim. God is the everlasting light which soothes our hearts and appeases our souls. He does not ask you to pour out the blood of your brothers, sisters, children, families, or neighbours. No! He wants to bestow each of you with his infinite grace, comfort you in this life and prepare you for the next one. Yes, I am telling you, you have been lied to, misled into centuries of deceit, and manipulated by those who claim they can save you, absolve you, and secure your passage to paradise. For millennia, under their calculated guidance, humanity has been compelled to commit atrocities in the name of God, corrupting the message he sent by not allowing Abraham's hand to sacrifice his son Isaac. Images taken in Jerusalem three years ago will now be screened before you. It reveals the truth your religious leaders want to hide from you. To achieve their purpose, religious officials killed a young cleric and subversively disposed of the lives of others. Back then, they called this footage a fantasy, a deepfake. They advised you to disregard them. And so they will again. Your religious leaders will try to convince you I am a false prophet, a limb of the Devil. They will focus on perverting your souls, as they have done over and over again for millennia, to ensure you continue to fall for their lies. And the majority of you will likely believe them because, for the most part, the truth is hard to accept. I know this. God knows this. But very soon, they will face retribution. The light which creates life and dispenses death will burn in the sky in a manifestation of God's almighty power. And your eyes will open; you will see his strength, feel his love, and understand you have been cheated. Prepare yourselves! This world is about to end and give way to a new one where justice will prevail, free from all lies. Prepare yourselves!"

The crowd stood silent, indecisive about how to react to the words proclaimed by their prophet, to the images visualised on the big screen. The sound of the voice saying *Joseph, son of Jacob, son of Isaac, son of Abraham,* kept resonating under the vaults. The Prophet suddenly looked pale and started to falter. Elend hurried to aid him down the stairs before escorting him silently through the vast assembly, still in shock. After several metres, the young commander looked at the leader.

"Noble Mahd, is it true? Is God going to show his wrath?"

"Not his wrath, Elend. His love. And we must prepare. You will bring that Jesuit priest to me. I want to hear what he has to say. Just let me rest for a couple of hours before."

***

Father Callejo got out of the armoured car, which had picked him up from his prison a moment ago, assisted by a guard. He stood handcuffed in the narrow courtyard, facing the main gate of a simple but elegant villa. *The Prophet's residence, most likely.* A young Peshmerga with a command insignia on his left shoulder waited at the door. He signalled the prisoner to follow him. They moved to the second floor of the building before entering a spacious room decorated with several rugs and a few modest pieces of furniture. There was a small kitchenette on the left where a man dressed in traditional Kurdish clothes was brewing some beverages. At the end of the room stood a vast terrace surrounded by jasmine bushes and colourful flowers, overlooking the Tigris River shimmering gently under the sun. A man sat directly in its centre, his legs crossed, his back to the priest, and a hood over his head.

The commander spoked in Kurdish. *Willem wasn't allowed to come with me, and I don't see any universal translator around, damn!* Followed a five-minute exchange in which the voice of the Peshmerga expressed anguish and frustration before becoming pressing. The only word Luca could recognise was *Maraj*, pronounced with great respect. *'The Above'. This is most certainly the man who calls himself the Prophet.* Then all of a sudden, the hooded figure interrupted the argument with a commanding tone. The officer bowed his head in obedience, then approached Father Callejo angrily. He vigorously seized the priest's arm to bring him closer before forcing him to his knees. The Prophet dismissed his commander with a single movement of his left hand.

"You wanted to talk to me, Priest?" he asked in English.

"Yes, Noble Prophet. It is an honour to be in your presence. His Holiness Pope Urban IX sends his regards—"

"Spare me that sweet diplomatic tirade, priest. I despise flatteries and palavers. Why are you here? What business do you have with me?"

The truth is always the best approach.

"I am here as an emissary from Rome. The Holy See is troubled by your actions and anxious about your motives."

"You speak with the voice of truth, Priest—a highly valued quality. I believe I made my intentions clear a few hours ago. I assume you overheard my address to the world?"

"Indeed, Noble Prophet. Your guards made us watch. But with all due respect, it was an assemblage of obscure unproven accusations and confusing divine omens. I doubt

His Holiness will be significantly impressed. What is your true objective? Destabilise monotheistic beliefs? Cause more instability to this already confused planet?"

"Seeing is believing, Priest. And your Pope will soon witness the full power of God, very soon. My sole purpose is to expose the truth to the world. Nothing more, nothing less. And again, this truth lies hidden in Jerusalem."

"About this, what other evidence can you provide than that meaningless fake video?"

"That video is no fake, Priest. It is a genuine recording taken by a friend long gone now. A young cleric who was swiftly eliminated by a group of unscrupulous clergymen who wanted to conceal the truth at all costs. This video represents his legacy. A legacy he entrusted me with. But I disregard all my obligations as a host. May I offer you something to drink, tea or coffee?"

"A coffee would be nice, thank you."

"Ferhad?"

The silent servant gave the priest a mug of hot coffee flavoured with cinnamon. The taste was pleasing and vivifying.

"Noble Prophet, let us imagine for a moment that I believe the content of this footage and your allegations. Where in Jerusalem lies this evidence that you pretend exists?"

"You should know. Rome was involved in its dissimulation. One of your own paid with his life in the conspiracy."

Cardinal del Pietro! "I swear, Noble Prophet, I know nothing about it. Another part of my mandate here is to investigate the circumstances of this death."

"Then the others covered it..." he said, almost whispering. "I can say nothing more until God reveals himself, Priest. But be aware that certain members of the High Council of Jerusalem hold the evidence. With them lies your proof. Learn where to watch."

"Another riddle... But what about—"

"I have nothing more to discuss with you and your Pope. You must content yourself with what I have given you. *If you continue in my word, you are truly my disciples, and you shall know the truth, and the truth shall set you free."*

John 8:31 and 8:82. The man knows his scriptures well.

"That meeting has now ended, Priest, and you have extended your stay in Mosul. I will ask my Peshmergas to escort you and your companion to the Israeli-Palestinian border from which you can easily reach Jerusalem. Whatever decision you take subsequently depends entirely on you. Employ your remaining time wisely. Goodbye, Priest, until we meet again. Elend!"

40

"Your attention, please, this is your Captain speaking. We shall begin our approach to the Lunar landing pad in a few minutes. Please, return to your seat and fasten your seat belt."

The three days journey was finally coming to an end. The space shuttle had departed from the lunar orbital station a few hours before, and Pierre-Antoine could see the lunar surface details on the large screen before them. Although it was their first space trip, each member of the small delegation seemed to have enjoyed the experience. They especially enjoyed the break in the guest quarters of the imposing station orbiting around the Moon. Its installations were more comfortable than the Earth Orbital, primarily used as a transit zone for all space travel. From the start, Liz Edwards had shown her excitement, behaving like a child being taken to a carnival. The rest of the group consisted of two European journalists, the deputy chief of staff, four special advisors and four special security officers. It was a low-risk trip, and President Lascombes had ruled out the idea of taking more people, primarily for financial reasons. He had left his half-brother Jorge in charge of the Government and the relief operations on earth. Preparing for this visit had already required numerous financial and human efforts. Postponing it would have been suicidal. Fortunately, everything was going well on the West Coast, mainly thanks to the enormous outpouring of solidarity the nation demonstrated following his call. *There is still hope out there,* he thought. The entire shuttle started shaking a little, and the lightning in the cabin turned red.

"This is your Captain again. For those travelling with us for the first time, the vibrations we are currently experiencing are completely normal. They result from the retrorockets slowing down our descent before landing. Don't be alarmed by the red light, it is the standard procedure. Just one more minute, and we will land at the astroport as shown on your screen."

The image displayed a large round landing area surrounded by powerful lights getting closer and closer. Next, they felt a significant tremor, and all the engines went off.

"Dear passengers, this is your Purser speaking. Please remain seated during the shuttle transfer to the arrival zone. Thank you for your understanding."

The platform on which the spaceship had landed slowly descended inside the lunar rock layer. After two minutes, the upper dome closed over their heads, and they heard a raucous hiss outside.

"This is your Purser again. I will ask you for a little more patience while Operation Control proceeds with depressurisation and fills the arrival zone with breathable air. Please remain seated in the meantime."

Liz grabbed Pierre-Antoine's hand with her thick glove.

"This is so exciting! I have not had so much fun in years! Thank you for giving me this opportunity."

"You are welcome."

Not everyone seemed as enthusiastic as she was. The colour of his deputy chief of staff's face oscillated between white and green, and appeared quite shaken. He tried to reassure her.

"It is alright, Maryse, it is over, I promise. The transfer to the base will be more pleasant."

"I... I hope so..." she answered, stammering.

"Dear passengers. We have completed the technical operations for the arrival, and the air is now perfectly breathable outside our shuttle. We will proceed with the disembarkation. We hope you had a pleasant flight and an enjoyable moment with us. Be sure to disconnect your magnetic boots, as they will be unneeded in the arrival zone."

A moment later, they all exited the spaceship. A detachment of ten soldiers lined up on each side awaited them, together with three people standing in the middle. Pierre-Antoine recognised Vince Johnson but not the remaining two. One wore a Russian uniform, and the other a Chinese one. The Administrator of the European Lunar Base headed to the president.

"Greetings, Mister President. It is a great honour to welcome you here today. I hope you had an enjoyable and comfortable trip."

"Mostly, Administrator Johnson, mostly. While I think I will speak for everyone here, saying we are glad to have arrived and walk on solid ground," Pierre-Antoine replied with a grin.

"Allow me to introduce you to Evgeny Kuznetsov, Administrator Principal of the Russian base, and his colleague Liu Chen, Administrator Principal of the Chinese base."

"A pleasure to meet both of you," the president said, shaking their hands. "Please, excuse my outfit. We have been enjoined to keep our spacesuits, especially as we still have some distance to cover."

"Do not formalise yourself, Mister President. We understand perfectly," replied the Russian Administrator. "On behalf of the Russian Federation and the members of the Russian Lunar base, allow me to express my country's sincere condolences for the recent tragedy which struck the United Federation of Europe. My government had urged me to renew its offer for any assistance required."

"Thank you for your kind words, Administrator Kuznetsov; they are greatly appreciated. Please again convey my thanks to President Alexeyevna and her generous offer. We have the situation in good hands now, but be certain I will contact her if we require any additional support."

The Chinese Administrator remained silent.

"May I quickly introduce my Deputy Chief of Staff, Maryse Demonceau, Julio Espinoza and Irina Kravchenko, journalists, and Professor Liz Edwards, our eminent expert in cybernetic intelligence and robotics."

"A pleasure."

"Evgeny, Liu, if you have no objection, we still have a long way to go. I am convinced the President and his companions are looking forward to getting some rest. I believe we will have the pleasure of meeting again at the reception tomorrow night."

"Of course, of course. We will see you tomorrow."

Half an hour later, the delegation was travelling at a moderate speed along the slopes of a crater. Pierre-Antoine was in the second moon rover with Vince, Liz, a security officer, his deputy chief of staff and Emile Dubois at the wheel.

"Well, it was certainly an experience, Vince. I never expected your two colleagues to wait for us."

"Hard to escape them. The landing pad is located next to Malapert Mountain, where their bases are. The elevated position gives them direct control on every arrival, even if the pad is considered as an international zone."

"Could not we consider building our own landing pad?"

"Impractical and very costly, I fear, Mister President, with minimal possibilities in our immediate vicinity. The site is regarded as the best possible and, as you know, both countries were there first. But we manage to cooperate quite well."

"That Chinese administrator did not appear to be the most pleasant."

"She is rather enigmatic. But I think her attitude was more a result of her suspicions about our little 'adventure' on the American base than a genuine antipathy."

"Both governments were briefed on President Wilson's consent when you set a date for the incursion. I did not want to have to justify it afterwards. Especially while we were dealing with the situation on the Atlantic coast. Surely, she was informed beforehand."

"Yes, but she is the suspicious type, especially since we left precipitously, not waiting for her investigative team."

"You left precipitously? What was the motive of the haste?"

"Something which requires your immediate attention as soon as we arrive, I fear, Mister President. It was simpler to wait until your arrival to discuss it. Unfortunately, you will need to keep your spacesuit a bit longer."

"You have me curious now. What is this about?"

"For your eyes only, Mister President, for your eyes only…"

In the middle of the afternoon, Universal Earth Time, Pierre-Antoine, Vince, and Emile, reached the entrance of a warehouse at the end of a long underground tunnel outside the Lunar base. After passing the airlock and removing their helmets and gloves, they entered a vast storage area filled with containers of various sizes and colours.

"This is where we mainly store substantial spare parts and hazardous materials. It is fully secured and separated from the main facilities. This way, please."

They walked along broad aisles where workers and robotic assistance units handled boxes and heavy pieces of equipment. Vince escorted them to an access door labelled *High Security – Restricted Access*. He placed his left hand on a screen while presenting his eye to a scanner. They heard a beep, and the door slid sideways. Upon entering the storage area, the light turned on to reveal its contents.

"Great Lord!" gasped Pierre-Antoine. "Are they…"

"X58-2 thermonuclear tactical missiles, Mister President, yes. I had heard about them, but I had yet to see any. Although small in size, they possess an intercontinental ability. Able to strike any corner of the Moon or even the Earth, with the proper alteration. Their primary purpose is surgical strikes, but they are powerful enough to level down a small city."

"Are they operational?"

"Fully. I even found launch codes and activation cards stored right next to them. The people who abandoned them seemed confident that they could not be discovered. According to the base manifest, they arrived shortly before the evacuation. The base personnel did not get a chance to position them. They likely thought they would return soon."

"How many are there?"

"Twenty-five, Mister President. I am surprised President Wilson did not mention them when you contacted him."

"I am not. A lot of confusion emerged following the Pentagon's destruction three weeks after the first ceasefire broke down. Something tells me he is most probably unaware of their existence. You did well to secure them, Vince. This could be a game-changer in the future. Who else knows?"

"Emile and the intervention squad. I have taken it upon myself to keep this discovery as quiet as possible."

"And it must remain as such. I shall consult our military command on Earth as soon as I return."

"Understood. Also…"

"What is it?"

"I need to take you to the research lab if you don't mind. We have one other issue to address."

"Mu blood pressure will explode at this rate, Vince, with all this unexpected news. And I thought it was just a routine tour."

"Let's get back to the main building."

Later, Pierre-Antoine spent half an hour in his private quarters, finally freed from the uncomfortable space costume. Just enough time to freshen up before Vince accompanied him to the facility's main laboratory. Liz was already there, playing with every available little toy and appeared in heaven. The minute she saw the president enter the research centre, she jumped on him.

"Mister President, this is simply a dream. I thought I had the best high-tech equipment in my lab, but it is beyond anything I could imagine."

"Well, our policy is to invest as much as possible in advanced technology to stay one step ahead. Our lunar research facilities are critical to our future space development."

"Say no more, Mister President. I accept your offer without a second thought! This is way too convincing. But, please, grant me the favour of not having to go back to Earth. I want to start right away."

"Well, this is completely unexpected, even if the purpose of this trip was to convince you in the first place. I will contact your employer to ensure they understand the situation. There will be some resistance, but the promise of extra funding should soften the pill. However, I do not want to be responsible for a breakup between you and Doctor Caracciolo."

"Do not worry. Our relationship is complicated. Thank you! Thank you!"

"Well, Administrator Johnson, please meet Liz Edwards, your new Head of Robotics Engineering. I do not doubt she will be a valuable asset to your team."

"Welcome to the Moon, Ms Edwards. It is a pleasure to have you among us."

"Please, call me Liz."

"Okay, that is resolved. Now, Vince, what would you like me to see?"

The Administrator waved to one of the scientists working in a corner.

"This is Doctor Richard Visser. He is supervising our astronomy unit. As you know, we are equipped with an assorted range of surface telescopes to survey the Universe around us, as well as the Sun. Aren't we, Richard?"

"Indeed, Vince." The short man looked at Pierre-Antoine with both excitement and nervousness. "Mister President, it's such an honour to meet you in person, and I'm so glad to have this opportunity to speak with you. I've addressed several reports to your administration over the past few weeks but still expect an answer."

"Although extremely effective, I fear my administration is not known for its speed of action. We have some urgent priorities to address right now."

"Of course, of course. What a tragedy this has been for us all."

"So, what does require my attention, Mister Visser?"

"Let me show you, let me show you."

He tapped on a portable keyboard and began to holo-project a dozen detailed pictures of the Sun, side by side.

"What exactly am I supposed to be looking for?"

"These are shots of our sun taken over the last three months. I'm sure you'll identify a few differences."

"I hate admitting I am not a big expert in astronomy, Doctor," answered Pierre-Antoine. He took a closer look. "Well, I certainly notice what resembles dark spots on our star's surface. They appear to increase in number and size on the latest photos."

"Exactly! These dark spots are actually called sunspots. They're a manifestation of the Sun's magnetic fields. When visible, they're usually concentrated on a small part of the surface and move back and forth according to our star's activity. But what the recent pictures show, Mr President, is a significant increase in the activity of the Sun—something we haven't witnessed in decades. The last time a similar activity occurred was in 2012, resulting in a solar storm that fortunately missed the Earth. And that was half of what you're observing right now. I fear we're witnessing the beginning of an unprecedented solar flare. Given the wrong alignment, we might be on the verge of a potential major catastrophe that could affect both the Earth and the Moon."

"Alright, but what time frame are we talking about?"

The scientist looked embarrassed.

"Well, that's the problem. Statistically, it could be now, just as in a couple of years, because this is only the fourth year of the current active cycle. Or it could suggest nothing. There have been active cycles in the past when nothing has taken place. It's not… an exact science, unfortunately."

"I see… No wonder no one took the time to investigate it in Strasbourg, Doctor. We are no big fans of probabilities."

"I understand. My apologies. But let me assure you that the danger is real…"

"That said, hypercanes in Europe were only a conjuncture. And look what happened last week. I remember that, alarmed by some eminent scientists on Earth a few years ago, we had invested in an alert structure as a preventive measure for this possibility. I will make certain they are up and running. Better safe than sorry.

Now, if you have any new suggestions, there is room for improvement, obviously. I will ask my chief of staff to send an alert before the end of the day. Could you possibly draft a brief for me on this before my departure? I will pass it on to the appropriate person for action personally."

"Definitely, Mister President. You'll get it tomorrow morning. Thank you, thank you!"

Pierre-Antoine looked at Vince with satisfaction.

"Well, despite the bad news, it seems I managed to please several people today. Let's have dinner. What is it you eat around here?"

41

The Prophet was enjoying another hot morning on the terrace of his villa, savouring a jasmine tea perfectly infused by his loyal Fehrad, when he heard the noise of footsteps rushing up the stairs behind him. His Commander entered the room and approached him respectfully.

"You asked to see me, Noble Mahd?"

"Yes, Elend. I received a vision last night. God is coming this morning. We must prepare for his arrival. Have you organised everything as I instructed you?"

"Yes, Noble Basheer. Everything is prepared."

"Very well. Then you must warn all cities immediately. We have just enough time left to brace ourselves."

"Shouldn't we first…"

"Now, Commander."

"As you order, Noble Haad. Forgive me."

He took off. A few seconds later, the courtyard resounded with orders to hurry.

"He contradicts you more and more, Noble One," said Ferhad. "Especially since you allowed the priest to go."

"He disapproves of my decision. He wanted me to keep him in jail for my safety. It is good to see he takes his responsibilities increasingly seriously. He finally realises the extent of what we are achieving. He is a charismatic leader with clear judgement and possesses a knack for people, like his father, if not better. I discerned this aspect of his nature from the moment we met. I have faith in him and stand by that decision. He will do good for this country. He just does not comprehend it yet."

"Aren't you concerned he may start to oppose you at some point?"

"He probably will, but not as you imagine. And soon, we will go our separate ways. He is questioning his faith now, as many of my followers are. They are all wondering why we suddenly stopped after so much success and why I refuse to take the lead and subjugate the entire region. My speech at the mosque added to their confusion. But very soon, all those thoughts clouding their minds will dissipate with the vision of God's glory. And you, Ferhad, are you doubting me too?"

"You already know the answer, Noble One. My pledge to you is unswerving."

"However, it shall be tested in the future."

"It will only reinforce my resolve, Noble One."

The Prophet smiled and looked outside once more. Suddenly, the clear azure sky started to flicker, shining in myriads of tiny dancing sparkles, until a massive blast of light completely shrouded the upper atmosphere.

"Serve me more tea, Ferhad, if you do not mind."

"Of course, Noble One."

***

The three clerics were running through the streets of Old Jerusalem, heading for the siege of the High Council, and led by Father Calleja, who was encouraging the two others. The instructions transmitted by Rome were explicit. He had to immediately shed light on the events that took place almost three years ago.

"Perhaps you should have rested a little, Father," said Cardinal Chehab, panting. "You barely returned from your ordeal."

"You read the answer from Rome as I did, Your Eminence. They regard the Prophet's accusations, however enigmatic, as crucial. The members of the High Council are definitely hiding something. And he did say we had little time, so hurry!"

They finally arrived at the Council building and rushed directly into the Great Hall. The other four members were all waiting, comfortably seated in their respective chairs. Patriarch Nicodemus II was presiding over the session, as usual. The usher closed the doors, and the cardinal took the stand.

"Your Beatitude, Members of the High Council, thank you for allowing this meeting on such brief notice." He took a few seconds to catch his breath. "May I present Father Luca Calleja, Jesuit priest and special envoy from the Vatican, on a mission to investigate the Prophet in Kurdistan. Brother Willem de Vries, a member of my delegation, accompanies him."

"In the name of the members of this Council, I welcome you to Jerusalem, Father," said the Patriarch. We were told

372

that you returned from Mosul last night and asked for an audience at the earliest. We look forward to hearing any information you can provide about this so-called prophet."

"Your Beatitude, thank you for your kind words and for accepting to see me so quickly. Sadly, there is little I can say about the Prophet. Despite our lengthy encounter, I was not allowed to stay in the city long enough to build up a clear picture of him before he ordered my return to the border. I can confirm he is a non-violent man. Brother de Vries and I saw how peacefully he took control of the country with the blessing of most of the local population. On the way to Mosul, all the villages and small towns we travelled through praised the one they called 'the Liberator'. He also initiated a process of establishing democratic institutions to stabilise the country. His followers seem extremely devoted to him, and his troops are certainly most loyal."

"So, in your view, a man of peace, with a more political than religious agenda. I am not quite persuaded this aligns with what we have gathered so far. Did he mention his intentions, especially outside the boundaries of the area that his rebels control?"

"I would not consider them rebels, Your Beatitude. They are extremely well organised, trained, and composed mainly of Kurdish Peshmergas. In terms of boundaries, his forces are all concentrated east of the Tigris River. And nothing during the brief time we were allowed in made us think they were about to move again. But I may be wrong."

"So, truly nothing but another warlord with religious delusion, more organised, and who will end up like the rest when a bigger fish comes along," said Rabbi Eliyahu mockingly.

"With all respect, Chief Rabbi, I think you are mistaken. The Prophet struck me as a devout man, respected by all. And he undoubtedly sees himself as a messenger of God. I assume you all have seen the broadcast aired a few days ago."

"Preposterous accusations!" suddenly burst the Grand Mufti, hitting one armrest with his right hand. "Who will believe the unfounded allegations made against this city by a deluded zealot threatening to unleash God's wrath on the revealed religions? On several occasions in the past, I have warned the members of the Council that he represents a danger and that he should be permanently silenced."

"My dear colleague, you are overreacting. We are talking about a remote danger," replied the Patriarch. "And which will eventually return to the anonymity from which it came, no doubt."

"*When the storm starts talking, no ocean can sleep.* You will recall my words when it is too late," Your Beatitude.

"So, what do you want from us, Father?" continued the patriarch, ignoring the Muslim leader.

Well, Your Beatitude, during our conversation, the Prophet specifically incriminated the members of this council regarding the tragic events that took place in 2064. He maintains the footage which emerged at the time and he played during his speech is authentic. Then he accused this council of a cover-up, especially regarding the death of Cardinal del Pietro and the existence of the stela seen in the images. I have received direct instructions from the Vatican to clarify those allegations with you."

"More unfounded accusations! And now carried by Rome!" blasted the Patriarch. "Listen to me, Jesuit. We have nothing more to report to you than what the investigation concluded. Cardinal del Pietro tragically died falling on the stairs of his residence. And the alleged existence of a secret chamber at the heart of the Rock of the Dome is sheer fantasy. There is no other truth or covert conspiracy." The Orthodox prelate moved closer to the Jesuit priest in an intimidating posture. "Naturally, if your Pope is interested in more details, he can always come here and request them himself."

"I will make sure to convey your answer to His Holiness, Your Beatitude. I am certain—"

Father Calleja was suddenly interrupted by an intense light overflowing the room as if the radiance of the Sun had increased considerably in intensity. They heard people screaming outside.

"God saves us! The sky is on fire! It is the end of the world! The Prophet was right!"

The clerics rushed to the windows and froze in terror at the vision before them. The azure sky had gone, and the heavens seemed to burn, ripped by apocalyptic waves of gigantic flames. Inside the hall, the lamps exploded as a powerful surge blew out every clogged equipment. They all took shelter under the large table in the centre to avoid being harmed by the shattering glass. The fateful event lasted about ten minutes before it came to a sudden end. Outside, the flames eventually disappeared, replaced by soft waves of greenish northern lights gently floating in the sky slowly returning to blue. They could hear people howling and weeping in the streets. Father Calleja picked up his holophone to make a call. A message was blinking on the screen: *Sorry, no service. Please contact your network.*

***

The presidential delegation had just left the Earth Orbital and was heading for the Cegled Starport in Hungary. The visit to the Moon had been reasonably productive despite a few worries. Pierre-Antoine hoped this would increase public and media interest, and convince Parliament to focus the space program there instead of the distant Mars. Everyone else was asleep, and he observed the sunrise on the starboard. He stared ahead at both pilots, methodically checking their instruments in preparation for landing.

"Control, this is the shuttle Charlemagne. Entering the outer atmosphere in six minutes," declared the captain.

"Roger that," answered back a voice on the radio.

The shuttle rotated its axis, presenting its shields to the atmosphere to absorb friction-generated heat.

"Control, we are ready to proceed with entry."

"Roger that, stand by for authorisation."

Suddenly, an alarm went off, and a red light repeatedly flashed on the right, taking the rest of the passengers by surprise.

"Control, we have a red alert. I repeat, a red alert. All systems are nominal here. What is happening? Over."

"Shuttle Charlemagne, this is Control. We have just been informed of an unexpected solar flare of extreme intensity heading straight for Earth. You must proceed with atmospheric entry immediately to avoid losing system control. Over"

"Copy that, Control. Please indicate the time to impact."

"You have five minutes, maybe less. Over" The voice sounded stressed.

"Copy that, Control. Initiating emergency entry procedure." He turned to the passengers. "Alright, people, we are going to make an emergency landing. Please fasten your seatbelt and place the oxygen masks that have dropped before you firmly over your nose and mouth. We will get through this, but it will be bumpy."

They all complied. Maryse was sitting beside Pierre-Antoine, looking terrified and having difficulty breathing. He grasped her hand and spoke calmly.

"Maryse, look at me, please. Just breathe slowly. One breath in, pause, one breath out. No need to panic. You heard the Captain. We will be fine. Again. One breath in, pause, one breath out. Yes, like that."

She calmed down a little. He felt remarkably peaceful and serene as if nothing could happen. After all, I already died three times. The spacecraft was moving slowly into the outer atmosphere when a tremendous flash of light burst inside the cockpit, glistening in a surrealist display. Alarms started to go off everywhere, and the pilots desperately tried to keep control of the shuttle.

"I have lost navigation!" shouted one.

"I can't shut down the boosters!" yelled the other. "Try to reboot. Hurry!"

The shuttle started spinning uncontrollably and accelerated its speed.

"Control, we have lost navigation! I repeat, we have lost navigation! On a crash course. Require direct assistance. Mayday, mayday!"

They all lost consciousness a few seconds later as the aircraft continued its rapid descent towards the ground inexorably.

42

"I am categorical; he is conscious. Mister President, do you hear me?"

Pierre-Antoine opened his eyes painfully. He quickly realised he was in a hospital room. A doctor was close by, examining him. A bright light passed through his eyes, and he heard the regular beep of a cardiac monitor. He felt something painful on his right arm. It was a needle from a transfusion valve.

"Just some hydrating fluid, Mister President," declared the voice. "I am Doctor Kastler. Do you hear me?"

"Yes, Doctor, I hear you."

"Can you give me your name and date of birth?"

"I am Pierre-Antoine, Louis, Richard, Lascombes. I was born on the 5th of September twenty-twelve, in Carcassonne."

"Excellent, Mister President. As I said earlier, there's no evidence of head trauma. The president responds very well to stimuli, and we detected no lesions or internal damage. Only several superficial burns on different body parts, and a few second-degree ones localised on the cranium, the left arm and the right leg. Nothing a good ointment and a little paracetamol can't fix. Every test we have conducted has returned negative. The patient appears slightly confused but is in perfect physical condition and can be discharged in the next two hours. I'll need that bed soon, so make sure he leaves on time. Now if you'll excuse me, I have more urgent patients to attend to."

The physician walked away. *He was not talking to me.* Pierre-Antoine looked further away and saw Monika and his half-brother seated in a corner, General de Soverosa and Fabijan opposite them. They were all silent, staring at him with bewilderment. The scene seemed like deja vu. He could now hear a cacophony of cars, sirens, and people yelling and screaming outside. It sounded chaotic.

"Where am I? What happened?"

Jorge approached him.

"You are at the Central University Hospital in Strasbourg. You were repatriated last night by a special convoy from Hungary, two days after we finally found your wreck. How do you feel?"

"I am alright. I feel fine. Why the faces?

"You… You had an accident four days ago."

"An accident?" His head was aching. He placed his right hand on his forehead. Confusing images formed in his mind. "Yes, I remember now. The shuttle… The lights. Is everyone else alright?"

"You… are the sole survivor of the crash. Most of the others were already dead by the time we discovered the wreckage. The remaining two are in the ICU, suffering from severe radiation burns. They are not expected to survive the night. It looks like one of the pilots managed to deactivate the thrusters and deploy the parachutes. But the shuttle was too close to the ground to reduce its speed significantly. After scouting the area blindly for hours, the rescue team eventually found the dispersed debris. Your body was discovered a few metres away from the main wreckage, most probably ejected during the impact. This was three days ago."

"Maryse?"

"I am sorry, hermano…"

"How terrible. But, how… how come I am still…?" He looked at his body and hands and saw only a few bruises. "… Intact?"

"Well…"

"Do not lie to him, Jorge," abruptly interrupted Monika rushing to his side. "You were in a terrible physical condition, Pierre-Antoine. We first assumed you were dead. Most of your body skin was burned, some up to the bone. And now… now…" She took his rosary in his hands and knelt. "God… it's a miracle!" Then she started crying.

"Monika, please sit down. Fabijan, please help her."

The Director took the crying Commissioner in his arms and walked her back to her chair.

"I… I do not get it, Jorge. What does she mean?"

"We are as mystified as you are, hermano. As Monika mentioned, when we discovered you, you could barely breathe; most of your skin was severely burned or fused with your clothes. We barely recognised you at first, if not for your damn gemstone pendant!" he said, chuckling. "And now… look at you…" He stared at him with apprehension. "… There are only a few scratches and bruises left. Even your hair had begun regrowing. By the time we decided to repatriate you to Strasbourg, your body had already half healed. The doctors here think we have all been hallucinating."

Pierre-Antoine remained perplexed.

"But what happened on that shuttle? Why did we crash? What were those lights I remember?"

"A massive solar flare caused it, followed almost instantly by a huge coronal mass ejection from the Sun. It hit Earth within minutes instead of the few hours calculated by most scientists in the past. The magnetic wave it generated impacted our planet on a global scale, knocking down all satellites, most of the generators and electricity grids. Communications, networks, and GPS systems have been inoperative for seventy-two hours. The entire world is literally blind, and shuttles and aircrafts are stranded on the ground. Our rescue team had to be sent by land, which explains why it took us so long to find you. But you saved Europe."

"I... I saved Europe?"

"Yes, you remember this controversial program that you fought so hard to convince President Kowalczyk and the Parliament to adopt despite its cost a few years ago? You know, the Emergency Preventative Blackouts System?"

"... Yes?"

"It worked, Pedro! It worked! Every main generator in Europe was turned off a few seconds before the major magnetic storm affected them. We are quite impacted. But at least we can still supply power and water to the main cities and are actively repairing the remainings. You are a genius, you know!"

He was interrupted by an officer who entered the room before standing at attention.

"Forgive my intrusion, Commissioner Sanchez, but they are becoming quite pressing outside."

"What is happening, Jorge?"

"It is a delegation from the Parliament led by the leaders of the main parties. When we informed them that you were doing well, they came here to urge you to assume the emergency powers under Article 46 of the Constitution. But—"

"Send them away!" screamed Monika. "He was in an accident just a few days ago, for goodness' sake! Are they without compassion?"

"It is alright, Monika. You heard the doctor. I am in excellent shape." Something popped into his mind, and he looked at his half-brother. "Was any official statement concerning my condition issued after I was discovered?"

"Are you joking? We have no working network. Only the people here and the rescue team know the details. We told the parliament and the press that you escaped thanks to a parachute and were only under medical supervision. I know, it is a bit far-fetched, but that was still better than trying to explain… that."

"Let us keep it that way, then. For now." Pierre-Antoine addressed everyone in the room. "Whatever happened to me, however extraordinary or miraculous it may seem, will have to wait for a reasonable explanation. The doctors have declared me fit, so I will accept the full powers they are offering me. The situation Jorge just described requires a prompt response. Especially since a little more than two weeks ago, we were already grappling with another significant crisis."

"Be careful, brother," murmured Jorge in his ear. "It is a trap in which these hypocrites wish you to fall into in the hope that you will fail."

"Well, I shall make sure to disappoint them, then," Pierre-Antoine whispered back. "Colonel?"

"Yes, Mister President!"

"Please, invite the Parliamentary Delegation in. I will see them now."

"Immediately, Sir!"

"An excellent officer; keep him close at hand. My first decision will be to declare a national state of emergency if that has not been done yet. Order and security are our primary goals in the coming days. And can someone remove this thing from my arm? It is increasingly annoying," he said, pointing at the transfusion pipe.

*** ***

The following day, Pierre-Antoine presided over the first crisis group with several members of his cabinet, his Chief of staff, the Director of the Department of External Affairs, and the commanding officers for air, sea, and land forces.

"...overnight we restarted all major electrical installations across the continent and restored power grids in the most densely populated areas. However, to offset the loss of power resulting from the devastation of the offshore wind turbines on the West coast caused by Hurricane Konrad and the shutdown of the nuclear powerplants following the flare, we had to bring back into operation some of the coal-fired power plants that were still in working conditions in

Germany, the Czech Republic, Hungary and Poland. The Federation has enough coal reserves to ensure three-month production, giving us adequate leeway to replace defective turbines and restart our nuclear facilities. This allows us to reopen most of the essential factories, with priority given to the food industry, basic electronics, and water supply—"

"What about communications, General de Soverosa?"

"That is a more complicated issue, Mister President. Like the rest of the world, we have lost all satellite networks. We are currently restoring landline capabilities, but only to prioritised bodies like the national government, state governments, critical administrations, and military and police forces. It should take a week or so for everyone else to have full access. In the meantime, we rely on the Hertzian network, which could be re-established rapidly. The internet is still down, but private companies work day and night to restore it through the optical fibre network. A week from now, they promised. Consequently, the entire banking system is still inoperative, and the European Central Bank has almost no reserve of banknotes to cover small transactions."

"Printing banknotes will be absurd in the current circumstances, and we will face the risk of counterfeit money circulating. Issuing food ration tickets is similarly useless. It could unlock Pandora's box and generate more troubles. The industries and the people will have to work for free for a limited period and receive free necessities in return." Pierre-Antoine turned to the Commissioner in charge of Food and Industry. "Peter, I want your team to contact the CEOs of the major industry groups and organise food chain supplies across the country with them. Prepare a basic shopping cart containing a list of essential groceries and cleaning supplies that will be distributed to each household according to their size. If they are reluctant, threaten them with a nationalisation bill without compensation. We have no time for pointless negotiations. I want their complete and unconditional cooperation. This is a difficult task, but I am confident you will work wonders. I am giving you twenty-four hours to issue an action plan for my approval. You are now being promoted to High Commissioner to ensure you have the necessary budgetary resources and authority."

"Thank you, Mister President. I will make sure not to disappoint you."

"And I want the banking system included on the priority list. In the meantime, Jorge, generals, ensure that the police and the military coordinate to protect our food supply. I wish to praise you for having already undertaken this initiative with my brother in the hours following the disaster and for quickly containing panic and riot movements. The curfew is maintained between 6 pm and 6 am, with a full lockdown. People should stay at home, as they did during the last pandemic. Any attempt to protest will be considered an act of sedition and, if necessary, put down with force. Civil liberties are curtailed until we return to a minimum of normalisation. Use military camps to contain sedition rather than prisons which would be too complex to deal with. However, I do not want excessive violence. Dialogue will be the first line of action. Sensitive areas identified as hotspots in the past should be closely monitored. We are obligated to maintain order. There will be considerable temptations from extremist groups of all political stripes to cause unrest. Given the cohesiveness that followed the hurricane, I expect the disruptions to remain at a minimal level. At least as long as we provide food, and until we actively restore some normality. The majority of the population has benefited from stability for too long to foster movements leading to chaos and anarchy. What they want is reassurance. This is why we should concentrate most of our efforts on restoring services. Jorge, I require the regional governments to fully collaborate. I shall pass a special decree to ensure a federal governor immediately replaces anyone objecting to our actions. It should calm down the seditionists. We have more fundamental issues to deal with than wrestling with self-absorbed politicians. I received every guarantee that Parliament will approve those measures tonight. My apologies for being a bit long, but I had to clear things up from the start. Anything else, General?"

"Actually, yes, Mister President. I must inform you that our nuclear and air capabilities are currently inoperative. We depend entirely on conventional land and maritime forces in the event of a threat. Essentially because we do not have any GPS systems available. However, according to my sources, all the other major powers are confronting the same issues."

Pierre-Antoine took a few moments to reflect.

"How about the Kourou Space Centre? Can it be contacted?"

"Yes, it can. An entire brigade was deployed to protect it. It is a part of our sensitive facilities."

"Excellent! As far as I can remember, there are seven weather satellites that, thanks to the inaction of this Parliament, are stranded on the ground. Our scientists can easily place them in orbit using one or two of our space shuttles and recalibrate them for communication purposes.

It will be a minimally risky operation as air traffic will still be virtually non-existent for several weeks. The air force will supervise it. Thank you, General. All right, let us take a quick look beyond our borders. Fabijan."

"Mister President, I fear I only have sporadic intel, and not very encouraging ones. Most world nations were not as cautious as us and have been severely crippled by the magnetic storm. I can report a major destruction of electrical capacity and a shortage of spare transformers to restore minimal power, except for the African Union, which also had a contingency system. Countries like Russia and China suffer a more worrisome situation. The global shutdown had destabilised some of their nuclear power stations, making them unable to maintain a stable cooling system. I have received reports of a Chornobyl-type incident in the southern suburbs of Moscow, forcing the Russian government to evacuate to St. Petersburg. In China, three similar incidents occurred in Beijing, Wuhan, and Shanghai. The situation there is even more alarming, given that the country seems to be experiencing large-scale riots. I await further information about the rest of Asia, North America and Oceania. All the authorities I have managed to contact so far have declared a state of emergency, provided a political structure is still in place. My only concern, however, is the potential window that this global instability provides to some groups to access mobile nuclear arsenals illegally and unnoticed. We must remain vigilant about this issue."

Pierre-Antoine sighed.

"That is rather disturbing. It offers me no choice but to close our borders completely now. This global instability and the influx of refugees it will create will turn us into a magnet, especially when the news gets out of our overall situation. We can only offer our help according to our possibilities but cannot afford to save humanity as a whole. See into it rapidly. I was informed by the United Nations a few hours ago that they will hold a general meeting in three days to discuss the global situation. I will attend in person, accompanied by Monika. Alright, let us reschedule for tomorrow. Thank you all. Monika, Fabijan, and General de Soverosa, I need you to stay longer."

Once everyone else was gone, Pierre-Antoine activated the intercom.

"Lief, is everything ready?"

"*Yes, Mister President.*"

"Connect us, please."

"What is this about?" enquired Fabijan.

"Well, I deliberately neglected to ask questions about our space facilities during the meeting. For specific reasons. Administrator Johnson will now join us via radio communication. I just needed time for IT to establish a secure connection." The speaker before them started cracking. "Vince, can you hear me?"

"*…hear you, Mister President. The… nk is not p…ect, I am afraid. Just hold …inute.*"

They heard a series of cracklings and distorted sounds.

"*Do you hear us now, Mister President?*"

"Much better, Vince."

"*Good. Liz managed to boost the signal. Communication should be fine, hopefully long enough.*"

"How is the situation on the Moon? What can you tell me?"

"*Our lunar base is barely affected, Mister President. I must say, thanks to our decision to build our facilities underground. It was expensive, but in return, it completely shielded us. Our observation equipment has suffered slightly but should be operational in a few hours. Our primary focus is on repairing the Sun monitoring telescope, just to ensure no more storms are coming our way."*

"That will be the end of us if it happens. The EPBS will only be operational again in a few days."

"Is the situation that bad down there?"

"Worse than you could imagine. The world is on the brink of chaos. But Europe is holding strong, thanks to the EPBS, which has remarkably limited the damage. Unless the devil interferes, we should be up and running in a couple of weeks."

"This is great to hear."

"Anything else to report?"

"The spaceport landing pad is operational, like all underground infrastructure. I checked it out a couple of hours ago. We can operate shuttles if necessary. As far as the Russian and Chinese bases are concerned, that is another matter. They are both erected on the surface and have been severely impacted by the magnetic wave. Dozens of fatalities have been reported, and most of their equipment is severely damaged. Administrator Chen died, along with her second in command. Chief Engineer Lee Chang has now taken charge. Administrator Kuznetsov is still in command. He is injured but will recover. They both requested our assistance, which I am organising as we speak. I have been unable to contact the Indian, Pakistani and Japanese bases on the North Pole so far, and I cannot update you on their status. The orbital station is less impacted technically, thanks to its automatic shutdown system. But they report serious radiation burns. Their shields were not sufficiently strong to completely contain the intensity of the solar proton storm. I am also putting together a rescue team to aid them."

Pierre-Antoine looked at his Chief of Staff.

"This is too good to be true. What do you think?"

"An opportunity not to be missed."

"My thoughts, precisely. Vince, listen to me carefully…"

43

It was half past seven in the evening, and Pierre-Antoine was losing patience. For almost six days, the world's nations had gathered in Geneva's United Nations Assembly Hall, represented by their permanent delegates or broadcast live on big screens. The world, as they knew it, lay in ruins. Still, they squabbled over trivial requests or argued that their country's condition demanded more attention than the others. Most did not even try looking at the positive side of the rapidly improving global situation. Like Europe, two large blocks, South America and Africa, were recovering rapidly, restoring their electricity and food supply to their largest cities. Russia had responded the way it had throughout its history. A nation not inclined to sudden revolutions and ready to make the necessary sacrifices for the good of the fatherland. As long as a strong leader was in place and the military had firm control. However, a failing nuclear plant had rendered half of Moscow uninhabitable, and a similar catastrophic accident had turned Nizhny-Novgorod into a no man's land. Nearby,

China was still experiencing unrest. The People's Liberation Army and communist leaders actively worked to *eradicate the bands of enemies of the people* that scourged the country's regional governments, weakened by decades of endemic corruption. For the first time in their history, India, Pakistan, and Bangladesh chose the path of collaboration over confrontation, sharing their resources and setting aside their divisions. The situation in the rest of the world was unclear, particularly in North America, which Monika had tried to contact several times without success. Some delegates based in Geneva still had no news from their government and abstained during the votes pending further new instructions. *A mutating world*, thought Pierre-Antoine.

Fortunately, food supplies were abundant enough to sustain most of the planet's population for at least six months, limiting restrictions until global agriculture and international trade resumed. The biggest challenge was still global communications. The network of satellites in space was inoperative. It had become a graveyard of pieces of trash orbiting in space, with no hope of repairing them. Without cooperation, each nation would take years, if not decades, to rebuild it. On the optimistic side, the fibre optic cable networks were primarily intact, allowing to partially restore the Internet almost everywhere, supplemented by radio networks. Europe was the exception, with its seven satellites placed in orbit three days before. Its functional GPS capabilities were the focus of all covetousness. But Pierre-Antoine did not intend to easily share this strategic leverage without obtaining significant benefits in exchange. *In the land of the blind, the one-eyed man is a king...*

The representative for Indonesia had just concluded his speech, and the Secretary-General was back in the gallery.

"Honourable Members, I would like to invite the President of the United Federation of Europe again to the stage to address the key points raised in the last hour about the global share of communication capabilities. Mister President, if you please."

"Madam Secretary-General, with all due respect, I have nothing more to add to what my Commissioner for Foreign Affairs had already declared to this honourable Assembly," Pierre-Antoine replied. "My country will not accept being threatened by some form of reprisal simply because we were better prepared than most other nations. Our satellites are not for sale, at least not at the pitiful price offered to us."

A clamour of disapproval spread across the hemicycle.

"Mister President, you can genuinely appreciate that the current situation requires all cooperation for the sake of global stability."

"I shall not deny this, Madam Secretary-General. What we are not in agreement with is how to share it. Cooperation, yes. Donation, no. I do not run a charity. Our advantageous circumstances result from costly investments. We are entitled to seek compensation in return if anyone wishes to access our facilities. With all due respect, I am tired of justifying my country's position whenever we are in session. After six days of debates, the only thing most of us have agreed with so far has been maintaining our state of emergency. And even then, I suspect some governments to resort to it as an excuse to protect their own political agenda instead of the well-being of their populations!"

Some delegates started booing him while others cheered.

"Those who do not find our terms acceptable can still wait until other nations offer them more appropriate options... several years from now."

"It's an outrage!" yelled the representative for Myanmar, followed by others.

"Are you sure not to push things too far, Pierre-Antoine?" whispered Monika.

"On the contrary, let me make the most of this moment," he answered with a smile. "Madam Secretary-General, honourable delegates, I delivered a speech ten years ago to nations that had lived through centuries of division, endlessly fighting against each other. I declared this was the pivotal moment where we reject our old demons, once and for all, and commit ourselves to secure the stability and prosperity of those to whom we are now accountable. I renew this appeal before this assembly. Despite our ordeal, we have a unique chance to move forward and work together to restore this planet, save it and save ourselves. Let us put aside our egoistic differences and act for the general good. We need the people we govern as much as they need us. It is a symbiosis, not a master-and-servant relationship. Some nations are proving, as we speak, that change is possible. Look at what is happening in Pakistan, India and Bangladesh; something unthinkable just a few weeks ago. They are showing us the way. Therefore, I repeat my terms. I offer the use of our satellites to the nations accepting a global cease-fire, renouncing any territorial claim, institutionalising the protection of its minorities, and agreeing to enter negotiations to establish a new international governance body with strong interventional powers!"

His words were followed by an uproar that lasted several minutes, some delegates yelling "Colonialism!" and "imperialism!".

"The Russian Federation accepts those terms!" suddenly declared President Alexeyevna on one of the monitors.

"So does India!" promptly followed by the representatives from Pakistan and Bangladesh, and several more.

"And what about those countries not adhering to your pledge, Mister President?" shouted a voice behind.

The whole chamber fell silent as everyone wondered who had just spoken. Wearing a white cassock, Pope Urban IX stood defiant at the entrance beside other leaders of the various monotheistic confessions based in Europe.

"Your Holiness, it is a privilege to welcome you and your distinguished guests among us," declared the Secretary-General. "May I invite you to sit while we continue with…"

"Madam Secretary-General, as head of state and as a Permanent Observer, I want to exercise my right to address this assembly and offer my ecclesiastical colleagues a voice. In that capacity, I wish to hear President Lascombes' response."

"Be careful, Pierre-Antoine," whispered Monika. "He is a snake in religious attire."

"A snake which speaks for the souls of a billion people and comes accompanied by representatives of even more," he replied. "Your Holiness, my answer to your question will depend on their actions. Those who attempt to undermine our commitment by force will be met with firmness when necessary."

"Is that a promise, Mister President?"

"It is an engagement, Your Holiness."

"Well, let us ascertain how you honour these words. Honourable delegates, we urge you to act promptly against an imminent threat to the voices of billions of faithful. Two days ago, the army of the so-called Prophet crossed the Tigris River and is now heading to Baghdad. While you were all discussing world peace, that agent of evil was addressing the masses. Claiming the geomagnetic storm that plagued our planet represented the awaited sign of God, he warned the world about two weeks ago. Once again, he progresses without opposition with the support of populations rallied to his cause, overwhelmed by his lies. He has indicated his intention to march on Jerusalem, where he intends, I quote, *to free the city of the corruption and evil perverting its governing council.* We, the representatives of the revealed faiths, cannot sanction this deliberate attack on the Status Quo. Neither can we allow another false prophet to forcefully challenge the foundations of our religious beliefs, as the Islamic State tried decades ago. Delegates, will you fulfil the commitment you made a moment ago and nip the snake in the bud before it is too late?"

"Certainly, Your Holiness, you cannot expect us to start a war in the current circumstances," the Secretary-General replied. "There are far more fundamental questions to be resolved at present than the possible fate of Jerusalem. Notably when the individual in question has, so far, only demonstrated peaceful intentions. I am confident we can persuade all parties to listen to reason by simply sending a diplomatic delegation."

"The possible fate of Jerusalem, as you call it, Madam Secretary-General, is vitally important to the billions of our followers. Allow me to remind this assembly of the words of the Apocalypse: *'And the second beast performed great signs to cause even fire from heaven to come down to earth in the presence of the people.'* And from our Lord Jesus: *'Beware of false prophets, who come to you in sheep's clothing, but inwardly they are ravenous wolves.'* Hear me!"

There were murmurings among the delegates.

"Your Holiness, if I may. This is the assembly of the nations, not a religious gathering. We are not here to debate the End of the World or some other theological fantasies."

"Pierre-Antoine, she is losing momentum," said Monika. "We must do something."

"Wait, I'm going to try and buy some time," he replied. "Madam Secretary-General, may I speak?"

"Please, President Lascombes. Reason with His Holiness and his honoured guests."

"Your Holiness, imagine for a moment that we answer your call and accept to act. What are your people offering in return? You do not expect us to intervene simply for the greater glory of God?"

"Pierre-Antoine!" muffled Monika in shock.

Most of the assembly looked at him in amazement, while others enthusiastically greeted his words.

"Ever faithful to yourself, President Lascombes," answered the Pope with sarcasm. "If you agree to intervene, we commit ourselves to sustain recovery with all our spiritual and material resources."

"To support the new world governance?"

"If necessary."

"And observe its decisions?"

"As long as they respect our beliefs."

"Well, hear my offer to you, religious representatives. I propose that each country dispatch a military contingent according to its capabilities. Those contingents will be regrouped into an intervention unit deployed within the next twenty-four hours to protect Jerusalem. But it will not serve as a weapon. These troops will operate as a peacekeeping force. In return, you will appoint some delegates to accompany us, agree to engage in talks with this Prophet, and negotiate an appropriate settlement."

"You seriously do not expect us to enter into negotiations with this messenger of Satan?"

"He possesses an army, and you have none. Madam Secretary-General, what is your position on this proposition?"

"I believe, Mister President, that it requires an immediate vote from our delegates. Those in favour of President Lascombes' motion, please raise your hands."

After a brief moment of hesitation, most delegates voted in favour.

"The motion is approved!"

Pierre-Antoine stared back at the Pope.

"These are our terms, Your Holiness."

44

Another scorching day in Jericho, thought Monika. *What on earth are we doing here when the world is struggling to recover? Sometimes, Pierre-Antoine's logic escapes me. Five days here and nothing. Nothing more than religious gibberish and endless confrontations.* She sighed. She was sitting on the lawn at the Russian Museum. It was a large building designed in a typical Russian neoclassic architecture where the different parties held discussions. The temperature was soaring this mid-afternoon, but she found that cool spot, enabling her to take a break from the constant agitation inside. The peacekeeping force —ten thousand soldiers mainly from Europe, Russia and Africa— was stationed on the edge of the allegedly oldest city in the world under the command of Colonel Wladyslaw Zielinski of the United Federation of Europe. The Pope had chosen to come personally, accompanied by the Patriarch of Moscow, to support the members of the High Council.

Across the Jordan River were camping the twenty-five thousand troops of the man who called himself the

Prophet. The miracle maker claiming to be the Servant of the Light, the Voice of God, and who foresaw the chaos the planet experienced. Monika looked at the rosary she held in her hands. Prayer had consistently brought her solace and clarity, even if the ex-chancellor was not profoundly a churchgoer or a priest-seeker. It was more of an instrument of meditation and self-therapy. Although born and raised as a Roman Catholic, she addressed God directly, especially in her moments of insecurity, believing he sometimes answered her through signs. It was a habit she developed during her youth in East Germany, where there was a more significant Protestant community. As a teenager, she frequently accompanied a close friend to her Lutheran church to listen to the minister preaching the existence of a direct link with God. But she was Catholic at heart, as her family had been for generations, even if she was probably one of the few to maintain religious convictions still. *We represent a dying race, and religion will ultimately die with us. At least as it stands.* Yet, she could not keep off her mind her recent images of people turning to religion out of desperation. *Even the most sceptics seemed to express doubts, wrestling with the logic of the celestial event and the coincidence of the Prophet's message. An ultimate surge, a swan song those religious leaders inside hang on to before the situation finally escapes their control. Once things are resolved, when the world returns to normality, people will revert to their previous dispositions, as they have done many times before. And this 'miracle' will be remembered as a delusion.* She heard Pierre-Antoine approaching her.

"Monika, we are leaving. I paused the negotiations for three days to allow things to calm down."

She slipped her rosary into her pocket, and they walked back to the vehicle waiting for them at the main gate.

401

"Five days we have been through this. And still no breakthrough?" she asked.

"Nothing. Both sides refuse to concede any ground, enclosed in a deadlock. I ran out of arguments and tricks. Hopefully, the pause I entitled them for reflection will open up new possibilities."

"We cannot afford to remain here indefinitely, Pierre-Antoine. We must return to Europe very soon before the political situation worsens. Jorge warned you about the Parliament's duplicity."

"I know, Monika. And believe me, if I were selfishly listening to myself, I would wash my hands of it and wrap things up before leaving. But I have a Pope, Christian and Muslim leaders threatening to call for a Holy War if the Prophet refuses to yield."

"A Holy War? What is on their minds? Bringing us back to the Middle Ages?"

"With all that solar firework, they can manipulate enough minds to unleash more disorder than we already have. We need to prevent this. And I must also deal with the Russians, who insist on neutrality. Minister Kozyrev keeps repeating that they agreed to dispatch troops only to enable the talks. But he refuses to exert its influence on the Orthodox Church. I am on my own."

"I know Kozyrev. He is a fox and is likely waiting for you to be desperate enough to pull a rabbit out of his hat."

"My thoughts as well. Finally, I have a Prophet who insists he will consider my proposals only if he is allowed to enter Jerusalem with some of his troops to access Temple Mount. To which the four members of the High Council —the fifth one is still absent because of his health— answer they will not accept this demand. These people are a nightmare! I should never have agreed to this masquerade. I am giving them another five days, and then I will leave, no matter the consequences."

Back at the residence, Pierre-Antoine freshened up and had dinner. Later, he examined the dispatches from Strasbourg. The situation was gradually returning to some normality. His half-brother was urging him to return rapidly before Parliament took advantage of his absence. Then he looked at a report by Fabijan summarising the movements of the Prophet's troops after crossing the Tigris. They continued to advance unopposed and peacefully from Baghdad towards Amman before reaching the Jordan River. Every village and city they passed through welcomed the peshmergas as a liberation army with joy and gratitude, allowing more soldiers to join their ranks.

That explains how the Prophet was able to bring along twenty-five thousand soldiers. We conveniently turned a blind eye to this chaotic part of the world, focusing on the events in North America and Asia. After freeing ourselves from fossil fuels, we cowardly abandoned the region, allowing anarchy to spread out because it seemed the best tactic to finally eliminate terrorist groups. We thought the best way to neutralise the threat was to arm the local warlords and encourage them to fight the religious factions and each other. We only succeeded in creating a massive Afghanistan without any remorse. No wonder those people readily turn to this man who promises them peace and stability when we just failed them...

A separate note captured his attention. The troops of Abdul Al-khawaldeh, the self-proclaimed Emir of Amman, had hastily evacuated the city before the Peshmerga arrived, disappearing without a trace. With no spy satellites at hand, no one knew where they had retreated. An even more disturbing intelligence indicated that much of the Emir's forces were former members of rampant religious fanatic groups that roamed the region up to a decade ago. The man could represent a potential new threat if not located. *Where have they gone? They cannot just have miraculously disappeared in the middle of the desert...* Knocks on the door interrupted his thoughts. It was the officer commanding the team protecting the building.

"Sir, I apologise for disturbing you, but two gentlemen out there insist on speaking to you. One says he is some kind of prophet, and the other looks like an officer from the Peshmerga army. They are both unarmed. Shall I dismiss them?"

Some kind of prophet... Priceless. "No, Lieutenant. Bring me to them. Allow me to judge for myself."

Pierre-Antoine followed him to the main entrance, where, much to his surprise, he discovered the Prophet accompanied by his first commander.

"Good evening, Mister President. May the peace of the Light be with you."

"Prophet, what an unexpected visit. You should have informed me earlier that you intended to come tonight. I would have made arrangements."

"I preferred this meeting to be discreet, and, to be honest, this is a last-minute decision. I hope you have no objection to Commander Barzani's presence, who insisted on coming with me."

"Not at all. Let them in, Lieutenant. Let's have a sit in the lounge." A few seconds later, the President and the Prophet sat comfortably under Elend's fierce watch. "So, tell me, what business brings you here at this hour of the night."

"Mister President, I have an important subject to discuss with you, and I hope it will receive your approval."

"I am listening, Prophet."

Meanwhile, in another part of Jericho, at the Zacchaeus Greek Orthodox Church. Pope Urban IX, Patriarch of Moscow Alexy III, Father Calleja and the members of the High Council of Jerusalem were meeting secretly.

"Father Calleja, thank you for organising this gathering tonight."

"You are welcome, Your Holiness. Unfortunately, Metropolitan Archbishop Tawadros cannot join us again as he is still ill. But he charged me to inform you that he is improving and should be present when the talks resume."

"Excellent news, the more we are, the stronger we stand up to adversity. Please, convey my blessings and those of Patriarch Alexy next time you see him."

"I shall, Your Holiness."

"Very well. Members of the High Council, Your Beatitude, let's take advantage of the time President Lascombes has graciously given us to develop a strategy to neutralise this heretical prophet once and for all. This farce has lasted on long enough."

"We completely agree with you, Your Holiness," declared Cardinal Chehab.

"But before that, there is a matter on which I would like some clarification: the mysterious circumstances surrounding Cardinal del Pietro's death three years ago. I mandated Father Calleja to inquire about them. Instead, it seems the members of the Council would be more inclined to disclose the details directly to me. So, here I am, all ears!"

"Your Holiness", said Patriarch Nicodemus, embarrassed, "this was undoubtedly a regrettable misunderstanding. I already advised Father Calleja that there was nothing more to say than what the official investigation concluded. This whole affair simply resulted from a series of unfortunate events."

"Well, my vision is quite different. I took the liberty to have Cardinal del Pietro's body exhumed and subjected to a new post-mortem. Its conclusions seem to differ by far from yours. A violent shock to a thick angular object that penetrated the skull before crushing the brain appears to have caused the head trauma. Quite a gruesome death, I must say. And one incoherent with a fall on the main staircase of the nunciature, as the official report states. Therefore, enable me to ask again, what happened that day?"

The Patriarch of Jerusalem, the Grand Mufti and the Chief Rabbi stared at him, ill at ease, like children caught red-handed, until the Muslim leader exploded.

"We need not answer you. You are not our superior! We are the ruling members of a free city and manage our affairs as we see fit. The official version is the only one you will receive from us."

"Therefore, you would have no objection to Cardinal Chehab publicly presenting the new investigation results and urging the competent authorities to reopen the case."

"You cannot do that!" squealed the Greek Patriarch. "You would unlock Pandora's box!" He looked at the Russian Patriarch. "Your Beatitude, assist us. There is a lot at stake here."

"Leave me out of this purely local issue, Patriarch Tawadros. And honestly, the more I hear about it, the more it catches my attention."

"Please! Let us forget this and—"

"Stop there, Tawadros!" interrupted Chief Rabbi Eliyahu. "You are making things worse. And you, Suleiman, are no help either. Your Holiness, let me tell you what happened. But perhaps you should sit down first."

Then the rabbi recounted the whole story. The two archaeologists, the Coptic Archdeacon, the stela; everything. As he went on, the faces of the Pope, the Russian Patriarch and the Jesuit Priest froze with astonishment.

"Holy Mother of God!" cried out the muscovite prelate. "If this is revealed, it is the end of all things, the ultimate Armageddon!"

"Why on earth did you keep this to yourselves?" the Pope added. "Do you lack common sense? You should have informed us immediately!"

"Informed you?" replied the Grand Mufti. "And multiply the risk to expose it by telling more people? With the death of the Cardinal and the Archdeacon, and the archaeologists neutralised, there was no need to act further."

"No need to act further? Are you out of your mind? Beneath Temple Mount still lies a hidden artefact threatening the very existence of our beliefs, patiently waiting to be rediscovered at any moment in the future. Its existence is both a sin and a threat. That stela must be destroyed immediately!"

"We have tried addressing this issue on several occasions, Your Holiness," said the Chief Rabbi. "The problem is getting it done without leaving any witnesses. We can trust no one, including our own police. Remember the video. Despite all our efforts to destroy it, it found its way to—"

"If I may," interrupted Patriarch Nicodemus, "I have a proposal to eliminate both the Prophet and the stela simultaneously. Although it implies accepting a small sacrifice for the greater good."

45

The European President and his High Commissioner for Foreign Affairs arrived early at the Russian Museum, accompanied by Colonel Zielinski. The talks would resume in the morning and, hopefully, conclude with an agreement this time. Pierre-Antoine prepared the day the night before. The information communicated by the Prophet was invaluable and finally provided him a powerful lever. The resulting action plan had received the approval of his people in Strasbourg and, to its great surprise, of its long-time friend, Monika. At first, she was reluctant but eventually gave her approval and support *despite the consequences*. He had to move quickly while still retaining emergency powers. Hopefully, the religious leaders will be persuaded to reason without using this last option. Whatever happens, the day will be decisive. If everything goes according to plan, he and Monika will return to Strasbourg tonight.

Pope Urban IX, Patriarch Alexy III, and Father Calleja arrived first, followed several minutes later by the members of the High Council of Jerusalem. Metropolitan Archbishop Tawadros looked pale and exhausted, quivering while being brought to his chair, helped by an acolyte. He had suffered a stroke a few months before, leaving him partially blind. Since, his health had steadily deteriorated, as if his frail body were losing its will to live. Finally, the Prophet joined them, accompanied by his commander and his faithful servant. He wore a black and white robe and held his golden staff. They all sat around the table, and Pierre-Antoine opened the session.

"Your Holiness, Your Beatitudes, Your Eminences, Chief Rabbi, Father, Prophet, welcome. We are resuming our talks today in the hopes that these three days of introspection have helped both sides resolve their differences and accept concessions to end the current impasse. We will start with His Holiness, Pope Urban IX."

"Thank you, Mister President. After lengthy discussions with my religious colleagues, I am pleased to announce that the High Council of Jerusalem has agreed to allow the Prophet to enter the Holy City for a few hours and present the *proof* he so vehemently insists exists."

Pierre-Antoine and Monika expressed surprise at the statement. That move was unexpected. *Something is wrong,* he immediately thought.

"But it will be subject to several requirements."

Here we go.

"The Prophet must wait until nightfall before entering Temple Mount. We want no publicity, no reporters, no witnesses except ourselves. His servant will only accompany him. His guards and his commander must remain at the gates of the Mount. We solemnly guarantee his safety. Assuming we are satisfied with the genuineness of his claim, we shall vote on accepting his request for a council of religions by a simple majority. Whatever the result of our decision, he will agree to keep his army behind the eastern shore of the Jordan River. Finally, Mister President, you will accept to remain with your troops in Jericho, waiting for our decision to be made public. We regard this matter as a divine question that should be evaluated only among men of God. Those are our terms."

Pierre-Antoine could barely believe it.

"My apologies, Your Holiness, you cannot expect I would—"

"Say no more words, Mister President," interrupted the Prophet. "I accept those terms."

"Noble Mahd," said Elend in Kurdish, "what are you doing? This is madness! You cannot go there only accompanied by Ferhad. You must take a few of my Peshmerga to escort you. I am confident the President will support this."

"My dear Elend," replied the Prophet in English, "do not fear for my life. I told you this moment would come. You must trust my resolve and God's plan. I walk in His truth, and He will protect me as He has done over the years. The time for redemption is upon us all."

"That... voice. That voice! I do not believe it. Lord Jesus!" That was Metropolitan Archbishop Tawadros. He stood up and stared at the Prophet with his eye open, his face shining joyfully. "I shall recognise this voice among thousands! Shenouda, my son, is that you?"

The Prophet remained silent. The old man approached him, trembling over his feet, and examined his face attentively.

"The years may have altered your appearance, but your eyes betray you. Yes, those striking, compassionate eyes. It is you!" he cried with tears of joy. "Praised be the Lord to allow this old man to see you again. Let me hug you once more, my son."

"Your Beatitude," replied Shenouda, "my heart rejoices in seeing you again. You to whom I owe my life."

The other members of the High Council observed the scene with dismay, frozen in their seats. The Pope and the Russian Patriarch gave them startled looks. Suddenly, the Grand Mufti Amin al-Sabri stormed to the Metropolitan, clasping him firmly by the shoulders.

"Look at me, Tawadros! What is this masquerade? Shenouda died years ago. I saw his body; everyone saw it. What demon possesses you? Answer me, old fool!"

Pierre-Antoine came to the rescue, separating the two clerics.

"Your Eminence! How dare you physically harm this man. Shame on you!"

He escorted the Metropolitan back to his seat.

"I am alright, Mister President. Thank you." The elderly priest took a minute before speaking again. "My dear colleagues, I do not have long before departing this world. May God be my witness. I must confess to you the unforgivable sin I committed several years ago. Following this dreadful night when Cardinal del Pietro tragically died, the High Council searched extensively to retrieve Archdeacon Shenouda's remains after he fell in the Sea of Galilee. One of my men discovered him unconscious two days later, along the banks of Ein Gev, dragged there by the currents created by the storm. When informed, I immediately travelled to the location covertly. Shenouda suffered from several burns but was still breathing, still alive. He was transported to the house of a carpenter and taken care of. There lay that unfortunate and vulnerable young man. The innocent victim of our appalling manipulations. At that moment, I knew my heart would not find the strength to bring him back to Jerusalem and endure another dreadful ordeal." Tawadros coughed a little. "This is when I did something shameful. God forgives me. A young villager of Shenouda's age and equivalent height drowned the previous night. I waited until the night, then ordered my man to dig up his body discreetly. With the help of an undertaker, a friend of mine, the corpse was submitted to atrocious mutilations and transformations to make it appear burned by lightning. I confess melting the handcuffs attached to the wrists myself." The coughing intensified. "Then, we threw the remains in the middle of the lake. Patriarch Nicodemus' men eventually recovered it two weeks later. After Shenouda's physical condition improved, I gave him clothes and money, and paid a smuggler to take him to the eastern border. There, he would be free to continue as he chooses." He was now coughing loudly.

The Grand Mufti burst into rage.

"Do you realise the consequences of your decision, you imbecile?! What your weakness initiated? How could you be so senseless?!"

The metropolis was now breathing with difficulty.

"As God… is my witness, I… I have… no regrets. I… only followed… what my conscience… was dictating… me." With one final effort, he looked at the Prophet. "Forgive… me… Shenouda, for… all the… wrongs I have

413

caused… you. Please, Almighty God… forgive my… sins…"

Next, he died in a final breath. Shenouda approached him and gently kissed his forehead.

"God forgives you, old friend."

Patriarch Nicodemus discreetly approached the Pope.

"We cannot wait till tonight," he whispered. "We must act now!"

"Very well, contact your friend. I will try buying some time." He approached Pierre-Antoine. "Mister President, in light of this new development, we would like to ask you to grant us time to pray for the repose of Metropolitan Tawadros' soul and discuss the situation between us."

"I understand your holiness. Of course, I will permit it. We will leave you alone. Prophet Shenouda, please accompany me."

"With pleasure, Mister President."

"Colonel, take two guards with you to move Metropolitan Archbishop Tawadros' body to a more private place until the Coptic authorities arrive to reclaim it."

***

Monika was nervous, circling through the main lobby.

"Two hours, Pierre-Antoine! They have been in there for two hours! What are they talking about which requires so much time?! Something is going on."

"My thoughts exactly. They are manifestly stalling, but for what purpose?"

They heard steps running in the hallway. It was Colonel Zielinski who appeared anxious.

"Mister President, terrible news. I just received a message from Jerusalem. Emir Abdul Al-khawaldeh and his troops forced their way into the Old City, executing anyone standing in their path. The religious police are overwhelmed."

"What? What treachery is that?! Monika, return to the residence with the Prophet. Colonel, arrange an escort and initiate the recovery mission we set up yesterday immediately. Let's hope we still have time."

"At once!"

"If you do not mind, Mister President, I would like to stay. I feel completely safe with my Commander."

"As you wish, Prophet."

Two minutes later, Pierre-Antoine stormed into the boardroom.

"Your Holiness, Your Graces, I need to inform you that the City of Jerusalem is under attack by the troops of a local warlord named Abdul Al-khawaldeh. I must ask you to follow Colonel Zielinski to a secure location until we assess the situation and initiate appropriate action."

"What nonsense is that, Mister President?" said the Pope with a gasp of amazement. "Assess the situation? If your information is accurate, there is no time to waste. You must intervene without delay! I should not have to remind you that the purpose of your presence here is to protect the Holy City."

"I will not act blindly and foolishly risk the lives of our troops by a reckless move. As a peacekeeping force, we agreed to avoid any armed conflict. We will open channels with the Emir and discuss his demands first."

A soldier rushed in and spoke to the colonel, who whispered at length in Pierre-Antoine's ear.

"Your Holiness, I have just received more troubling news. It seems Abdul Al-khawaldeh has proclaimed himself Caliph of Jerusalem, Commander of the Believers, and is demanding an unconditional surrender of the Holy City. His troops are wreaking havoc on the streets, slaughtering every person resisting them or considered, I quote, an infidel. The population is fleeing by the thousands, taking refuge in the Western territories under the protection of Israeli-Palestinian forces, which refuse to intervene without our consent. The Church of the Holy Sepulchre, St Anne's Church, the Four Sephardic and the Hurva Synagogues are in flames. The invaders are now besieging the Temple Mount complex where the remains of the Religious Police have barricaded themselves, opposing a fierce resistance."

"What! This is impossible!" The Catholic Church leader turned angrily to the Greek Orthodox patriarch. "Nicodemus! What have you done?! You assured us the man was only willing to resolve our problems. That he would be accompanied only by a few men, and the losses would be minimal. Not that he intended to bring an army and spark a bloodbath!"

"I… I apologise, Your Holiness. I'm as surprised as you are. I have known the emir for years. I consider him trustworthy. We used his influence to protect the eastern banks of the Jordan River from various threats. It must be some kind of misunderstanding. Let me speak to him, to—"

"I cannot believe my ears," interrupted Pierre-Antoine. "I came here in good faith, genuinely willing to assist you in finding a reasonable solution. However, all this time, you were scheming behind my back for your benefit when the entire planet desperately needed help. Were you planning on eliminating the Prophet as well? And you dare to call yourselves men of faith?"

"Mister President, you are mistaken. Allow me to set out the facts and explain the entire situation. Just take a few minutes to—"

"I will no longer listen to your lies, Chief Rabbi. You are all a disgrace. For far too long, you people have interfered in human's affairs and aspirations. You revolt me and leave me no choice. Colonel, proceed immediately with Operation Amaterasu."

"Mister President! I would advise caution before considering extreme measures."

"It is an order, Colonel. I will assume full responsibility for the consequences of my decision. Escort these *holy men* to their new quarters."

46

It was almost midnight, and Abdul Al-khawaldeh, the now self-proclaimed Khalifat Al-Quds, walked through the silent streets of Jerusalem, protected by his closest men. Not that he needed them. The inhabitants had fled the city now in the hands of his brave warriors. Less than an hour ago, his forces finally pushed through the main gate and entered the Temple Mount complex, where the remaining resisting police squads were entrenched. He recalled the moment when his most trustworthy lieutenant came to see him at the headquarters after securing the site.

"Mighty Caliph, Commander of the Faithful, the place is ours! We are removing the last pockets of resistance as we speak."

"Very good. You are a loyal servant, Ahmed. God will reward you. Return when the entire operation is completed." The soldier hesitated. "Is there anything else, Ahmed?"

"We... we found a large group of civilians gathered at the El-Marwani Mosque, about a thousand. They are claiming sanctuary in the name of Allah the Magnificent."

"Are all those people Muslim? Only the faithful followers of our Noble Prophet Muhammad are allowed into the sacred grounds of the Haram-al-Sharif. Any infidel found desecrating our holy place would have to be cleansed by the sword."

"I understand, Amir al-Mu'minin. But what shall I do, for I cannot distinguish between the Mumins and the Kafirs?"

"Kill them all; God will know His own."

The warlord passed through the Bab al-Atim Gate, then headed towards the centre of the complex where the Dome of the Rock patiently stood, the Qubbat al-Sakhrah. The long wait will soon end, and the splendour of the caliphate will be restored for millennia to come. It was Al-Khawaldeh's long-awaited moment of glory, the culmination of all these years of sneaky alliance with those greedy imbeciles of the High Council. Nurturing them, gifting them, deceiving them with his honeyed words while he was building his army step by step. *Fools!* And now, the ultimate price was finally within his grasp. *Next, Medina and Mecca!* The emir wore a white thobe and walked barefoot as a sign of humility and obedience to God. The ground around him was saturated with blood, splattering on the immaculate robe with each step. *The blood of Abraham's sacrifice purifies the world from its sins and bestows eternal redemption.* He finally reached the main plaza, facing the magnificent, tiled monument crowned with its golden bulge. The Beacon of the Faithful, lit by dozens of tall torches his disciples had carefully displayed around in

419

circles. At that exact moment, the Moon's silver crescent rose from the darkness above the Dome, majestically radiating in the heavens. *God approves. God is pleased. God rewards me with his blessings.* The surrounding stars glittered brightly, dancing in the sky to celebrate his achievement. The magnificence of the scene before his eyes aroused his soul, and he knelt to thank God for so generously repaying him, his humble servant. Right beside the Moon, a star shone more brilliantly than the others, its light pulsating vividly among the firmaments. As time passed, it seemed to increase in intensity, getting bigger and bigger. The emir took a closer look, intrigued.

"Are you alright, Noble Amir al-Mu'minin?" asked her lieutenant, wondering why his master suddenly stopped praying.

"Do you see that glittering star other there, Ahmed? The very bright one above the moon. Does it appear normal to you?"

The warrior looked in the direction the commander pointed up in the sky. But before he could answer, they were suddenly engulfed in a violent flash of intense light and heat, instantly converting them into minute particles of matter.

***

The clergymen were assembled on the upper terrace of the St John's Greek Orthodox Convent, near the Jordan River, where they had been convoyed earlier *for their safety*. Patriarch Nicodemus, Chief Rabbi Eliyahu and Grand Mufti Amin al-Sabri sat together at one end in complete

420

silence, crestfallen. Father Calleja and Cardinal Chehab were a few steps further, lost in their thoughts. The Prophet rested on the opposite side, meditating, Elend, Ferhad and a few guards beside him. In the centre, Russian Patriarch Alexy was watching with amusement Pope Urban IX walking anxiously in circles around the golden dome standing in the middle. The Pope suddenly stopped and approached him.

"We have been detained here for hours now! What is this man waiting for?"

"I am sorry, Your Holiness. I wish I had an answer, but I am as clueless as you are."

"You seem remarkably calm looking at the circumstances. Can your government not assist us?"

"Unfortunately, I was not permitted to contact Minister Kozyrev. And my calm only reflects my inability to act. Like you, I can only wait and see what lies ahead."

The Pope scoffed at him and gazed at the others.

"You are all worthless, none better than the other. Forgive me for not giving up. And you, you!" he said, pointing a shaking finger to the members of the High Council. "Look at you, the Three Wise Men! So confident in your egos and helpless to foresee the consequences of your despicable actions. You are an offence to the clothes you wear!"

They remained silent. Then the Catholic leader turned his anger to one of the soldiers guarding access to the stairs.

"I demand to talk to President Lascombes immediately! I am the Pope, the Sovereign Pontiff of our Holy Mother, the Church. I should be treated with respect and consideration. All that waiting is unacceptable. Go and fetch him!"

At the same moment, a vivid orange flash burst into the western part of the horizon, illuminating the night and rapidly increasing in intensity. They all stared at the sky with stupefaction. A few seconds later, a howling sound broke the silent night, followed by ferocious gusts of wind. A formidable ball of light rose in the atmosphere before dissolving. All turned calm again. The Pope stared at the Prophet with fear.

"What... is this sorcery? Another one of your tricks?"

"I apologise for the disappointment, Your Holiness, but I fear the talents of Prophet Shenouda have nothing to do with the phenomenon you have just witnessed. Although, I am certain he is most certainly flattered by your sudden creed in his divine abilities."

Pierre-Antoine appeared, followed by Monika, Colonel Zielinski, and a detachment of guards.

"I am the bearer of the most unfortunate news. A minute ago, a nuclear-related incident devastated our beloved Jerusalem."

They all gasped in shock, except for the Prophet, who remained stoic.

"What... what happened?"

"I decided to remove a thorn that has poisoned humanity for millennia. I put an end to the unfinished work left by the Babylonians and the Romans. The Jerusalem you knew, the religious battlefield that caused so many wars and atrocities, is no more. Temple Mount and its direct surroundings have been obliterated, reduced to ashes, erased from history. In its place now stands a barren radioactive crater. It will take some time before anyone can access it safely."

The pope backed away before losing his balance and falling to the ground. Father Calleja rushed along to aid him. The others just stood there horrified.

"The world has grown weary of your evil schemes, of religions constantly plotting against each other, of centuries of feeble rivalries. All for the sole purpose of establishing your influence and controlling people's minds. Again and again, this vicious circle persisted, each rising religion not better than the previous, and its message inevitably perverted by its advocates. What about the people whose souls you are meant to guide, help, and comfort? Where is this redemption you are supposed to offer them? Where is God in all of this? If he exists, he must feel like the saddest and loneliest creature in the universe, contemplating what his beloved creation has become. Three times he tried to instil reason into men. But, like Peter in the Gospels, by three times he was betrayed of his efforts."

"You are mistaken in your judgement, Mister President. We do follow God's words as much as men require our guidance," replied the Russian Patriarch. "Without us, they would be lost, unable to comprehend his message. Eliminate us, and there would be nothing but chaos, a world without ethics, morality, suffering from the original sin, and people fighting like Cain and Abel. Even you, as a politician, need us to ensure stability, directly or indirectly. We are inevitable."

"Hear your words, Your Beatitude. In your opinion, human beings are no better than irresponsible little children needing to be maintained under your benevolent control. And I thought the primary mission of religions was to prepare people for the hereafter while comforting their existence. Instead, they must live in constant fear of the punishment of an invisible supreme being under the compassionate guardianship of the good shepherds you embody." He designated the Prophet. "Maybe this man does speak to God. Maybe God has still not given up on us and is making a final attempt to transcend the differences by bringing together those who have been divided for so long, unifying the creeds into one. Who am I to contradict his truth? All I see is that if you are capable of pulling together when your survival is threatened, nothing prevents you from finding common ground for the practice of faith, for the greater glory of God."

"You want to subjugate us, erase us, but we will resist you!" replied the Pope, regaining his composure. "Thanks to you, this malevolent creature, this so-called Prophet, possesses no power over us anymore. Judge us however you like, Mister President. You are a finished man, a mass murderer. And we will ensure you will be held accountable for your crimes!"

Pierre-Antoine laughed at him before removing a small tablet from his pocket and presenting it to Father Calleja.

"Your Holiness, if any of your words referred to a certain artefact inside Temple Mount, I suggest you watch the little video stored on this tablet. I believe you will find its content rather entertaining. It captures the moments when a detachment of my special forces, taking advantage of the little chaos your accomplices initiated earlier today, retrieve a piece of compelling historical evidence. I am certain its existence will captivate the little children you people are desperately keen to keep under your guidance. And before you ask, allow me to reassure you. It was diligently transported to a secure location, ready to be examined by international experts eager to confirm his authenticity, if needed."

"You would not dare!" the pontiff replied with fear.

"Come, Your Holiness. I am confident you understand how desperate I am. I have been tasked with rebuilding and preserving a world at the edge of destruction before it is too late. Your unconditional support will be greatly appreciated and heavenly rewarded. Instead, I stand accused of a terrible deed. Come on! Everyone here knows this dreadful bombing was the unfortunate result of the mishandling of a weapon of mass destruction by a bloodthirsty terrorist. My intelligence services are actively investigating how he successfully obtained the weapon illegally. As you can see, Your Holiness, I have no time for your pathetic little games when so much is at stake. You are accurate on one thing, though. It would be unwise to deprive the world of the stability provided by the various faiths. But I can still try and tame them. Monika, please get in touch with Turkish President Burakgazi and inform him that a rare honour has been conferred upon his country. The city of Istanbul will soon hold a Grand Council of the Faiths in the presence of the main religion's representatives to promote spiritual peace. I am certain Your Holiness and Your Graces will find the perfect motivating arguments to persuade other religious leaders to participate in this historic event. In the meantime, Colonel Zielinski and his troops will kindly escort you to a transport currently waiting for you to take you all to Rome. Naturally, Prophet Shenouda will accompany us."

"No!" The Kurdish commander swiftly deployed his soldiers around the Prophet, pointing their weapons at the others. "The Noble Haad is staying with us!"

425

"Stop Elend! Lower your weapons. All of you. I will go willingly."

"But, Noble Basheer, you cannot abandon us. We need your guidance."

"My dear Elend, I am not abandoning you. But you no longer require my guidance. The past few months have clearly demonstrated that you and Elfesya are more than capable of leading our people without me. I told you our paths were about to part, and that time has come. God is now calling me away to attain a greater purpose. My mission in Kurdistan is accomplished, and I must obey His command. Do not worry; my faithful Ferhad will stay with me and diligently look after my person."

"Commander," said Pierre-Antoine, "I guarantee you the protection of Prophet Shenouda. You have my word. And when your future government assumes power, my country will be among the first to recognise it unconditionally. The days of betrayal are over."

"Go, my son. Go back to our land, our children, our families. Build a new future based on peace and prosperity. Your work here is over." Shenouda hugged the young man who was weeping. "Do not cry. It is only goodbye. You can still reach me. And we shall meet again in the future. God promised me." Shenouda grabbed his staff. "Colonel, Ferhad and I are ready to follow you."

"Colonel," said Pierre-Antoine, "I entrust these men of God to you. Take all necessary steps to ensure their comfort and security on their memorable journey in the service of the Lord."

"You can count on me, Mister President."

The pope stared at the European president, his face distorted by anger and hate. He slowly raised his right arm to point an accusatory finger.

"You… you! You just exposed your true self. I recognize who you are. Antichrist! The Beast from Hell! You believe you are victorious, but you are mistaken. God's wrath will fall upon you and return you to the depths you should never have left. Hear my words, Demon!"

"Your Holiness, you seem rather pale and exhausted. You are having me worried. Father Calleja, I suggest you attend quickly to His Holiness, who appears deeply affected by all recent events. We should avoid risking further stress by hastily escorting him to the safety of the Vatican. I am confident the Holy See will provide all the necessary help there. The world would be saddened if another leader of our Holy Mother, the Church, were to step down from the Throne of Saint Peter a second time in this century."

The Jesuit priest stared at the man standing before him. A man who, with his kind looks and good manners, was just another human being. A creature of God experiencing his life the same way he was, with moments of joy, sadness, hope, and disappointment. He sounded so harmless. And yet, there he was, the ruler of one of the most powerful nations on earth. The man who, without hesitation, ordered the destruction of one of the most prominent religious symbols on the planet. The man holding in his hand the power to ruthlessly shake the structures of long-established systems of beliefs. *And God, the very God we, men of faith, worship and fear, did nothing to prevent it.* It was an unsettling and terrifying thought. He supported the pope by the arm and assisted him down the stairs. A passage from Matthew's Gospel echoed in his mind. *Jesus left the Temple, and as he was*

427

going away, his disciples came up to draw his attention to the Temple buildings. He said to them in reply, 'You see all these? In truth, I tell you, not a single stone here will be left on another: everything will be pulled down."

***

A pleasant late evening in Scotland. Three men, wearing red and saffron robes, sat under a majestic oaktree standing in the park of a vast mansion in the western suburbs of Edinburgh. Their eyes observed the starry night and the bewitching large greenish ribbons floating lightly above. Everything was peaceful around them except for the sound of the small creatures of the night.

"What's on your mind, Rinchen?"

"I am thinking of my parents, Kalsang. These northern lights remind me of the bands my mother used to tie her hair with when I was a child. It seems such a long time ago."

"Do you miss your parents? I miss mine."

"Sometimes I do, Jamyang. The thought of not knowing what happened to them is even more painful. It is like a wound in my heart that can never heal. I take solace in the Buddha's infinite compassion and wisdom. Wherever they are, I am convinced they found peace."

"I love looking at the stars," says Kalsang. "I always had this strange fascination for those tiny lights shining in a vast dark ocean. The sky here is not as clear and majestic as in the Himalayas, but it is still beautiful to contemplate."

"My mother used to say the stars were precious jewels sewn in the heavens by the Goddess Ratri. Each born from

428

a compassionate act performed somewhere in the world. Ratri collects them and sets them up in the firmament for all living things to hold onto hope, even in the gloomiest times."

"This is a beautiful story, Jamyang. Your mother always possessed a gift for telling stories."

"And cooking momos!"

They laughed like children.

"Do you think we shall someday journey to the stars, Rinchen?"

"I do not know, Kalsang. Is that something you would like to do?"

"Some nights, I have this weird dream where the three of us sail on a large boat in the middle of a vast, calm Ocean. We look content. Then a giant black eagle appears in the blue sky and circles around us. He circles and circles until suddenly diving to catch me and flying away. I see you below, smiling, waving at me. I wave back. I am flying, and feel free. The eagle flies higher and higher until we reach space. Surprisingly, I don't feel cold but warm and protected while it squeezes me tight in its talons. The stars shine evenly around, but one glows brighter than the others, flashing frenetically as if calling me. The eagle heads in its direction. And..."

"And?" asked Jamyang, dying to hear the rest.

"And... I wake up! Boom!"

"This is not funny..." he replied, crossing his arms.

"Is my dream merely a dream or a vision sent by the Buddha? What do you think, Rinchen?"

"I have no idea, Kalsang."

"What do you mean you have no idea? You are the Dalai Lama. You are supposed to know everything!"

And they laughed again.

APPENDIXES

APPENDIX I
The World in 2057

Simplified map of the World in 2057

APPENDIX II
Short Chronology

2020-2022: the First Pandemic, caused by a mutated Coronavirus, resulting in around five million deaths worldwide.

2030: Russia and China's moon bases completed on the Moon's South Pole. Followed by the USA in 2031 and the European Union in 2032. Pakistan, India and Japan establish theirs on the North Pole in 2033.

2046-2047: the Second Pandemic, caused by the apparition of a new virus strain combining SARS-CoV and MERS-CoV, killing fifteen million people worldwide.

06-11-2052: Republican Presidential candidate John Alistair Simons refuses to concede defeat against incumbent Democrat President Julius Theodore Thomas, claiming voting fraud after losing by only two electoral college votes. He asks for a recount in several states and starts legal proceedings. Conspiracy videos flood social media with alleged 'evidence' of vote rigging. The authorities temporarily close social media to protect the democratic process.

16-12-2052: the Electoral College officially confirms the election of President Thomas with 270 votes despite several states trying to overturn the votes.

08-01-2053: the joint session of Congress objects to the counting of the votes by one vote. Republican Congressmen ask for a new election and petition the Supreme Court.

15-01-2053: the Supreme Court Democratic Majority rejects Congress vote. As a result, some Republican states threaten to secede from the Union.

20-01-2053: President Thomas is sworn in for a second term. The states of Texas, Oklahoma, Arkansas, Louisiana, Mississippi, Alabama, Georgia and Florida declare secession from the United States, forming the Southern Confederation based on Biblical rule and followed by other states the next day. The following day, President Thomas imposes federal martial law, triggering the Second American Civil War. The rest of the country forms the Union of Democratic States.

October 2054: offensive of the Confederate troops in Washington. The Confederate army destroys the Capitol and the Pentagon. The Union troops are repelled at the Battle of Rivercrest.

Mars 2055: the Southern Confederation invades Canada accused of conspiring with the Union. President Thomas is assassinated, splitting the Union into two factions.

24-03-2055: the United Nations moves its headquarters to

Geneva and abolishes the system of permanent seats.

09-05-2055: Pierre-Antoine Lascombes elected President of France.

June 2055: Russia invades Belarus and Ukraine. President Grigory Alexeyev orders the massacre of the resisting population in Kyiv, earning the title of 'the Butcher of Kyiv'. The European Union sends coalition forces after talks collapse. Russian forces retreat on the Eastern bank of the Dnieper River. A few days later, China invades Mongolia, Taiwan, and North Korea.

26-06-2055: Jorge Sanchez becomes Prime Minister of Spain.

July 2055: cease-fire between Russia and the European Union. Russia permanently occupies Belarus and Eastern Ukraine. Western Ukraine integrated into the European Union. The Member States decide to vote for further integration. Creation of the Commonwealth of Independent States under the protectorate of Moscow. Nepal and Bhutan join the Indian Federation.

September 2055: all the Middle East countries collapse into anarchy. Revolution in Iran and creation of the Persian Republic. Treaty of Perpetual Alliance between Turkey and the European Union.

25-09-2055: Monika Richter elected German Chancellor.

06-12-2055: creation of the Pan American Union.

24-02-2056: Russian President Grigory Alexeyev dies unexpectedly of a heart attack, and is succeeded by his daughter, Yekaterina Alexeyevna.

08-05-2056: the African Union adopts more integrated institutions.

10-07-2056: Israel, Palestine and Lebanon form the Israeli-Palestinian State. Jerusalem becomes a Free State.

25-03-2057: creation of the United Federation of Europe.

APPENDIX III
Glossary of terms used in this book

A

Admonitor: title given to the advisor of the Superior General whose responsibility is to warn (or admonish) the General honestly and confidentially about *what in him he thinks would be for the greater service and glory of God.*

Aleem: Quranic title meaning *the Knowledgeable.*

Amir al-Mu'minin: Arabic title meaning *Commander of the Faithful.*

Anaghnostos: a Deacon of lower rank.

B

Basheer: Quranic title meaning *the Bringer of good news.*

C

Cassock: a long, loose, piece of clothing usually worn by clergymen.

Christ Pantocrator: Christ Almighty.

D

Deacon and Archdeacon: members of a clerical order next below that of a priest, appointed or elected, performing variously defined religious duties and sacred rituals.

Dhonka: wrapped shirt with cape sleeves, part of the traditional Tibetan robe.

F

Fasiq: Arabic term meaning *sinner, he who violates God's laws.*

Fellahin (sing. Fellah): Egyptian farmers or agricultural labourer.

H

Haad: Quranic title meaning *the Leader.*

Holoscreen: television monitor using holographic technology.

Holophone: smartphone using holographic technology.

K

Kafir: Arabic term meaning *infidel* or *nonbeliever.*

Khalifat Al-Quds: Arabic title meaning *Caliph of Jerusalem.*

Khor (Land of): region South of modern Syria under Egyptian control during the New Kingdom period (c. 1550 BCE – c. 1077 BCE).

Khatag: a traditional ceremonial scarf used in Tibet and Mongolia.

M

Mahd: Quranic title meaning *the Guided one.*
Maraj: Arabic title meaning *the Above.*
Minbar: pulpit in a mosque where the imam stands to deliver sermons.
Mumin: Arabic term meaning *faithful* or *believer.*
Musharifin: Arabic term meaning *Seraph.*

P

Peshmerga: word traditionally associated with the military forces in the autonomous Kurdistan region of Iraq. Literally meaning *those who stand in front of death.*

R

Rinpoche: honorific term used in the Tibetan language meaning *precious one.* It may refer to a person, place, or thing.

S

SEV: Space Exploration Vehicle. Concept name given to the man-operated rovers used on the lunar surface first designed by NASA.
Shemdap: maroon skirt made from patched cloth.
Simar: black robe with scarlet piping silk, stitching and buttons, with an optional elbow-length shoulder cape, traditionally worn by cardinals.

Z

Zhen: sometimes spelt *Zen*. Traditional Tibetan shawl wrapped on top of a monk's attire.

AKNOWLEDGEMENTS

A beginning is a very delicate time. With these words, Frank Herbert started the first line of what was to become his most famous novel, *Dune*. Despite the impact of his work during my adolescence, I won't presume to have Frank Herbert's talent. But here is my first book, whose narrative has haunted my mind, waiting for the right moment to materialise.

While writing fiction is mainly a solitary work, a lone challenge of putting extravagant ideas into words with the hope of pleasing readers, it cannot be achieved without the help and support of the people close to you.

I want to thank my mother, who taught me to stay true to myself, respect others the way you expect to be respected, and that dreams come true. My grandmothers, who nurtured my mind, fed my spirit and challenged my convictions. Anne and Emmanuelle, who spent their spare time making more sense of my senseless words. Yannis for his invaluable mental and spiritual support. Stephane, Bernard, Valentine, Lea, Lionel, Stuart, Ian, among others.

I also wish to acknowledge the people who indirectly inspired some of the events and characters in this story. The anonymous ones I had the privilege to meet through my travels and previous job. You have made the journey memorable through your little gestures, your help, and your patience under challenging moments.

Finally, a special dedication to you, the reader. Without you, a writer's writings remain silent, nonexistent, lost in the Void. You are our strength and our weakness.

Printed in Great Britain
by Amazon